USA TODAY bestselling author **Stefanie London** is a voracious reader who has dreamed of being an author her whole life. After sneaking several English Lit subjects into her 'very practical' business degree, she got a job in corporate communications. But it wasn't long before she turned to romance fiction. After leaving her hometown of Melbourne to start a new adventure in Toronto, she now spends her days writing contemporary romances with humour, heat and heart. For more information on Stefanie and her books check out her website at stefanie-london.com or her Facebook page at Facebook.com/stefanielondonauthor.

Anne Marsh writes sexy contemporary and paranormal romances—because the world can always enjoy one more alpha male. She started writing romance after getting laid off from her job as a technical writer—and quickly decided happily-ever-afters trumped software manuals. She lives in Northern California with her family and six cats.

D0682496

If you liked *Unmasked* and
Inked, why not try

Her Dirty Little Secret by JC Harroway
The Marriage Clause by Alexx Andria

Discover more at millsandboon.co.uk

UNMASKED

STEFANIE LONDON

INKED

ANNE MARSH

MILLS & BOON

First Published in Great Britain 2018
by Mills & Boon, an imprint of HarperCollins*Publishers*
1 London Bridge Street, London, SE1 9GF

Unmasked © 2018 Stefanie Little

Inked © 2018 Ann Marsh-Flores

ISBN: 978-0-263-26642-9

MIX
Paper from
responsible sources
FSC® C007454

This book is produced from independently certified FSC™ paper
to ensure responsible forest management.
For more information visit www.harpercollins.co.uk/green.

Printed and bound in Spain
by CPI, Barcelona

UNMASKED

STEFANIE LONDON

MILLS & BOON

To Canada, thanks for letting me stay.

CHAPTER ONE

LAINEY KLINE STARED at the chocolate cake, which had the words *sorry I'm leaving you* piped in shaky white icing. Was an apology dessert over the top? Subtlety had never been her style, and announcing that she had secured a new job—and planned to relocate from Melbourne to London—required a special touch. A special *chocolate* touch.

Her two best friends, Imogen and Corinna, stared at her. "You're breaking up with us via cake?" Imogen said. "Seriously?"

"This isn't a breakup," Lainey replied, trying her hardest to replicate the positive spiel she'd practised in front of her mirror. "I'm simply suggesting a long-distance relationship."

Imogen shook her head. "A month is *not* enough time to say goodbye."

"I can't believe you kept it quiet for a whole week." Corinna grinned.

The three of them sat at the picnic table in Corinna's parents' backyard. Even though Corinna had moved out two years ago, the three women still loved to congregate at the McKnight family home, especially during the summer. Their lush, sprawling garden was filled with native trees that attracted colourful birds like rosellas and galahs. Their song usually soothed Lainey, but not today.

"It wasn't easy, believe me." Lainey watched the bubbles race to the top of her champagne flute. "When I booked the flight, I wanted to scream it from the rooftops. But I had to tell you both at once, and you two are so difficult to coordinate."

Between Imogen's long hours and Corinna's bustling social schedule, it'd taken a week to find a day where they were both free. But that was their deal— all news had to be shared as a group. Easier to avoid the whole "three's a crowd" issue if there were no favourites. But it wouldn't be like that for much longer. Worry stabbed Lainey in the gut. She knew her best friends would grow closer once she left; hopefully they wouldn't forget about her altogether.

Hence the cake. Hard to forget about a person who piped her apologies in buttercream.

"So, hairdresser to the stars, huh? Maybe you'll end up doing the royal family." Imogen forced a smile, but her eyes glimmered with moisture. "Well, Prince Harry, anyway. Poor old Wills hasn't got much left. He's already in comb-over territory."

"I doubt they'll let me near the royals," Lainey said, reaching for the big knife next to the cake and slicing straight through *sorry*. "Besides, I'll be more focused on the social media side of things."

Lainey had been a hairdresser ever since she

walked out of school on her sixteenth birthday. Now she had eight years in the industry, which was by far the longest time she'd ever stuck to anything. Certainly longer than her failed attempts at reading tarot cards or working as a Red Bull promo girl. Two years ago, bored and desperate for creativity, she'd started posting her hairstyles on Instagram. Within a year, she'd amassed over a million followers and had brands foaming at the mouth to work with her.

Then she'd parlayed that into a gig as a social media consultant with a well-known celebrity hairstylist in London.

"But the contract is only six months, right?" Imogen asked as she handed a slice of cake to Corinna. "Then you'll come back?"

"I'm hoping they'll put me on permanently." The finality of the move settled in the pit of Lainey's stomach.

"Of course we'll miss you," Corinna said, shooting Imogen a look, "but I'm glad you've found a way to turn your passion into a job. This sounds like an amazing opportunity."

With the scent of eucalyptus on the breeze and the late-afternoon sun beating down, Lainey wondered if she should have picked another location for her big announcement. There were so many memories here. And, as excited as she was about her new job, the thought of leaving her best friends behind made her feel ill. Like her body physically rejected the idea of them being apart.

It's for the best. You've been miserable, and a fresh start is exactly *what you need.*

"I'm happy for you, too," Imogen said, her words a little blurred around the edges. The girl was a total lightweight—two champagnes and she was already entering tipsyville. "But I *do* wish you'd been able to find such a cool job here."

"I need to get away." Much to her horror, Lainey's voice wobbled.

Imogen frowned. "Get away from what?"

A confession hovered on the tip of her tongue. She wanted to blurt her secret, but what was the point? The decision was made. She was leaving in one short month, and Lainey made it a rule not to dwell on the negative.

"I just meant there are more opportunities overseas," she said carefully. "I'm going nowhere here. Marsha didn't seem to care that I resigned, since she thinks we're all replaceable, and it's not like I have a relationship to tie me down. Thank *God*."

She hoped the booze would prevent Imogen from noticing how false Lainey's voice sounded. Corinna raised a brow but mercifully didn't press for more information.

"But you're sworn to secrecy," Lainey went on. "I want to tell everyone else myself." She looked them both in the eye and smiled when they nodded. "I'd rather people hear it directly from me."

Although the interview process for this job had been going on for almost two months, Lainey hadn't breathed a word of it to anyone until she'd signed a contract and booked her flight a week ago. Part of her hadn't really believed it would happen. Even now, the whole thing felt a little surreal.

"Have you got a 'before I leave the motherland' bucket list?" Corinna asked. "There must be something you want to do before you go."

Not something, but some*one*. Lainey's move was as much about chasing her career dreams as it was about escaping the futility of her situation in Melbourne. She'd done something dumb. Idiotic. Monumentally stupid.

An action that might one day be documented in her memoir, under the title "Ways I Like to Torture Myself."

Over the years, Lainey had developed a gigantic crush on the one guy who was totally and utterly out of reach. The one guy who wouldn't look twice at her—Corinna's big brother.

Worse, seeing Damian McKnight get married, divorced and then pimped out on *Australia's Most Eligible* had torn her up inside. All her dreams for turning her adoration of rom-coms into a romantic reality had vanished. The only solution was to be somewhere else, so she could focus on the important stuff—like her career—and forget that she was doomed to have a miserable love life because she wanted the one man she couldn't have.

"This is the perfect opportunity to go wild," Corinna said. "You can do whatever you like here, then flit off to England without consequences. Surely there's someone you've always wished you could have it out with. Maybe a crazy customer that you hate?"

"Or maybe I should tell your brother I think he's hot," Lainey said with a wink. Corinna pretended to stick her fingers down her throat, and the three women laughed.

It was a running gag—both Lainey and Imogen considered Damian McKnight to be the highest level of hotness—usually reserved for the Hemsworth brothers and Prince Harry. But jokes were the only thing keeping Lainey's deep-seated attraction a secret—because the more she overplayed it, the less they believed it was anything serious. Therefore, she could hide in plain sight.

He was her Prince Charming, her Mr. Darcy, the Harry to her Sally. The Danny to her Sandra Dee. The only guy who'd ever truly known her.

"Speaking of Damian," Corinna said, "did you know he scored a ticket to the Carmina Ball?"

"Wow." Imogen blinked. "My sister's stupid fiancé is going…without her, I might add, which has shocked absolutely no one."

The Carmina Ball was something Lainey only knew about from drooling over red carpet dresses online. It was invite only and distinctly too upper-crust for lowly hairdressers like her.

"Apparently it's five grand to attend," Imogen added. "Five. Freaking. Grand!"

"I bet that's a drop in the ocean to them," Lainey said, rolling her eyes. "But still, Damian must be excited he scored an invite."

"Who knows with him?" Corinna shrugged. "That guy seems to have a permanent scowl on his face these days. I told him to be careful—the wind might change and then he'll be stuck with that ugly mug for the rest of his life."

Lainey snorted. "I'd still do him."

Imogen almost choked on her cake as Corinna visibly shuddered and said, "You guys are disgusting."

"He's cute, Cori. I know you're related, but you have to admit it." Imogen grinned.

"We are *not* talking about my brother," Corinna said. "Besides, I want to know what the gossip is with your sister, Immie. You're telling me Richie Rich couldn't afford to get her a ticket?"

"He said that it's going to be all business and that he'd rather spend the money to take her on a romantic getaway to some fancy-pants resort in Thailand than get her a ticket to the ball." Imogen's lips curled back into an uncharacteristic sneer. "But *I* think it's because he's cheating on her with someone who'll be there."

"Whoa." Lainey held up her hands. "Since when is he cheating on her?"

"Penny said something that has been bothering me for ages. Dan goes to Sydney a few days each month for work." Imogen toyed with her pearl earring. "Last month I was at the Boatbuilders Yard in South Wharf having drinks with people from work, and I saw him."

"But he was supposed to be in Sydney?" Corinna asked.

"Yep, and I'd spoken to Penny that afternoon. She said he wasn't coming back until the following night." She gritted her teeth. "I didn't know what to do. He was with this blonde and they looked like they were flirting, but I lost him in the crowd."

"Did you tell Penny?" Lainey asked.

Imogen sighed. "I tried to, but she accused me of hating him from day one. She wouldn't listen."

"Perhaps he came home early," Lainey suggested. "He might've been called back for a meeting. It could be completely innocent."

"I can't explain it…" Imogen sighed. "I know something is going on. I'm *sure* of it."

"What are you going to do?" Lainey asked.

Imogen fished her phone out of her pocket and pulled up a photo of a woman wearing a mask. It was covered in pink stones, the colour of rosé. White feathers sprayed up from the top, and lengths of superfine chain in rose gold hung down in elegant loops on either side.

"Is that you?" Lainey asked, and Imogen nodded. "I'm not following."

"I'm going to sneak into the Carmina Ball. Then I'm going to catch him in the act and make sure my sister doesn't walk down the aisle with the wrong guy."

Lainey squinted at the picture, the intricate design of the gems and beads mesmerising her. It was impossible to see Imogen's features. Add some dramatic makeup and a wig or change of hair colour, and her identity would truly be concealed.

"You're crazy," Corinna said with a shake of her head. Her phone buzzed and she snatched it off the table. "Sorry, ladies, it's Joe. I need to take this."

"Hi, Joe!" Lainey and Imogen chorused when she answered the phone, dissolving into laughter when Corinna rolled her eyes and headed into the house.

"Where's the loyalty?" Imogen said as she reached for her champagne and sloshed a little over the edge. They were *definitely* getting an Uber home tonight.

"He does seem like a decent guy," Lainey said. "She has better luck than me, that's for damn sure. I haven't been on a date in months."

Imogen laughed. "That means your life hasn't been unnecessarily complicated for months."

"I thought you enjoyed hearing about my dating disasters." Lainey grinned and scooped some icing off what was left of the cake. Her message was now an incoherent mess. "Solid entertainment value there."

Disasters was certainly the right word. While Corinna always attracted cute, decent men, Lainey ended up in every kind of impossible, couldn't-make-it-up dating scenario there was. She'd dated a guy who turned out to be as old as her father, two ex-cons and a circus performer who liked to watch her walk around wearing only a pair of mismatched socks.

"In a kind of masochistic way...yeah, I do." Imogen forked some cake into her mouth.

"Why is it masochistic?"

"Because I know I'll be picking up the pieces when it goes bad." Imogen's eyes sparkled as an amused smile formed. "What happened when that guy wanted you to move to the hippie commune in Nimben? I told you not to go with him."

"I didn't go with him...well, not all the way." Lainey bit down on her lip to stifle a laugh.

Okay, so Imogen was usually the voice of reason. Which made her plans to sneak into the Carmina Ball all the more interesting. The thing was, if anyone was going to break the rules and do it properly, it would be Imogen. She'd have plans and contingencies and all the necessary details worked out.

"I drove all the way to the state border to drag your butt home," Imogen said, crossing her arms. "And what about the time you decided to go camping in the middle of nowhere with that guy who got arrested and left you stranded?"

"I didn't know the car was stolen." Lainey shrugged. "Besides, I'm pretty sure Damian bailed me out that particular occasion."

Imogen chuckled. "Speak of the devil."

Lainey's head whipped around. The object of her fantasies was in the doorway. Damian McKnight, in all his panty-singeing glory, wearing a pair of faded blue jeans that hugged his thighs to perfection. His blue checked shirt was open at the collar and rolled back at the sleeves, inviting Lainey's eyes to linger on smooth olive skin.

"What were you saying about me?" he asked warily as he walked over.

As usual, Lainey gave him a saccharine smile, which he didn't return. He might have been all biceps and close-up-worthy eyes, but Damian McKnight was the sworn enemy of all that was fun. Mr. Stick Up His Butt, she'd called him once.

It was truly baffling why she found his seriousness so damn appealing.

He used to be fun before Jenny broke his heart into a million little pieces. Maybe you need to show him how to have fun again...

Yeah, right. Damian had always acted like she was a little bug that buzzed around him, invading his space. Hanging around where she wasn't wanted. And the one time she'd gotten drunk and tried to kiss him the year after he got divorced, he'd made it clear he wouldn't go there with her, despite the fact that he'd been giving her eyes all night. She was twenty-one then, and fully aware of what she wanted with him.

"We were reminiscing about some of Lainey's finer dating moments," Imogen said.

Damian smirked. "Like that time you had to climb out that lawyer's window because his other girlfriend came home early?"

"He told me he was single," Lainey protested, reaching for her drink. "I would *never* have dated him if I'd known."

He shook his head. He often did that around her... they *all* did. "Where's your third musketeer?"

"Inside, talking to her lover boy," Lainey replied.

"And what about you?" His gaze skated over her. "Any recent victims?"

Lainey drained the rest of her champagne and tried to appear as though she hadn't noticed the searing look. Damian had the Blue Steel thing down pat, and she knew for a fact that women all over Melbourne would give their right arm to be on the receiving end of it. And since his stint on TV, the guy even had a fan club on Facebook. A freaking fan club!

"I love being single, you know that. But I might head out later, see if anyone takes my interest."

His jaw tensed. *Interesting.* "If you do, be sure to give him my condolences."

There was a strange undercurrent in Damian's tone, a little hum of tension that sent ripples of curiosity through her. Was it because he didn't care or because he didn't like the idea of her chatting someone up?

She never could tell with him. He said he wasn't interested, but his body language told a different story.

"And what are you up to tonight?" she asked.

"Not much. Mum needed a hand with the pipes in the kitchen, and Dad's back is still giving him a hard time," he said with a brisk nod. "I'm exchanging hard labour for lasagne."

Well, damn if that didn't make her insides melt. Despite his sharp rise in business and wealth, Damian never forgot where he came from or who was important in his life. He was dedicated to his family, always making himself available for his parents or his sister.

It still baffled Lainey why his wife had left. Who in their right mind would walk away from *him*?

Damian's eyes flicked over her once more, and she felt it all the way down to her toes. "Anyway, I'd better get to it. Behave yourselves, okay?"

"Never." Lainey had to contain a laugh as he rolled his eyes, walking away without a backward glance.

The man had an ass so perfect it should be in a gallery.

"So uptight," Lainey muttered, her eyes locked onto the way his hips rolled as he disappeared into the house. "But so *smoking* hot."

Imogen snorted. "I think you mean 'so unattainable.'"

"Potato, po-*tah*-to." Lainey tapped her nails against the table. "So, I want to know more about this whole Carmina Ball plan. I'm intrigued."

"I was going to keep it a secret." Imogen dropped her face into her hands. "But Corinna kept topping up my glass and then with the shock of your news, I...ugh. Please don't tell anyone."

"My lips are sealed." Lainey mimicked turning a key in a lock. "How are you going to get in without an invitation?"

"I know the caterer." Imogen leaned forward. "I'll arrive with her team and then slip off to change into my costume after the party starts."

Lainey sucked on her lower lip. The plan was totally insane. Absolutely and utterly bonkers.

Speaking of Damian, did you know he scored a ticket to the Carmina Ball?

Corinna's words rang in her head like a siren song, along with the teasing thought of being able to do anything she wanted before leaving for London. If Imogen could sneak into the ball in disguise, Lainey could, too.

What the hell will you do once you get in?

Anything. A wicked smile curved on her lips. She could do anything at all.

"I don't suppose there's room for a sidekick on this grand adventure?" Lainey asked.

"Now why would you want to do that?"

While Lainey was confident in her seduction abilities with men in general, Damian seemed to be her white whale. He resisted her where other men didn't, and she had her suspicions it wasn't due to a lack of physical chemistry. They had it in excess. Her body sparked whenever he came near her. And as for him... well, she'd caught him looking at her before with that heated blue gaze. But for some reason, he never acted on her flirty suggestions, never returned any teasing innuendo.

But the whole point of a masquerade ball was to have a little fun without revealing your identity, right? She could test her theory that they did have something between them.

Damian McKnight had a hold over her unlike anyone else. He was a man among boys. A total and utter fantasy.

In quiet moments, she'd wondered if he was the reason she chose to date flighty, flaky types. She could never have Damian, so she went for the opposite—the loose cannons and the jokers. The guys who would never tempt her into falling in love.

"Let me revise that," Imogen said, narrowing her eyes. "Do I *want* to know?"

"Probably not," Lainey admitted. Her eyes snagged

on the empty doorway where Damian had exited a few minutes ago.

"Are you doing what I think you're doing?" Imogen asked, tracking Lainey's gaze. "Not a good idea."

"Please, Immie," she said. "He won't know it's me. I'll keep my mask on and I'll get out of there if things go bad."

"I thought you were only trying to wind Corinna up." Her friend gripped her drink, her hand hovering in midair as though she'd forgotten about it. "Were you serious about him this whole time?"

"I was," she admitted. "But he never treated me as anything more than a little sister type. Please. This might be my only chance. Once I'm gone...that's it."

After a moment, Imogen threw her hands in the air. "Fine. But I will not take sides if this blows up."

Lainey bit her lip, trying to trap the excitement inside her. One night to see if her fantasies could come true. Then she'd move on and pretend it never happened.

CHAPTER TWO

DAMIAN'S WEEK HAD started bad and ended in a steaming pile of crap. Seeing Lainey over the weekend had distracted him with all kinds of inappropriate thoughts, which made him guilty and snappy. He was like Snow White's rejected eighth dwarf.

Distraction he could handle. Failure, on the other hand...that was *not* tolerable.

"How'd the meeting go?" Aaron reached for his gin and tonic. They'd arranged to meet at their usual place, an older bar that was no longer trendy, which therefore meant you could get decent service. Plus, with the Carmina Ball happening tomorrow night, Damian was sure he'd need to store up all his energy. Parties weren't really his thing, but getting an invite was akin to being accepted by people who mattered. And while everyone would be in masquerade dress, he'd been told a lot of business was conducted if you knew the right people and asked the right questions.

It all sounded a little secret society to him.

He grunted. "Don't ask."

"That good, huh?"

Damian tossed back his drink, trying to drown the sick feeling in his stomach. Tonight's meeting was supposed to have been the start of a new era for his management consulting business. Another rung climbed toward the shining carrot dangling a hairbreadth out of reach. Validation. Retribution.

Instead he'd gotten a big fat face-to-face rejection. In under five minutes, which was salt in the wound. Not that Damian had ever been frightened of the word *no*. People had knocked him back left, right and centre when he'd first struck out on his own. But this client was different.

This client was personal.

"He said he didn't want to have his family-friendly image associated with someone like me. Like I'm a fucking social pariah. It was one reality show, for Chrissakes."

He regretted going on *Australia's Most Eligible* more than any other cock-up he'd ever made in his career. He hadn't been looking for love, like the show proclaimed—none of the contestants were. They wanted publicity. Name recognition. At the time, his PR person had assured him it would bring his fledgling Melbourne-based business to a national level… and it had. Damian had come across well on-screen, and his business had seen a hearty boost in attention after the show aired.

But mostly it was small stuff. And Damian wasn't happy with bread crumbs—he wanted the whole damn loaf.

Only hard work had allowed him to take his business to the next level. He'd put in long hours and hustled to get clients. Now he was operating at a level most people could only aspire to, but his reality TV show days still hung around like a bad smell.

"And the damn thing is scripted. They turn you into a character—everyone knows that." Damian shook his head. "But he said people who used 'cheap tricks' to get ahead were not the kind of people he wants to do business with. Oh, and apparently those kinds of shows are the reason our society is falling to pieces. Because nobody has 'good, old-fashioned values' anymore."

"He sounds like a dick. Anyway, you always land on your feet," Aaron replied with a shrug. "You'll get another client."

"Of course I will. But I want this one." He turned the empty whisky glass over in his hands. "I just need to figure out how to look more family friendly."

"You?" Aaron laughed. "No offence, mate, but you're not exactly the family-friendly type."

Irritation prickled under Damian's skin. He *knew* that. Getting divorced six months before he turned thirty had put a sour taste in his mouth when it came to families. And relationships. Which meant he dated with an immovable expiry. It worked for him, kept things mess-free, but after his TV stint, more people took notice of his dating habits. Potential clients included.

"What company is it?" Aaron asked.

"McPartlin & Co."

The company had started out with a single restaurant and now owned seven fine dining establishments across the country, plus another recently launched in New Zealand. The owner had also signed a lucrative deal with Coles supermarkets. They even had plans for expansion into Singapore, Hong Kong and Dubai, all within the next five years.

But the owner of the company was notoriously uptight and traditional. Hell, he'd fired one of the best chefs in the world for swearing in the kitchen, because "foul language" shouldn't be tolerated. Given it wasn't unusual for chefs to have a colourful vernacular, the news had made headlines.

"Jerry McPartlin's company." Realisation seeped into Aaron's features. "Your old boss's client?"

"That would be the one."

"Okay, buddy. You need to take a breath and think about this." Aaron put his drink down and planted a hand on Damian's shoulder. "I know you're pissed about what happened, but—"

"He was screwing my wife, Aaron."

That was what this was about. Revenge. The McPartlin & Co. deal had launched Ben's boutique consulting firm into the big leagues. They were his flagship client.

And Damian was going to do everything in his power to take the business from him, the way Ben had taken something precious from Damian.

The memory made red flash before his eyes like a matador's cape. "Then he had the audacity to tell me I'd never make it. That I'd never even come close to playing at his level."

"He's a prick, that's a fact well established." Aaron shook his head. "But you need to let it go. It was four years ago. It's not healthy to hang on to this shit for so long."

"Are you done, Oprah?"

"Sticks and stones, mate. I'm only saying this because you're like a brother to me." He sighed. "Have a few drinks, find a woman and forget about Ben. Forget about Jenny while you're at it. They're not worth the energy."

Aaron was the only person outside his family who knew what'd happened with his divorce and his abrupt departure from Ben's firm. Trust wasn't something Damian had in large supply, especially these days, but he'd put his life in Aaron's hands if the situation called for it.

However, the guy had married his teenage sweetheart and lived a life of sunshine and roses. He didn't understand Damian's need to settle the score.

"Having a few drinks and finding a woman is exactly why McPartlin & Co. thinks I'm wrong for them. I need a change of image."

"And how are you going to do that?"

"Maybe I should get engaged. That'll make me look like family material." Damian drummed his fingers on the bar, his mind whirring. Searching for a solution. "I could be the guy who finally settled down for the right woman."

Aaron looked at him like he was crazy. "And who would you get engaged to?"

"Someone I don't care about." In other words, someone who wouldn't be able to screw him over.

"I'd always assumed if I was going to be in a barn naked, there'd at least be a sexy cowboy involved." Lainey shimmied on the spot, pulling the dress over her hips. It was a touch too tight, but it was a loaner, so she'd have to make do.

"Are you saying I'm not good enough for a roll in the hay?" Imogen grinned. "Now, quit complaining and zip me up."

Both dresses had come from a friend of Imogen's who owned a boutique in Malvern. The sizing options for borrowed dresses had been limited. But since Lainey couldn't afford to shell out a few thousand dollars for a fancy dress, she had to suck in her stomach and avoid eating. One, because the boning in the bodice wouldn't allow for any expansion, and two, because the dresses could not get dirty under any circumstances.

And yet they were changing in a stable. Go figure.

Lainey reached for the zip at Imogen's back and tugged. It stuck at the halfway point for a moment, then slid up. It was a snug fit, but it would do.

"How do I look?" she asked.

Imogen's dress was all black lace and vampy satin—a far cry from her usually sedate approach to fashion. Her jewelled mask hid most of her face, and with a plummy stain coating her usually bare lips, Imogen was transformed.

"Incredible."

"And you…" Imogen squealed. "That hair makes you look like a totally new person."

Lainey had spent years trying to get her naturally dark blond hair to the perfect shade of Gwen Stefani platinum. But earlier that week she'd thrown years of careful bleaching and maintenance down the drain to turn herself into a fiery redhead.

The shade was a vibrant ruby colour that made her fair skin seem even more porcelain. It also warmed up her hazel eyes and gave her total *Little Mermaid* vibes. So much that she was starting to wonder why she'd never been a redhead before.

Imogen reached up to adjust the glittering fabric on Lainey's dress. "You're going to cause trouble for every man in that ballroom."

The skimpy straps and plunging neckline left no room for a bra. And there was a slit up the side of the twinkling silver skirt, which made her feel all kinds of exposed. But that was exactly why she'd picked it. If she was going to do something stupid and reckless, then she was damn well going to look hot while she did it.

"One wrong move and I'm going to flash my boobs," she said with a rueful grin. "Chances are Damian will totally ignore me and I'll end up scandalising Melbourne's society crowd."

"At least you're here for a positive reason," Imogen said. She sounded stressed, though it was hard to tell with the mask covering her face.

"Everything will work out okay. You've thought

this plan through. You're looking after your sister," Lainey said. "But you're not doing anything wrong."

Imogen nodded. "Exactly. I just want to get evidence that he's cheating."

"Wouldn't you'd rather find out he's *not* cheating?" Lainey raised a brow.

Imogen pressed her lips into a flat line. "Don't judge my plans and I won't judge yours, okay?"

"Fair enough." Lainey held her hands up. "I solemnly swear not to mention it again."

"Good." Imogen nodded and scooped up the uniforms they'd worn to sneak into the venue with the owner of the catering company. "We can leave these here and Marie will pick them up later."

Lainey nodded. "What's she getting out of this, by the way?"

"I'm putting her on the preferred suppliers list at work," Imogen said. "We use caterers all the time, so it would be a big chunk of business for her. We're supposed to put all new suppliers through a panel vetting process, but I just told my boss we should use her and he said okay."

"Privilege of being the CEO's right-hand lady?"

"Exactly, and I know she's amazing at her job so I don't feel *too* bad about doing it. You know I don't normally bend the rules, but I figure she's going out on a limb for me…" Guilt flickered across Imogen's expression, but she quickly refocused. "Anyway, let's get this show on the road."

"Knock 'em dead." Lainey gave Imogen's hands a

squeeze and then hung back while her friend headed along the building toward the side entrance.

Imogen paused at the corner, where a path curved through the garden, and peeked around. She held up her hem, a handful of black lace and satin exposing some strappy silver sandals with a sensible midheight heel. Lainey smiled. So there *was* a hint of the real Imogen under her costume.

A second later, Imogen flashed Lainey a thumbs-up. And then she was gone. The plan was for Lainey to count to thirty and then make her way down the same path.

Digging into her clutch, she pulled out a round compact mirror. Unlike the sleek dress, fancy shoes and glamorous mask, the compact was rough around the edges. Well loved. The gold clasp was tarnished and the embroidered rose on the lid had seen better days. But tonight it was her talisman. The compact had belonged to Lainey's grandmother, a woman who'd done fearless things in the name of love. Like giving up marriage to a wealthy aristocrat and forgoing a life of privilege, causing her family to cut her off and cast her out. She'd given it all up for him— her comfort, her security, her family.

She would understand why Lainey was doing something outrageous to have one night with the guy of her dreams.

"One cat dog, two cat dog, three cat dog," Lainey murmured, forcing herself not to speed through her count using the technique her mother had taught her when she was little. "Four cat dog, five cat dog…"

Around twenty cat dogs, she couldn't take it anymore. Touching her fingertips to the black lace mask, she stifled a nervous giggle. Glimmering beads brushed her cheeks every time she moved her head. Combined with the scandalous dress, it made her feel fiercely powerful. Sexy in a way she hadn't ever experienced.

Lainey's high heels made clicking sounds against the stone path. As she turned the corner, a courtyard opened in front of her. The area was large, surrounded by standard white roses and gardenia trees. The scent was intoxicating. Two large glass doors opened to the ballroom, and music spilled out into the air. Lainey's stomach fluttered.

A waiter holding a tray of wineglasses passed by, and she flagged him down. She'd seen him earlier when they'd entered with the catering assistants. But his eyes swept over her without a hint of recognition. *Phew.*

Lainey headed toward the open doors. She wanted to get the lay of the land—see how many people were inside and figure out whether it would be hard to find Damian. The Carmina Ball was in full swing.

Sucking in a breath so big it caused the boning in her dress to dig into her ribs, Lainey stepped into the ballroom. It was like something out of a movie— mysterious masked men in tuxedos, women in incredible gowns, the glittering chandeliers that looked as though they belonged in the castle from *Beauty and the Beast*. It was all her fairy-tale romance-movie dreams come to life.

Was it even real?

She brought her wineglass to her lips, revelling in the flutter of her heart against her rib cage. Yes, it was real. And tonight, she was going to bring her longest-held fantasy to life.

CHAPTER THREE

DAMIAN DIDN'T MIND wearing a suit. Hell, he didn't even mind wearing a tux. But being forced to look like a cross between the Phantom of the Opera and an *Eyes Wide Shut* reject was pushing the limits.

The ballroom of Patterson House stretched out before him, resplendent with gold detailing. The building had been erected in the late 1800s, but the ballroom had been remodelled in the '30s. It was a fitting location for such an event—heaving with history and old money, blue blood to the very core. The women were dressed in spectacular ballgowns and the men in tuxedos. *Everyone* wore a mask. Some were simple scraps of lace or filigree, leaving most of the face bare and recognisable. Others were more ornate, heavily beaded and elaborately designed, a feature of a person's outfit rather than an afterthought.

He tugged at his own black leather mask. It had been designed to resemble a crow, and included sculpted satin feathers. Apparently, it made him look mysterious. That's what he got for letting Aaron's wife pick out a mask for him. But he'd made sure to ask her for one that only covered half his face. He didn't see the point of attending without letting people know he was here, especially since an invite to the Carmina Ball was supposed to be life changing—acceptance from the people who "mattered." A chance to get in with Melbourne's power players.

But the invite had come with strings attached… to the tune of five thousand dollars for entry and expected participation in the night's charitable events. Not that Damian had an issue donating to charity, of course. But he'd told his folks a little white lie about coming tonight so they didn't worry he was frittering away his recently acquired wealth.

"Don't you look handsome," Jessie, Aaron's wife, said as she placed a hand on his arm. "I knew you'd be a good addition to this circle."

"Why, because you wanted some eye candy?" Damian smirked when she slapped her palm lightly against his bicep.

"Watch it," Aaron said, sliding an arm around her waist. "You don't need to worry about me getting jealous, but Jessie plots revenge in the way only a woman can. Hell hath no fury like a grammar girl scorned."

Unlike Damian, both Aaron and Jessie had grown up as part of the elite, with expensive private school educations and safety nets padded with zeros. But regardless of their privilege, both were incredibly hardworking people. He'd met Aaron when they were in their early twenties as graduates at a big four consulting firm, doing grunt work and jumping every time a partner made eye contact. They'd learned the ropes together, climbing the corporate ladder in tandem until Damian left to work at Ben's firm, and he and Aaron had maintained a valuable friendship ever since.

And it was because of Aaron and Jessie that he was here tonight, so he really *should* try to have fun.

"No denial, huh?" Damian said, nudging her with his elbow.

Jessie laughed. "They wouldn't have put you on TV if you didn't look the part."

"Don't encourage him," Aaron muttered. "I had to find an extra ticket so his ego could attend tonight, too."

Damian chuckled and scanned the room. "So, give me the lowdown. Who's who around here?"

"That's Arthur Wentworth and his sons, Parker and Ian," Jessie said. "They own the Wentworth Group. Department stores, luxury vehicles, couture fashion—you name it."

"They're one of my clients," Aaron added. "Don't even think about poaching them."

Damian smiled. Aaron had worked his way up to partner at that firm where they'd started their careers. Some days Damian wondered what might've been if he'd stayed there, too, instead of following Ben. Would he still have his positive attitude...or his wife?

"I won't dip my hand in the cookie jar, I promise," he drawled.

"Who else would be of interest?" Jessie clucked her tongue. "The Allbrook family is here—they own a huge architecture firm that does a lot of high-end residential towers in the city. We've got judges, politicians, CEOs, barristers, even a few celebrities. I heard a rumour that Cate Blanchett might be coming."

"Excellent. I'll ask for her autograph," Damian said with a straight face.

Jessie looked horrified for a moment before she realised he was joking. "Damian, please."

"Your South Yarra is showing," he said. "You might want to cover that up."

"Not here." Aaron chuckled. "It's practically a requirement for entry."

Jessie rolled her eyes and pushed on, pointing out people across the room. "Oh, and my friend Amelia told me the restaurateur Jerry McPartlin is going to be here. I ate at his new place, Gilt, last week. It was absolutely divine."

Damian's ears pricked up, ignoring Aaron, who was giving him a stern look. "Really?"

Suddenly, the evening had gotten a whole lot more interesting. This would be the perfect opportunity for him to chat with the uptight family man in a social setting and try to figure out exactly what he needed to do to secure the guy's business.

Did he need a girlfriend? A fiancée? Promise to give up his firstborn? Whatever it was, Damian was ready to sign on the dotted line. Snagging McPartlin & Co. would be the best possible thing he could do, because another big-name client was extra security. Relying only on one or two big fish meant your business balanced on a knife's edge, and keeping the client happy often overtook the uncomfortable but necessary process of crafting the right solution for them.

The fact was, any big client would help him. But he *wanted* this one.

Signing McPartlin & Co. would give him the closure he needed to finally shut the door on his past. Or rather, slam it in the faces of those who'd broken his heart.

A while later, Damian stood at the edge of the crowd, watching. He felt like a kid at the zoo, his face pressed against the glass of the reptile enclosure. Everything happening in front of him was foreign. Alien. This wasn't his world...yet.

Sure, he was rich by most people's standards. He lived in a luxury hotel that cost more per week than what he'd spent on his first car. But that would be nothing to these people.

And he knew that an evening like this could make or break him. Get the right connections and his business would soar. Piss off the wrong person and... well, he could easily be back to doing grunt work for some asshole.

Damian clenched his fists and let the fantasy of punching his ex-boss in the face roll through him like a wave. The betrayal was no less raw today than it had been four years ago when he'd come back to the office late one night to pick up his laptop and found his wife spread-eagled on Ben's desk.

The Carmina Ball was the key to it all. To revenge. To *closure*.

If only he could get close to Jerry McPartlin.

The man stood a few metres away, surrounded by a group of women who wore dresses so large they created a barrier around him. And it looked like he was loving the attention, too. Damian could wait. Patience and determination were two of his greatest strengths, and he would find the perfect moment to strike. Before the night was out, he *would* have a plan.

"I wasn't expecting to find such good company playing wallflower," a silky voice said.

A woman sidled up to him, her shimmering mask of white lace studded with gems that winked at him. Black hair flowed over one shoulder in stark contrast to a floor-length white ballgown. Her full lips were painted red and they curved into an inviting smile.

"That depends. What kind of company are you looking for?" He stuck out his hand. "I'm Damian."

"Hannah," the woman replied. "You have a familiar face."

Ugh. He could almost guarantee what was coming next, the one sentence that made him cringe every bloody time.

You're that guy from Australia's Most Eligible.

But instead she cocked her head, the gems on her mask shimmering, and said nothing.

He was about to respond when a blur of red stole the words from his mouth. Moisture soaked through Damian's dress shirt and the sound of glass shattering pierced the subtle din of the ballroom. He'd been hit.

"Oh my God." A woman with blazing-red hair reached out to touch his chest, her fingertips sending fire through his veins. "I am so sorry."

Damian looked down. Wine streaked his chest, a slash of angry red against the crisp white cotton. The broken glass glittered in a pool of liquid on the floor, its stem rolling across the parquet.

"You got me good." He brushed his hands over his chest in a futile attempt to clean himself up.

"Excuse me." The redhead waved to get the attention of a waiter, but there was already a small army descending to clean up the mess.

Her silver gown was bunched in one hand, revealing a finely boned ankle encased in a strappy, high-heeled shoe. She tried to take a step but couldn't shift her full weight onto her foot.

"You might have some glass in your shoe," he said, reaching out to her. "Come on. Let's get you cleaned up."

She accepted his hand. Her mask was so detailed it was impossible to see much of her face—it covered her entirely from above her brows to above her lips. "I'm so sorry, my hem got caught…"

Damian narrowed his eyes at the sound of her voice. It was familiar, but he couldn't place it. Maybe she was a business acquaintance? Or someone he'd met during filming? She seemed the glamorous type who might be part of the entertainment industry. But without seeing her face, it would be impossible to tell, and there couldn't be too many people he knew who could afford the Carmina Ball's ticket price.

Plus, he was *sure* he would have remembered a woman with hair the colour of rubies. A woman whose touch stirred something impossibly primal and strange inside him.

He looped her arm around his neck and supported her slight weight. But a few hobbling steps later, when it was clear she was frightened to put pressure on her foot, he lifted her into his arms and strode through the ballroom with what felt like the whole city watching.

CHAPTER FOUR

BROKEN GLASS AND bloodshed weren't supposed to be part of the deal. Not to mention the fact that she'd come precariously close to getting red wine on her borrowed finery. But it was the stupid dress that caused the problem in the first place. Who was tall enough for these damn dresses? Amazonians?

The fabric had gotten caught under her heel and she'd stumbled, the wine splashing across Damian as the glass escaped her grip. She was only supposed to slosh a little over the edge, just enough to interrupt him and the glamorous woman in the white dress who was about to go in for the kill.

But oh no. That would have been too easy, and Lainey never could seem to take the easy route.

So elegant, Kline. Like a drunk baby llama on roller skates.

But being weightless in Damian's arms was more than she could have hoped for, at least within the first five minutes. Now all she had to do was cross her fingers that she hadn't embedded glass in her foot.

"You okay?" he asked as they exited the ballroom and headed to the powder rooms.

The mask covered only half of his face, one eye and cheek, Phantom of the Opera–style. That was how she'd spotted him so easily. Tonight he was freshly shaven, his olive skin smooth. By the end of the night he'd have a shadow there, a hint of darkness impressing itself on his clean-cut image. Like a reminder that he was more than he appeared.

"I'm not about to pass out from blood loss, if that's what you mean," she replied in the voice she'd been practising all week. She spoke slower and breathier than normal, trying to disguise the very last thing that could give her away.

"I should hope not." His tone was heavy with amusement. "I doubt they'll take the tux back if it's got blood on it."

A five-thousand-dollar entry price and Damian had rented a tuxedo? For some reason that made her grin like an idiot. No matter how rich he got, there would always be a hint of where he came from lurking beneath. And damn if that didn't make her heart swell.

No hearts, no flowers, no chocolates. Cut that shit out right now. This is a fantasy. Nothing more.

"At least you'd have a story to tell."

"I have a lot of stories to tell. That's not my problem."

"What *is* your problem?" Her heartbeat kicked up a notch when his eyes shifted down to hers. With the black surrounds of the mask, the sharp blue of his irises was even more stark and breathtaking. "Maybe I can help."

The corner of his lip quirked. "You'll do the opposite of that, I'm afraid."

"Try me. You never know when a stranger might be exactly what you need."

A little seed of guilt unfurled in her stomach. She was no stranger and everything about this encounter was for her own selfish gain—to appease the fantasy that'd plagued her for years.

You're not forcing him to do anything. If this goes somewhere, it'll be because he accepts your offer, not because you held a gun to his head.

They reached the private powder rooms. There were no cubicles for the guests of Patterson House, that was for damn sure. Each powder room was spacious, with a single private sink and toilet. Lainey thanked her lucky stars for the diva-like needs of the rich, because it would afford them some privacy.

Holding her, Damian nudged the door open with his foot and let it swing shut behind him. The click of the automatic latch was like a single firework in the quiet room, the sound echoing off the tiles and rattling around in her brain. He set her on the marble countertop. Lainey glanced around. The room was like no other bathroom she'd ever seen—the taps were gold and ornate, and fresh flowers sat in a vase that was most likely crystal. They even had a fancy hand soap dispenser that resembled a Fabergé egg.

"Let's have a look at the damage." He crouched in front of her, pushing her dress up so he could get to her foot. His fingers made quick work of the strap on her sandal, and with one hand bracing her ankle, he slipped the shoe off.

The action was so soft and caring that Lainey's heart caught in her throat. The warmth of his fingers was like an aphrodisiac, potent. Intoxicating. Her blood hummed at the contrast of it all—the firmness of his grip mixed with the careful, tender touch.

"I think you can keep the foot," he said, his tone serious. But the twinkle in his eye gave him away.

It appeared Damian *did* still have a sense of humour, much to her delight.

"You think?" Lainey peered down and wriggled her toes. The light glinted off the shimmery black nail polish she'd chosen because it reminded her of the stars against a night sky. "The word *think* isn't something I want to hear when we're discussing amputation."

He chuckled and lifted her foot higher to inspect the sole. "I'm going to rub my thumb across the ball of your foot. If you feel any pain, then there could be glass under the skin."

She nodded, her breath stuttering like a car engine failing to turn over. Lainey wasn't sure she'd be able to detect pain—or anything else—as Damian inspected her. For an encounter that shouldn't have been in the least bit sexual, every nerve ending in her body was singing as though it was Christmas Day and New Year's Eve and every other damn holiday all at once.

"Do you feel anything?" He looked up.

Seeing a big man like him on his knees, looking

up at her through that sexier-than-sin mask, touching her as though she were the most precious thing in all the world...

"I think I'd be a statue not to feel something," she said, her voice low and soft. "But I'm not in pain."

He held on to her foot for a moment, his eyes fixed on her. Her calf was cradled in his palm, the heat from his skin working its way through her, turning her veins to threads of fire. Thank God she had a mask on so he couldn't see her face heating up. They stayed there—locked in that moment, frozen by intimacy—until he cleared his throat and slipped the shoe back onto her foot.

"So I'll be alright, Doc?"

"Better than alright." He stood. The tuxedo fit him perfectly, hugging his shoulders and tapering down to his waist in a line so mouthwateringly divine, it stole Lainey's breath. The only thing ruining the effect was the red wine stain. "I'm glad we checked—the last thing you want is a glass splinter."

"Exactly. Cinderella had glass on her feet, and look how that turned out."

He raised a brow. "She got the prince, didn't she?"

"The prince had to rely on the fit of a shoe." Lainey shook her head. "What she got was a dude with a bad memory and a foot fetish."

Damian chuckled. "Not into fairy tales, then?"

"Oh, I am." She swung her feet, relishing the swish of the beaded material around her ankles. "But Cinderella isn't my favourite. What woman wants a man who can't remember her face?"

"Good point." He pulled a hand towel out of a small basket beside the sink and ran it under water. "They're all kind of messed up when you think about it. Sleeping Beauty, especially."

"I prefer my romances a little more grounded in reality." Lainey swallowed as Damian dabbed at the stain on his shirt, turning the fabric damp so that it clung to his chest muscles.

If bodies were supposed to be temples, his was the Parthenon.

Maybe if you'd been able to recall that kind of crap during exams instead of checking out a hot guy, you would have done better at school.

"Do you mean the kind of movies where the woman splashes the man with red wine and seduces him in a bathroom?" He caught her gaze in the mirror.

"I haven't seduced you yet."

"Yet." His smile turned from amused to wolfish, his lips revealing a perfect set of white teeth. "So there's still hope."

"You don't even know my name."

No, he didn't know her name. And he was supposed to be focused on seducing his client, not a mysterious redhead. But having her alone, feeling her energy sparking all around him put him in his element. Not like out there, where he was an anomaly.

If she's here, then she's one of them. A rich princess type who'll be more trouble than she's worth.

Just like his ex.

But something gave him pause. There was an inkling, more the potential for a feeling than a feeling itself, that said he was wrong. When she'd dropped her glass, the first thing out of her mouth had been an apology—not an excuse or accusation. When he'd offered her help, she'd graciously accepted. And now she was teasing him. Playing with him.

The redhead was like him, an outsider looking in. He knew it.

"Maybe I can guess your name," he said, giving up on the stained shirt and throwing the face towel into the basket below the sink. "Wasn't that in a fairy tale?"

"Rumpelstiltskin. It's not a very romantic one." Her legs swung back and forth over the edge of the marble countertop. Though they didn't know each other, she seemed completely at ease. "But you can try. I'll give you three guesses, and if you lose…" She tapped a finger against her chin. "You have to share a drink with me on the balcony upstairs."

He braced his hands against the countertop, leaning toward her. She smelled like vanilla and peaches. The black beads on her mask glittered, reflecting his hungry expression in miniature, over and over.

"How many names are there in the world? I'd be a fool to take such a bet." He grinned. "Do I get any clues?"

"You don't look like a man who needs a clue."

"Some might argue that," he said drily. Damian himself thought a clue would be good right about now—one that would give him the hint to leave this woman alone and head back out to the ballroom so he could corner Jerry McPartlin.

She turned to look in the mirror for a moment. "My name has nothing to do with my hair colour."

"So not Ruby or Scarlett or Rose?"

"Nope." She tucked a strand of fiery-red hair behind her ear.

"That doesn't really narrow it down. Can I get a letter?"

"This isn't *Wheel of Fortune*."

His lip quirked. "How about a year of birth?"

"Tsk, tsk." She waggled a finger at him. "That's the one thing you should never ask a lady."

He thought for a moment, cycling through some options that would be appropriate for someone in her age group—which was tough to narrow down without being able to see most of her face. But from the smooth, unblemished skin and the way she sat, comfortable and swinging her feet...he'd put her at her midtwenties. Maybe less, although he didn't want to think about her being over a decade younger than him.

"You're holding all the cards."

She grinned. "Which is exactly how I like it."

"You're not a negotiator, are you?"

"No. I'm a romantic and a dreamer."

"Ah, so you're unemployed?"

She threw her head back and laughed, the sound striking him right in the chest. But it cut off before he could grasp hold of something that flickered out of reach. A memory.

"Do we know each other?" he asked, looking closer.

"No." The answer was immediate, her reaction drawing a line between them that made him curious as hell.

"Will you take your mask off before I guess?" He cocked his head. "Help me even the playing field a little?"

"Tonight is all about the mystery, don't you think? Strangers without faces."

Ah, so she was looking for something anonymous. He wasn't sure why that unsettled him—hell, *he'd* looked for exactly that on countless occasions. No names, no phone numbers. No repeats.

And certainly no fucking regrets.

Maybe it was because Jerry McPartlin had gotten Damian's head all messed up, but he accepted her terms. "Okay, three guesses it is."

She drew her bottom lip between her teeth, as though stifling a grin. The mysterious redhead knew she was going to win, little minx. She held up three fingers. "Go on."

"Is it…Samantha?"

One finger curled down toward her palm. "Strike one."

"How about…Natalie?"

She shook her head. "Strike two."

"Lucky last guess." He blew out a breath, enjoying the way she shifted on the countertop, a faint flush colouring her chest. "Amanda?"

She made a buzzer noise and dropped her hand down. "You owe me a drink now."

He wanted something else. No doubt she would taste better than the top-shelf stuff they were serving in the ballroom. A drink seemed far too tame for her lush, full lips and creamy skin. For that bold, flaming hair and the dress that was cut to a deep V at her chest. For the slit that flashed a shapely leg and hinted at sex and sinfulness.

He stood in front of her, his hands falling to the countertop on either side of her thighs, hemming her in. He watched her pupils flare—no fear, just desire. Her chest rose and fell with quickened breath, and her lips eased open a fraction. Taunting him. Inviting him in.

Lust battled with logic—telling him to stay and kiss her. To leave and go after Jerry McPartlin.

A series of thumps rattled the door to the bathroom, frantic and quick. "Excuse me? Is anyone in there?"

Damian stepped back and helped the redhead down from the countertop. "Looks like that's our cue to go. Can you walk okay now?"

She nodded. "Yeah."

He opened the door, allowing the redhead to exit before him. A man in an elaborate gold mask bounced up and down on the spot, clutching his stomach. He pushed past Damian and the redhead with an angry huff. "You know these bathrooms aren't for fooling around. Some people have to *use* them."

Giggling, the redhead grabbed his hand and pulled him down the corridor, away from the ballroom, to a grand curving staircase. "Come on, this way."

"I don't think there's anything up there, Ariel."

"So that's my name now?" The hazel of her irises shifted in the light, making the small amber flecks look like gold dust. "Ariel?"

"Seems fitting. Long red hair, mysteriously showing up out of nowhere." His eyes dropped down. "Great legs."

She laughed and tugged him farther along. The back of the corridor was deserted, but the sound of clanging grew louder. Just before they hit the staircase, a waiter exited from a swinging door, his uniform crisply pressed. The redhead marched right into the kitchen, as bold and brazen as anything, and plucked two champagne flutes from a silver tray that was waiting to go out.

"What are you doing?" he asked as she breezed back into the hallway as though it were totally normal for ball gown–clad guests to steal drinks.

"There's no service upstairs." She handed him a flute. "Come on, you promised me a drink on the balcony."

Damian looked toward the entrance to the ballroom, where a group of men in tuxedos were gathered. Their rich, booming laughter floated down the hall, the sound of stuffy voices discussing boring things ringing in the air.

Last chance. Go back in there and work on your plan. Or be the man McPartlin thinks you are.

The redhead leaned in close, the beaded strands on her mask brushing his cheek. Warm breath whispered over his skin as the scent of her perfume grabbed hold of his heart. "You know you want to and *I* know you want to."

He turned, his face so close to hers he could have captured her mouth. "Fine," he said. "One drink."

CHAPTER FIVE

LAINEY'S HEART HAMMERED like a toddler beating tin pots together, the feeling vibrating through her body right down to her thankfully uninjured toes. That moment in the bathroom, where Damian had asked if they knew one another, she'd thought it was all over.

James Bond she was not.

But her response must have satisfied him, because his suspicion had drained away.

Holding her hem tightly in one hand, she lifted the fabric as they ascended to the next floor of Patterson House. According to the little sign at the bottom of the stairs that politely directed guests back to the ballroom, the balcony was supposed to be off-limits. But Lainey figured if they really wanted people to stay downstairs, they would have roped it off.

In any case, she needed to get Damian in private again. He'd been about to kiss her before that bumbling idiot and his digestive issues had interrupted them. She was sure of it. And that kiss was dancing in her head. She wanted it. Bad.

As they stepped out onto the balcony, warm air

swept over Lainey's skin, reminding her how much she had on display. A shiver rippled through her.

"It's a beautiful house," Damian said.

"It is."

The balcony was as ornate as the rest of the building. White fretwork closed the balcony in while letting light filter through. The sun had started to set, and shades of orange and pink streaked the sky, making the greenery of the Patterson House gardens seem all the more vibrant. Lainey felt like a star waiting for nightfall.

"Cheers." Damian held his glass up, and she clinked her own against it. "Here's to masked strangers and wayward wineglasses."

"And fairy tales and guessing games." She sipped her drink.

"I notice you haven't asked for *my* name," he said.

Shit. She'd been too busy worrying about protecting her own identity that she'd momentarily forgotten that she wasn't supposed to know him.

"You're awfully hung up on names," she replied, walking to the edge of the balcony and peering down at the garden below.

"And you're awfully evasive." He smiled, his head tilted slightly. She recognised that look; he was trying to figure her out.

"Let's just say that being able to wear a mask was the reason I decided to come here tonight."

The scent of gardenias floated past on a breeze. The balcony overlooked the garden rather than the courtyard, and she could see two people stealing away.

Was it Imogen? Lainey tried to get a better look, but the haze of dusk made it hard to tell.

"Are you hiding from someone?" he asked. "Or pretending to be someone else?"

"A little from column A and a little from column B." She took another sip of her champagne. "And that's the truth. I'm not trying to be evasive."

"You can still be things even if you're not trying." His lip quirked. "Tell me, Ariel. If you're not yourself tonight, who are you?"

He was close. So close she could smell the cologne on his skin and the bare hint of his soap underneath. He'd used the same sandalwood soap since forever. The clean, woodsy notes were burned into her brain—and never ceased to shock her with a mix of memory and fantasy.

The visuals played like a film reel in her head, flickering images from that day years ago when she'd been studying at Corinna's place. She'd watched him strip down to his board shorts and dive into their pool. She'd imagined what would come next. Following him into the water, pulling him close, running her hand over his naked chest...

"I'm no one."

He reached for her champagne and placed the two flutes on a table. Then he did the same with her clutch. It was like being stripped down, and her empty hands felt naked without something to do. "You are most certainly *someone*."

"Maybe I'm a figment of your imagination."

"I hope not." His voice lowered, the sound rough yet silky. Like satin dragging over gravel.

Her breath hitched as his fingertips came to her waist, confident and firm. With the dress sucking her in, his hands looked enormous against her. He could overpower her, control her. She wanted him to.

The voice in her head shouted at her to press against him, but she wanted to draw this moment out. Stretch it like toffee and give her brain time to soak in every minute detail. This moment would have to sustain her for the rest of her life and become the thing she could cling to late at night. Her fantasy come to life. She couldn't—*wouldn't*—rush it.

"Why?" Her hands came to his chest.

Beneath the thick cotton of his dress shirt, he felt like sculpted stone. Hard and unyielding. Powerful. She had to remind herself to breathe, not to lose herself entirely and let something slip. Like his name.

"Because imagining things is a waste of time. Why spend energy on something that isn't real?" His hand slid around her back, pulling her closer.

"Life doesn't always measure up to a fantasy." Her voice was barely a whisper now, thin and soft and unnatural. The rest of her body struggled to function with all the adrenaline coursing through her veins.

"That's sad, Ariel."

"It's the truth." Not just that, it was the story of her freaking life. The world she'd created in her head—the world that matched the romantic stories she loved so much—was *way* better than reality. If real life truly lived up to her fantasies, then she wouldn't be wearing a mask tonight.

His head lowered to hers, hovering for what felt like her life three times over, before he ended the torture. He crushed her to him, his lips landing on hers and opening in a hot kiss, delving and exploring and tasting. Making her head spin and the world shift beneath her feet.

God help her, she was done for. Ruined for all other men. For all other kisses.

His lips were soft and full, the taste of champagne and the scent of something earthy and male lingering in her senses. Heaven. Her hand found the back of his head and her fingers thrust into his hair, pulling him closer, hoping it might stop her from levitating in his arms. From floating up into the night air.

When his hand slipped up her thigh, parting the slit in her dress, her body sang out: yes, yes, *yes*.

She ached everywhere. In her head, in her heart, between her legs. For him. Because of him.

His palm was hot against her skin, his thumb moving in slow circles against her inner thigh. Inching higher, then retreating. Moving forward and back in a maddening, teasing dance that left her breathless with need. She tightened her grip while her tongue ran along his lower lip. She nipped at him, dragging a groan from deep in his throat. The sound rubbed her nerve endings raw, heightening her sensitivity.

He kissed her as if all of his pent-up lust and attraction and protective urges spilled forth at once. As if he'd fantasised about this for the past decade just as she had. This was everything she'd wanted, and holy *hell* did it live up to expectation.

"My God," she groaned into his mouth, thrusting her body forward so their chests pressed together.

He backed her up against the railing, keeping one arm around her waist and pushing his other hand up higher so he could slide it around to cup her ass. Warm air caressed her everywhere, the tiny scrap of lace masquerading as underwear covering only the necessities. He moaned into her mouth as he grabbed bare flesh.

"You feel so damn good," he gritted out as his teeth scraped along her neck. "And you taste like heaven."

"Touch me," she whispered into his ear. "Please."

He traced the lines of her body, the curves of her hips, and felt for the heat between her legs. Pinpoints of light danced behind her shuttered lids as he finally brushed his fingers over her sex. The thin silk and lace of her underwear hid nothing. He crushed his lips against hers, kissing her rough and hard and dirty. With teeth and tongue. Ferocious. Demanding. Every cell in her body fired as if fighting for life. Fighting for survival. Fighting to hang on for that one moment of pleasure.

"Please," she whimpered. "I need more."

"The next step is you coming against my hand, princess." The growl in his voice rippled over her skin. "Because once I start, I won't stop until you're shaking with my fingers inside you."

"Yes," she gasped as he toyed with the edge of her

underwear, the back of his knuckle rubbing against her sex.

"Be sure." His teeth were at her neck, scraping the line from her jaw to her collarbone.

"I am." Her eyes fluttered shut. "I couldn't be surer. I am *so* sure right now."

He chuckled against her neck. "I like a woman who knows what she wants."

"And I like a man who's good with his hands." She arched her back as he pushed her underwear to the side, biting down on her lower lip to keep from crying out.

The last thing she wanted was to attract the attention of the people milling below. But it was hard not to let the groans fall from her mouth as he stroked her. Played with her. His fingers pressed into her, dragging the moisture from inside her sex and rubbing it over her clit. Her whole body throbbed.

"That's it." He dragged one of her legs over his hip to open her further. "Let me feel how wet you are."

His hand moved against her sex, his thumb strumming the swollen bud of her clit like he knew exactly how to make her fly. The edge of release rushed toward her, tremors starting in her thighs and spreading out, until it felt like she was going to fall. But his other hand held her steady, cradled her with a gentleness that belied the demanding fingers between her legs.

"It's too soon," she gasped, trying to hold on—to draw it out—but he knew her body too well. *Way* too well.

"It's perfect, princess." He pressed his lips to her temple. "Don't fight it."

She couldn't, even if she'd wanted to. Release rose up from her depths and blanked everything out—sound, sight, smell. It was all lost. Nothing but the electric feel of the orgasm rocketing through her.

Her hands clasped his head, her nails biting into his scalp as she tried so very hard to muffle her cries against his neck. His voice broke through as the intensity ebbed, soft and low. A whisper.

Princess.

She melted in his arms, liquid in the wake of her pleasure. But he had her. She wouldn't fall.

"That was so fucking beautiful," he whispered, grabbing her hand and bringing it down to his cock. He was like marble, hard and rigid beneath her trembling fingers. "You got me all worked up."

She righted herself, smoothing her dress down with one hand and keeping her other on him as his body pinned her to the balcony railing. "I did?"

"Those quiet little cries as you came are going to haunt me for the rest of my life."

She swallowed. This man…he was everything she'd known he'd be. Her body and soul were alive, filled with a satisfaction so vibrant, she wondered why she'd never realised that she was only half-awake before.

But when she opened her mouth to respond, the sound of footsteps froze her.

"Ahem." Three men stood at the edge of the balcony, all in tuxedos and without masks. "Looks like we're interrupting something," the one in the middle said.

Lainey wanted to shout that they were and tell them to get lost. Her perfect moment with Damian had been interrupted, and for what? So these beefcakes could judge them? She had to fight the urge to slap the smarmy smirk off the middle guy's face.

"Looks like you are," Damian said.

"Can I see your ticket?" one of the goons asked.

Lainey's heart leapt into her chest. She hadn't counted on being asked for her ticket once she was *inside* the venue. Crap. How was she going to explain that issue away?

"We've had a report of someone sneaking into the event," goon number two added. "We take the privacy of our guests very seriously."

Damian slipped his hand into the inside pocket of his jacket and handed his invite over. *Mr. Damian Edward McKnight* was written in scrolled font across thick cream paper. Lainey would bet money they'd spent more on having the invites printed than she forked out for rent each year.

"Damian McKnight," he confirmed. "My apologies to have to interrupt you, Mr. McKnight. I'm sure you understand that we have to take these matters seriously."

Damian nodded. "Of course."

Just as the goons turned to Lainey, someone came up behind them. This man was in a mask, so obviously he wasn't one of the security staff.

"I thought I heard a familiar name," he said. "I was

coming up here to get away from the crowd, and it looks like you two had the same idea."

"Mr. McPartlin." Damian's tone was flat.

As in Jerry McPartlin. *The* Jerry McPartlin. Lainey knew his name because her parents were huge fans of his first restaurant, Ora. They couldn't afford to eat there regularly, but once a year on their wedding anniversary, they splurged.

"Are you going to introduce me to your lovely guest?" Jerry motioned to Lainey.

Fuck. Of *course* it had to be Jerry McPartlin who stumbled across him with a gorgeous, nameless girl in his arms in an area of the building they weren't supposed to be in. He and the redhead had broken apart the second the security team had walked in, but why else would two people be hiding up here on a private balcony? Any hope he had of changing the man's opinion had vanished into thin air. Unless…

An idea sprang to his mind. Hadn't he been saying to Aaron that he needed to look like a family man? Like a guy who'd finally settled down?

This was either going to work brilliantly, or everything he wanted—needed—was going to come crashing down around him. Saying nothing would mean certain failure, and his motto had always been Go Big or Go Home.

"I'd like to introduce you to my fiancée, Ariel." He squeezed the redhead's hands in what he hoped was a silent plea for her to go along with his plan.

"Your fiancée?" Jerry cocked his head. "You never mentioned that you were getting married."

Damian glanced at the woman beside him, who'd stayed mercifully quiet. "Didn't think it was a necessary part of doing business."

"It's a pleasure." Jerry stuck out his hand, and the redhead hesitated a moment before accepting the gesture.

"Likewise. I'm a huge fan your restaurants, Mr. McPartlin."

"Please, call me Jerry." He kissed the back of her hand before looking back at Damian. "Charming and glamorous. Looks like you're a lucky man."

"Not lucky enough to secure your business, on account of my image." He couldn't resist the little barb, especially since it appeared as though his story had been bought. "You can't blame a man for wanting to steal a moment away with his soon-to-be wife, can you?"

"Perhaps I was too quick to judge." His gaze lingered on the redhead's hand, which wasn't wearing a ring. "Didn't you propose with a diamond?"

Shit. His mind whirred again.

"We're having something custom-made," she said, her voice silky smooth as though she hadn't been panting and breathless a few moments ago. "Damian knows how much I like things to be perfect."

She knew his name? He turned to the woman and her face tilted up to him, her lips full and pink. They curved into a smile. Of course, the security staff had said it aloud when they'd checked his invite. At least that bit of detail could lend extra authenticity to their story.

"That's my Ariel." He slipped an arm around her shoulders and drew her close. He sensed McPartlin's eye lingering on her. "She knows exactly what she wants."

"Well, I'm glad we cleared that up." McPartlin nodded.

"We still need to check your invite, miss," one of the security guys said.

The redhead stiffened beside him. Her hand tightened around his, squeezing in a way that told Damian she was *exactly* who they were looking for. No wonder she wasn't keen to give up her name.

"I'm afraid Ariel's invite met with an unfortunate end," he said. "In the bathroom."

The guards looked at one another, unsure how to handle that information.

"It's my fault," the redhead said, her voice perfectly pleasing and yet slightly breathy. "I was at the sink and my clutch got caught and spilled open."

"It's not your fault, darling." He rubbed her back in slow circles, the role of doting fiancé taking him over fully. A wicked smile curved on his lips. "I shouldn't have been so rough."

A small gasp sounded on her lips, but it was cut off by one of the guards clearing his throat. "Well, then. We should get moving."

"It was great to see you again." Damian nodded to McPartlin as he turned to leave, as well.

"Yes." The older man looked them both over once

more, as if trying to figure something out. "Enjoy the evening."

Damian and the redhead stood close together on the balcony without saying a word until the men had descended to the ground level. Her relief was palpable in the evening air, and she sagged against him.

"So you're a gate-crasher, huh?" Damian glanced down into her wide hazel eyes. "That's a bold move. This is a very important event."

"It certainly is," she replied smoothly. "Oh, dear future husband of mine."

He chuckled. Neither one of them was in a position to judge—they were both liars. Or both saviours, depending on how you looked at it.

"I guess this means I'm stuck with you for the rest of the evening, then?" she said, resting her head against his arm.

"Looks that way."

He could think of worse ways to spend an evening—and at least having company would keep him from going crazy with all the snobbery in the ballroom. However, he'd put himself into a tight spot with Jerry McPartlin. While letting the man think he had a fiancée could work to his advantage, he'd have to make sure that Jerry McPartlin didn't need to see his "future wife" ever again.

CHAPTER SIX

LAINEY COULDN'T BELIEVE her luck. Damian had practically done all the work for her—the whole thing about her being his fake fiancée meant they *had* to spend the evening together. And since he was the one who'd made that happen, she'd been able to relax and enjoy his company.

Or, more accurately, quietly freak out and enjoy his company.

They'd danced, eaten tiny, fanciful foods; she watched him bid on the silent auctions and talk to people whose names she knew from the papers. There'd been a lot of business talk, too. But he continued to introduce her as his fiancée, Ariel, and so that meant playing the supportive, doting future Mrs. McKnight. Of course, they'd had to explain the ruse to his friends, who'd eyed her with suspicion.

Now they were in the ballroom, and Lainey had her arms looped around his neck while his hand pressed into her lower back. It wasn't dancing, per se. More like swaying in time with the music. But Lainey could have died right that second and been the happiest person on earth. Even in the whole Milky Way. This was the night of her dreams...but hopefully with a dirtier ending.

"You know what this means, don't you?" he asked.

"What?" She tilted her face up to his.

"We need to leave together." He'd bowed his head, his lips brushing her ear as the gravelly words made her knees go weak. "In case people are watching."

"Of course."

Damian held her close, his hand smoothing over her lower back, exposed by her dress. "No protest? I could be anyone."

"So could I." Her fingertips found his jaw, tracing the hard angle softened by smooth skin. "But that's the whole point of a masquerade ball. We get to be anyone we want for a night."

"Why did you come here?"

"I was hoping to get swept off my feet." She grinned. "But a fake proposal will have to do."

"If memory serves me correctly, I literally did sweep you off your feet. I might even have saved your foot."

"That's not what I meant."

His forehead pressed against hers, mask to mask. Beads brushed her skin as she tilted up to him, her lips hovering a hairbreadth from his.

"What did you mean, Ariel? You wanted a man who was going to whisk you away to his castle and turn you into a princess?"

"No." She shook her head. "I wanted a man who

was going to treat me like a queen right now. A fantasy for one night—that's all I want."

Something stormy and electric shifted in his eyes, his lips tightening. But Damian wasn't a man to hide his feelings. His hands shifted lower, cupping her behind and pressing her flush against him. He was harder than an algebra exam.

"One night?" he growled in her ear. "And nothing more?"

"I promise to turn into a pumpkin at twelve on the dot." She dented her lower lip with her teeth, desperate to rub against him—to get the friction her body cried out for—but trying not to draw attention to them any more than they already had. This obviously wasn't the kind of dancing the Carmina Ball was used to. "Then you'll never hear from me again."

"That's really what you want?"

No. She wanted what he'd said—for him to whisk her away and make her his. For that proposal to be real. For the lust in his eyes to be something more. But Lainey was a pragmatist, if nothing else. And she knew there was no point wanting what she couldn't have.

"Yes," she lied. "That's exactly what I want."

His hands dropped suddenly and she stepped back, her body raging at the loss of contact. Her need chanted like a drumbeat in her bloodstream: *more, more, more*. The rushing sound in her ears drowned out the rest of the ballroom, her focus narrowing to him. Only him.

He was like a strange man-god hybrid in his black

tuxedo and mask. The curve of the design high-lighted his perfect nose—aquiline and aristocratic—the black leather making him darkly handsome. His lips formed a smile that sent a tremor through her. It wasn't friendly, wasn't romantic or caring or any of the other smiles she'd seen in the past. It was preda-tory. Delicious.

"Let's go." He held out his hand. "Now."

Lainey glanced around the room—the ball was coming to an end. Guests were already leaving, though the waiters still lingered with drinks on their trays. "Now?"

"Right now. I've done enough business for one night." He grabbed her hand and pulled her to his side, his head dropping down to her ear. "And if we don't finish this soon, I'm liable to drag you behind one of those potted plants in the next few seconds."

"That could be fun," she teased.

"I don't like being quiet, Ariel." Each word tugged on her nerves. He was playing her like a harp. "When I'm inside you, I want to make as much noise as I can so you know how incredible you feel wrapped around my cock."

Her breath stuttered. Holy. Freaking. Shit. Damian wasn't a man god—he was pure sexual divinity. That one sentence had taken her from being excited and warm on the inside to drenching her lacy underwear. He was right, they had to go now. Because that potted plant was starting to look like the perfect place to be.

"Hurry up, then." She strode away from him. "Time's a-wasting."

Chuckling, he followed her to the front of Patterson House. The grand foyer was a sight to behold—an intricate parquet floor gleaming under an enormous chandelier that looked like something straight out of a royal palace. Two security guards stood by the front door, but Lainey couldn't tell if they were the ones who'd caught them on the balcony.

They joined a short queue of people leaving the building, and Lainey tapped her foot impatiently.

"Good evening, sir," a man in a dark suit said as they reached the front of the line. "Can we get you a car or do you have one booked?"

Damian nodded. "A car would be great, thank you."

The man stepped out onto the path that framed the circular driveway in front of the estate and raised a hand. A moment later, a black limousine appeared.

She'd never been in a limo before—never had a reason to. Her life hadn't been littered with special occasions that required fancy dresses and fancy cars and drivers who held the door.

"After you." Damian motioned for her to enter first.

She slid onto the seat as elegantly as she could, the length of her dress in one hand and her clutch in the other. Damian followed her, and the bang of the door filled her with electricity. With excitable, nervous energy. She pulled her grandmother's compact out of her bag and touched up her gloss, because she had no idea what was supposed to happen next.

Her plans had never taken her this far, because, in

the back of her mind, she'd been certain she would fail. Or be discovered. Or that he would have no interest in her, even with the disguise.

But he did.

"They went all out," she said, snapping the compact shut and running her thumb over the embroidery. "Limousines for that many guests must have cost a fortune."

"Well, the ticket holders pay for it, really. Not that you would know that." His lip quirked. "How did you get past security, anyway?"

"I would tell you, but…" She shrugged. "You know how it goes."

"Blood and mayhem and all that."

"Exactly. Don't make me ruin such a pretty dress."

"If that dress is going to be ruined, it won't be by bloodshed. Trust me." He leaned back and stretched his arm along the back of the leather seat. The pose—coupled with the way his gaze burned her up—was so unabashedly male. She'd always envied his confidence in the space he occupied. "Now the mask, on the other hand—"

"It's staying on." She'd come too far to ruin it now. Her body was primed and ready for him—the one little taste from earlier had only stoked her appetite. "No negotiations."

He rubbed a hand along his jaw, a grin forming. "But I'm a brilliant negotiator."

"I'm sure you're wickedly talented, but I'm not interested. The mask stays on or you can go home and have a cold shower."

He laughed and reached for a bottle of champagne stashed in a small refrigerator that Lainey hadn't noticed. Obviously, Damian had a lot more experience with limos than she did. He expertly eased the cork out of the bottle with a soft pop and poured the liquid into two glasses.

"I can handle a little mystery," he said, passing a flute to her. "But I need you to tell me one thing."

"What's that?" she asked warily.

"You're not married, are you?"

His words were a punch to her heart. It hadn't even occurred to her that he might assume she was married, but it made sense. With his history and her desire to hide her identity, it was a logical conclusion. As much as he acted like he'd moved on, it was clear he still carried the scars from his divorce.

"No, I'm not married," she said softly. "I'm not in a relationship of any kind, I promise."

Damian raked a hand through his dark hair and nodded. "I gave something away, didn't I?"

"Just that you're a guy with morals." She sipped her drink. "But I won't push you for more information."

Damian leaned back against the plush seat, toying with the stem of the champagne flute. Tonight he'd crossed a line that he'd promised himself he wouldn't—at least for a little while—and he wasn't the sort of guy who changed his mind once he'd made a decision.

He was supposed to be off women. Off sex and

head games and all that fuckery, because he needed to concentrate on his work. After finding Jenny and Ben together, he'd screwed his way into oblivion for twelve months straight, and it had done nothing but cause him grief. It hadn't filled the gaping chasm in his chest, nor had it quietened the critical voices in his head. So he'd become very selective about who he let into his bed. And even more selective about who he let into his life.

But then this redhead had bowled him over and flipped everything on its head. Back on the balcony, he'd been powerless to resist her demands for more—and she wouldn't even tell him her name.

"I, uh... I don't do this normally," the redhead said.

"Have a one-night stand?"

"At least not without dinner first." She drained the rest of her champagne. Looking for some Dutch courage, perhaps? He was tempted to remind her that he'd already brought her to orgasm once, so what was there to be nervous about? But he kept his mouth shut.

"We had canapés, so that's dinner covered."

She smiled, but it wasn't seductive or sexy. She seemed...shy. "You know what I mean."

"No judgement," he said, finishing his drink.

Right about now he would have preferred a scotch—two fingers, neat—but this would do. Really, he didn't want *anything* to dull this experience. Something told him that the redhead was special. That this whole crazy thing wasn't going to be regular "good in the moment, but forget it the morning after" sex.

"You don't have to be nervous," he said. "I want this, you want this. All we need to do is settle on a location."

"How about right here?" she whispered. Her cheeks were flushed beneath her mask, the pretty pink extending down her neck and colouring her chest.

"In the car?"

"Why not? As you said, your ticket paid for it."

He stifled a groan as she crossed her legs, the long slit falling open to reveal miles of creamy, pale skin. Knowing she wore nothing but a scrap of lace beneath had made him impossibly hard. He wanted her in his lap, legs spread, moaning his name. Now.

Damian dropped the privacy partition and instructed the driver to circle the botanical garden a few times. With Saturday-night traffic, that should give him ample time to lose himself inside this beautiful, mysterious woman.

Her eyes grew dark, the muscles in her neck working as she swallowed. The low light danced across her skin, highlighting her smooth paleness where the dress exposed the sensual curve of her breasts. Light caught on the shiny silver beads, glimmering like stardust.

His cock hardened even more, straining against the wool of his tuxedo pants. Adjusting himself, he counted to ten in his head. His self-imposed dry spell would work against him if he didn't keep his urges in check. If he was doing this, he wasn't going to blow it in the first five minutes.

"You should know before we go any farther that I'm not going to tell you my name," she said. Her fingertip traced the beading on her thigh. "Is that a problem?"

He clamped his teeth down on his lip and imagined sinking them into her, leaving a perfect indentation on her inner thigh. The idea of such a personal mark on her skin filled him with excitement. How would she react to the sharp sting mixed with all the pleasure he planned to give her?

"It's not how I usually do things," he said, holding out a hand. "But no, it's not a problem."

She slid across the limousine's seat until her thigh touched his, her shallow breathing music to his ears. He grabbed her by the waist and hauled her into his lap so that she straddled him, the slit in her dress riding up even higher to expose the tops of her perfect, creamy thighs.

His cock ached to be inside her. Cupping her head with his hands, he smoothed up her jawline to thread his fingers into her hair. His thumb traced the shell of her ear as he stared at her mouth, watching her lips as her breath stuttered in and out. She sank lower, pressing the heat of her sex against his straining erection, sending sparks of need shooting through him.

"Stop moving," he commanded, whispering into her ear.

The scent of peaches and vanilla invaded his nostrils and filtered through him like a drug. She stilled in his arms and he brought his lips to her jaw, kissing along the gentle angle until he reached her lips. They were plump and juicy.

Slowly, slowly.

Hovering above her lips, he waited to see if she would break. Not a muscle twitched as she waited, compliant. He pressed his mouth to hers, coaxing her lips open so he could taste her fully.

Knotting her hair in his fists, he held her head in place while he devoured her. She moaned into him, the muffled sound awakening every nerve ending in his body. He was going to savour this.

CHAPTER SEVEN

IF KISSING WERE an Olympic sport, Damian would take home gold, silver and bronze. No contest. The man had a mastery over his tongue that was borderline indecent.

He tugged her hair, moving her head into place so he could take what he wanted. How he wanted it. This kind of kiss should have been accompanied by a crash of cymbals or the roar of the ocean. It could have its own soundtrack. But in reality, she was only aware of the slow sizzle of her nerves frying as she slowly melted into him.

"God," he moaned into her ear as he sucked her lobe into his mouth.

Hot breath warmed her skin. He enveloped her, supported her. Held her in place. Only her mouth moved as she kissed him back, her body his to manoeuvre as he saw fit.

He released her hair, smoothing his hands down her neck, his thumb tracing the little hollow at the base of her throat. She could feel her pulse fluttering wildly, and she sucked in a breath, relishing the power he had over her. She willed him to fuck her right here, to tear her underwear to one side like he had on the balcony and release the tension bundled up tight between her legs.

But it seemed Damian had other ideas. Slower ideas. He leaned forward to suck on the skin at her décolletage, his tongue tracing the bones pressing against her skin before he moved down. Safe in his arms, she leaned back to give him the access he needed. He tugged the dress over, revealing her breast and drawing a nipple into his mouth.

He sucked, teeth scraping over the sensitive peak. Was it possible to come from only this? Lainey often orgasmed by her own hands rather than with a partner. The men she slept with thought breasts were more for jiggling and bouncing, but Damian treated hers like the centre of his world. He worshiped them.

She stifled a moan, flooded with the realisation that they were in a car, surrounded by windows. Tinted, thank God, but windows nonetheless. The rush of tires over bitumen flowed through her as Damian nipped at her breast. His tongue circled her before he drew her back into his mouth, the pressure building inside her. Rising until she felt like she'd explode.

"I'm going to get you off again."

"Again?"

"Yes, princess."

The soft words made her tremble, her sex pulsing hotly. Begging. Pleading. She nodded.

"Don't be quiet, okay? I want to hear you this

time." He pressed his lips to her breast as his hand trailed down her stomach and landed on her thigh. "Can you do that for me?"

"Yes."

Hot palms slid up her thighs, pushing the fabric of her dress up to her hips. He moved aside the triangle of lace covering her sex and eased her open with gentle fingers. Probing. Teasing. A gasp caught in her throat.

"You're so fucking wet," he groaned into her ear.

His eyes were dark and smoky, his mouth slack with desire. *She* had done this to him. Feminine power hummed through her body, mixing with the excitement that flamed as he teased her clit with his thumb.

He knew exactly where to press, how hard to push and when to ease back. Orgasm welled within her, threatening to crash over her at any moment. True to his promise, he brought her to the brink and let her hover there, suspended. Weightless. Wanting.

This time he didn't rush her, choosing to toy with her instead. "We're almost there. Just hold it for a little longer."

He traced slow, maddening circles around her clit. She forced her hips not to buck, to let him give her this experience. He controlled the pace and therefore controlled her pleasure. Controlled *her*. Nails bit into her thighs as she resisted the urge to thrust against his hand. She was so close...so very close.

"Take it," he growled.

He applied the last bit of pressure she needed to tip

over, and the air evaporated from her lungs as she fell, fell, fell. She pressed her face into his neck, letting her cries of pleasure vibrate against his skin. Shudders ran through her body, deadening her limbs as she rubbed against his hand until there was nothing left. Until she'd squeezed every last bit of pleasure out.

Lainey wondered if she'd died and gone to some kind of sexual nirvana. She'd been with a few guys who liked the thrill of a public grope—alleyways, nightclubs, taxis. But it had never been her thing.

Until now.

She had a feeling Damian could make her want sex in any possible way, in any possible position. And maybe a few impossible ones, as well. He had a power over her that should have been frightening…only it wasn't. It was the most thrilling, liberating thing she'd ever experienced, and they'd barely scratched the surface.

The sounds and sights of the world cut into her hazy post-sex glow. The honk of horns, tram bells ringing and sirens wailing. Lights flashed in her peripheral vision as they passed the hustle and bustle of the Flinders Street railway station.

Thank God for tinted windows.

"Do you feel like a queen yet?" His hand came to her jaw, tilting her face up to his as he brushed a thumb across the string of black beads shadowing her cheek.

"I'm certainly in the realm of royalty, but I'm not done yet." She leaned forward, endorphins emboldening her, and slid her hand between their bodies.

Through the thin wool of his tuxedo trousers, he was hard. And long. And thick. Perfect. It was like he'd been created with pleasure in mind. Lainey's heart skipped a beat. She was really going to do this—have sex with her best friend's older brother in the back of a limo while he had no idea who she was.

A chord of unrest struck her, sending tiny pulses of worry through her system. The downside of this situation—of her carrying out her mission perfectly—was that he was willing to sleep with her without knowing a thing about her.

Are you really complaining because you're about to get everything *you set out for?*

"Why did you agree to this?" she asked, immediately cursing herself for ruining the mood. "With me?"

"Do you mean because we're strangers?" He removed her hand from his crotch and ran his palms over her shoulders and arms, caressing her. Soothing her. "Because you're beautiful and interesting. Mysterious. Do you want me to try harder to convince you to take off your mask?"

"No." Her gaze dropped. What *did* she want?

"I'm not in the habit of sleeping with anyone who offers, in case that thought is dancing through your mind." He held her hands. "And I can't quite explain it, but I feel like I know you even though I don't. There's something about you that has me quite…"

Lainey looked up, smirking. "Aroused?"

"Yes, but I was going to say 'enraptured.'"

Enraptured. The word summed up everything she'd always wanted to be to him but never was.

Lainey, the crazy magnet. She'd thought once that being wild and impulsive meant she was interesting, but one day she woke up and realised that it exhausted people. But without that persona, who was she? The doubt had plagued her while she made her plans to leave Australia, the little demons in her head telling her to start over. To try her hand at being someone else. Maybe this time she would get it right.

"I don't think I've ever enraptured anyone before," she whispered.

"I sincerely doubt that."

The shocking thing was, he sounded sincere. But he didn't know who was behind the mask, so he couldn't possibly mean it. It was lip service. Superficial. Words to keep the night moving along so he could get what they'd agreed to. Sex.

"You know all the right things to say." She shoved the worries aside and planted her hands against his chest. "Now I guess it's my turn to make you feel good."

If Damian's cock was any harder, he'd be at serious risk of busting the zipper on his trousers. Which would make returning them an interesting experience. Although he already owed Aaron an explanation after he'd quietly demanded that he and Jessie play along with Damian's "fiancée."

Yeah, in the scheme of things, a busted zipper was the least of his problems.

The redhead pulled her dress back into place and shimmied down his body, dropping to her knees at his feet. Between the sight of that smooth porcelain skin, the pressure of her hands on his thighs and her glossy lips parting in anticipation…oh, hell. He'd be carrying this image to the grave.

He'd meant what he said earlier. It *did* feel like he knew the redhead, like they had some existing bond, but that was impossible.

She reached for his zipper and drew it down. Damian shifted his hips so she could pull his pants and jocks down to his ankles. He probably looked ridiculous in a stuffy tuxedo jacket and mask, naked from the waist down, but he wasn't physically able to give a fuck at that point. All that mattered now was the anticipation of having the redhead's lips wrapped around him.

"Do you want it?" She looked up at him, eyes huge from the extreme angle.

She looked doll-like, with lips glistening and open, waiting for him. She hovered, teasing, testing.

"Fuck, yes."

"Then take it."

He growled on hearing his words come from her lips.

She didn't move, she simply opened her mouth and stuck her tongue forward in invitation. He drove between her lips in a single, smooth thrust, and she closed around him tightly. The hot wetness consumed him and stars danced behind his shuttered lids as he gave himself over.

Both hands burrowed into her hair, controlling the bobbing motion of her head. It was pure, unadulterated bliss. With each flick of her tongue, each stroke, he grew closer. Pressure built at the base of his cock.

"Christ," he gasped. "Those sweet lips feel so fucking good."

He tried to pull back but she held him tight, the snug ring of her mouth sending dizzying shock waves through him. He hovered for what felt like eternity before she pulled back at the last minute, leaving him desperate and wanting.

Her lips curved into the most delicious smile he'd ever seen and he hauled her into his lap. "What do you want to do to me?"

Holding her tight with one arm, he leaned forward and fished his wallet out of his pants. He always kept a condom there, though it'd been an eternity since he'd needed one. Lights flickered outside the window, and it looked as though they were rounding the gardens again. He made a mental note to tip the driver generously.

"Tell me," she repeated, plucking the foil from his hands and extracting the rubber. "Exactly what you want."

It was hard to speak with her handling him, slipping the condom over him with sure fingers and her breasts rising and falling against the deep V of her dress. "I want to slide my cock into that tight little pussy of yours and feel you stretch around me. Then I'm going to hold your hips and grind into you until I feel you shake."

She pushed up higher onto her knees and positioned herself over him, holding her dress in her hands. "More."

"I'm going to fuck you until you come so hard that you squeeze every last drop of cum out of me." His voice was a saw now, hard and cutting. So roughed up and dangerous.

"Oh, God." Her breath stuttered in and out as she lowered herself onto him.

The feeling of her tight, wet heat was so sublime, Damian thought he might have been dreaming. But as she sank all the way down and his hands found the curve of her ass, he knew it was real. Nothing that good could come from his mind.

She wrapped her arms around his neck and whispered into his ear, "Make me feel good. Make me forget everything except how you fill me."

There would be no stopping him now. His fingers bit into her sides and he bucked up into her, dragging a groan from her lips. The edge of pleasure was too close already, but he didn't want to hold back. Didn't want to give her slow and sweet and sensual. No, this could only be hard and fast. Passionate. Furious.

He held her tight as she rocked against him, his hips thrusting up to meet her. Her teeth were at his neck, biting and scraping. Tugging. He smoothed a hand down the back of her head, feeling the ribbon holding her mask in place. Then he fisted the lengths of her silky hair and pulled so her face was tilted up to his. Her eyes rolled back and her lips parted, her cries soundless as she hovered at the precipice.

"You're starting to shake." The flutter of the muscles in her sex dragged him closer. "You're so close. Remember what I said. I want you to come around my cock. Take every last drop."

She trembled in his arms, her breaths turning to gasps as orgasm took hold of her. She squeezed him, her hips grinding as she wrung the pleasure from him. Dragging it out of them both until they peaked. He roared into her hair as the release shook him, his cock pulsing inside her.

Thankfully, Damian had a good grip on her, because that was the only thing stopping Lainey from tumbling back onto the floor of the limo. How long had they been driving? Had the driver heard everything going on back here? She reassured herself that if the guy drove limos for the rich and locally famous, he'd probably seen or heard a lot worse.

"Wow," she breathed, her head resting against his shoulder.

"Wow, indeed." His lips brushed her hair. "That was incredible."

If only she could freeze time and stay here forever—in his arms, before the cold reality of what she'd done came crashing down like an avalanche. But it was officially time for Cinderella to turn into a pumpkin. Or something like that.

No doubt Damian would be a gentleman and offer to have the limo drop her home first, which couldn't happen. He'd been to her place a few times. She'd have to give a fake address. Somewhere close enough for her to walk home safely, without giving the game away.

As she moved to climb off his lap, something shifted against her face. The mask slipped, and Lainey's hand flew to the back of her head as shock seized her heart. She felt for the ribbon that held the mask in place, but all she could find were the frayed edges of where it *should* have attached.

Crap! One wrong move and she was about to have the mother of all wardrobe malfunctions.

"Is everything okay?" He reached out for her. But the gesture sent her into panic mode.

He could *not* find out her true identity. She couldn't risk losing his respect, not to mention putting her friendship with Corinna on the line right before she was due to leave the country.

Just hold the damn mask and get the hell out of this car.

"I'm fine," she said, but her voice was tight. "I... I need to go."

Damian glanced out the window. "Right now?"

They were driving down Swanston Street in the heart of the city, not at all close to her apartment. But there were plenty of people around, and she could hail a taxi. Besides, once Damian was gone, she didn't need the mask. And then she'd just be a girl in a dress...a revealing, slightly too tight, impossibly expensive dress.

"Yes, please. Right now." She searched for her clutch but couldn't find it. Shit. Where had she left it?

Her breath came in shallow bursts, her ribs flexing against the tight fabric of the dress, which only served to amplify the panic. She needed her clutch— she wouldn't be able to get back into the house without it. It had her keys, her money and ID. Oh, God, her ID!

If Damian saw it...

She spotted the bag on the floor of the limo. It must have been knocked down in their passionate encounter. She snatched it up and pressed it to her chest as though it were a life jacket.

"We can take you home," he said. "I don't like the idea of dropping you on the side of the road."

"I live in the next block. It was...good timing." Her voice was about as convincing as a politician telling people he had their best interests at heart. She wasn't about to get into acting any time soon. "Please, ask him to stop."

Damian sat still, his large frame seeming even more imposing in the wake of her panic. His lips pressed into a line, but he relented and zipped himself up before pressing the button to lower the privacy partition. A second later the limo pulled over.

"I don't suppose you'll give me your number?" he said. "Even if I promise not to ask your name."

"I can't." She shook her head, tears pricking her eyes.

Why was she being so emotional? This was exactly what she wanted—a night with the perfect man. *Her* perfect man. No consequences...except that she hadn't factored in her stupid heart.

"Thank you," she whispered. She leaned forward

and stole a kiss before pushing the door open and stepping out onto the street, her hand still holding her mask in place.

Lainey waited, her muscles tense and aching, until the limo pulled into the stream of Saturday-night traffic. It disappeared around a corner at the next intersection, and the air flew out of her lungs. Her chest hurt. Her head hurt. The tender spot between her legs hurt, but in the best way possible. Damian had left his mark on her, and she would never be the same.

"Just great," she muttered to herself as she stuck her arm out to hail a taxi. "You're ruined for other men."

As the yellow vehicle pulled over, she opened her purse to dig out her phone. That was when she realised that her grandmother's compact was missing.

CHAPTER EIGHT

DAMIAN SAT BEHIND his desk, turning the compact mirror over in his hands. No matter how hard he tried, he couldn't get that night out his head. It was odd, since he didn't usually mull over a one-night stand. Especially when it was clear up front that it would be a onetime-only thing.

But something about the redhead had got him all tangled up. For the first time in four years, he was thinking about something other than work.

He frowned at the compact. It'd been sitting on the floor of the limo, and he'd almost missed it. Must have fallen out of her bag when they'd knocked it to the floor.

How on earth was he supposed to return the damn thing without a name or phone number? It looked old, possibly a family heirloom. An important item. But there were no distinguishing marks on it—no engravings or product details. Nothing that might help him identify the mysterious masked woman.

Placing it carefully on his desk, he turned to stare out of the huge window that framed the city view like a piece of art. From his level thirty-six office, he could see everything: the tracks running into the Flinders Street railway station, the ribbon of water cutting through the city, the spire at the Arts Centre, and the great stretch of green from the gardens. Ever since he'd walked into his first office job, he'd had his eye on a big corner office just like this one.

It'd taken a few years of slumming it, first working out of his apartment and then—when he'd hired a team—out of a crappy, falling-down building in the inner suburbs north of the city. But his collection of smaller clients had led to some medium-size fish. And those had led to bigger fish. Now he had two blue-chip clients and a healthy list of medium-size businesses that made him very good money.

But he wouldn't be satisfied until he had McPartlin & Co.

"Damian?" His assistant, Leila, poked her head into his office. "I've got a call for you, but you're supposed to be meeting with Corinna in five minutes."

"Who is it?" He swung back around to his desk and raked a hand through his hair. "If it's the tax office again, put them through to Greg. I don't have time—"

"It's Jerry McPartlin," she said. Leila's expression didn't reveal a thing, but Damian had worked with her long enough to detect the hint of judgement in her voice. Since he'd poached her from his ex-boss's company, she knew the history.

"Put him through."

Leila frowned but didn't argue, and a second later the red light on his desk phone flashed. "Hello?"

"Mr. McKnight, how are you?"

"Call me Damian." He reached over to his laptop and pulled up the file he'd been working on before his first meeting with McPartlin. It had everything he knew about the guy and his company—from personal and professional achievements to the AFL team he supported. "I'm well. Did you enjoy the Carmina Ball?"

"I did. The TAFW charity thanks you for your generosity."

The charity were the organisers behind the Carmina Ball. They had a lot of powerful people in their ranks and worked to raise money for various recipients, most notably the Royal Women's Hospital.

"I wasn't aware you were affiliated with them." Damian scanned his file, but nothing about the charity appeared there.

"It hasn't been announced yet, but I'll be joining their board soon." He cleared his throat.

Damian leaned back in his chair. This was going to go one of two ways: either McPartlin had decided to give him a shot at his business, or he was calling to ask for a donation. "So are you calling to tell me you've decided to come across to McKnight Management after all?"

"Let's not get ahead of ourselves," the man replied in what Damian could only imagine was his "stern father" voice. "But I thought we could have dinner."

Damian had to force himself not to fist pump. This

was the opening he'd wanted—a chance to show what he was made of. And really, that was all he needed. Because once Jerry saw Damian on his game, that asshole Ben wouldn't stand a chance of hanging on to McPartlin & Co.

"And by we, I mean including my wife and your lovely fiancée," Jerry added.

Shit. "You really want to put them through the tediousness of a business dinner? I'm not sure about your marriage, but Ariel and I have a no-shop-talk policy at the dinner table."

"It's not a business dinner. It's a social dinner." McPartlin paused. "For now."

"Right."

"And maybe your fiancée could let us know where she got that incredible mask. Sandra is dying to find out." There was a hint of amusement in the older man's voice.

"Of course," Damian said smoothly. No way in hell was he going to pass this opportunity up, and if he couldn't locate the redhead, he'd find a substitute. Because the one thing no one had seen was her face.

Not that anyone else would even come close to her. This woman was the first in years to leave him wanting—wishing. But he knew nothing about her. He had no leads...other than the compact.

"I'll get my assistant to call your office tomorrow and set it up," Jerry said. "I look forward to seeing you both."

The message hung in the air—his fiancée had better be there.

Damian ended the call and stared up at the ceiling. He'd figure something out—he *had* to. For the last four years it had felt like he was moving through quicksand. Work had kept him busy, but the other areas of his life had stalled. One beer-fuelled night a few months ago, he'd seen Jenny and Ben out together. That night he'd packed a suitcase and walked out of the apartment he'd once shared with his ex-wife. He hadn't returned.

Movers had put his things in storage, and he'd been living in a hotel room ever since. He was in limbo. Not wanting to be living in the past, but unable to move forward. If only he could get one back at Jenny and Ben, then he might feel as though he'd levelled the playing field and be able to move on with his life.

He needed a redhead. He wanted *the* redhead.

"Damian?" Leila's voice came through on the intercom. "I've got Corinna here for your lunch date."

"Send her in. I need to finish up an email before we go."

He was tapping away at his computer when his sister walked in. As usual, she looked perfectly fashionable. Her grey eyes—identical in colour to his—were accentuated by a pair of chunky black glasses that would have looked awkward on most people, but looked chic on her.

"Ticktock," she said, dropping down into one of the chairs facing his desk. "We can't be late. I've got a class at two."

"You need to graduate and face the real world sometime, you know."

"I've graduated once already." She grinned. "No one said I couldn't go back for more."

"You're a glutton for punishment."

"There are worse vices in the world than academia. Not all of us are so desperate to become corporate slaves," she teased.

He shook his head, refusing to take the bait. Despite the decade between them, they were as close as a brother and sister could be. Different, yes, but they had a deep bond. Maybe it was because he'd been like another parent to her. He'd cooked her meals, driven her to ballet class and cheered like a maniac as she'd received her bachelor's degree.

But that meant she knew what buttons to push and made a sport out of winding him up. Not today, though. He had bigger fish to fry than letting his sister get under his skin.

"What are you doing with this?" She reached over his desk and picked up the compact.

"Uh…" Close as he and Corinna were, their sex lives were *not* up for discussion. "I need to return it."

"No shit." She flipped the compact open to check her appearance. "Lainey must be having kittens."

Damian blinked. "Excuse me?"

"This is her compact. Well, it belonged to her grandmother, but it's hers now. I've been telling her to put it somewhere safe, but she carries it *everywhere*." She shook her head. "Like a good luck charm. Wait, no…what did she call it?" Corinna snapped her fingers. "A talisman."

Lainey.

There's no way she could have...

A cold fist enveloped his heart and squeezed. But her voice had been different. And her hair had been different.

She's a fucking hairdresser. You don't think she could have dyed her hair?

He forced himself to remain calm...at least on the outside. "You're sure it's hers?"

Corinna looked at him strangely. "Positive. There's a little set of initials in the embroidery, and Lainey has the same initials as her grandmother." She put the compact on the desk and pointed to one of the roses, where a very subtle shift in the colour of the threads revealed the letters *LK*. He'd never have noticed it if she hadn't pointed it out. "She's had this thing since her grandmother passed away years ago. I'd recognise it anywhere."

Fuck. Fuck. *Fuck.*

He couldn't flip out right now, because the last thing he wanted was to explain to his little sister that he'd accidentally screwed her best friend. He needed to play it cool.

"It must have fallen out of her bag last time I gave her a lift." He shrugged. "I found it under the seat of the Audi when I was cleaning it, but I had no idea who it belonged to."

"Because so many women ride in your car." She rolled her eyes. "Do you want me to drop it off to her?"

"No." He shook his head. "I'll return it myself. I'm heading out her way tonight anyway. I should stop in to see her—it's been a while."

"Okay." Corinna looked at him strangely. It wasn't like he'd ever mentioned "dropping in" on Lainey before. But Corinna's stomach rumbled and she huffed. "Can we go now? If I don't eat soon I'm going to turn into Bitchzilla."

"I definitely don't want that." He pushed up from his chair and pocketed the compact.

Tonight he'd call in to see Lainey and confirm if his fears were true—that he'd found the redhead right when he needed her, but that she was definitely someone he shouldn't have slept with.

Lainey stood in her tiny kitchen, cradling a mug of coffee, and quietly tried not to lose her shit. This week had been a complete fucking disaster. First, she'd had *zero* luck in tracking down her grandmother's compact. The limo company had been sweet and checked multiple times for her, but to no avail. Then she'd dropped her phone into a sink full of water and now the damn thing wouldn't turn on. And, like the cherry on top of a giant fuck-you sundae, Imogen's friend refused to accept the masquerade mask back because of the broken strap. Which had meant forking out more money she couldn't afford to buy a broken mask.

Frustration bubbled like lava in her veins. It was karma, for sure. Karma for tricking Damian and keeping secrets from Corinna. And to what end?

"Only the best sex of my entire life," Lainey grumbled.

And not the best sex in the way people tended to

fling those words around. It was *literally* the best. It was the Ferrari of sex. The Chanel of sex. The kind of sex that people scoffed at in romance novels and labelled unrealistic, because nobody could come like that on the first try with a new partner, right?

Wrong.

It was like Damian had been in her head every time she'd reached between her legs in the dead of night, thinking about what she would do with him if only she had the chance. Like he'd saved up all her fantasies and distilled them into one perfect, never-to-be-repeated experience.

And instead of feeling over the moon that she'd gotten exactly what she wanted, she felt bloody miserable, because one taste wasn't enough. Nowhere near it.

She twirled her hair around her finger and startled herself with the bright red hue. She still wasn't used to it. Every time she walked past a mirror she gave herself a fright. But the longer she wore the vibrant colour, the more she liked it.

A knock at the front door snapped Lainey out of her worries and she put her coffee down before going to answer it. "Hello?" she said as she swung the door open.

Time seemed to slow as her brain tried to catch up with what she was seeing. Damian McKnight, standing on her doorstep, looking hot and pissed as hell. He wore a charcoal suit with a white shirt and baby-blue tie, which brought out the subtle blue tones in his grey eyes. But the soft colours did nothing to lessen the impact of his ice-cold stare and the hard set of his jaw. His nostrils flared as his gazed raked over her.

Oh my God, he knows.

"Uh, hi, Damian." She swallowed. "Are you looking for Corinna? She's not here right now."

"I wasn't looking for her," he said. The words squeezed out between his teeth, the razor-sharp edge of his anger palpable in the night air. "I came to see you."

"Oh." She stepped back and held the door, unsure what to say.

Maybe he doesn't know and you're being paranoid. Perhaps he's had a bad day...

He stalked past her and made his way to the kitchen. Everything about his movement screamed agitation—from the stiffness in his shoulders to the fists bunched by his sides. He wasn't saying a word and Lainey had to fight the urge to fill the silence, because she was bound to say the wrong thing.

They were in a nonverbal stand-off. Damian leaned against the counter, stuffing his hands into his pockets, encouraging her eyes to drop down to that general area. Like she needed help in the gawking department. His legs were crossed at the ankles, showing off a pair of expensive black shoes. The position could have easily been mistaken for a relaxed stance, but Lainey wasn't a fool. She knew he was about to strike.

She dropped down into one of her rickety dining chairs and waited, sucking on the inside of her cheek to keep the words from spilling out.

"Haven't you got anything to say to me?" His tone was frigid. "A confession, perhaps?"

Hell, he made Frosty the Snowman look warm and fuzzy.

"Fine," he said after a few beats of silence. "Have it your way."

He pulled one hand out of his pocket and placed her grandmother's compact on the table in front of her. She snatched it up, her breath releasing in a long *whoosh*. Having it back in her possession made the world feel right again, but one thing was now clear: Damian knew *exactly* what she'd done.

"What do you want from me?" she asked, her thumb stroking the embroidery. The worn threads and familiar habit soothed her.

"I want to hear you say it."

The rough, gravelly sound of his voice flooded her with memories of their evening together—it was so similar to the dirty way he'd growled into her ear. A tremor rippled through her, warming her body from the inside out, almost as if anticipating a repeat performance. But that wasn't going to happen. Not since he looked as though he was about to strangle her.

She sucked in a breath. "Why? It won't change things."

"Because I deserve the truth," he said. "You owe me that, at least."

Shit. It shouldn't surprise her that he wasn't going to back down. The man was a bull when he wanted something.

"I snuck into the ball." Her chest constricted, the

enormity of her actions suddenly weighing on her like great big boulders. "I lied about my identity."

"And?"

"I slept with you." Dammit, why did her voice have to fail her now? The words came out jagged and panicky.

"I didn't quite catch that." He folded his arms across his chest, the intimidating breadth of his shoulders casting a shadow over the table.

"I slept with you," she said in a louder, although no more steady, voice.

"You *fooled* me." His eyes were like fire, ready to burn her up until she was nothing but ash. "Why?"

Because I've wanted you ever since I laid eyes on you. I've wanted you in every sense of the word—from the most innocent to the most possessive to the things I could never say aloud.

"I don't know," she lied.

"So I could have been any man, then? You snuck in to have anonymous sex with someone, and I was the guy who happened to end up between your legs?" His jaw ticked.

"No." She shook her head, confused by the hint of jealousy in his voice. Was he bothered that she might have wanted anyone? "It wasn't random."

"Then you targeted me?"

Her chest rose and fell, her breath becoming rapid. What would he say next? Was he disgusted with her? Disgusted with himself? Did his desire lessen now that he knew who Ariel was?

"Yes."

"You've put me in a very hard place, Lainey." He raked a hand through his hair. "A very hard fucking place."

"I'm sorry, I—"

"I don't want your apologies." He sighed.

"Then what *do* you want?"

"Your help."

Lainey raised a brow. "What?"

"We told someone important that you were my fiancée," he said. "Jerry McPartlin. And now he wants me and my nonexistent fiancée to accompany him and his wife to dinner."

"And you want me to pretend to be your fiancée?"

"You did a pretty good job pretending last time." He planted his palms on the table and leaned closer. Next to him, it looked like dollhouse furniture. "Very convincing."

She gulped. "Was I?"

"You screamed in my ear like you were having the time of your life, and I had no idea you were pulling the wool over my eyes." His expression told her nothing. "You got me good."

The feeling was annoyingly mutual. "I didn't hold a gun to your head, Damian. You agreed to the terms."

"If I'd known it was you, I wouldn't have slept with you."

The rejection stung like a thousand blades. "Right."

"So I need you to come to dinner with me next week and play along with your new identity. Okay, *Ariel*?"

"You've got a lot of nerve." She sucked in a shaky

breath, humiliation and anger and frustration roiling in her chest.

"No, *you've* got a lot of nerve. I don't want to do this any more than you do, but here we are." He glowered. "And don't get your knickers in a knot because I said I wouldn't have slept with you if I'd known who you were. It's nothing to do with attraction."

"Then what is it?"

"You're like family." He shook his head as if she were an idiot. "Why would I risk making a mess of that?"

"You don't think it was worth it?" The words popped out before she could think about their consequences.

He looked at her for a long, hard moment, and Lainey seriously wondered if he'd be able to melt her with his stare. "I'm not answering that," he said eventually. "I need you to give me one dinner. Nothing more."

Her heart skipped a beat. "And what do we tell Cori?"

"We don't breathe a word of it to anyone." He pushed up from the table and pinned her with a stare. "Promise me."

"I promise," she whispered.

"Good. I'll send you the details."

Lainey sat, rooted to the chair, as Damian left the apartment. The bang of the door shutting behind him echoed through the quiet space. Then the only thing she could hear was the sound of her heart pounding in her ears.

One more night with Damian, pretending to be his fiancée. She couldn't stop herself from grinning.

CHAPTER NINE

DAMIAN PUMPED HIS arms and legs, gaining speed as his feet pounded the boardwalk planks that lined the Yarra River. No matter how fast he ran or how loud he blasted the music through his earphones, he couldn't get Lainey out of his head.

Knowing the mysterious redhead was in fact his little sister's best friend *should* have put a stop to the dirty dreams. But instead the knowledge fuelled them, gave them life and depth and the sharp snap of reality that had him turned upside down and inside out. Every night was a battle of wills—his carnal self paired with vivid imagination versus his moral core.

It was a terribly one-sided battle.

After his evening run, he was itching to get out of his workout clothes. The soaked cotton clung to his back and chest like a second skin, and he peeled it off quickly. A light ache spread through his muscles, a sign that he'd pushed himself hard today, and he'd need to spend some time on the foam roller to ease out the knots.

He'd been tighter than usual. Stress, his trainer had

said. Lack of stretching, according to the remedial masseuse. Working too hard, his assistant claimed. But he knew it wasn't any of those things.

Desire. He'd felt it burrowing under his skin ever since he'd seen Lainey on Monday night, niggling at him in the quiet portions of the day. In the dead of night. In the dark corners of his dreams.

He shook the thoughts off and stepped under the running water, sighing as the warmth seeped into his muscles. He lathered up, working the bar over his skin. Tonight was going to be an exercise in restraint.

Because sleeping with Lainey again—this time knowing it was her—would only create trouble.

You don't fuck people you care about.

Sex had no place getting mixed up with feelings, that much he knew. But since the Carmina Ball he'd only had thoughts of one woman. And his libido had come back to life like a bear out of hibernation—hungry and desperate for the bounty of springtime.

Just one night.

Temptation rolled around in his mind. Would it be so bad to act on the fantasy that Lainey *was* his fiancée? God, she was gorgeous. Porcelain skin and ruby-rich hair that looked so perfect it should have been natural. Perky breasts that went uninhibited by a bra most of the time. The memory of running his thumbs over her nipples, the stiff little peaks pressing against his touch, rocketed through him.

He was hard as stone remembering it. Without thinking, he reached down and wrapped a soapy hand around his cock. He'd spent every day trying to deny his urges—to deny his fantasies about her—and now all the sexy thoughts had piled up. Testing the heft of his length against his palm, he let the air rush out of his lungs.

The muscles of his ass and thighs clenched as he squeezed himself, sliding his hand up and down slowly. Deliberately.

Bracing his other arm against the cool tile of the shower wall and shutting his eyes, he thrust into his hand. It would never be as good as the real thing, but his flickering reel of fantasies was vivid and bright. He could practically feel the soft wetness of her mouth against his cock, the slippery slide of her tongue and the tight ring of her perfect pink lips.

Orgasm welled within him, pulling his balls up tight against him and making his muscles harden. When he came it was hard, his grunts bouncing off the walls of the shower as he emptied himself, his mind filled with Lainey.

This would have to do. He couldn't let himself get fooled again.

Lainey had expected an email with the details for their dinner date, or whatever the hell she was supposed to call it. Maybe a text. Even a phone call. You know, normal-people communication methods. But Damian didn't do things the way most guys did.

The day after he'd dropped by the house, a parcel had been delivered via courier with a handwritten note.

*I'll pick you up at 7:00 p.m. on Friday. Don't
open the box until then.*

Ever since, she'd been on edge, each night willing
sleep to come. But her dreams were no less restless,
and the silver box winked at her from across her bedroom. Tonight she'd see him again.

Gripping her towel tight, Lainey skimmed her
hand over the subtly embossed pattern, enjoying the
feel of the tiny ridges beneath her fingertips. Heart
in her throat, she lifted the lid and stared at the layers of frothy, candy-coloured tissue paper.

It crinkled as she opened the edge to reveal a dress.
One of those formfitting bandage-type dresses. The
straight lines were enhanced by panels of mixed fabric—leather, brushed silk, something reflective and
glossy—all in a shade of purple so dark it was nearly
black. A fine zipper in gold ran the entire length of
the dress from the bust to the hemline.

She steeled herself and glanced at the swing tag,
blinking at the neatly printed price label. Surely that
last zero wasn't supposed to be there. Lainey's stomach pitched. She could cover a few months of rent
with that!

She dropped the dress onto the bed as though it
had burned her. In no universe could she accept such
a gift. The dress she'd worn to the Carmina Ball had
been this expensive, but it had been a loaner and she'd
almost ruined it.

Lainey had a thing against charity. The second
you accepted it, you admitted that you couldn't take

care of yourself. Sure, she might need rescuing from funny situations on occasion, but she had a job that she was damn good at. Opportunities on the horizon. She was her own woman and she paid her own way.

Lainey fingered the fabric. She had to admit Damian had impeccable taste.

Who says he *bought it for you? He probably had an assistant do it for him.*

She bit her lip. Was he testing her? Getting the upper hand back by dictating the terms of their next evening together, dressing her up like a doll so that she would look pretty enough to please his dinner guests?

She stared at her reflection in the vanity mirror as she held the dress up, the gold zipper glinting. Maybe this was exactly what she needed right now—another costume to boost her confidence and help her get what she wanted. In this, no one would look at her like she was lesser. Like she didn't belong on Damian McKnight's arm.

She wriggled into the dress and slipped on a pair of pencil-thin stilettos. Her hair hung in soft waves and her makeup was dark and sultry.

Mask firmly in place.

If he wanted her to act like a smitten fiancée, then she was going to give an Oscar-worthy performance. Without the limitations of her Carmina Ball disguise, she'd be able to tell if he wanted her rather than "Ariel."

She swallowed back her guilt. It felt wrong to be going behind Corinna's back like this, but Damian had set the rules. They weren't to breathe a word of it to anyone. Besides, what harm would one more night do?

Her flight to the UK was booked, and she left in twelve days. It wasn't like they were entering into long-term arrangement, and Lainey had no illusions she possessed that "forever" quality. She was fun—she'd been told it time and time again—but fun didn't make for happily ever after.

One little fling before you leave the country and forget about men altogether.

Before she started her life as a career go-getter—Lainey, the creative. Lainey, the social media guru. She had plans, big ones. Long-term ones. And they didn't include falling in love.

After Damian picked her up, it was all business. He'd briefed her on his plans for signing McPartlin & Co. as a client and gave her an overview of their expansion strategy. Then they agreed on the details of their "relationship." Dating for a year, engaged for two months. They were keeping it quiet because Lainey—*Ariel*—didn't want to deal with the media. No date set for the wedding, but the plan was for a small and private event. Be general but not too vague, avoiding unnecessary details that might make it hard to keep track of the story.

Damian parked beneath the Crown Entertainment complex, and they got out of the car.

"Think you can handle all that?" he asked as they walked toward a set of elevators.

Lainey's high heels made echoing sounds that bounced off the concrete walls. "A few white lies? Sure."

"I guess you *do* have practice."

She jabbed the call button for the elevator. "If you don't want me to apologise, then stop bringing it up. I tried to say I was sorry."

"Apologies are useless." He stared straight ahead, his hand coming to the small of her back as the doors opened. The touch burned through her dress. "You knew exactly what you were doing."

"And I take responsibility for my actions."

"Do you?" He raised a brow. "For as long as I've known you, you've skated through life, leaving mass destruction in your wake."

Her cheeks burned. How was it possible that she could be so attracted to a man who thought she was a hot mess? "Yes, you were incredibly upset after we fucked. I'm sure you'll have mental scars from it."

He was on her in a flash, hands gripping her shoulders as he held her fast. His dark brows knitted into a frown. "Do you have any idea how I felt when I found out it was you?"

She wasn't sure she wanted to know, so she opted for sarcasm instead. "Were you sick to your stomach?"

"I was."

She snorted. "Just what every woman wants to hear."

"I was sick to my stomach because I couldn't get the thought of your body out of my head. I wanted you again. I can't stop thinking about how good it felt to be inside you." His face was inches from hers, his breath puffing across her cheeks. "I was sick over how much I wish you'd come back to my place that night so I could have stripped you down and explored every fucking inch of you."

Her sex throbbed and she squeezed her thighs together, but it did nothing. There would be no satisfaction unless it was him there. All of him. *Only* him.

He continued. "And I can't think about you like that."

"Why? I'm *not* family." She rolled her eyes. "We're not related. We wouldn't be doing anything wrong."

"Yes, we would. Because, as crazy as you are, I don't want to screw things up with us. It's not worth the risk."

She blinked. It was far from the answer that she expected. In her mind, he'd never viewed them as having anything to screw up. "What do you mean, it's not worth the risk?"

"Sex creates tension. I don't like being jealous or disappointed or resentful, and sleeping with someone I care about makes that difficult."

The words her hit like a fist to the chest. "You care about me?"

Damian opened his mouth to respond, but the elevator dinged and the doors slid open. Their private little bubble was gone. "Come on. We don't want to be late."

They walked through the bustling building and approached two large gilt doors. The name of the restaurant wasn't visible from the front, but judging by the clientele, it seemed to be the kind of place where if you had to ask then you didn't belong. She knew it was one of Jerry McPartlin's restaurants, but that was it. Would he be able to pick her out as a fraud right away? She was wearing a ridiculously expensive dress, but it might not be enough.

She glanced furtively at the maître d' as they stepped inside, wishing for a second that Damian had taken her for a burger and fries instead. But this wasn't a social catch-up and she was playing a role— Ariel, Damian's fiancée. Confident, cultured. Definitely *not* the kind of woman who would gate-crash a society ball.

She swallowed. They'd be able to pick her out like a cheap knockoff among rows of the real deal.

"Mr. McKnight, what a pleasure." The maître d' greeted him warmly, her hand gravitating to his arm as he leaned in and kissed her on the cheek.

"Good to see you, Marcella."

"We've got our best table reserved for you. Mr. McPartlin and his wife will be joining you shortly."

Marcella's eyes swept over Lainey, curiosity apparent. With a warm smile, she gestured for them to follow her into the restaurant. Large light fixtures created a twinkling ambience, though the overall effect was still darkly intimate and sensual. Gold trimmings tastefully adorned the walls. The vast area housed small round tables and was lined with booths in dark wood and rich, plum-coloured velvet.

Lainey followed, still clutching Damian's arm, and held her breath as they navigated the tight space between the tables. The last thing she needed was to trip and make a fool of herself. History told her the chances of that happening were as likely as the sun rising tomorrow.

"Relax." Hot breath caressed her skin as Damian whispered into her ear. "You look like you're about to have a heart attack."

"I'm fine," she said tightly, the words sticking in her chest.

They reached a secluded booth at the back of the restaurant. Ornate fabric hung from the ceiling. It looked like a curtain that could be closed for privacy if needed. She ran her hand down the silk, her fingertips grazing over the faint gold embroidery.

"I've got our most experienced server looking after you tonight," Marcella said. "But please reach out to me if you need anything at all."

Lainey's jaw clenched automatically. Marcella looked exactly like the kind of woman Damian *should* be dining with. Articulate. Smooth. Polished. All the things that Lainey had given up hope of mastering.

"Of course."

Damian motioned for Lainey to take a seat and he watched as she slid into the booth awkwardly, the tight fabric of her dress and towering heels making her feel like a circus performer on stilts.

"She's got it for you bad," Lainey observed. "Do you know her?"

"She's a friend." He removed his jacket and hung it on a little hook at the entrance to the booth before sliding into his seat with easy grace. "But I don't want you thinking about Marcella or anyone else tonight. I need you on your A game."

Nodding, she wound a strand of hair around one finger, watching the light catch on the vibrant pigment. Her nerves jangled, and anticipation swirled through her. With the mask on, she'd felt confident and in control. But now she was exposed. Maybe Damian was right. Sex with someone you cared about stirred up a whole mess of emotions, and she was unprepared. Woefully so.

But that was no excuse. Lainey might have come to rely on her friends to bail her out, but she didn't shy away from her decisions.

You've made your bed—now you have to lie in it.

CHAPTER TEN

THE DINNER PROGRESSED better than Damian had expected, despite the fact that McPartlin steered the conversation away from business every time it came up. However, the older man seemed to have lost his suspicions, mainly thanks to Lainey's brilliant performance.

She'd brought the mask with her and spent a good ten minutes cooing over the design with McPartlin's wife. Every so often, her eyes would flick to Damian and something would pass between them. A ripple of tension, electric with the force of her energy. It was like she wanted to communicate, and though he didn't know exactly what she was thinking, the heat in her expression had his whole body lighting up. Crying out for more.

Crying out for *her*.

The dress he'd bought for her looked incredible. The dark fabric clung to her curves the way his hands had that night. The zip was mostly done up—less than an inch remained open at her bust. It didn't reveal a thing, but it *did* make him think about undoing the dress and tracing the line of the zipper with his tongue.

He didn't know what had gotten into him when he'd bought that dress. He'd only planned to send her the details for the dinner—but he'd walked past the boutique and handed his credit card over before he knew what he was doing.

"I can't believe you've managed to keep the engagement a secret," Jerry's wife, Sandra, said as she raised a gold-trimmed coffee cup to her lips. Her red lipstick left an imprint behind on the white china. "The media is relentless with stuff like that. How did you do it?"

"It hasn't been easy," Lainey said, placing her hand affectionately on Damian's thigh and leaning closer to him. Her expression was as sincere and sweet as apple pie, but under the table her hand inched higher.

She'd been testing his boundaries all night—touching him, planting sweet kisses on his cheek and smiling as she swiped the lipstick mark away with her thumb. Playing the doting fiancée with aplomb.

"Sometimes I feel like I've made the whole thing up," she added with a twinkle in her eye. "I haven't gone to many events with him, but the masquerade ball was the perfect opportunity since I could keep my face covered. We could be together without anyone knowing who I was."

"Sometimes I felt like *I* didn't even know who you were that night," Damian said drily.

Lainey squeezed his thigh, the top of her finger precariously close to where he was doing his best to will away a burgeoning erection. They really needed to stop talking about the ball, because he was struggling to keep the image of Lainey straddling him out of his head. He wrapped his hand around hers, interlacing their fingers and guiding them away from his crotch.

"You'll have to go public at some point," Jerry said. "People talk."

"To be honest, I don't want a life in the spotlight anymore." Damian shrugged. "My company is where I'm focused. I had my fifteen minutes and frankly hated every bloody second of it."

Jerry laughed. "It certainly has its ups and downs. But you do have a face for television, I'll admit that."

"I have a mind for business," Damian corrected. "Television didn't really work out for me. All it did was give me a reputation that I'm not proud of. I'm not fame hungry, and I'm not a womanizer."

He couldn't blame McPartlin entirely for having a low opinion of him. While Damian had come across well on the show, the people who made *Australia's Most Eligible* knew exactly how to interview contestants and edit the footage to tell the story they wanted. They could create villains and heroes out of ordinary men. Or, in his case, men who would do anything to get ahead.

He'd watched half of the first episode the night it aired and had cringed the whole way through. The Damian on that show wasn't him.

"Ah, yes. Well, even those in the industry fall prey to believing what they read." That was as close to an apology as Jerry was ever likely to give, but Damian would take it. "Call me old-fashioned, but I think people today don't value the sanctity of marriage like they used to. Monogamy is a wonderful thing."

"I couldn't agree more," Damian said, reaching for his wine in the hopes of washing the bitter taste from his mouth.

Sandra shot Damian and Lainey a look. "He also thinks today's music is abominable. I'm sure when time machines are invented he'll go back to the '50s and never leave."

"Nothing wrong with having morals," Jerry huffed.

"Well, now that he's on his high horse, it's probably time we leave." Sandra shook her head. "One glass of wine and he gets philosophical."

Damian stifled a laugh. He'd once thought of Jerry McPartlin as intimidating, but it was clear his wife was the one running the show behind the scenes. For some reason, it made him think of Lainey. On the outside she appeared one way—flighty and silly and a little bit crazy—but on the inside she had a fierce determination to go after what she wanted. As much as he disliked her methods, he had to admire her resourcefulness.

"I need to check in with the kitchen," Jerry said, pushing up from the booth. They were seated near a set of doors that led into a high-tech kitchen, which had allowed not only privacy for their dinner but meant Jerry had been able to keep an eye on his staff all night.

"Always working," Sandra commented, shooting Lainey a look. "I suppose Damian is the same."

"Absolutely." She nodded. "He's so dedicated. It's inspiring."

Jerry stuck his hand out to Damian. "Enough with the hard sell already. I'll give you a meeting, but I'm not making any promises. You need to prove you can offer me more than my current firm, which is going to be tough. And at a better price, too."

"It won't be tough." Damian gripped the older man's hand.

"Cocky." Jerry laughed. "There's another problem with young people today."

"All right, grumpy old man," Sandra said as she slid out of the booth behind him, shaking her head. "Time to go."

"There's a VIP bar through the doors over there," Jerry said, pointing. "Marcella has your details if you'd like to go in for a drink. It's very private, so you don't need to worry about people bothering you. But you can stay at the table as long as you like."

"That sounds wonderful, thank you." Lainey smiled, and the room felt as though it'd brightened by a million watts. She stayed seated by Damian's side, blocking the entrance to the booth and waiting until Jerry and Sandra had left the area. "Would you like to get a drink?"

He shouldn't encourage bad decisions—or rather, a repeat of bad decisions. "I should take you home," he said.

"Should?" She raised a brow. "Come on, it's one

drink. You're trying to get this guy's business. It would be rude to decline."

"One drink," he said, giving her a firm look. "And that's it."

Looking far too much like the cat who'd got the cream, she slid out of the booth and headed toward the VIP bar without waiting for him. He stared after her—admiring the curve of her shapely behind through the tight fabric of her dress.

His cock stirred and Damian cursed himself. Normally, it was easy to maintain platonic relationships. In fact, not a single one of the women in his circle had ever made him think twice about his "no sex between friends" rule. Not a single one had even come close to tempting him. But Lainey had him hot and bothered like nothing else.

"Get your head in the game," he said to himself as he followed her.

In the VIP area, the lights were dimmed, a soft glow emanating from the bauble-like chandeliers that hung around the room. The atmosphere held a pleasurable intimacy, perfect for secret sharing and arm touching. He recognised a few of the patrons— a local politician, a TV host he'd met during his time on *Australia's Most Eligible*. No one even looked in their direction. Damian let out a breath.

Lainey headed to the bar and ordered a drink. When it arrived she traced her finger around the rim of the shot glass, the movement slow and languid. It was all too easy to imagine her circling the tip of his cock like that.

"Drink up," he said. "Then I can get you home."

"I meant one drink for *you*." A smile quirked on her lips. "I'm not going to limit myself."

He sighed. "What are you doing?"

"Having a drink with my *fiancé*." Her eyes were piercing, like polished amber. "You invited me—the least you can do is let me enjoy a few drinks."

"We're not having this argument again," he grumbled. "You set these wheels in motion."

"That's the adult version of saying 'you started it.'"

"You *did* start it."

"And you finished it. Three times." She smirked. "Always the overachiever."

A few strands of her hair slipped seductively over one eye. She dipped her pinkie into the shot glass and sucked it clean. The creamy liquid moistened her lips, and Damian felt his mouth run dry. He reached down to adjust himself, finding his cock fully hard and pressing against the zipper of his pants. Christ, how did she manage to do that?

"What are you drinking?" he asked, forcing his mind away from the cleavage peeking out of the top of Lainey's dress.

"Buttery nipple," she replied with eyes wide and purposefully innocent.

Heat flooded his stomach, and he felt his cock clench in response to her full lips wrapping around the shooter's name. And she was doing it on purpose, the devil. She brought the squat glass to her lips and tilted her head back in one liquid movement. Desire blanked out Damian's senses so that all he could see was the ivory column of her neck and the thrust of her breasts as she threw her head back.

"Delicious." She licked her lips. "You should try it."

Stifling the impulse to reach out and pull her into a kiss, Damian pressed his hips against the bar in an attempt to dispel his throbbing hard-on. But all it did was give him the friction he craved and bring him another merciless inch closer to Lainey.

"Are you drunk?" He pulled on his arsenal of big-brother interrogations to force some distance between them.

"Not yet." She grinned, and he could see the tip of her pink tongue between her teeth. "But I could be."

"Behave yourself, Lainey," he warned, though it was more for himself than it was for her.

She rolled her eyes and blinked her long, sooty lashes at him. "Learn to have a little fun, *Damian*."

He had to get out of there. If he watched her down another shooter, he might be tempted to kiss the flavour from her lips, and who knew where that would end up. It was impossible not to notice her body or the sexual energy that swam thick in the air around her.

And now, knowing how sweet she tasted...

"Your brand of fun is a little too over the top for my tastes." He nodded to the bartender so he could order a drink. Something stiff, which seemed fitting. The quicker he downed it, the quicker he could leave. "Why don't you call it a night? I'll get you a cab."

Lainey reached for his wrist, her fingers burning

him as she angled his watch toward her. "It's only gone eleven—the night is young."

"Don't underestimate the value of sleep."

Bloody hell, he sounded like an old man—and compared to her, he was. The extra decade had made him jaded, untrusting. And she was like a ray of fucking sunshine, so happy and optimistic it terrified him.

"I'll sleep when I'm dead," she replied with a wink.

His scotch arrived and Damian snatched it up, sending a good portion of it down his throat in one gulp. The warmth burned pleasantly in his chest.

"I'm leaving soon," she said, suddenly.

"Good," he said. "I want you to text me when you get home, though."

"No, I mean *leaving*. As in, the country." She ordered another drink, this time a glass of champagne. "For good...probably."

"Probably?"

She looked up at him. "Hopefully."

The word socked him in the chest. A few weeks ago he would have sent her off with a wave, wished her the best. But now...things were different. "Why?"

"I've got a job in London, doing social media for a celebrity stylist." She smiled, but not happily. "I felt like it was time for a change of scenery."

"Congratulations." The word stuck in the back of his throat like cactus prickles. He tried to swallow but found a lump there. "Have you told Corinna and Imogen?"

She nodded. "Yeah. I leave the week after next."

He should have been breathing a sigh of relief—

the source of his temptation would soon be gone. But it felt like something had shifted beneath his feet, unsettling him. Throwing him off balance, because what he *should* have felt in no way described the outcry in his head.

"That's not long."

She shook her head. "Nope." When her drink arrived, she raised it to his. "Here's to new beginnings."

"And old friends."

She sipped, a strange expression passing over her face. "Are we friends? I always thought you saw me as some annoying little sister type."

"Those two things aren't mutually exclusive."

She swatted him. "So you *do* think I'm annoying?"

"Well, you are the girl who insisted on telling everyone in which order they could open their Christmas presents."

He remembered it vividly—Lainey as a loud-mouthed ten-year-old telling him and his friends who could go first for their Bad Santa present swap. She hadn't even been invited to the event. But along with Corinna and Imogen, she'd crashed into his family's lounge room and demanded to be part of the festivities.

"Well, I never had any of my own siblings to boss around." She grinned. "You were the next best thing."

"I'll miss you," he said, the words flying out before he could stop them.

She stared at him, her eyes intense and focused. Something flickered there—a hint of emotion? Not positive. But Lainey was as good at hiding her weak points as he was.

"I'll miss you, too," she said.

"You're not planning to come back?"

"Nope." She cocked her head. "So that means you've got two weeks to make use of me as your 'fiancée' before you need to make up an excuse as to why we broke up."

The idea of making use of Lainey in any capacity filled his bloodstream with the snap, crackle and pop of anticipation. Maybe an expiration date would be good for them. Insurance against things getting out of hand, because how much damage could two people do in two weeks?

A lot. Don't kid yourself.

He cleared his throat. "I'm sure I'll be able to come up with some reason for why I screwed our relationship into the ground."

"Maybe you were unable go with the flow and my free-spirited heart couldn't take all that rigidity." She grinned. "Or perhaps you simply couldn't keep up with me in bed."

His nostrils flared. "You should know by now that I can hold my own in that area."

"One night isn't really enough to say for sure." She sucked on her lower lip. "It could have been a fluke."

He leaned closer, dragging in the scent of perfume on her skin mixed with the alcohol on her breath. Her cheeks flushed pink, and her breasts strained against the neckline of her dress as she breathed a little heavier. A little faster.

"It wasn't a fluke, Lainey, and you know it." Against his better judgement, he slipped a hand around her waist and pulled her closer. God, she felt good—so warm and soft and smooth. "I certainly know it."

"That we're good together?" Her lips parted.

"In bed," he clarified.

"Then why won't you let this happen?" She raised a palm to his chest, her fingertips brushing the buttons on his shirt. "Why won't you tell me the truth?"

"About what?"

"How you feel about me." Her eyes were wide, luminous. How on earth had he not recognised them at the ball? Her hunger radiated like a cloud around his head, messing up all the things he should be saying and tying his words into a knot.

"What do you want to know?"

Her lips lifted. "Have you fantasised about being with me?"

Her face was streaked with curiosity. He gripped her hip tightly, fighting back the urge to wedge her against the bar and take her right there on the spot. That mouth was asking to be plundered.

"Yes."

Her hand toyed with the zipper on her dress. "Tell me."

"Why do you want to hear this?"

"Because I've spent a good deal of my life thinking what I felt was one-sided."

She'd never hidden her feelings. Well, not effectively, anyway. When she was young, she'd looked up at him with adoring eyes—the big brother she never had. But as she got older, that adoration turned into something else, something decidedly more adult.

"It's not one-sided, but I knew it couldn't go anywhere, so I never acted on it." He brushed a strand of hair over her shoulder, grazing his knuckles along her exposed skin.

"But you're attracted to me."

He lowered his gaze, taking in her long, lean silhouette, the gentle curves at her waist and the swell of her breasts. "How could I not be? I doubt any straight man could resist you."

"So it's just biological?"

"No." He shook his head. "But that doesn't mean I think we're compatible, either. And regardless, I'm not looking for a relationship."

She stretched up onto her tiptoes and brushed her lips against his ear. "Neither am I."

Aided by her stilettos, she lined her hips up with his. Snaking one arm around his side, she hooked her thumb into the belt loop at his lower back. Claiming him. Being so close to Lainey had made his heart rate skyrocket and his skin hot enough to sear a steak.

"You should go home," he said in a last-ditch effort to maintain his rules. "Come on. We'll get a taxi."

"No." She snuggled closer to him, pressing her face into the base of his neck.

Her perfume wafted up and made it hard to breathe. She smelled like a summer garden, ripe and tempting. Her hair tickled the skin exposed at the collar of his shirt, and he brushed it from her face without thinking.

"Take me back to your place," she said.

It was a bad idea for so many reasons. Lainey was far too important to him for anything to get screwed up. Sure, she was crazy and pushy and reckless, but she'd been part of his life for years. His sister loved her, his parents loved her. As for him... He didn't know how to label it. He felt too old for her, too jaded. But he cared about her, that much was true.

"That's not a good idea," he said.

"What's the big deal? It's just sex. You want it, I want it. Why not have a good time?"

His restraint was like a rubber band pulled too tight—holding on, but threatening to snap at any moment. Excuses swirled in his head, words that encouraged him to have his way with her because it would be temporary, consequence-free. They could hide it until she left—and then they'd be on opposite sides of the world. No chance of awkward run-ins or a slip of the tongue after too many drinks.

"Tell me what you fantasised about," she urged. Her body pressed against his, the gentle back and forth sway of her hips making his cock ache.

Damian gritted his teeth. "Lainey," he warned.

"Do you think I can't handle it?" She narrowed her eyes. "Pretty sure I've proven I can. Or is it that *you're* afraid?"

"Of what?"

"That we might be amazing together...that we're already amazing together? Why does that scare you?"

She was baiting him and doing a damn good job of it. But he couldn't let her know that he *was* scared—

of ruining things with her, with his sister. Vulnerability, however, wasn't something Damian did. Not anymore.

"You really want to know?" he asked.

She nodded.

"I've thought about bringing you to the brink over and over. Holding you back until you beg me to let you come." Images danced in front of his eyes, all the fantasies of her he'd stroked himself to merging together. His control was slipping, dissolving. Turning to dust. "I've thought about fucking you so hard that you forget how to speak. So hard that you can't take a step the next day without remembering how good my cock felt inside you."

Her eyes widened.

"I've thought about that night," he said. "Over and over and over."

"And what do you do while you remember?"

"I think you know," he growled.

A tiny noise escaped her mouth, and already her eyes had taken on a glassy sheen, her movements becoming stiff and jerky. "Take me home," she whispered.

Their conversation was interrupted as the bartender arrived to check in with them. "Can I get you anything else?" The man looked at him expectantly.

Damian downed the rest of his scotch, though the expensive top-shelf liquor tasted like sawdust. "No. I think we're done."

None of his senses would be satiated until he got Lainey to his bedroom. Anticipation bubbled like boiling water, threatening to spill over and burn if left unattended for too long. But waiting was the best part, dragging out the exact moment that he would allow himself—and her—to go someplace new. Someplace terrifying.

The point of no return.

"Have you touched yourself while thinking about me?" She swallowed the remainder of her drink demurely as she waited for him to respond. There was no teasing in her tone now.

"Yes." He swallowed. "Have you?"

She hesitated for a moment. "I have."

"When was the last time?"

"Last night."

He raised a brow.

"Thinking about seeing you again... I was so wound up. I couldn't sleep." Her lashes touched as she closed her eyes for a moment. "But it wasn't the same. I didn't want to come unless you were there with me. I want all those things you said." She spoke slowly, controlling the words.

If he didn't have at least a taste, he was going to burst. Or he'd come quicker than an inexperienced teenager during his first fuck.

"Tell me what you thought about when you were touching yourself," he commanded softly.

She closed her eyes and sighed. "I imagined you taking me to bed, ordering me down to my knees so that I could take you between my lips. I wanted you to tell me what to do, to tell me to suck you until you came in my mouth."

Fuck. Was someone up there trying to test him?

She tilted her face up to his. "I want to try everything with you."

"Fine." The word popped out before he could stop it, warning bells sounding in his head like a cacophony of sirens. "But it's just sex."

"Just sex." She nodded. "Nothing more."

This was a *very* bad idea.

CHAPTER ELEVEN

LAINEY'S HEART THUNDERED like fists beating against drums as Damian led her from the restaurant. This was the moment she'd never dared to hope for—having him, without disguises or trickery. She might have said it was just sex, but her heart knew differently. With him it would always be more, even if she wouldn't admit it aloud.

At least she knew Damian would look after her. He was *exactly* the kind of guy she'd always wanted but never chased. The kind who had his head screwed on properly, who made her feel boneless and tingly. He was the complete package, perfection in man form... well, except for his inability to loosen up. But she was going to help him with that.

His clear eyes searched her face, trying to figure her out as they walked along the boulevard. The night air was balmy against her bare arms and legs, doing little to cool the inferno inside. Focusing on the strength of his arm around her, Lainey put one foot in front of the other and concentrated on keeping her balance in her stilettos.

The world felt like it was spinning around her, due as much to the way reality had rushed back as to the drinks. They rounded the corner and walked through the doors of a fancy hotel. Damian's face was hard, his mouth a slash across his movie star–handsome features. The hotel lobby gleamed, every surface polished and trimmed in gold. A heavy chandelier hung in the centre of the room, sending fractured light in all directions. Her eyes couldn't focus for all the blinding, dazzling finery.

"Why are we here?" she asked.

"You said you wanted to stay the night."

Her stomach dropped. "You're outsourcing me to a hotel?"

Heat crawled up her neck, blooming in her cheeks. So he was happy to fuck her but he wouldn't take her back to his place? Had she really read him that poorly?

He raked a hand through his short, black-brown hair. "I'm taking you home."

"Here?"

"Yes, here." He steered her away from the reception desk and toward a set of gleaming elevators.

"I don't understand."

It didn't make sense. Damian McKnight didn't live in a hotel. She and Corinna had crashed at his apartment plenty of times. He had a glorious view of Southbank and the river, a coffee machine that made the perfect cappuccino, and a couch that was softer than the clouds in heaven. He had a *home*. A real one.

"I live here." He sighed and jabbed the up button with his forefinger. "For the moment."

"And you've been keeping it secret?"

"Not specifically." His voice sounded brittle. "But Corinna knows I'm a private guy, in case you're wondering why she didn't tell you."

Strange. It *definitely* sounded like there was a story there.

An elevator chimed and the doors slid open, beckoning them inside. Mirrored walls reflected her confusion as she searched Damian's face. But he avoided her gaze, pressing the button for the top floor. Her ears popped as they rose higher and higher, the silence only broken by the chime that let them know they'd arrived.

The hallway of the hotel was quiet, and only a few doors dotted the walls. They stopped at the first one and Damian let them in, holding it open for her like he always did. *The perfect gentleman.*

"Whoa."

Melbourne's skyline painted the windows that ran the length of the room. Lights in every colour blinked and bathed everything in a twinkling glow. Damian deposited his key card into a slot by the door and the lights came on.

The suite was larger than most city apartments. It even had a dining table and a study area. Lainey rushed forward and stood at the window, her palms pressed against the glass. The view at his old place had been good, but not as good as this. It felt as though she were suspended in midair, flying above the city and away from her doubts.

"This is amazing." Her breath fogged the glass and she turned to find Damian watching her intently.

"It's temporary," he corrected, and held out a hand to her. "Come on, it's bedtime for you, princess...before you turn into a pumpkin."

He looked as though he belonged in this room, his crisp shirt and inky suit every bit as luxurious as the gold trimmings and soft lighting. She, by comparison, felt awkward in her too-tall heels and too-expensive dress. What *was* she doing here?

He led her to the bedroom, and her breath caught in her throat. Damian loosened the collar of his shirt, revealing a smattering of dark hair. She knew for a fact that it sprinkled the rest of him, too—decorating him in all the right places.

She wondered how it might feel to have the weight of him pressing her into the bed. To straddle him and watch his face contort with pleasure in the moonlight. She reached for him. Her movements were clumsy, nerves stripping away her motor skills.

He watched her, eyes wide and pupils blacker than night, while he drew a long breath and squared his shoulders. Lainey knew the signs well; she'd seen them that first time she'd tried to kiss him, three years ago. His first instinct had been to respond, but as quick as it had started, he'd pulled back. Now he looked the same, with tension bunching his muscles. She would not let Damian run, not when she'd finally found a way to make the sadness in her heart seem conquerable. Under his gentle exploration she felt renewed, alive. Safe.

"I promised myself I'd never go here," he said.

The conflict in his voice called to her, and she wanted to kiss him until he forgot how to speak. "Too late."

"It's not too late for me to do the right thing." He pulled back, breaking free of her greedy hands. "I can go back outside and we can wake up tomorrow morning and act like this never happened."

"As if you'd be able to forget me," she teased.

"I said *act* like it never happened...not forget." He shook his head, dark hair gleaming in the moonlight. "Unfortunately, I'll never forget."

She drew her zip down slowly, the sound cutting through the quiet room. His eyes tracked the movement, swallowing up every inch of bare skin as it was revealed. And she was bare all the way down.

"Christ." His muttered curse sent anticipation zinging through her as she dropped the dress to the floor and stepped out of her heels. "You were sitting there naked under that dress the whole evening?"

"Uh-huh." She stepped forward and reached for him, brazenly drawing her fingers along his fly. "Now strip."

This time there was no argument. He disposed of his suit jacket and popped the buttons on his shirt one by one. His bare torso looked paler in the glow of the city lights, but each muscle was defined to perfection. He was a powerful, virile, intoxicating man.

She slid her hand over his thigh and felt the muscle

twitch in response. Emboldened, she ventured farther by brushing her fingertips over his straining erection, eliciting a gasp from him. His hand shot down, fingers wrapping around her wrist as he yanked her hand away.

"Lainey," he growled. "Wait—"

She cut off his words by pulling his face down and kissing him. Hot, hard, wet. She explored him ruthlessly, revelling in the taste of him. A guttural moan reverberated in his throat, and he ground against her.

Balancing on her tiptoes, she fused their bodies together. Sighing into him, she thrust her hands into his hair and tugged. Hard. The buckle of his belt dug into her belly, and his mouth seared a trail from her lips to her collarbone, each kiss hungrier than the last. She had to have him, had to have every glorious inch of him.

The moment when the fight left his body filled her with a roar of power so loud and forceful it shook her to the bone. She had him *exactly* how she wanted him—without disguises. Without pretence. His shoulders dropped and his kiss intensified. It was as if the temperature in the room shot up a hundred degrees, and the air around them sizzled and popped. His fingers bit into her hips, teeth nipping at her skin. He was marking her, claiming her with his touch.

Then she was being lifted, wrapping her legs around him while he spun her. Two steps and her back met with the glass of the hotel window. It was cold on her bare skin while the front of her burned brightly, flames licking and growing with each stroke of his tongue. She traced the corded muscles in his neck, her fingertips smoothing over his Adam's apple.

Stubble scratched at her skin as he devoured her with gentle nips of his teeth. She wanted to see the marks, to see the evidence of his desire. A shiver shot down her spine, deepening the ache between her legs.

"Put me down," she whispered. "I want to touch you."

"Not yet."

He carried her to the bed and dropped her onto the mattress, settling on his knees and pressing his face between her legs. He kissed her there, swirling his tongue over her clit and wrenching a cry from her.

"You're so fucking perfect." He trailed kisses along the length of her heated sex, each one sending shock waves through her.

What had he done to deserve this incredible woman in his bed? He traced the sensitive curve of her inner thigh, chuckling as she bucked against him. He was going to draw it out, make her beg. He'd been hungry for so long, and she was a hot meal, a cold beverage, the light at the end of the tunnel. Every fucking cliché in the book...but it felt real. Special.

She writhed on the bed as he took his time getting to every line of her body. He drew his tongue up to flick over the sensitive bud of her clit.

Nails bit into his skin, delicious pain slicing through the fog in his head. He grabbed her hands and brought them together, easily encircling both wrists in one strong grip. He held her steady, making sure she couldn't move to touch him while he pleasured her. Her hips lifted from the bed, pressing shamelessly against his face.

"Patience," he said, swirling his tongue against her mercilessly. Each stroke was gentle, designed to wind her up but hold orgasm out of reach.

"You're a cruel man, Damian." She threw her head back. "I can't take it."

"You *will* take it." His voice came out edgy, raw.

Familiar desire crowded his senses. He was losing his grip. Restraint was slipping through his fingers with each groan and under-the-breath curse out of Lainey's mouth. She was a firework, ready to explode and burn them both.

He wanted to be burned. Tonight, he wanted it more than the air in his lungs.

"Damian, please." She lifted her head and her hazel eyes caught his attention. "I'm not too shameless to beg."

She laughed then, the breathy sound sending heat coursing through him. Her wrists tugged in his one-handed grip, but he held on, restraining her. That action alone had him hard beyond anything he'd experienced in a long time. And those smudgy, smoky, needy eyes…fuck.

He bit back the words swirling in his head. The filthy things he longed to say to her. But Lainey was someone he cared for…and you didn't speak to princesses the way he wanted to speak right now.

"Please." She drew the word out, long and agonisingly delicious. "I need to come."

He plundered her without warning, so that her gasp rang in his ears for what felt like hours. He dipped a finger into her core, delighting in the way her muscles clenched around him. Ecstasy could be found right here, with a woman on the brink of an orgasm he controlled. She hovered at the precipice, body grinding and writhing and desperate for release, while he dangled her over the edge.

"You taste so sweet," he murmured against her, breathing her in and savouring every second of it. "You're so soft, so perfect."

He drew the tight bud of her clit between his lips. The soft murmur of eagerness at the back of her throat swelled into a crescendo of pleasure as she shattered. He held her wrists tight, her muscles flexing as she came apart with his name on her lips.

He only released her when the last waves of her orgasm subsided and she lay sprawled on the bed, skin damp and glowing in the moonlight. Her eyelids fluttered and he crawled up on the bed to hold her. He pressed a kiss to her lips and she curled into him.

"I always knew you'd be good at that." Her hand traced the flat circle of his nipple, fingernail scraping gently over the sensitive peak. "You've got a good mouth for giving head."

He chuckled. "That so?"

"Yep." Her hand dipped lower, cupping the bulge

of his ready-to-burst cock. "Full lips, stubble for the right amount of friction…"

Her fingers wrapped around him, stroking the length of him through the thin material of his suit pants.

"I think we need to relieve you of these," she said, a coy smile on her sweet lips.

He couldn't strip down quick enough; if he didn't have her now he'd burst. Need thrummed in his veins, urging him to move quicker. He threw open the drawer next to the bed to grope for the little foil packets. It'd been so long he wasn't sure he had any left, but when his fingers brushed the telltale crinkled material he sighed with relief. He sheathed himself and then came back to the bed, his hands pressing down on either side of her head. The mattress shifted, accommodating his weight as he nudged her legs apart with his knee.

"I've been thinking about this nonstop since that night," he said.

She shot him a smug look. "Even when you were telling me it was a mistake?"

"Just because I was trying to do the right thing doesn't mean I wasn't thinking about burying myself inside you." He lowered his head to hers.

"And now?" Her lashes touched, lips parted and glistening in the lamplight.

"And now…if you keep talking I'm going to have to gag you, because I don't want to wait a second longer."

Her mouth opened as if she wanted to say something more, but it snapped shut a second later.

"Wise choice, princess," he growled, slipping his hand between them to find her slick and needy. "Brace yourself. You've got me all worked up."

He pushed into her, burying himself deep. When her hands came to his chest he grabbed her wrists with one hand, forcing them above her head. She whimpered, her sex clenching around his cock as he thrust.

Fantasy didn't even begin to compare to reality. On the nights since the ball, when he thought of her, his mind hadn't been able to accurately conjure how tight and hot and perfect she was in real life. She was made for him, a perfect fit. And that one crazy night in the limo was nothing compared to this.

Because this wasn't just about her tight body or sexy, smoky stare. It was *her*...all of her.

Her hips bucked against his, her arms straining against his grip. "Keep your hands above your head," he growled. "Don't make me stop."

He released her and her hands immediately fisted in the duvet, her knuckles white. "Please don't stop."

"Tell me what you want, Lainey."

"I..." She stopped to moan as his hand came between them and found her clit. "Oh, my God. I want to come again."

He bent his head down to her ear. "You want to come again, greedy girl?"

"Yes," she panted, her head lolling back and forth. "I want to come against your hand."

Sweet fucking hell.

As if it wasn't enough that she'd been so perfectly responsive, the desperation in her voice as she told him how she wanted to come was…everything.

He applied pressure to her clit, working his hand in circular motions until he felt her clench on his cock, as shock waves raced through her, her body trembling beneath his. It was all he could take to hold on a second longer before he felt his balls draw up and he tumbled into the abyss after her.

Rolling onto his back, he took Lainey with him. Her face pressed into the curve of his neck, her breath hot against his already flaming skin. She murmured his name and an incoherent pleasure sound that washed over him like a warm blanket.

When his strength returned, he pushed up, cradling her in his arms. He carried her to the bathroom and set her down, keeping an arm around her waist as he flicked on the large tub's tap.

"Let's get cleaned up," he whispered in her ear.

She nodded mutely, her body sagging into him, and her arms tucked up against his chest. In the mirror he could see the faint pink marks where he'd gripped her hard. By morning, evidence of their night together would be gone, with only memories to keep him going.

He tested the temperature and helped her into the bath, disposing of the condom before following her and drawing her back to his chest. Her head rested against him, the length of her hair swirling in the water as the tap ran. Tracing circles on the inside of her thigh, his mind whirred with tomorrow's possible outcomes.

"Stop thinking," she said, grabbing his hand and interlacing her fingers with his. "Everything is going to be fine."

CHAPTER TWELVE

DAMIAN WOKE THE next morning feeling as though he'd been transported to Eden. Rolling over, he reached for Lainey but found an empty mattress. Rubbing the heel of his hand into his eyes, he sat up. Clinking sounds came from the kitchenette, and he got up and pulled on a pair of pants.

"Rise and shine," Lainey sang as he walked into the main area of the suite, the chime in her voice making him smile.

He raked a hand through his hair. It'd been a while since he'd felt this exhausted in the morning. Sleep deprived in the best way possible, but still…what he needed was a nice strong cup of—

"Coffee?" Lainey appeared in front of him, holding out a steaming mug.

"You're an angel." He reached for the cup.

It was an apt description, considering how she looked right now. Endless legs extended out from the bottom of a soft white T-shirt—*his* T-shirt—which barely covered her. Her breasts were unrestrained beneath the fabric, nipples peaked and tantalising.

He frowned. "You're still here."

"Did you expect me to bail?" She dropped down onto the coffee table in front of him, one long leg draped over the other.

He'd hoped in the light of day she'd be easier to resist, that without the tight dress and heels he might stand a chance. But no…this was a hell of a lot worse.

Karma was a cruel and enticing bitch.

"I wasn't sure you'd want to stay."

She cocked her head. "Do you want me to go?"

Ah, this old dance. It was one he avoided with most women by getting the fuck out of Dodge before it was necessary to communicate. But that wasn't how he wanted to handle things with her.

"I didn't say that."

"You look sleepy." She grinned when he rolled his eyes. "Drink up."

He shook his head and sipped his coffee. "Same old bossy Lainey."

"I have a proposition for you." She kicked her feet up onto the couch next to him so that all he could see was miles of peaches-and-cream skin. "I'm going to stay here, and if by the time midnight comes around tomorrow you don't want to sleep with me again, I'll go and I won't ever mention it again."

"Is this some kind of messed-up Cinderella sex thing?" He watched her over the rim of his cup.

She poked her tongue out at him. "More like Beauty and the Beast."

"Charming."

"So we're on?" She put her hands on his shoulders and leaned forward so the ends of her hair tickled his bare chest and stomach. "No offence, but my money's on me."

Her lips hovered close to his, her knees nudging his thighs apart. His blood fizzed and raced as though she'd hooked him up to an electrical outlet. Each breath was an effort, desire crushing him from the inside out. Holy hell, if the girl could do that from mere proximity…

She winked and released him. "I'm having a shower—feel free to join me."

Then she sashayed off as though it was her place, not his. Hair swung behind her like a band of scarlet silk, brushing the hem of the T-shirt. Her arrogance should have grated on him, but he found it oddly charming and comforting. She made no attempt to adjust herself to him, no attempt at false niceties or trying to please him. Since his stint on television, he'd noticed how people acted differently around him, and it pissed him off to no end.

The sound of the shower snagged his attention. It was tempting to join her…oh, so tempting. But he had to get his head straight and figure out just how long he was going to play her game before one of them got burned.

Water poured over Lainey, warm and soothing. Last night she'd seen another side of Damian. It had been every bit as perfect as she'd hoped for—hot sex, no head games. He'd wrapped her up in his arms and held her all night.

Unease settled in her stomach. She was already trying to convince him to give her another night—another hit. She was an addict, craving her next fix, chasing satiation that would never come. She turned her face against the spray and chuckled. She must be crazy after all. Who else would chase a man so hard knowing it wouldn't go anywhere?

The door to the bathroom hadn't budged an inch. Hmm, so he wasn't taking the bait. She rinsed the conditioner from her hair and turned off the water. Fluffy white towels hung from the gleaming silver rack—one of the perks of living in a hotel. Her brows crinkled. Why *was* he living here? He'd sold a perfectly good apartment to live in a hotel that probably cost as much per night as she earned from a month of hairdressing.

It was definitely something Corinna would usually have told her. The fact she hadn't meant this wasn't simply a change of scenery for him.

She gave her body a quick wipe-down and then wandered, stark naked, into his bedroom contemplating what to wear. Her dress from last night had barely been appropriate for an evening on the town let alone for the bright sunshine of the morning after…but it wasn't like she had much choice.

She tugged on the stretchy dress and riffled through Damian's wardrobe, plucking out a clean white shirt. She slipped it on, rolled up the sleeves and located the emergency ballet flats in her handbag. There she also found her touch-up makeup palette. It wasn't perfect, but at least she wouldn't look like something the cat had dragged in.

"Going through my clothes again?"

Lainey whipped around. "Thought I'd make an effort to look respectable. So, what are the plans for today?"

He folded his arms across his chest. "I don't think we should be playing games like this."

He was probably right. The little bundle of doubts was already growing, the voice in her head warning her that she was going to be flying to London with tears in her eyes. But if the end was nigh, then she'd go out all guns blazing. What was the point of small regret? Might as well go hard.

"We made a deal, so I'm staying. You can ship me off at midnight if you want. But until then...you're stuck with me."

"I don't remember agreeing to that." He closed the distance between them in two long-legged strides. "Besides, you're too young for me—"

"Too young? I'm almost twenty-five."

"You should go for someone your own age..."

"Ugh." She rolled her eyes and flipped her hair over one shoulder, fully aware of just how much that action supported his argument. "You're not that old, Damian, but you sure do act like you're a hundred sometimes."

"See?"

"No, I don't see. Like I said, I'm sticking around all day, so you can stay here and argue with me—which would be pointless, because I'll outlast you—or you can take me for a coffee. A real one."

"What if I told you straight up I don't want to sleep with you again?" He pulled her closer, staring down at her in what might have been an attempt to intimidate. Instead it made her body burn, need gnawing at her insides.

"I'd call bullshit."

A smile twitched on his mouth. "Fine. Coffee it is. It's probably safer to have you out there than in here."

She grinned. "You'd like to think that, wouldn't you?"

The day was already hot. Sunshine filtered through the trees lining the café strip, sending dancing speckles of light across their table. They'd found a quiet spot on the courtyard of a café, private enough for them to talk. Because Lainey had questions.

Swiping at her croissant, she tore off one end and stuffed it into her mouth. "So what's the deal with the hotel room?"

He sighed. "It's a long story."

"We've got all day."

He stared at his coffee cup for a moment before looking up with a blank expression. "I couldn't stand to be in the apartment any longer."

Lainey had known Jenny well enough to know she and Damian were completely and utterly wrong for each other, though she'd never said it to his face. They'd gotten married at twenty-four—a conservative ceremony without passion—and cracks started showing less than a year in. Jenny had been over-bearing. Her family was even worse. Then one day the marriage ended suddenly and Damian had never spoken of his ex-wife again.

Not even to explain *why* the marriage broke down. To this day it was a mystery.

"Why?" Lainey asked. "What changed?"

"Nothing, that's exactly the point. I thought I'd have gotten my shit together, moved on...something."

"But you have moved on." She sipped her coffee, shielding her eyes from the sun with her hand. "You're like a completely different person now. Well, like how you used to be before."

He shook his head. "I'm not."

"Yes, you are. You were so uptight when you were with her. You were tense all the time. It was like you were always trying to force something when she was around, like you were trying to be something else." She sighed. "You weren't yourself."

Damian quirked a brow. "Really?"

"Yes." She swatted him across the table. "And don't look at me like that. I can say insightful shit from time to time."

"'Insightful shit'?"

He was mocking her, the bastard. "I know what I'm talking about." She crossed her arms, self-conscious for the first time.

She could be stark naked in front of him, in the throes of orgasm, and be confident. In control. But the second it came down to the personal stuff—she couldn't have felt more exposed.

"No need to get defensive. I'm quite partial to insightful shit." His eyes swept over her, skimming the neckline of last night's dress and her bare skin exposed between the open lapels of his shirt. Was he remembering the way he felt when she lowered the zipper? When she'd bared herself to him?

She leaned forward. "Why do you think you haven't changed?"

"This is a bit heavy for breakfast conversation, don't you think?" He raked a hand through his dark hair and the front sprang forward rebelliously.

"We might be eating breakfast, but it's hardly early. Besides, I get the impression it would be heavy conversation for you no matter what time it was."

"I prefer to keep things light. Sue me."

He attempted a look of nonchalance, but his gaze flicked over her. Hot and intense. Sunlight streamed down over their table, shifting so that the trees around them no longer provided protection. Lainey slipped the white shirt off and bundled it on top of her handbag. The sunshine felt good on her bare arms.

"I could tempt you to get heavy." She smirked. "I convinced you to sleep with me, after all."

Damian's Adam's apple bobbed and his gaze narrowed, two flintlike eyes challenging her. "Once."

"Twice," she corrected.

"The first time doesn't count."

"Then I'll do it again." She shrugged. "You're just buying time now."

"I'm not buying anything."

"Yet." She jabbed a finger in his direction. "I've got all day."

"You're going to need all weekend at the rate you're eating that croissant." He nodded to the barely touched pastry sitting in front of her.

"Would you prefer it if I stuffed the whole thing in my mouth at once?" She sucked on her lower lip, stifling a smile. "That's not very ladylike, is it?"

Damian's serious expression broke, his eyes crinkling at the corners, and he laughed, low and throaty. She needed to see him laugh more often.

"Since when are *you* ladylike?"

"Good point." She grinned.

Her phone vibrated against the glass table, Corinna's picture flashing up on the screen. Lainey's smile faded; she didn't want to talk to her best friend right now. Guilt twinged low in her gut.

Ugh, why did they have to be related? Or rather, why couldn't she only want the physical with Damian? Why did she need more than their memory-obliterating night in bed? There was nothing wrong with some serious, scream-the-roof-off fucking. She knew that. Dirty, impolite sex was her favourite kind.

But with him…it was always going to be more.

"What's with the expression?" he asked. "You look like you're plotting a murder."

Lainey wrinkled her nose. "Plotting a murder, huh? How would you know what that looks like?"

"I picked you up from that freak's house one time, remember? I'm pretty sure if I'd walked past a mirror my face would have looked exactly like that."

"Which freak?" She rolled her eyes. "There have been so many."

"Why *do* you always have to date idiots?" He drained the last of his coffee and tilted his face up to the sun. "Aren't there any normal guys left in Australia for you to choose from?"

"Despite what you might think, I don't always get my pick of the litter." She rolled her shoulders back, stretching her arms in front of her. "Besides, you rejected me."

He pressed his lips into a flat line.

Yeah, and it has nothing to do with Corinna or Jenny. It's because you're not forever material. You're not good enough for him.

She would ban all doubts until the weekend was over. She would get Damian back into bed and she *would* forget about the fact that she was leaving everything she knew in under two weeks, all because she couldn't have the man she wanted with all her heart.

CHAPTER THIRTEEN

GIVEN THE EVENTS of last night, Damian didn't want to heap his personal problems on Lainey. Because that would take them squarely away from casual sex and into...not-so-casual sex. Either that or he was still so ashamed about the divorce that he couldn't bear to talk to anyone about it. Not even her. His family and Aaron knew what'd happened, but they'd all been sworn to secrecy.

It was *his* business. His private shame that he hadn't been able to keep his wife happy.

"So you sold the apartment because you think you haven't gotten over the divorce?" she pressed as they exited the café.

"Well, it was never going to be *my* place," he said, slipping on a pair of sunglasses to shield himself from Lainey's intense stare. "No matter how much time passed, I could still feel her there."

"And you want to move on?" She looked at him with earnest eyes, glimmering with hope. That was exactly what he *didn't* want from her.

He knew Lainey had a crush on him when they

were growing up, because she was as subtle as a sledgehammer. Problem was, as time went on, he grew more and more attracted to the chaotic girl with the heart of gold. It pained him to admit, but she'd been in and out of his fantasies since his divorce.

He shoved the conflict aside, making a silent promise that it would be a single indiscretion. An isolated incident—well, except for the night of the ball, since that time had been out of his control—and that he would send her home…later.

"I'm ready to move on, yes." He paused. "But I'm past that whole fairy-tale bullshit thing now. Moving on does not mean looking for someone else to marry."

She considered that for a moment, her head bobbing slowly. He wondered if she might want further details. And he was ready to shut her down if she did.

"Sounds like you made the right decision to move…but a hotel? Really?" She frowned, her brows crinkling. "That's not a home. You don't even have a proper kitchen."

"I want to find the right place, and I'm not going to rush things this time." With the apartment or with a woman. "And the hotel owner is a client."

Trees lined the patch of greenery that ran parallel to the river. Chairs dotted the edge, most of them occupied by couples and families enjoying the summer warmth. Arm in arm, Damian and Lainey would have looked like any other couple. Their footsteps dropped in perfect unison, a synchronicity that only developed after years of being around one another.

"I can help you move on, you know." Her voice

turned coy, a sly smile spreading across her lips. "I want to help."

"I don't need your help." Against his better judgement, he reached out and touched her hair; the long red waves looked as though they belonged on a mermaid. On a mythical creature. Not on this crazy, impulsive woman.

"But you might *want* my help." She stepped closer.

"I don't." The words stuck, and Damian had to force them out. "Want" was too high up in his vocabulary when it came to Lainey.

"Why are you so uptight?" she asked, tilting her head. A cool breeze swept past and ruffled her hair, sending the vibrant waves across her shoulders. "What are you trying so hard to repress that you've turned into this…"

"Curmudgeon?" he offered.

"I don't even know what that is, but it sounds about right." She threw her hands in the air and huffed.

"It means killjoy."

"Yes, killjoy. That's *exactly* the word I was looking for." She grabbed him by the shoulders and shook him. "I am going to make you have some fun."

He wrapped his hands around her wrists and lowered them, hanging on to her for a moment longer than necessary.

"Why don't we find you an apartment?" she said.

Now, that wasn't a bad idea. A few property inspections would keep them away from his hotel room, and talking about kitchen layouts was a hell of a lot easier than talking about his divorce…or why Lainey was such a risk to him.

"Fine, apartment hunting it is."

Half an hour later they were following a brisk-mannered real estate agent into a penthouse apartment in Southbank. Turned out she was a huge fan of *Australia's Most Eligible* and the name Damian McKnight meant she dropped her other appointments quicker than a hot potato.

"This apartment was previously owned by a CEO who lived in Sydney and needed a base in Melbourne," the agent said as she held the door open for them. "As you can see, it looks brand-new."

"It would have to be for three million," Damian said under his breath.

Lainey stifled a smile, standing close to him as he inspected the kitchen fittings. Marble benchtops gleamed as sunlight poured in from floor-to-ceiling windows. The kitchen was sizable, and all the fittings looked as though they'd never been used. He could correct that.

"Couldn't you see us in this kitchen, Damian?" Lainey asked, loud enough so the agent could hear.

Her hazel eyes sparkled with mischief, hands knotted in front of her as she beamed at him. He shot her a look. What the hell did she think she was doing?

"We could make such a mess in this great big space." She smiled at the agent, wrapping an arm around Damian and giving him an affectionate squeeze. "You know, I do most of the cooking at home."

The agent arched a brow, her gaze sweeping over Lainey as one might inspect something on the bottom of their shoe. Lainey's dress left miles of long, creamy leg on display, and her smudgy, sexy eye makeup was more suited to midnight than midday, but that didn't give anyone the right to judge her.

"I'm sure you'll find all the fittings here to be of the highest quality, Mr. McKnight," the agent said, continuing to move through the room. "It would be a shame for a man like you to waste your money on something not up to standard."

He didn't miss the quick flick of the agent's eyes toward Lainey. Luckily, she was too busy trailing her hand along the edge of the marble countertop and looking out at the view to take notice. Damian's jaw clenched.

"I make it a point never to waste my time on things that don't meet my standards. My fiancée knows I have very particular tastes."

Lainey's head shot up and she grinned at him. "Yes, dear. You are *very* particular."

The agent looked at him in disbelief, her mouth popping open for a second before she snapped it shut and walked toward the lounge room. "The living area is open plan, as you can see, but there is an additional space for recreation. If you follow me through here…"

"Recreation, hmm?" Lainey tugged him after the agent. "That's very important. We should make sure it will fit all our recreation…equipment."

Damian stifled a laugh. The agent's face had turned the deep shade of a tomato, and she scurried along in her heels, changing direction and gesturing for them to follow her to the bathroom. He knew it was wrong to pay the agent back for being a bitch… but it had been so long since he'd had any fun.

It was true. All work and no play had made him a very dull man indeed.

"You can see the bathroom is very generous. There's a double shower and a deep tub. The towel racks are heated. You can control them with the switches here," she babbled, unable to look either of them in the eye.

"Double shower would be great," Lainey said in mock seriousness. "The last thing we want is to break the glass like we did at that holiday house."

Damian smothered his laughter with a cough. "Yes, that was rather expensive."

"We had fun, though, didn't we?" She walked past him and brushed her hand brazenly along his crotch.

Unfortunately for Damian, while the words were joking, her touch had a very real effect on him. As she wandered out of the bathroom, she shook her hair out so that it tumbled unrestrained down her back, and his pants tightened considerably. That merest touch, a graze of her fingertips, had made him rock hard in an instant.

He followed Lainey into the master bedroom, watching her walk. The hem of her dress was borderline indecent, but she had such fantastic legs it would have been a crime for them to be hidden away. He was thrust into a memory. Last night. His lips on her, those smooth, perfect thighs parted for him. Only him.

"Is this a king-size bed?" Lainey asked the agent, who looked more than a little annoyed that she'd ended up dealing with his fiancée.

"Of course it is, ma'am." The agent nodded stiffly.

"Please, don't call me ma'am," Lainey replied with a saccharine smile. "I'm way too young for that."

If Damian had a drink he would have choked on it. Perhaps his earlier assumption that Lainey hadn't noticed the older woman's attitude toward her was incorrect. She seemed to be enjoying herself far too much.

Stop it, he mouthed at her.

As the agent made her way into the enormous walk-in closet, Damian grabbed Lainey by the arm. He brought his lips close enough to her ear that he brushed her earlobe as he spoke. "If there's a report on some gossip site tomorrow that I enjoy dating young women, I'm going to blame you."

She laughed, the deep, throaty sound sending whatever blood was left in his brain straight down to his cock. Turning her head, she batted her eyelashes at him. The bronzy smudges of makeup around her pale eyes wound him up even more. He wanted those eyes looking up at him while he drove into her mouth. He wanted to see her blink as he pressed between those lips. Pushing as far as he could, seeing how much she could take.

Stop that shit. Right. Now.

"I haven't even told her how you like me to dress up as a schoolgirl yet," she teased.

"Liar." He squeezed her arm, pulling her tight against him. "Don't. You. Dare."

"Or what?" She blinked at him. "You'll punish me?"

He wanted to press her up against the bedroom wall and kiss her until her knees gave out. "Don't tempt me."

She stepped out of his grip, following the agent into the closet. Bending forward, she pretended to inspect the finish of the built-in shelving. Her hem rose higher, inching toward the pleasures that lay beneath. Knowing there was nothing to cover her under the dress was bad enough. Waiting to see if he'd catch a glimpse was pure torture. He turned, facing the endless stretch of glass that revealed Melbourne's skyline and adjusted himself. His cock strained against his jeans, and he had nothing with which to hide himself. Nothing to conceal that Lainey had far more of a hold over him than he wanted.

Her laughter rang in his ears as she materialised beside him. Up close, the smell of his soap on her skin stoked his desire. The heat of her body pressing gently against his tested his barriers.

"Enjoying the view?" she asked.

"It is a fantastic one," the agent chimed in. "People pay a lot for a view like this."

Lainey cupped her hand over her mouth, trying not to laugh. Damian watched her from the corner of his eye. Pink had spread across her cheeks, her red-lacquered nails shimmering against porcelain skin.

"I do appreciate the view," he said, not daring to look at her directly.

"Can't you imagine waking up to it every morning? Going to sleep with it every night." Lainey pressed on, linking her arm through his. "Watching the moon."

He snorted and tried it cover it with another cough. He needed to get out. The longer he imagined what it would be like to see Lainey standing stark naked against the window, the creamy flesh of her backside presented for him, the harder it was going to be to compose himself.

"So what do you say, Damian? Do you want to pay for the view?" Her hand squeezed his bicep.

"I need to think about it." He nodded at the agent. "Thanks for showing us around. We have to talk before we can make a decision."

"There are several other properties I could show you." The agent hurried over to him, plucking a business card from a fancy silver holder in her leather notebook. "We could make a time—"

"I'll get in contact if I'm interested in seeing more." He cut off her sales pitch and made his way to the front door, Lainey in tow.

"Oh, you're interested," Lainey whispered as they left the apartment and headed toward the elevator. "I can tell."

"What makes you say that?"

"Apart from the fact that your jeans look a little... snug?"

"A little?"

She laughed. "A lot."

By the time they made it out to the street, Damian

had managed to calm himself down. Okay, so he was attracted to Lainey. He knew that already. She was fun, hot and confident. What wasn't to like? Any guy would have the same reaction.

It wasn't a big deal. He'd simply sit her down when they got back to his hotel and tell her that he cared about her too much to have her as anything but a friend. He'd made a mistake, but he wouldn't let it get between them. In the meantime, he had to deal with this crazy, pent-up sexual frustration. But screwing his way out of it wasn't going to work...that much was damn clear.

"It's boiling," Lainey moaned as they wandered back to the river. She fanned herself with one hand. "Let's get ice cream."

"You haven't had lunch yet."

"Thanks for the nutritional lecture, *Dad*." She swatted him. "I can have ice cream for lunch if I want."

He shrugged. Ice cream actually sounded like the perfect antidote to his overheated state. They strolled along the tree-lined boulevard as he tried to settle his mind. Everything about this situation screamed potential disaster, but he couldn't force himself to put an end to it.

Does it matter? She's leaving the country soon. You have an end date.

But that was the thing with Lainey—she never played by the rules. Never stuck to the plan. He needed her to know why he couldn't engage in anything serious.

Perhaps he should tell her the truth about his divorce. Then she might understand his actions better.

Even thinking about it brought heat to his face that made his skin prickle and his chest feel tight. It'd been four years, and still the shame burned as brightly as it had the day he'd caught Jenny and Ben. All he'd ever wanted was for his marriage to fulfil him and his wife, and he had believed that Jenny wanted that, too. Unfortunately, when tested, it was clear that what Jenny had really wanted was for him to sacrifice his career ambitions to spend more time with her...or else she'd get revenge.

The sun beat down on them as they walked. Lainey had ditched the white shirt again, and perspiration beaded along her bare arms and her chest. The dress clung to her like a second skin.

"Why so serious?" Lainey asked, tilting her head up to him and shielding her eyes.

"I was thinking about the apartment," he lied, fishing his sunglasses out of his pocket and handing them to Lainey.

She slipped them on, the large mirror-like lenses obscuring her eyes. "Why were you frowning, then?"

"It's a big decision." He spotted a café with an ice cream counter up ahead. "I'm weighing up my options."

"What are your must-haves? The things that you absolutely won't compromise on."

"You mean aside from a great view?" He smirked. "Space for a big desk, a bigger bedroom."

"What else?"

"Somewhere to relax and zone out. A place where I can think."

Lainey shook her head. "You think too much."

"I thought we were talking about the apartment." They joined the long, snaking line for ice cream.

"We are, but the apartment is a representation of you." Lainey pushed the sunglasses on top of her head.

"How so?"

"You want a big desk because you're ambitious and your business is a huge part of your life. You want a big bedroom because you have a lot of shit to deal with and you need somewhere to be yourself."

His shoulders rose, fingers balled into fists by his side. "What does the bedroom have to do with being myself?"

"Because you hide things when you're out in the world. When you're at home, it's just you. You can stop pretending." She smiled. "Maybe that's why you moved into a hotel without finding a new place first. You know you don't want to be who you were with Jenny, but you haven't figured out what the next step looks like."

He gaped at her, unsure whether to laugh off her comments or immediately drag her back to his hotel room. Perhaps he too was guilty of underestimating Lainey; she obviously saw deep into him. She knew him far better than his ex-wife ever did.

"You really *do* say some insightful shit."

She grinned. "I sure do."

As they approached the ice cream counter, Lainey's attention locked firmly on the rainbow selection of treats. She tapped a finger to her lip.

"What flavour are you having, Damian? I'm buying."

"No, you're not." He pulled out his wallet, but she slapped his hand.

"I said *I'm* buying. You paid for this ridiculous dress and left the tags on. So I know you should be broke by now." She winked at him.

"Vanilla bean," he replied. "Single scoop."

Lainey turned to the woman behind the counter. "I'll have two waffle cones, single scoops. One rocky road and one caramel crunch."

"No vanilla then?" Why did she even bother asking?

"You're not a vanilla guy, Damian. I know that much."

"Does this mean we're done with the amateur psychology hour?" he asked drily, accepting the two cones from the woman behind the counter as Lainey paid. "Which one do you want?"

They walked away from the café, and she contemplated her options before plucking the caramel cone from him. Her tongued darted out to capture the ice cream and she sighed. "So. Damn. Good."

Lainey and Damian walked along Southbank, past the busker in the Super Mario costume playing guitar and the chalk artist drawing people's faces on the ground. They ate in silence, mouths working quickly before the sun melted the ice cream onto their hands.

Damian tucked in to his rocky road with enthusiasm. And he'd wanted vanilla? She smiled to herself, remembering the way he'd hardened when she'd touched him during the apartment inspection. Vanilla was for guys with unsteady hands and fumbling fingers, and Damian wasn't one of those guys.

They came to a stop at a bench that overlooked the aging beauty of the Flinders Street station. It rose up, magnificent and unusual among the sleeker office towers in Melbourne's skyline. The old building had character. Though weathered, it held a certain charm in its mustard-coloured facade and iconic green dome. There was beauty in its age and history, the scars of decades making it even lovelier than it would have been when brand-new.

"Are you shocked that I know you so well?" Lainey asked, still looking out over the water.

"You don't know me as well as you think. One accurate psychoanalysis doesn't change that."

"But you *do* hide from the world," she pressed.

She had an inkling that he covered up his true self for the same reason she relied on zany antics and a crap ton of eyeliner—for fear that people wouldn't like what was underneath. She fought against a memory of being dumped because she'd dropped out of school.

Not like she had a choice. School had been slowly stifling her—trying to stuff her into a box that was too small and too dark. She couldn't seem to follow the rules that were designed for kids with long attention spans and the ability to make sense of numbers. Lainey's skills lay in areas that weren't marked on paper.

Nowhere in the curriculum had she been praised for her ability to defuse a tense situation or cheer someone up. The fact that she could instinctively tell what colours would look good on people meant nothing. Not even in art class could her creativity flourish because, even there, the rules had stifled her.

After that, she'd learned to be someone else. She wore short skirts and acted out. She attracted guys who didn't care that she still counted on her fingers, guys who were only after one thing. All so she could call the shots. So she never again had to face the humiliation of being dumped because she wasn't good enough for the longterm.

"It's something I have to do," he replied, concentrating on his ice cream. It was torture watching his tongue and lips devour the treat with surgical efficiency.

"Why?"

He shook his head, and a smile tugged at the corner of his lips. "Things have happened that make me wary of putting myself out there."

"I haven't done anything to criticise the way you are."

"Other than calling me boring or stodgy, you mean?" He took a bite out of his waffle cone. "What about that one time you said I was the Antichrist of fun?"

Lainey's cheeks burned. "Okay, so maybe I said those things. But it's because…"

"I'm no fun?"

"You are when you allow yourself a little breathing space." She shrugged. "You always act like it's your job to protect everyone around you."

"It is," he said without hesitation.

"No, it's not. I appreciate all the times you've bailed me out, I really do." Lainey finished off her ice cream and put her hand on Damian's knee. "But you need to stop worrying about everyone else and start worrying about yourself. Or else you'll be a... what did you call yourself?"

"A curmudgeon?"

"Yeah, that."

"I'm never going to stop worrying about you." He turned and Lainey got the full force of his Blue Steel stare.

Could he see right into her soul? Did he know that she was a woman who wanted to run away from her life? Away from the fear that she would forever be in one-sided love with him?

The feeling slammed her in the chest with the force of a freight truck. Sure, she'd thought it so many times before—that she had a thing for Damian. An insatiable, unending schoolgirl crush on her best friend's handsome older brother. Harmless...until it wasn't.

Love. How was it possible to love someone who didn't love you back? It was cruel that humans had been designed that way. She tugged on the hem of her dress, paranoid that her fear and devastation were shining out of her.

"You don't need to cover it up, Lainey. I saw it all

last night." His words hitched, his voice rough and ragged around the edges.

Was he referring to her body or to the unwieldy mix of terror and desire warring inside her?

She swallowed, her hand lifting to cup the side of his face. A light stubble showed along his jaw, and her thumb swiped against his lip to capture a tiny smear of chocolate. The only movement he made was the quickening of his breath, hot against her hand. He kissed the pad of her thumb, then caught her hand and pressed his lips to the inside of her wrist.

Darkness engulfed his eyes, grey irises shrinking until there was nothing but a mere rim of it around two bottomless black holes. "I hide because I'm afraid that I might hurt you."

Lainey puffed out her chest, chin tilted up to him. "I won't let you hurt me."

She wouldn't. *Couldn't.* Because if she allowed him to crash through the careful fence she'd set up around this encounter, he'd railroad her heart until it broke for good. This was just sex—fulfilment of a fantasy. And that was all it could ever be.

CHAPTER FOURTEEN

LAINEY SAT IN the middle of her room, surrounded by boxes. They were labelled—not with descriptions of the items inside, but with names. Imogen. Corinna. Mum. She'd divided her not-so-worldly possessions into two piles—keep and discard. The keep pile was further sorted into boxes for the person who would appreciate the items most.

For some reason, it reminded Lainey of a will reading. She was going, and all that would be left of her was an insanely large shoe collection and her childhood set of *The Powerpuff Girls* on VHS. She should have appointed an executor for her stuff. That way she could whisk herself off to London and leave someone else to deal with it all.

She popped the lid on a dusty plastic tub that was packed to the brim with memories—her grade-six polo top with all the signatures of her friends written in puffy fabric pens. A tattered-looking friendship bracelet with the silver beads containing the initials *C*, *L* and *I*. A photo album wrapped in a *My Little Pony* pillow case, the cover dusted with pink glitter from some stickers that had shed sparkling particles all over the place.

She flipped it open and grinned. The first page had three almost identical shots of her, Corinna and Imogen in some awful-looking hipster jeans with super-wide belts, strappy metallic halter tops and silver lipstick. In each photo, one of the girls was making a silly face while the other two laughed. They'd never been able to get a shot with the three of them looking good all at once. The Goof Balls, her mother had called them.

Lainey flipped through the album, her heart sinking with each page. Through every up and down, these girls had been by her side. Through every terrible hair phase, every eyebrow-plucking accident, every celebrity obsession and every tearstained heartbreak, Imogen and Corinna were woven into her life. There was no part of Lainey's history that didn't include them.

She flipped to the last page and found a loose photo. The image caused her heart to stutter. Scrawled in pen was a date ten years ago. New Year's Day. Lainey had still had her natural mousy hair then, and it hung down to her waist without a kink. On her head she wore a plastic tiara with "Happy New Year" in glittering letters. She held a giant slice of watermelon.

But her eyes weren't on the camera or the food. They looked up to Damian. He'd been in his early twenties then, muscular and tanned. Yet his face was soft and free, his grey eyes crinkled with laughter. The emotional scars hadn't yet turned his jaw to stone.

The memory shot through her like a firework—she'd gone to Corinna's place to celebrate with the McKnights. They'd bought a watermelon and hacked it into pieces. Damian had been a little hungover and thus, not paying attention, he'd bit into the melon and a pip had shot across the table and hit Imogen square between the eyes. They'd laughed until tears had streamed down their faces.

Lainey didn't remember staring at Damian, but the open adoration was captured brilliantly in the photo. On the back, she'd written "if only" and the date in purple ink.

If only he hadn't let Jenny ruin his heart. If only they hadn't wasted the years since his divorce with her being too chicken to tell him how she really felt and him looking at her as though she was too young, when she wasn't.

"Is it safe to come in?" Corinna asked as she and Imogen poked their heads into Lainey's room. "Are we likely to die under an avalanche of stilettos?"

"It's safe." Lainey found her throat tight, the words struggling to slip past the lump blocking her airway.

"What's wrong?" Corinna's smile disappeared as she kicked off her work pumps and dropped down cross-legged next to Lainey.

"Ah, you're taking a trip down memory lane." Imogen bent down and picked up the album, flipping through and laughing. "Oh, God, Corinna. What were you thinking with that hair?"

She turned the album around and Corinna cringed. "I look like a skunk with those chunky highlights."

Lainey swallowed against the lump in her throat and forced herself to smile at Imogen. "So, what's the latest with your sister and Dan?"

"Ugh, don't ask." Imogen shook her head. Ever since the ball, she'd been quiet about her mission. "It's a mess."

Corinna raised a brow. "Why?"

"I had to get someone else involved. A guy from work who knows him." Her cheeks flushed pink. "But I feel like he's trying to hold it over my head. I never should have asked him to help me."

The pink flush turned darker still, and Lainey had a feeling there was a whole lot more to the story than that. But there was one thing she knew about Imogen—she'd only talk when she was ready.

Pushing her for information never went down well.

"Are you taking all your albums with you?" Corinna asked, turning to Lainey.

"I can't." She shook her head. "No space."

Imogen patted her arm. "I can babysit them for you."

"I thought I'd be okay with all this." To her horror, hot tears pooled in Lainey's eyes and no amount of furious blinking would chase them away. They splashed onto her cheeks and rolled toward her chin. "Am I making a huge mistake?"

"No." Corinna put an arm around her shoulders. "Not if you're going *to* London rather than running *from* Melbourne."

"How can I do one without the other? It's two sides of the same coin." She sniffed and swiped the back of her hand along her cheek.

"If you're going somewhere, it's a forward-momentum thing—you're chasing an opportunity or an experience. If you're simply leaving Australia because you want to run away, and London is where you happen to land, then it's not moving forward, is it?"

"Do you remember that day?" Lainey asked, scooting over so the three of them could sit together in the small space between her bed and her closet.

"Yeah, I feel like I still have an indent in my head from that damn pip," Imogen said drily.

Corinna laughed. "How could we forget it? We had that slip-and-slide thing in the backyard and you decided to take the cat on it."

"I did!" A heartfelt laugh burst from Lainey's lips. "She scratched the hell out of my arm and wouldn't go near me for months. We were so stupid back then."

"We?" Imogen asked in mock indignation. "Speak for yourself. I *knew* that was a bad idea at the time and told you as much. You were too busy trying to impress Damian and his mates."

"Not his mates," she said with a sigh. Worry coiled tight inside her. She'd never seriously admitted to her feelings in front of Corinna before. All the previous times she'd covered the words with bluster and exaggeration. "Just him."

Guilt gnawed at her. This was the only thing she'd ever kept from Corinna, without at least having the intention to fess up at a later date. How had she thought it possible to walk away and act like none of it ever happened—the ball, the weekend with Damian? Dragging Imogen into her lies?

"I told him once to stay away from you," Corinna said, wrapping an arm around Lainey's shoulder. "After the divorce. I said if he ruined our friendship I'd never forgive him."

"You did?"

"Yeah. I don't think he took me too seriously. But I saw how he looked at you then." Corinna sighed. "And I was jealous. You two always had this spark and I knew you had a crush on him and, well, *all* the boys had crushes on you. Ever since we were teenagers."

"They did not." She rolled her eyes.

"That summer you dyed your hair white-blond and got your braces off, I don't think I've ever been more jealous. *Everyone* looked at you, and I was still in my ugly duckling phase." She adjusted the glasses on her nose. "After he split with Jenny, I caught Damian watching you when you came over for a swim, and I was furious. It was so stupid, but I wanted someone to look at me like that. In hindsight, I wish he'd ended up with you instead of her."

"I slept with him." Lainey blurted the words out, unable to carry the guilt a second longer. Then the fear of knowing she'd crossed a line whipped through her—confessions could never be taken back.

Corinna sat up straighter and snapped her head toward Lainey. "When?"

Imogen bit down on her lip, her eyes swinging

back and forth between her friends. But she didn't say a word.

"Recently." Lainey swallowed. "I had it in my head that since I was leaving…"

"It might be your last chance?"

"Yeah."

Corinna's expression was hard to read, but she didn't look as though she were about to fly off the handle. "And you're still leaving?"

"Sex doesn't change that." She waited for Corinna to make her usual fake-disgusted reaction, but her best friend was uncharacteristically serious.

"Is that all it was?"

"Do you even want to be talking about this? It's your brother." The tears prickled her eyes again, and Lainey tipped her face upward, begging them to stop. "I know how you feel about something happening between us. I thought you'd be furious."

"It's not like I didn't see it coming a mile away." She brushed her thumb over the photo. "Honestly, I thought one of you would have caved earlier than this."

"You're really not mad at me?" Lainey asked.

Corinna shook her head. "Like I said, there's always been something between you two. And I know now that sometimes you can't help who you fall for. Joe wasn't the man I thought I would end up with."

"You seem so perfect together."

"We are, but I had it in my head that I'd marry some ambitious lawyer type. A career guy who wanted the great Aussie dream." She shrugged. "Instead I met a schoolteacher who wants to move to the beach and have a veggie garden and a couple of chickens...and I couldn't be happier."

"You two are total opposites." A strange expression washed over Imogen's face. "It's nice. Balanced."

The pressure slowly eased out of Lainey's chest. Keeping secrets from Corinna had been weighing her down, forcing the spring out of her step. But worse still was the growing fear that running away to London would do nothing to ease the ache in her chest. That no matter how many continents and oceans she put between them, Lainey would never be over Damian.

"He didn't treat you badly, did he?" Corinna picked at a frayed patch on Lainey's carpet. "I know he doesn't mean to be a dick, but he hasn't been himself the last few years. Sometimes I feel like I don't even recognise him anymore."

"He was great," she said. "Treated me like I was special even though I'm not."

"Don't say that." Imogen frowned. "You *are* special."

"Not enough, apparently. If I was that great, he would have wanted me for more than a weekend."

Corinna looked at her pointedly. "Did you ask him for more?"

Lainey bit down on the inside of her cheek. "Well, no... I mean, he knew I was leaving. There was never any discussion about it."

"Then why would he suggest more if he knew you had this amazing career opportunity overseas?"

Lainey wanted to scream at her friends to stop giving her hope—to stop inviting her to leave room for that tiny, blissful bubble of what-if, because it wasn't going to happen. If she went to Damian now, heart on her sleeve, he would break her. Ruin her.

Aren't you already broken? If you were fine, you wouldn't be sitting on the floor crying over an old photograph. Whether you tell him or not, you'll never escape how you feel.

"What if I go to him and it *was* just sex?" she whispered.

"Does that change anything in the grand scheme of things?" Corinna cocked her head. "I mean, if you're leaving anyway, isn't it better to know?"

"Cori's right," Imogen said. "You can't get closure if you're still wondering how he really feels."

Lainey had no idea which option she preferred. Leaving now without seeing Damian would mean a lifetime of asking herself what might've happened. But if she went to him and he rejected her…

Would she be able to move on? She honestly didn't know.

Lainey caught a glimpse of herself in the full-length mirror across the room. Her hair gleamed like scarlet silk, rich and bold and vibrant. It wasn't a colour one wore to blend into the background, even though it had been intended as a disguise. Pushing up from the floor, Lainey went to her handbag and pulled out the compact.

"That damn compact." Corinna laughed and shook her head. "How did I not figure it out then?"

This one little item had brought her back to Damian after that fateful night. What might've happened if she'd never dropped it in the limo? They might not have spent last weekend together. She might never have known that they were perfect together. That they were perfectly balanced. She ran her fingertip over the *LK* embroidered in the flowers.

Do it.

The voice in her head started as a whisper and grew until the words pounded in time with the rush of blood in her veins.

Do it. Do it. Do it.

She sucked in a breath. Her friends were right—there *was* a difference between going to England and leaving Australia. She didn't want her doubts following her to a new country. It was confession time.

She loved Damian McKnight and had for as long as she could remember. And now she was going to tell him.

Damian couldn't stop the grin spreading across his face as victory pumped through his veins. He'd been staring at the email for a full five minutes, revelling in the knowledge that he'd won. Jerry McPartlin was going to sign as a client.

They'd met earlier this week, and Damian had pulled out all the stops. He'd worked with his top consultant, the two of them dazzling McPartlin & Co. with all the ways they could improve the business—cost-cutting through efficient processes, giving him more money without the need to lay off employees, not to mention implementing a talent-retention program to lower their turnover rate, thus keeping the people they'd invested in. The pitch had required back-to-back all-nighters, meaning Damian had slept on the couch in his office. But it'd been worth it.

Victory.

He couldn't wait until his phone lit up with Ben's number. His old boss would be livid. Served him right—karma was going to bite that bastard where it hurt.

The strange thing was, Damian's natural instinct made him want to call Lainey, to share his good news with her, to thank her for her role in helping him land the biggest deal of his career. Because his hard work would have meant nothing without her by his side—she'd charmed the McPartlins, played the perfect sweet and sassy balance to his harder personality. All without judging him, without making him feel bad for chasing his career with an insatiable hunger.

She got him. Understood him. Had never once tried to change him.

He scrolled through the contact list on his phone until he found her name. But before he had a chance to call her, his intercom buzzed.

"Damian, your 4:00 p.m. conference call has been pushed. Stacy said they needed another twenty-four hours to get the information you've requested for the case study." The sound of fingernails clicking against a keyboard filled the pause. "And Lainey Kline is here to see you, but she doesn't have an appointment."

"That's okay." His heart thumped. "Send her in."

A second later, Lainey walked through the doors like the very embodiment of his desires. She always sent a jolt of electricity to his libido, and the feeling had only grown stronger since their weekend together.

"Hey," she said, her hands fiddling with the end of her long red ponytail. Today she looked different. There was no dramatic makeup, no fitted clothing or sky-high heels—none of her usual attention-grabbing tactics, in fact. "I hope I'm not interrupting."

"You're always welcome here," he said, gesturing for her to have a seat. "I was going to call you, anyway."

"You were?" A smile ghosted across her lips.

"I signed Jerry McPartlin." He clapped his hands together and leaned back in his chair. "And I owe you a celebratory drink. Couldn't have done it without you."

"I'm sure that's not true." She ran her hands over the floaty hem of her white cotton dress. The stark contrast with her flame-red hair made her look like a firework against a black-and-white background—like she was the only bit of colour he could see.

"My first meeting with the man was a disaster." He laughed. "If it wasn't for you going along with the whole fake-fiancée thing, I doubt he would have given me a second chance."

"I'm glad I could help. I know he's an important client."

"He is." For some reason he felt a little less victorious than he had the moment the email had popped into his inbox—would Lainey still be happy she helped if he told her the full story? "He was my old boss's client."

Her brows dipped into a frown, as if she was unsure of the significance of that detail.

"Jenny was having an affair with him. My boss… ex-boss." He cleared his throat, startled by the rush of anger that resurfaced fresh and raw. How many years would pass before those feelings stopped? "I found them. Together."

She blinked. "I had no idea."

"I didn't want you to know. I didn't want *anyone* to know." He sucked in a breath. "The worst thing was that it started as a revenge screw. She didn't want me starting my own business because it would mean even longer hours and she thought I neglected her enough as it was. She told me if I was a good husband then she never would have had to go elsewhere."

"That's a load of bullshit." She pursed her lips. "And it certainly doesn't excuse an affair."

"Well, my boss was a bastard, and when I resigned he told me I'd never make it to the big leagues, that I'd never be on his level. He'd hired me to be his gofer and nothing more."

"So you stole his client?" Lainey asked.

"His favourite client."

She picked at the embroidery curving around the hem of her dress. "Why are you telling me this?"

"You were involved." He shrugged. "I thought you had a right to know."

"If you thought that, you would have mentioned it

before I got involved." She looked up. "Do you still love her?"

"Jenny?" He reeled. "Fuck, no. Not after what she did."

"But you're still clinging to her." Her expression was soft and sad and not at all what he'd expected. "This whole revenge thing says you're not over what happened. You said yourself it's the reason you couldn't stay in the apartment. She's still part of your life even if you don't want her to be."

Damian's mind whirred. He knew he didn't love Jenny anymore. *That* was a certainty. But her betrayal haunted his every move. Mocked his every step toward success, telling him it would never be enough. *He* would never be enough. Not until he proved that they'd been wrong to doubt him.

That was why McPartlin was so important. Landing this client was the key to him being able to move on, because it was proof he'd become successful... wasn't it?

Is that really the kind of success you want?

"She's not part of my life anymore," he gritted out.

Lainey shook her head. "But you haven't had a real relationship since."

"Because I don't want one." He swallowed. "I told you that."

"Why did that change?" Frustration gave her voice an edge, subtle enough that most people wouldn't hear it. But he did, because he knew her. "Was it due to her cheating, or something else?"

"I was sick of having to take sides between her and my career. I didn't want to be in that position again."

"Bullshit." She folded her arms.

"You think I'm lying?" He planted his hands on his desk, his fingers curling against the polished wood.

"I think you're deluding yourself. If what you said was true, you would have broken things off with her *before* you found her cheating. Or if you knew things were going to end anyway, you wouldn't still be pissed about it years later."

Her ability to see right through his facade was borderline terrifying. No one had ever done that before. He was damn good at projecting the image he wanted, cultivating a persona that kept the real him safely tucked away, protected from harm. But Lainey was smashing through his defensive walls with a battering ram.

"And I'm supposed to take relationship advice from you?" He regretted the words the second they slipped out in a misguided need for self-defence.

Way to go, dickhead. You've attacked the person whose opinion you care about.

The realisation chilled him. He *did* care about Lainey's opinion. A lot. Why else would he be airing his dirty laundry to her? He didn't want to lie.

"The thing is, I know where my issues come from. I'm not in denial about who I am." Her voice wobbled, and that unsteady sound was like a knife through his heart. "The reason I date all those idiots is because I know I can't have the man I truly want."

The blood stilled in Damian's veins. She could

only say one of two things next, and he didn't want to hear either of them. Because if she loved some-one else, he wasn't sure he could stand it. And if she loved him…

Shit. How could he have let this get so out of con-trol? He never should have taken her back to his place the night of the dinner. It was the stupid strength of lust and desire that had allowed him to ignore his own rules. No other woman had gotten to him after Jenny. He'd only ever satisfied physical need. Sure, he'd felt attracted to other women. But that was it. Something he could swallow down as easily as a pill.

But with Lainey his control slipped away like water through his fingers.

Her lip trembled. "Aren't you going to ask me?"

She'd led him to a fork in the path, forcing him to stop and look ahead. Forcing him to decide. When she left his office, something would be cemented—either she would be part of his life or she'd leave for good.

"I'm not sure I want to know," he said.

"Well, I need to tell you." She dropped her hands into her lap. "I love you, Damian. I always have."

CHAPTER FIFTEEN

LAINEY HAD ALWAYS thought the way people described time as standing still after an important moment was a bit of a wank. But now she understood. It was like God himself had planted a hand on the earth to stop its rotation, slowing things down so that each breath dragged into her lungs with agonising slowness.

Damian's expression remained unchanged. His heavy brows crinkled slightly, and the hard set of his jaw was devastating as ever. The lack of reaction was telling.

She'd made a terrible mistake.

"You can't love me." He cringed as soon as the words shot out of his mouth because Lainey jumped, ready to flee. Clearing his throat as if trying to put his thoughts in order, he said, "Stay...please. Let's talk this through."

Oh, God, this was it. The "well, this has been fun but..." talk that she'd always avoided by being the first to cut and run. And now she was going to have to sit and pretend like her heart wasn't shattering into a billion jagged pieces.

Why did you do this to yourself? You know a guy like him will find a picture-perfect wife, not some crazy woman who goes commando and does shooters and dresses up in disguise to seduce men.

Not men. Just him.

"You're panicking." He furled and unfurled his fists, and her hands twitched in response. "I can see it."

"Well, nothing good ever comes after 'we need to talk.' That usually comes before 'I'm not mad, I'm disappointed.'" She tried to muster a smile, but it felt like the bottom had fallen out of her world.

"I worry one of us will be saying that." He frowned. "And it won't be me."

"I know you don't want long term." She couldn't even look him in the eye. "But I thought…"

The weight of his silence pressed down on her heart.

"You're right," he said, eventually. "I *don't* want long term."

Her chest squeezed. "Then maybe we can skip to the part where I leave the country and we forget this ever happened."

Dammit. How pathetic are you? Why don't you drop your heart on the ground so he can stomp on it, already?

"I don't want to forget." His expression was deadly serious. "Lainey, I…fuck, I don't know how to say this."

"Do it. Like a Band-Aid." Her heart stuttered in her chest, tears prickling the backs of her eyes so that she had to blink repeatedly to push them away. "You say, 'Lainey, this has been fun, but you're not the girl for me.'"

He shook his head. "It's not like that."

"Then what *is* it like? Because from where I'm sitting, it looks as though we want different things." She knotted her hands in her lap, praying that the tears would hold off until she was alone.

Alone. It was an idea she had better get used to, because very soon she'd be a whole hemisphere away from her family, her friends. And the man she desperately loved.

"You're supposed to be leaving," he said.

The words were like a bullet ripping her insides to shreds. In his mind, there had always been an end date. She had a ticket and he'd banked on avoiding this conversation. He never had any intention of taking it further.

Did you? You hadn't planned on more than one night. And he wasn't even supposed to know.

But walking away had been so much harder than she'd anticipated. Going back to him without her disguise—being with him as herself—had been everything. The culmination of all her childish, heart-fluttering wishes, of all her lust and desire. Of all her secret dead-of-the-night prayers. And now he'd blown her wide-open. Taken a verbal shotgun to her heart.

"I *am* leaving," she said. "And I shouldn't have come here."

"Lainey, please. Let's not ruin what we had."

"What the hell does that mean?" She stood and

wrapped her arms around herself, taking a step back. But distance wasn't going to save her. Not even when she left Australia. Hell, flying to Mars probably wouldn't help at this point.

She was done. Broken.

Goddammit. Why had she let Corinna and Imogen get into her head? As if he was going to throw up his hands and say "I love you," just like that. But she'd hoped for something…anything. A flicker of feeling. Not the excuse that he thought she was leaving.

He cursed under his breath as he came around the desk. "I don't want to lose you. But that doesn't mean I have anything more to give."

"You have plenty to give, Damian. But you refuse to take the risk." She retreated, taking a step back for every one he took forward. "Or maybe it's that I'm not worth enough for you to try."

Her resigned tone twisted like a blade in his gut. Lainey was the most generous, beautiful, interesting person he knew, and that she felt worthless made him want to rage. His reluctance to enter into a relationship had *nothing* to do with her.

"It's not about that."

"It's probably for the best, anyway," she forged on, her eyes glimmering. "We'd never be equal. I'd end up living in fear, waiting for you to find someone better."

"There isn't anyone better, that's precisely the point." The words came out in a rush—too loud and too close to the bone.

"That doesn't make any sense. Why don't you want to be with me if there's no one better?"

"Lainey, what do you want me to say? I never promised you anything, and there was a bloody good reason for that." He reached for her, but she stepped away so sharply that he froze on the spot. "But that doesn't mean I don't care. I do. So much. *Too* much, which is exactly why I wanted to keep things platonic."

"I never realised how selfish you were," she said. "How self-preserving."

Jenny had looked at him the same way the morning after he'd found her with Ben, when she'd packed her bags to leave for good. Those wide, accusing eyes and that defensive posture that'd screamed *why didn't you try harder?* had frozen him with guilt.

He wanted to fight, but there was nothing left. It would take him some time to process what'd happened—to figure out how to move on. How to repair his relationship with Lainey so that she stayed in the box he needed her to be in—one that wouldn't allow her to get too close.

Walking away now was the smart thing to do—to give them both space to let the heat die down. He had no idea if he could fix things in a way that didn't make her feel rejected.

But he knew one thing for sure: that wasn't going to happen today.

"Self-preservation is important," he said.

"Apparently." Her eyes dragged over him, tears shimmering in a way that made her hazel irises look more green than golden brown. She was so beautiful it was painful to look at her. "Seems like I needed to learn that lesson."

"I didn't want to hurt you." He closed his eyes for a moment, using every ounce of willpower to jam his hands in his pockets so he wouldn't bundle her up in his arms.

"But you did," she said. "I blame me, though, not you."

His head and his heart were at war—one telling him to comfort her and the other telling him to pull the trigger. To end it. He was immobilised by competing tensions—the desire to move forward in opposition with the fear of the past repeating itself.

Words danced on his tongue, so close to tumbling out that he had to hold his breath to keep them in.

I want to be with you.

No. It was guilt and desire talking, and he knew they weren't his allies. He had to stay strong.

"I'm sorry."

"Don't be. You're right, you never promised me anything. I must have heard what I wanted to rather than listening to what you were actually saying." She headed to his door. "I guess I'll see you around... or not."

A second later the door shut with a soft *snick* and Damian stood stock-still, his hands itching to throw something as he listened to her fading footsteps. When the elevator dinged in the outer office, he returned to his chair and slumped down.

He tried to tell himself he'd done the right thing. So why, then, did he feel like the world's biggest bastard?

Damian had a go-to when it came to dealing with problems of the heart: denial. Along with that came an increase in workload so that he didn't have time to think about all the ways he'd fucked up his life. Because there were many. Damian was sure he was successful in his business in spite of himself. In relationships…not so much.

Corinna and Imogen had thrown Lainey a going-away bash the day before, rounding up all her friends and family for a sensational send-off. He hadn't gone. Instead, he'd sat in his suite and pored over the photo that had been waiting for him at the hotel's concierge desk. It was old, slightly discoloured. But he remembered the occasion well. New Year's Day, all those years ago.

She'd left this morning, flying from Melbourne to London via Dubai. According to Google, they'd departed on time and she'd been in the air exactly seven hours and forty-six minutes. He'd set up a notification on his phone so he'd know when she landed.

Why? He had no idea. It wasn't like he was going to call her. What could he possibly say to make things better? Only turning back time could do that. But he had to know that she'd landed safely.

Outside, the sky was vibrant. Below, a festival took place where men dressed as dragons danced along the Southbank boulevard. Their costumes were ruby red, bold and rich. Fierce, like her. His stomach churned in anticipation the way it did every time he thought of Lainey—an uncomfortable mélange of lust, need and regret.

Damian strode onto the balcony and curled his hands around the railing. The area was decorated with a series of fancy potted plants, and he stifled the urge to kick them all over. This itch for destruction would fade…it had to. Because Lainey wasn't coming back, and he wasn't going to change his mind about love. No matter what his dick—or his heart—had to say about it.

A knock on the front door startled him. Who the hell was interrupting his pity party? He hadn't ordered food and had barely eaten a full meal in days. Food wasn't appealing to him right now. He walked inside and grabbed a T-shirt from the back of the sofa, pulling the thin cotton over his head before yanking the door open.

A greeting stalled in his throat when he saw who it was.

"Long time no see." Ben still had the same smarmy grin he remembered. Still wore the same obnoxious red-and-black-striped suit that made him look like a wannabe mobster. Still smelled of too-strong cologne and chewing gum.

"Ben," Damian said flatly. "What the fuck do you want?"

"Is that any way to greet your old mentor?" Ben made a *tsk* sound. "Where are your manners?"

"You weren't my mentor." Damian planted a hand

on the door frame, making it clear that Ben would not be invited in. "And you're not welcome here."

"Can't exactly order me off the property since it's not *your* property, now can you?" His grin widened. "Living in a hotel room is an interesting choice. I know you paid way over market value to get that apartment from Jenny, and yet you're here. Interesting."

He clenched his back teeth, swallowing down the stream of profanity that threatened to erupt. "I've got a new place. Just waiting on the sale to go through."

Lies. But it wasn't any of Ben's business.

"Right." The other man nodded, disbelief painted in his raised eyebrows and cunning smirk. "So, I heard you've managed to seduce one of my clients away from me. I would have come sooner, but it took me a few days to track you down."

Hmm, so clearly Ben hadn't wanted to show his face at Damian's office.

"Not one of your clients, Ben. *The* client." He tilted his chin.

"No, just one client. You see, when you get to where I am, no one client is that important. It's the sum of the portfolio, young grasshopper."

Damian cocked his head. "Your lips are saying one thing, but your eyes are saying something else."

Ben was livid, as predicted. He was trying to act like it didn't matter, like Damian's actions hadn't bothered him in the slightest. But why was he here if he didn't care?

"You can have McPartlin & Co. The old man was

a prick, anyway." Ben shrugged, but the gesture was stiff. "I'm curious, though. What did you say to make him leave? Did you tell him all about how I stole your wife out from under your nose?"

Damian watched his former boss for a minute, letting his loathing roll through him. This man had been his friend once. "I did my job, Ben. I presented him with a plan that will help him save a significant amount of money. Something your people should have already done. If your company was running well, he wouldn't have left."

"You think you're so high and mighty, don't you? The great Damian McKnight, a man of ethics. It's a load of crap. You're no different to me." Ben's jaw ticked. "I thought you were above stooping to our level."

"I'm not fucking someone's wife," he said, coldly. "Don't you dare compare me to you. We're nothing alike."

"You think the fucking is the important bit?" He shook his head. "It's the breach of trust that stings most. You *know* what you're doing is wrong, but you're doing it anyway because you're selfish."

The word was like a slap across his face. Hadn't Lainey said the same thing?

"Hey, don't get me wrong." Ben held up his hands. "I never thought you had it in you. You do have some balls, despite what Jenny has said."

His blood boiled, but he would not let Ben see him lose his shit. The days of wearing his emotions on his sleeve were over. He would *not* be vulnerable in front of this vulture—or anyone like him—ever again.

"Glad to see you and Jenny have been discussing my balls at such length." He yawned. "Was there a reason you came over, or was it just so we could braid each other's hair and shoot the breeze? Because I'm not interested."

"I wanted to hand-deliver this." He pulled a white envelope out of his jacket pocket and handed it over. The front was embossed with Damian's name, and two doves decorated the bottom right corner.

A wedding invitation.

"That's right, we're finally tying the knot. As you well know, it'll be Jenny's second go-around, but there's nothing wrong with a practise run." Ben preened like a ridiculous peacock.

Damian waited for the wave of rage to flow over him, but strangely, it didn't come. It struck him that he didn't give a shit if Jenny and Ben got married because, as far as he was concerned, they deserved one another.

"I wish you a long and happy life together," he said.

Ben blinked. Obviously it wasn't the rise he'd been expecting—or hoping—for. But something Lainey had said had struck him.

If you knew things were going to end anyway, you wouldn't still be pissed about it years later.

It dawned on him that he *had* known things were going to end with Jenny before he caught her with Ben. In fact, he'd thought about how to end their marriage more than once. Naively, he'd assumed she wouldn't want that, despite their numerous arguments. And it wasn't the fact that she'd moved on that'd hurt him. It wasn't even the cheating, now that he thought about it. It was the fact that she'd targeted his boss—someone Damian had once admired and respected—that made him see red.

She'd wanted to hurt him as much as possible.

And how is that different from you specifically targeting Jerry McPartlin? You wanted to hit him where it hurt, too.

Holy shit. Clarity struck him with the force of a head-on collision: by prioritising revenge, by aiming to inflict pain on someone else for his own emotional gain, he'd acted exactly like Ben and Jenny. He'd let what they'd done turn him into the very thing he claimed to hate.

And all the while he'd pushed Lainey away because he was too chicken to put himself in a vulnerable position again. Talk about being a hypocrite.

"I mean it," Damian said. "I hope your marriage is better than what we had. I don't want to wish that on anyone. Not even you."

"Excuse me?" Ben spluttered.

"I won't be attending. But I guess you knew that already." Damian handed the envelope back. "Stop thinking about me and start thinking about your future wife."

He left the other man standing there, shell-shocked, and closed the door. Lainey had been right all along—instead of getting on with his life, he'd been clinging to his own history. Signing Jerry McPartlin hadn't been the key to moving forward—it was simply another rope tying him to his past. A way for him to *feel* like he was making progress, while still trying to protect himself.

But all he'd ended up doing was losing the one woman who saw through all his shit and still wanted him. A woman who was so maddening and intoxicating and wonderful that he should have done everything in his power to make her feel like the goddess she was. He'd failed her. Miserably.

"Not anymore," he said, reaching for his phone. He swiped at the screen and called his assistant, hoping she was still in the office even though he'd left early because he couldn't concentrate.

"McKnight Management, Leila speaking."

Thank God. "Hey. I need you to book me an urgent flight to London. Tomorrow morning."

He grabbed the small suitcase that had his essentials already packed for emergency consulting trips.

"You're meeting with Mr. McPartlin tomorrow," Leila said. Rustling sounded in the background. "Eleven thirty."

"Reschedule it." He hoisted the suitcase onto his bed and flipped it open.

"But it's your first meeting. Mr. McPartlin specifically requested—"

"Reschedule it," Damian repeated. "I need to get to London. His business is running fine. It won't fall apart if he has to wait a few days. And if he can't wait, then he's welcome to leave."

The shocked silence on the other end of the line dragged on for a few minutes before his assistant agreed. Ten minutes later the flight information came through.

Now all he had to do was find out where Lainey was staying and figure out how to make it up to her. It wouldn't be easy, but that was alright. She deserved something honest and real and raw, all the things he'd been afraid of. All the things he knew could hurt him.

But it was time to let go of his safety net. He loved Lainey Kline, and if that made him crazy, then so be it.

CHAPTER SIXTEEN

LAINEY SHIFTED ON the spot, trying to subtly tug at the bodice of her dress. This was the second time she'd stood at a fancy party in a borrowed dress, feeling wholly out of place. Only this time she didn't have a mask to protect her.

"Try to smile, darling," her new boss, Andre, said in his clipped British accent. "There are a lot of important people here."

He wasn't kidding. Though Lainey wasn't up on the who's who of British society, she certainly recognised many of the guests. Vivienne Westwood, Rosie Huntington-Whiteley, Stella McCartney. It was basically a London fashion week party minus the runway show.

"Of course." Lainey nodded and pasted on a smile, but inside it felt like someone had dug her heart out with a spoon.

She'd been in London for only a day and was due to start work on Monday. Her boss was eager to take her out and introduce her to people, and she'd been ready to throw herself into work. She had started helping him pull together some sneak peeks for Instagram stories. But it wasn't giving her the thrill she'd expected or hoped for.

Lainey had worked something out very quickly about Andre Lawrence-Jenkins. His social media strategy was less about building his business and more about making it seem like he lived a charmed life. Lainey would help him see that he needed a more well-rounded approach, but three days in wasn't the time for that conversation. So she dutifully took pictures and made small talk and tried not to wish too hard that she was back in her apartment—wait, no, her *flat*—and tucked up in bed.

"Excuse me a minute." She nodded to her boss, but he barely turned his attention away from the male model who'd come over to chat.

Thankful that she could slip away without argument, she headed toward a courtyard and put on her coat. A few people were smoking by the door, but they hadn't ventured far due to the weather. It was the first time since Lainey landed that the rain had ceased, but it was still bitterly cold. However, air was necessary right now. Between the tight dress and the loud music and the ever-present threat of tears, she needed a moment alone.

Plonking herself down on a wrought iron bench, she shivered as the cold bit through her clothing. This should have been everything she wanted—an exciting new job, an invitation to an exclusive party, opportunities glittering in front of her like city lights. But she was as miserable as the weather. All she wanted was to hear Damian's voice, to feel his lips on hers and the reassuring strength of his chest beneath her cheek.

But he'd rejected her. Confirmed that she would never have what she wanted with him. That her fantasies were stupid and childish, and she'd be forever alone. Or at least destined to continue dating morons because they didn't remind her of him.

She pulled her grandmother's compact out of her clutch and flicked it open. Inside she'd stashed a tiny photo of her with Imogen and Corinna, tucking it into the worn antique frame to keep it secure. The sight of her friends' smiling faces made her heart hurt. She missed them already. She missed her family. And as much as she hated herself for it, she missed Damian, too.

It had been a surprise to learn that homesickness could manifest as actual sickness, and Lainey's stomach had been tied in knots since the second she walked through the security gate at the airport. It was like her body rejected being away from them. People said the feeling would ease over time, but she wasn't sure. Perhaps coming here had been a mistake.

"Is there room on that bench for one more?" A figure loomed over her—dark and imposing. The man wore an immaculate suit with a crisp white shirt and bloodred tie. Covering his face was a black mask.

But they weren't at a masquerade ball.

Lainey shook her head. It couldn't be him. He was supposed to be at home and she was supposed to be here, licking her wounds and trying to figure out how to deal with never having him. Maybe her homesickness had started to cause hallucinations as well as an upset stomach.

She pressed the back of her hand to her forehead. No fever.

"You know this isn't a costume party, right?" she said, frowning.

She stood and wrapped her arms around herself as she moved away from him. But he stopped her with his hand—gentle, yet firm. No one else walked that line like he did.

"Aren't you going to ask my name?" he said. His fingers burned a hole through her coat, his warmth cutting through the layers of wool and cotton.

There was no doubt in her mind. Damian was here. With her. *For* her?

"I don't need to ask." She swallowed. "I know who you are, Rumpelstiltskin."

"Ugly name, isn't it? Curse my parents." His full lips curved to a wicked smile beneath the mask. It made him look even more darkly handsome now that she knew what pleasure and havoc he could wreak on her. "And here I was hoping we'd get to play our guessing game again."

"I'm done with the games."

They were alone in the courtyard, the smokers having retreated as thunder clapped overhead. The rain would arrive any minute, and standing in the open was encouraging danger. But Lainey couldn't move away—she was frozen. Stunned. And still not entirely certain this wasn't a dream.

"So am I," he said.

"Yet you're here, wearing a mask. Why?"

"I needed to see you." His cologne mingled with the heavy air, the scent of impending storm making it feel like she was experiencing him through a veil. It was otherworldly. Dreamlike. "I needed it like I have never needed anything else in all my life."

Her breath stilled. Believing him was hard, because she'd fallen for him over and over again—her heart couldn't take another hit. She was battered and bruised and still in recovery.

"How the hell did you even get in?" She glanced at the doors, which glowed with warm light. "This party is pretty exclusive, in case you didn't know."

His lip twitched. "I have my ways."

"Are you trying to tell me you gate-crashed a party in a mask just to talk to me?"

His soft chuckle rolled over her like a wave, threatening to pull her under and hold her there until the last bit of air was suffocated out of her. "I wish I could say I was as successful a gate-crasher as you, but no. I pulled strings…a lot of them. All of them, actually."

"All of them?" She tilted her face up, terrified of the glimmer of hope in her voice.

"I bribed Imogen and Corinna to find out where you were. I called every person I knew on this side of the world until I found someone who could get me into this party, and I got a call with the lecture of my lifetime from Jerry McPartlin because I bumped his meeting to get on the earliest possible flight." He laughed. "The bastard fired me and went back to Ben."

And he didn't sound the least bit cut up about it. Lainey blinked and shook her head. "But you worked so hard to sign him."

"It was all worth it to see you." His hand came up to tuck a strand of hair behind her ear and she shivered—not from the cold, but from fighting the need to launch herself into his arms. "I love that you kept your hair red. It's perfect on you."

"Damian, stop." She closed her eyes for a second, trying to ground herself. "Why did you do all that?"

"Because you were right. I was chasing revenge and clinging to the past. I wanted to sign him for all the wrong reasons. I would never have pretended to be engaged for any other client, but I was so hell-bent on getting back at Ben that I was willing to do anything."

"Even pretend to be engaged to me," she whispered.

"That part wasn't a hardship, trust me. But it was still wrong."

"And you came all this way to tell me that our fake engagement was wrong." Bitter disappointment clawed at the back of her throat. "Sounds like a waste of a flight."

"I came here to tell you I'm sorry." He cupped her face, brushing at her cheek where an errant tear had fallen. She hadn't even realised her eyes had welled up until she saw the moisture on his thumb when he pulled his hand back. "I shouldn't have involved you in my personal problems. I especially shouldn't have asked you to act for me. But more than that, I'm sorry I was too fucking stupid to acknowledge that you stopped being a friend a long time ago."

"How long?" she whispered.

"Too long. The night you kissed me... God, I wanted to kiss you back. But it wasn't appropriate." He shook his head. "You were so young and vibrant, and I was terrified I was going to drown you with all my baggage."

"Screw being appropriate. I left school the second I could because I was sick of all that *thou shalt behave* bullshit. I won't be forced to fit into someone else's box."

She knew that now. Trying to mask her feelings—whether with a physical mask or with loud clothing and lewd jokes—wasn't working for her. Some of it was real, but much of it was a front. A way for her to pretend like nothing hurt.

But it did. Walking away from Damian that final night had been as painful as any real blow.

"You always danced to the beat of your own drum, didn't you?" he said.

"Yeah. Too bad you wanted some perfect wife who wouldn't buck the rules." She was baiting him. "I can't be that person. I *won't* be that person. I need to be me."

She had to—it was the only way she could be happy.

"You should be you. But I do love that you're crazy enough to dress up in disguise and take what you want." He lowered his forehead to hers. "I love that you don't take no for an answer and you find your own solutions when life doesn't give you what you want."

"Even if I fooled you into sleeping with me?"

"If you hadn't, we probably wouldn't be here now. And I'd still be blind to the fact that I've wanted you for too goddamn long."

"What are you going to do about it?" She squared her shoulders and met his gaze, telling him with her whole body that she wouldn't settle.

The rain fell, drenching them with fat, pelting drops. Her tights clung to her legs, chilling her and making her yearn for the warmth of his lips and hands and tongue. But she wouldn't move an inch until she had what she wanted. Him. All of him. The only man she'd ever loved.

"I'm going to be honest with myself. With you." He gripped her hands, the water running in rivulets over them. "I love you, Lainey Kline. I love your antics, your determination, your loyalty, your incredibly sexy body. I wanted you and I always have, even when I couldn't admit it."

"Why now?" Her voice trembled.

"Because I lost you and it was the single most painful experience of my life." His Adam's apple bobbed. "It felt like someone had ripped my heart out, and I wasn't prepared for it. So I'm here. I gave up McPartlin & Co. and I will give up everything else in my life if it means I can have you. I will move my whole fucking life to this godforsaken storm cloud of a country, if that's what it takes."

The flicker of hope had turned to a blaze, the fire in her heart kindled by his words and his touch. "You'd move here for me?"

"For you, princess, I'd go anywhere."

She threw her arms around his neck and mashed her lips to his. It wasn't a kiss fit for a fairy tale— it was messy and hot. Open and seasoned with rain and tears. The weather continued to bear down, but Lainey wouldn't let go. It was nothing like how she'd dreamed it would be as a girl. But it felt so right. So perfectly imperfect. Like her. Like them.

"I guess I'll have to take you inside now and introduce you around." She grinned. "How are we going to explain the mask?"

"Tell them it's payback." He coaxed her lips apart for another searing kiss. "You fooled me once and now I'm getting you back."

"You're a vengeful man, Rumpelstiltskin." She tugged him toward the light. "You're lucky I love you."

"I am so incredibly lucky." Even with his mask, she could see the sincerity shining in his piercing grey eyes. "And I promise I'll spend the rest of our lives making up for all that time I wasted."

Her eyes darted to the door. "Ah, screw the introductions," she said, pulling him deeper into the shadows of the garden. "Time's a-wasting. Let's start making it up now."

EPILOGUE

Three months later

DAMIAN BOUNCED UP and down on the balls of his feet, jittering like a fighter waiting to swing his first punch. Adrenaline pumped through his veins, turning his usually calm and collected self into a bundle of nerves. Tonight was a big deal. The *biggest* deal.

He *finally* had Lainey back home. All to himself. Her job in London had kept her busy, and she had settled in. Eventually. But doing the long-distance relationship wasn't easy, and she'd insisted he keep his business in Australia. Because she was going to see her six-month contract to completion and then she'd bring all that knowledge home and use it to find her dream job in the place where she belonged. In Melbourne. By his side.

But there was only so much Skype sex that could satisfy him, and with their schedules—not to mention the twenty-four-hour travel time from Melbourne to London—he'd been missing her like crazy. He hadn't seen her in a whole damn month, and it was killing him.

Tonight, however, would be everything he'd been waiting—and planning—for. It'd had taken him a bit longer than he'd wanted to get things arranged. But time had been required to get the stars—or in this case the moon—aligned.

He tapped his foot as he stared at the stream of people in the arrivals area. They all seemed to blend into one human blob, until she appeared. Her bright red hair was a shocking contrast to her all-black outfit. She looked like some kind of sexy superhero ninja.

And it sure as hell felt that way when she launched herself into his arms with all the force her slender frame could manage. He kept his feet firm on the ground and enveloped her, pressing his lips to hers and inhaling the oh-so-familiar scent of her perfume. His hands were in her hair, at her back, holding her so tight because the fear that she would evaporate into thin air was terrifyingly real. His throat felt raw from the emotion rushing up out of nowhere.

Damian wasn't the kind of guy to get all teary, but fuck if he didn't feel a prickle at the back of his eyes. Who the hell was he right now?

"I missed you so much," she said, her own eyes sparkling. "And I really can't wait until they invent teleportation so people don't have to be on a plane for that long."

"Cool your jets, princess. You were in first class. That is nothing to complain about."

She grinned. "I *was* comfortable. But it was way too long before I got to see you."

"You're here now." The words clogged in his throat. "We're together. Everything is right again."

The drive was quick. Lainey filled the car with her chatter and every little update on her life in London, her excitement and happiness radiating out and tangling him up. He'd planned the evening meticulously—every detail was carefully arranged, from the venue to the dessert to the view. And now he found himself as anxious as a teenage boy on his first date.

"So what's your angle tonight?" she asked as he navigated them farther into the city.

"My angle?"

She narrowed her eyes at him. "I feel like you've got something up your sleeve."

He stifled a grin. The sky was darker now, but the city lights were a wash of glitter around them. He pulled up to the building that contained his new home and drove into the underground car park.

"Where are we going?" Lainey peered out of the window, but there wasn't anything to see except concrete pylons and rows of cars. "I thought you said you were staying in the hotel so we could find something when I came back."

"I never said that specifically." He pulled into his parking spot and killed the engine. "Now will you stop it with the questions?"

"Never." She shot him a grin.

How had it happened that he'd fallen head over fucking heels for this crazy girl who was a decade younger than him, who was wild on the surface but loyal and fierce underneath? Who had an open heart and an open mind and a set of legs that totally undid him?

They sat in the car, the silence only broken by the sound of their breath. "Do you trust me?" he asked.

She looked at him with love shining in her face. "Absolutely and completely."

He got out of the car and retrieved her suitcase from the boot. Its wheels squeaked as they walked toward the elevator, and he made a mental note to send her back to London at the end of her week off with a new one.

The second the elevator door opened, Lainey squealed. "I know this elevator!"

"Damn, and I was hoping to keep it a surprise until the big reveal." A roguish smile tugged at his lips and he ran a hand along his jaw.

"When did you move in?" They arrived at the top floor and entered the apartment.

"Last month. They had trouble selling it, so I had the chance to negotiate."

"I know how much you love doing that." She grinned. "I can't believe you bought this place."

The apartment was almost unchanged from when they'd inspected it together, because he wanted her input when she finally returned from London.

"It's perfect," she said, her eyes wide and her hand clamped over her mouth.

"We're going to make it ours, Lainey. Together, as partners." He gently tugged her hand down and scooped her up in his arms. "We're going to decorate it together, and we're going to mark it with memories. When I said I would spend my life making up for lost time, I meant it."

He took her to the bedroom and laid her down on the bed, her red hair fanning out all around her. She looked like a goddess. A vision.

"Don't even think about it," she said, squirming under his grip. "I showered at the lounge on my stopover in Singapore, but that was eight hours ago. You're not getting into my pants yet."

"Don't think about it?" He laughed, crawling up over her body and nudging her legs apart with his knee. "Baby, it's all I'm capable of thinking about. You don't know how hard it makes me to know I've got the woman of my dreams in my bed. *Our* bed. I'm not letting you go until I've felt those beautiful thighs shake around me, until I've heard that sexy, raspy voice begging me to go harder and deeper."

"You think you're so enticing," she teased, looping her arms around his neck. Her back bowed as he pressed his hips down to hers. "And for the record, I know exactly how hard you are."

"It's so good to have you home. Skype doesn't cut it." He pressed his lips to her neck, slipping one hand under her top to find her breast. His cock pulsed, desperate from weeks of knowing nothing but his own hand.

She reached down between them and pulled his zipper down, wrapping her fingers around his cock. "Hmm, home. I like the sound of that."

"Enough talking." He tugged her pants down in one smooth motion.

When he slid into her, it was like everything he'd been waiting for—the feeling of rightness rocketed through him and he bundled her up in his arms the way he'd dreamed of every night since he'd come back home from that first trip to London. Her lips were on his, her body needy and demanding, hips meeting his thrust for thrust as he buried himself inside her. They were still mostly dressed, but he didn't care. Because he needed her now, and not one second could be wasted.

"Lainey," he sighed into her ear as he cradled her, taking and giving with everything he had. "I love you so much."

"I love you, too." Her eyes were heavy-lidded, her cheeks flushed. And the little dent her teeth made in her lower lip was enough to make his entire body shudder with pleasure.

"I'm in this for the long haul, you know." He brushed a strand of red hair from her forehead, touching his lips to hers. "Forever."

"And ever," she whispered, her body trembling as he nipped at her skin. "Just like I always wanted."

* * * * *

INKED

ANNE MARSH

MILLS & BOON

For Jimmy the Cake Guy.

Clearly, the best guys bake, make cupcake deliveries, and look out for the women in their dorms and their lives.

Thank you!

CHAPTER ONE

Vik

BEFORE I TOUCH even so much as an inch of sweet, creamy skin I know I want to spank her, mark her. Make her mine. Take her heart-shaped ass and all the softness she's hiding from me. Doesn't hurt that she's wearing plain white cotton panties, the kind designed to cover up rather than to showcase but that instead makes a man like me think about turning good girls bad. She's tucked the waistband down to give me more room to work. Thoughtful as fuck, right? I can't stop looking at the tattoo chair where she's spread out, waiting for me to ink her. I'll be her first because nothing but virgin skin meets my greedy eye.

And here I'd thought tonight would be boring.

Located on a busy if seedy street in East Las Vegas, the tattoo parlor I run when I'm not taking care of Hard Rider business specializes in flash tattoos for the impulsive crowd. Ink Me fronts the sidewalk and passersby can look through our windows and watch whatever ink's in progress. Maybe my new client doesn't care if she gives lookie-loos a show. Maybe she loves the thrill. I won't judge. Christ knows, my list of guilty pleasures reads like an encyclopedia of vice. Won't make excuses or apologize, either. I know what I like and I make sure I get it. I'm a hedonist, not a fucking saint, and inking this pretty bitch is the much-needed cherry on today's shit sundae.

People like company when they dive into the deep end of the pool of sin and debauchery and virgin ass's blonde companion looks like an expert. The teeny black cocktail dress, mile-high heels and red leather choker scream fun. The hair flat-ironed into an immaculate curtain adds a note of sophistication that in no way matches the grit of East Las Vegas. Someone who pays attention to the wrapping paper will take even more care with the contents. Bet she waxes or goes full Brazilian with one of those clit piercings I love to roll around my tongue. Usually, Blondie would be my favorite kind of present and I'd be halfway to unwrapping her using that goddamned choker as a leash, but tonight the gorgeous ass in my chair trumps all.

"Ladies. What can I do for you?" I nod at the blonde, a wave of strawberry and tequila hitting me hard. Hope to fuck the woman in my chair is more sober. Not good to ink anyone with more alcohol than blood in her veins.

"Harper wants a tattoo," Blondie announces.

What kind of name is Harper? It sounds uptight and tidy, way too organized for the lush pair of thighs hugging my chair even if it fits the clothes. The white cotton blouse folded up her back matches the no-nonsense panties...and is that a *business* skirt unbuttoned and unzipped to give me access? When you've banged as many women as I have, you learn a thing or two about clothes, and Dolce & Gabbana is expensive shit. Ups the odds of her not being underage, though. As long as she's not a lawyer or a judge in the daylight hours, we're good.

Or bad. Lady's choice.

The shirt, panties and skirt might come from the Good Girl closet, but her shoes are pure sex. The black suede laces up the front, showcasing the cutest toes. I see her feet all tied up with a fucking bow and I start thinking about getting some rope on the rest of her body and showing her just how good a little kink can feel.

You got to admire a woman who can dress for success from the ankles up and then make a guy come on the spot when she flashes her feet at him. From the length of her legs, she's tall—and the heels give her another four inches. I'm a big bastard, but she'll come up past my shoulder no problem. Not too skinny, either, thank fuck. She's generous in all the right places, not some fragile flower that can't take a hard pounding.

"Start on her ass and work your way up," Blondie orders.

Gladly.

Been doing that my whole life. Grew up rough, just me and my old man. He rode for a local club, giving me a dozen honorary uncles who had my back and kicked the shit out of me whenever I needed it. First beer at twelve, first woman at fifteen and first bike at sixteen. Since I'd been a stupid shit, I'd barely made it out of high school, too busy enjoying the open road and free pussy to think long-term. A few years in the US Navy fixed that. Wasn't cut out to be a career soldier but I picked up some things from Uncle Sam's crew—discipline, training, a love of ink and the ability to cut loose when onshore. The life of the fiesta, that's me. I'd boozed and cruised my way around a dozen different ports of call and I'd left my mark on them all.

Party never ended.

My old man didn't like my constant fiesta, but his right to give me shit ended the day I turned eighteen and signed my life over at the local recruiting station. When I'd come home at twenty-one, we'd shared a beer and awkward small talk. Wasn't that my old man looked smaller and older, just…less big. Not sure where my genes came from but my club brothers call me the Viking for more than one reason. Not only do I fight like a berserker, but I look like one, too. My pretty face is just the party favor on a package of lethal. Ladies, you've been warned.

The beauty in my chair shifts impatiently. "Are we starting?"

I jerk my eyes up to Beauty's head. Gotta stop staring at her ass. She has dark hair, a glossy brown so dark it's almost black as it spills from the crown of her head in a long, sleek ponytail. Christ, it's like she looked inside my head and picked out all my favorite fantasies. If we were alone, I'd be fisting that soft length as I pounded into her from behind.

I need my sex dirty and rough. *Nice* has never been part of my vocabulary.

"You better tell me what you want. Not sure the front desk got the memo." Gia's a sweetheart but she's not the most organized person. Probably should get around to firing her but that would require finding a new receptionist. Plus, she's got a great smile and never gives me shit. Wouldn't be easy for her to find another job, either, since she's got a two-year-old and never-ending day care issues.

"A tattoo." She drums the pretty nails that match her toes, foot tapping like she's Queen of Sheba. I'd like to say that imperiousness makes her not my type, but who am I kidding? I fuck anyone who smiles my way. I don't like alone time, commitments or longevity.

"Put my ink right here." She reaches around, pointing to the top of her ass.

I grab my sketchpad from my rolling table. "You got a design in mind? Special occasion to commemorate?"

I ask more to keep her talking. Women like her— ironed, pressed and slumming in East Las Vegas— usually request rainbows or flowers. They demand teeny, tiny piece-of-crap tattoos rather than living large. Sometimes, they ask for the name of a lover or a boyfriend. Dead people and dead relationships are also popular—because if you're not celebrating the hell out of the living, you're mourning their loss.

Not that I have a problem tattooing *Property Of* on a woman's ass. Fuck no. The problem comes when she busts back in a week or a month later, demanding I cover the words up with "something pretty." There's nothing pretty about sex when it's mistaken for love, and love is as likely as a unicorn and a dodo bird getting it on.

"The douche," Blondie slurs.

Awesome. Tonight we're celebrating a death and the douchebag who's blown his chance fatally.

I drop onto my rolling chair, scooting closer. While Blondie smells as if she's rolled around in a gigantic strawberry margarita, my face almost brushes my girl's shoulder before I catch a hint of scent from her. Something subtle and discreet, the kind of thing the club girls try on at Macy's because no way can they afford it for real. Beauty's skin smells like vanilla and coconut, a warm, sweet invitation to eat her for dessert.

Sitting behind her on my stool, I glimpse her face in the storefront window. I deliberately brush my shoulder against hers as I offer her my hand. "Vik. Pleased to meet you, Harper."

My hands are large, battered and scarred, the knuckles inked with Cyrillic symbols until there's not an inch of bare skin. I was born here, but my old man came over from Russia when he was twenty. He pulled plenty of shit before and after he patched into his club, and he made a few introductions on my behalf after my Navy stint. Those connections left a mark.

"So you wanna give me more words about what you want?"

"Not flowers and hearts," she says decisively. "Fuck that shit. Today's been a bad day."

"Tell Doctor Vik all about it," I purr.

"I came home from work," she says. "Seems like no big deal, right? Kick off my heels, heat something up, fall into the tub and then bed."

The barest hint of a liquid slur to her words warns me she's not quite sober. I nod, filling in the blanks. Another woman in her bed, a we-need-to-talk moment, a fight. A, B, C, or D—all of the above. Beauty doesn't seem like a screamer, but she also doesn't seem like the kind of woman who gets ink. I grab the Sharpie from my back pocket and uncap it.

"He'd kicked me out."

He being the dead-to-her douchebag.

"Fucker," I say agreeably, tucking her ponytail over her shoulder.

"Absolutely," she agrees. "He had a service pack up my stuff and leave it in the garage for me. I didn't even get to pick and choose which parts of our life I kept. He pointed and strangers put my pieces in boxes. He kept my *cat*."

"I could go over there and kick his ass. Pull a little repo action for you."

A smile ghosts over her mouth. "You have no idea how tempting that is."

"Offer stands." When I smooth my hand over her skin, she jumps. "Touching you is part of my job, babe. Your job is to tell me what you want."

In bed, out of bed, up against the wall—I'm at her command.

"Give me something to celebrate getting free of him even if it wasn't on my terms," she demands.

"How much have you had to drink tonight, sweetheart?"

Her brow puckers as she holds her hands out in front of her. She's wearing a bracelet, a pretty little toy with a heart and key on it. Had that fucker given it to her or had she bought it for herself? "Four. No—five drinks."

"You trust me?"

"Absolutely not," she says, proving she's as smart as she looks. "Tell me what you're thinking."

"Firebird." I drag the Sharpie over her skin, bringing to life the image I see in my head. Maybe she won't appreciate wearing a Russian fairy tale on her skin, but she's not timid; and bold black, orange and red lines tracing the equally strong lines of her back feel right.

"You're a man of few words, Vik." Her lashes drift down as she exhales.

"Don't fall asleep on me."

She shakes her head. "Then don't bore me."

"Bitch," I say tenderly. "Firebird's a thief and hard to catch. She almost gets busted stealing the king's apples when the king sets his sons to catch whoever's been trespassing on his shit. Ivan gets a hand on her, but all he's left with is a single feather. She leaves and he spends fucking forever chasing after her."

"That's the entire story?" She yawns, turning her face into the leather.

"Only part I'm inking here. Yeah?"

"Okay."

I embrace the familiar adrenaline rush as I draw on her lower back, sketching the outline of a bird, wings outstretched to take flight to freedom. Her tail curls down, teasing, flirting, broadcasting a fuck you to the man she's leaving behind in the king's orchard. This is my skin, my piece of her to ink, to own, to give back to her filled up with the story she's shared with me. Right now, I own her and she's mine. She relaxes into my touch, my calloused fingers scraping gently, carefully over her skin, preparing her. Fuck playing by the rules.

I grab my needle and brush my mouth over her ear. "This is gonna hurt so good."

CHAPTER TWO

Harper

VIK DOESN'T REMEMBER ME.

The hottest man I've ever touched—and thank You, Jesus, I've touched this man—introduces himself as if I'm a stranger. As if he's never kissed me, never put his dick inside me, never made me see stars because he felt so damn good. High school seniors, a keg of beer and a wild party were apparently a recipe for oblivion.

Even through the rubber gloves he wears, the heat and strength of him sears me. It's weirdly seductive, his soft touch. Or maybe I'm lonelier than I thought to find comfort in the simple brush of fingers against skin. I'm paying him to give me this contact, and I'm far drunker than I should be if I'm in a tattoo parlor.

Today—tonight—is a day for firsts.

He hums, blond hair falling around his face as he sets the needle against my back. The first touch stings, the bright, rough bite blossoming into something rougher and darker. I push down into the seat to escape the burn but there's no out for me. Why am I here?

Because the man you thought you'd marry locked you out.

Because you do the same things over and over and you want different.

Because your life plan just hit an unexpected brick wall.

The sound that escapes my mouth is embarrassingly weak. I don't have to do this. I can go. He finds new skin with the needle and I whimper.

"Breathe." He pins me in place with one big hand. I should get up. Should tell him I've changed my mind. I had no idea this would hurt so much but when he scratches that needle over my skin, thin, wicked lines cut into me so deep I feel them everywhere. His thumb rubs back and forth over the untouched, un-inked part of me in soft counterpoint.

I twist my head to glare at Brooklyn. "I blame this on you."

She cackles, fishing her phone out of her jacket. Instead of offering sympathy, she immortalizes me for Facebook posterity. "You said you wanted to move on. That you wanted to do something bold and brave to commemorate this particular life milestone."

"I said that after two dirty martinis," I protest.

Vik hums, leaning closer. He hurts me. Part of me wants to kick Brooklyn's ass for talking me into this, but the rest of me just wants Vik closer and closer. To touch me more, to ease the sting his big hands create. Or maybe it's the quiet strength in the way he holds me in place, soothing and hurting and making something beautiful out of the pain.

Thankfully, Brooklyn provides a distraction. "Still counts."

"She's an IRS auditor," I mutter as Brooklyn flips me the bird. She's minutes from passing out hard, her eyes already half-closed.

Behind me, Vik snorts. "That true?"

"Brooklyn doesn't look like a CPA, but trust me. You should be really, really scared if she ever goes through your books. She'll find every secret you tried to hide."

"You could come join me on the dark side," she crows. "But nope. You have to hang with the investment crowd, making all that lovely money. You didn't need the douchebag for his bank account, so I hope the man had a magic dick."

The needles buzz, the pain burning and melting into something fiercer as Vik works. I take a deep breath, counting through the waves of pain. I can do this.

I *want* to do this.

Vik

"Tell me more about this magic dick." Harper tenses as I move the needle over her skin, but a grin lights her face.

"He was pretty," she says. "Everywhere."

Blondie—Brooklyn—raises a brow. "But did he

know what to do with his joystick? Because otherwise it's just a handle to lead him around by."

Harper snickers. "The man could play games for hours. He always made it to the bonus level and he's my all-time highest scorer."

"That's because you hadn't met me yet," I tell her.

Might be a good idea to keep my mouth shut. I consider the possibility for a handful of seconds before discarding it. Why hold back?

"Are you aware that you have no filter?" Harper's hands flex on the bench, opening and closing as she takes what I give her. She starts to say something else, but then winces, sucks in a breath and freezes. This is the point where some people quit, abandoning my chair, and others bitch and curse. You have to ride out the pain, find its rhythm, lose yourself in each wave. There's a magic moment when you pop to the top, finding the crest, and you're fucking flying in a whole other place.

I lay another, deeper line of ink into her skin. "Why putt down the highway of life when you can ride balls-out?"

"Do you like riding, Vik?" Harper's voice is husky and amused, a thread of discomfort just beneath the surface. She has the strangest, sexiest effect on me. I shouldn't want to lean down and kiss each raw line I've etched into her back. Lick the straight, strong line of her spine until she melts for me. She's a client, and whatever fucked-up shit goes on in my head, it stays there.

"Yeah," I say roughly. "I ride. I'm a member of the Hard Riders MC."

"MC?" She turns her head so she can watch my face.

"Motorcycle club."

"Isn't that illegal?"

"Depends on who you're asking, babe. Also on what kind of business we've got. Most days we're practically Boy Scouts. Even do a toy drive at Christmastime."

"And the other days?"

"We take care of business."

I give in to temptation and run my thumb down the straight line of her spine. Woman's got more knots in her back than that macramé shit my brother Cord learned in prison. Supposed to be therapeutic and relaxing as fuck as Cord can attest. He tied up a few strippers and taught them the finer points of bondage when he got out.

"You need to move on." Blondie's words come out soft and slurred. I don't disagree with her, and if Harper wants to forget the douche, I'm the man to help her.

Harper winces as my needle finds a particularly sensitive spot. "How many minutes until we're done?"

"Sweetheart," I say, brushing my mouth over her ear, "we're barely started."

I know firsthand what the needle feels like when it bites through skin, how the pain doesn't ever quite ease up. Shit hurts. Life hurts. But this pain is a choice and it leads to a thing of fucking beauty at the end if I do it right. My firebird slowly takes flight on Harper's back, first the wings, and then the head. I lose myself in between the lines, drawing and coloring, pulling something from her and putting it on the outside for everyone to see.

Harper's quiet for long enough that I lean over to make sure she hasn't passed out on me. Not that she's a constant talker, but some sign of life would be good. Her eyes are closed, her lips parted when I need her to be here with me.

"Hey. You okay?" I drag the back of my knuckles over her cheek, cursing the latex between my skin and hers.

Her lashes lift slowly. She's got the prettiest, softest eyes. "It hurts."

"Good hurt or bad hurt?"

Her forehead gets this cute little pucker like my question doesn't compute. "Good hurt?"

"Yeah. The kind where the burn eats you up and you get lost in all that feeling and you just have to let go and ride it out. You feel me?"

The crease in her forehead deepens, so I'll have to show her. I lay down a new line of ink. She's a squirmer. She wriggles against my bench, working her pussy into the leather like it'll open up and give her a way out of here.

"You chose this," I point out. "You put your cute little ass in my chair. You can endure the pain, or you can let go and lose yourself in it. I think you might like it."

I drag my thumb down the outside of her spine,

working against one of those knots. Investment banking doesn't sound like a fucking picnic, and her body seems to agree with me. She lifts into my touch, the muscle beneath my fingertip loosening. Then she wiggles against the seat again.

"If this makes you feel better, it's a good thing," I say roughly. The ink I'm tracing into her skin certainly is—the bright red feathers almost fly off her skin, they look so fucking real. "You deserve good things, you hear me?"

"Yeah," she says, so softly that I almost don't hear her. "I do."

Blondie's head hits the window with an audible thunk. I can't tell if she's passed out or fallen asleep, but girlfriend looks painfully uncomfortable.

"Give me a moment." I set my equipment down and strip off my gloves. "Sleeping Beauty needs an assist."

"Sleeping Beauty?" Harper twists her head and takes in her friend sprawled half on, half off the window seat. Not my circus, not my fucking monkeys, but she's here with Harper.

I brush my hands down my thighs. "You need a chaperone?"

Harper outright laughs. "Are you planning on hiding Brooklyn's body?"

"Nah." I shake my head and cross the room to Blondie. Harper watches like she can't quite figure me out as I scoop her friend up in my arms. "I'm offering relocation services. Think she'd be more comfortable on the couch."

I take her out front and set her down on the leather couch. Gia never looks up from whatever game she's playing on her phone. The room's chilly from the air-conditioning that ran for most of the day so I shrug out of my leather jacket and drop it over Harper's friend. The nipples poking the front of her sequined tank top advertise loud and proud that the woman's cold. It may be August in Vegas but it's also two in the morning. The sun's not up, and I don't need her to fucking freeze to death—or wake up—before I'm done with Harper.

When I go back into my studio, Harper gives me a smile. The sight of her bent over my bench, waiting for me to put my hands back on her, makes me hard, but then everything about this woman gets me going.

"You're a nice guy." She sounds surprised. Not sure why everyone seems to think bikers do nothing but kill shit. We've got other hobbies and mayhem's just one of my many talents.

"Everybody loves me." I wink at her reflection in Ink Me's windows. "So what does an investment banker do all day, Harper darling?"

"I make other people money."

"Are you good at what you do?" Harper doesn't strike me as the kind of person who'd settle for half-assing anything in life.

"I'm the best." A small, self-satisfied smile licks up the corners of her mouth. I'll bet she goddamned is the best. I know better but I press my fingers a little harder against her skin, spreading them so I can feel the little shivers as the needle bites into her skin and then the moment when she relaxes. She'd feel like that when I was deep inside her, too, making her come.

"Me, too." Either you rock your shit, or you don't, and I'm the best goddamned tattoo artist in Vegas. I already know that tonight's ink is my best ever. My firebird looks ready to streak into the sky—or curl up and dig in because it's hard to imagine a sweeter spot than the curve of Harper's back.

"This is the hard part," I warn.

Sure enough, when I start shading the feathers, she tries to hold it all in but a groan escapes her mouth.

"You don't have to pretend for me," I tell her. Mean it, too. "You do whatever you fucking feel like doing."

She nods—and then she reaches down, feeling for me with her hand. The fuck? My dick may be hoping for a hand job, but instead her fingers find my thigh and pinch. Fucking hard, too. She can't get a good purchase on me thanks to my jeans and my being built like a medieval Viking, all hard and no soft.

Christ, she's amazing.

Still, she needs to understand that she doesn't get to be the one in charge here. "Do that again and I'll spank your ass."

Not the smartest thing I could say, seeing as how it doesn't just cross the line of what's appropriate and what's not. More like my words blow the goddamned line up and bury it in a mountain of TNT.

"You said I could do whatever I wanted." Did she just blush? Been a long time since I've been with a woman who got embarrassed.

"Sure thing." I draw her hand up by her head and

pin it there lightly. "But if you make me jump, sweetheart, you're gonna end up with a mutant firebird. This next part hurts the worst."

"How long?" I can hear the tears in her voice. Fucking sucks. Harper's made for smiles, not crying.

"Not long. Be good and I'll kiss it better."

"Be specific."

I've got a lot of bare skin to fill in. This won't be quick or easy. "Forty minutes."

"Are you shitting me?" She shifts and I back off.

"Kisses," I remind her. "I'll make everything feel better if you hang in here."

"You've got magic kisses?" That's her drunk talking, laughter blurring the edges of her words and pushing away the tears.

"You can find out."

"I already know how you kiss," she announces, that cute pink blush getting deeper. "We've met before."

Shit. I rack my brain trying to remember her. Women come and go in my life. Pretty sure I wouldn't have fucked Harper and forgotten her, though, so maybe she's just messing with me. Fair enough, seeing as how I'm planning on getting her out of those cute little panties just as soon as I can.

"That so? We've shared adult naptime? Done the bedroom rodeo?" I start in on the skin over her spine.

"It doesn't matter." She shrugs like whatever memories she's got are NBFD—no big fucking deal—and I tap her ass.

"Freeze," I remind her. "Or you'll make me color

outside the lines. And while you're holding that thought, give me details about what we did together."

"Nope." Now I get the smile I wanted earlier, a big, wicked grin that lights up her entire face.

"A hint," I suggest.

"We met in high school," she concedes.

Huh. I do some more thinking while I work on her ink. High school wasn't my finest moment. I was too busy being angry at the world to stop and think. Used my fists, my mouth, my dick—whatever got the biggest rise out of my audience. Guess Harper here must have been on the receiving end of my dick.

"Tell me all about it."

"Not a chance." I see her roll her eyes in the window. I forgo smacking her ass, seeing as how we're in a public venue and all. I don't need the shit Prez would give me if the club's lawyers had to get me out of an assault charge. Instead, I try my words again. I can work miracles with my tongue, but that's in the eating-her-out department. Once I start working her clit over, she'll tell me what I want to know.

Not that *she* seems to remember things that way.

"You don't want to piss off the guy holding the needle, sweetheart."

She narrows her eyes. "I'm paying you. You have to do what I say."

Christ, she makes me laugh. "Do I look like I follow the rules? Remind me."

She rolls her eyes. "You're impossible."

"But you like me."

"And you don't remember me," she counters. "At all."

"I was your best, right? So fucking awesome that the Douche couldn't hope to compare?" I squeeze her shoulder with my free hand. I can feel her bra strap beneath the silky fabric, so I nudge it downward an inch just to piss her off. "No. Don't tell me. I'll guess."

CHAPTER THREE

Harper

"MOVE YOUR HAND and I won't have to sue you."

The words fly out of my mouth automatically, the way you blurt out *excuse me* when you stand on a stranger's foot in the train or accidentally slam your boob into someone. They're just words, things that should be said. I have no clue what I'd do if he actually acted on them.

Okay.

I might know.

I suspect—but can't confirm—I'd beg him to keep on touching me because he's right about one thing. The pain has melted into something else, a throbbing, hot sensation that makes me squirm against the leather seat and imagine dirty, depraved acts. It's wrong. It's completely unprofessional and I'm entirely certain I could be thrown out of Ink Me with a half-finished tattoo on my back for propositioning the talent and getting the seat all wet.

"You're really not gonna tell me?" Swear to God,

the man is pouting—and he's got the face for it. He could model for an underwear company. His billboard would stop traffic, he's so damned pretty. I had no idea I was this shallow but his cheekbones and that mouth... I'd happily look at every inch of him, in or out of his briefs.

I really need to have sex again.

"We did it in the gym," he suggests, big hands moving over my skin. I know he's just doing his job, but I'm having the most inappropriate feelings for him. Fortunately he has no filter himself.

"Earth to Harper." He taps my back to get my attention. "Did you check out like this when we made love? Because you might have scarred me."

Ordinarily, his inability to recall me—naked no less—would be humiliating, but my recent breakup with Mark has set the bar high.

"Definitely the gym," Vik murmurs. He's changed since that night in high school—filled out and gotten even bigger. The football coach was always after him to play, although he never would.

"You think?" The constant pleasure-burn of the needle loosens something inside me and not just my tongue. I can't hold on to any kind of anger right now. It leaches out of me.

"Yeah." I see Vik nod in the window. His hair slides around his face, longer and sun-bleached, a thick, shaggy mane better suited to a tiger or some kind of wild animal. "Bet we got nasty on the mats beneath the bleachers. Bet you were worried someone might walk in on us."

"Not the gym." The needle bites into my skin again, but the burn isn't so bad now. It's a deep, insistent rhythm of its own, this sharp scratching as he remakes me.

He's silent for a moment, but he's not done. "Empty classroom, then. Fucking loved those big teacher desks they had."

"You didn't." God, I hope no one did the whole apple-for-the-teacher thing after he'd done the nasty. Talk about unsanitary.

"I can't believe I don't remember you." I have to give him credit. He sounds like he means it.

I point out the obvious, however. "Maybe you have a volume problem."

He winks at me in the glass. "Practice makes perfect."

I roll my eyes. "There's a time and a place for overachieving. Do you even know how many girls you've slept with?"

"Do you know?" he counters.

"Zero," I say promptly. "Absolutely no girls."

"Tell me it's not so." He sighs. "All guys know that you college girls go wild and crazy in your dorms as soon as it's lights-out. Tell me you lived at home and I'll forgive you."

"On campus. All four years. Pick a new fantasy."

"Do you promise to help me reenact it?"

"When hell freezes over," I say companionably. This is crazy. Despite our brief but memorable (on my part, anyhow) past, I don't really know Vik. He's changed, I've changed and his idea of conversation would get me fired at my own job. On the other hand, I wanted to start over. New Me is getting her very first tattoo because Old Me wouldn't have so much as glanced at a tattoo parlor. So perhaps New Me can also trade witty sex jokes with the crazy-hot tattoo artist. New Me wouldn't give it up in the back seat of a Dodge Charger and then head home panty-less. If nothing else, New Me will be a thong girl all the way.

I think about this to pass the time, but there's only so long I can meditate on my past underwear choices. The more Vik works, the harder it gets to stay still. No one warned me that getting a tattoo sounds way too much like we're having sex. The sound of his hands brushing over my skin is followed by the rush of my breath as I exhale a little harder. Bite back a moan when he finds a particularly sensitive spot with his needle. I'm not quite to the point of screaming *oh, oh, oh*…but I'm getting there.

"Can I ask a question?" he says eventually.

Thank God. At this point I'd take a recitation of the dictionary from front to back over the interesting sensations building up where he's touching me. Especially since those sensations don't seem to stay put—they insist on migrating lower.

Because he's inking my lower back, his hands brush the top of my butt. It's unavoidable. It doesn't mean anything, but certain parts of me take notice. Plus, there's the delicious, wicked burn of the needle. At first the needle hurts, but as I relax into the sting, the feeling changes.

Because even if it hurts, it also feels good.

I want him to do it again and again, so that I can figure out why I like this. He lays another line of ink against my skin, and this time I push up toward him rather than away. The burn becomes something else, a heated sensation that's mine, that I own, that I crave.

I've never been into kink. I'm as vanilla and boring as they come and I don't *mind* that. I like who I am. I may be vanilla cake with cream cheese frosting surrounded by more exotic, colorful flavors, but I go with everything. As long as you're in the mood for cake, I never disappoint.

And yet my panties are wet and the sensations get stronger and better until I'm fighting not to clench or rub myself against the bench.

"Your boyfriend broke up with you, right?"

"Yeah." I'd really rather not think about that right now.

"So how come you're the one who's out on the street, looking for a new place to live?"

You know what? I don't have a good answer for that. I take a stab at it anyhow.

"Because his name was on our lease?"

Vik makes a dismissive noise. "If he's the one who wants change, he changes. You stay and he goes."

It's dark outside, and the few people walking past the window are either staggeringly drunk or so wrapped up in each other that they don't look inside Ink Me's windows. It's liberating knowing that everyone and no one is watching, that Vik and I are alone in this pool of light inside a bigger sea of darkness. I suddenly understand why all those detectives in

TV shows shine a spotlight on their targets, willing them to speak.

The words spill out of me with each question that Vik asks. He can't care about my answers, not really. He's working, filling the minutes and the silence the same way he colors in the blank spots on my skin, and yet it feels both surreal and good at the same time. It has nothing to do with my noticing how powerful his thighs are in those wash-worn, threadbare jeans of his, or how his motorcycle boots make me think really, really dirty thoughts.

"There was no magic putty for my relationship with Mark. The problem is I get distracted by a pretty face and Mark had that in spades."

"I'll be your booty call," he says as he presses a bandage over my lower back.

"Excuse me?"

I sound like I have a stick up my butt. Prissy. Uptight.

And he repeats the utterly ridiculous, totally crazy thing he just said.

"If you need a pretty face for sex, you can call me."

CHAPTER FOUR

Harper

VIK SHOVES A tattooed hand in my face. "Up," he says.

His voice is phenomenal. Low and rough, full of heat and humor, the man could make a fortune as a sex line worker. He could read bedtime stories, dirty limericks, the stock report…anything, and I'd be jilling off on the other end of the line because he's that goddamned sexy.

Danger, danger.

Getting up is exponentially harder than lying down. Not only am I more sober, but I'm stiff. There's also the whole business of my skirt and my blouse, and even though what goes up must come down, my skirt is a challenge. The fabric clings to my legs, and the strong possibility of flashing my high school lover-turned-biker my cotton-covered butt makes me self-conscious. Frankly, I'd feel better about putting myself on display if I wasn't wearing sensible white cotton.

Vik solves my logistical issues for me. Large hands

close around my waist and yank me upward. I try not to giggle, but a squeak escapes me anyhow. I'm painfully ticklish, and his fingers dig gently into every spot I wish he'd avoid. At least he's quick. I don't even have time to worry about the doughnuts I've been stress-eating because he flies me through the air and sets me gently on my feet. I'm not a small woman; I started growing up when I was ten and then out two years later. And while I haven't achieved Jolly Green Giant proportions, I'm not precisely sylph-like, either. I'm tall, I'm sturdy *and* I'm wearing four-inch heels.

"Warning would be good." I dig my nails into his forearms trying to find my balance. The skin beneath the dark scrolls of ink is sun-bronzed. It's also totally lickable, but I need to *not* think about that.

"Vik Air at your service," he deadpans. "Although you either have to let go or come home with me."

We both look down at the death grasp I have on his arms.

Right.

I let go.

Vik strips off his gloves and tosses them into the trash. I guess we're done here. He might be hot and talented, but this isn't personal. Sure, I've felt this man's hands on my body, his breath on my skin for three hours, but it's a business deal. His ink in exchange for my money. Anything else was absolutely not on the price list the girl at the front desk gave me.

But I want more.

God help me, but I do. I don't want tonight to end. Right now, it feels like I've lost everything. In the morning, I'll end my pity party, but right now, I don't remember what's right with my life. I just remember the crap. I don't have my place anymore. My stuff's packed up in a storage pod. My ex hijacked our Siamese. All I have is work on Monday and…this night. The tattoo, this man's hands on me waking me up in places I didn't know I was asleep. Would you want it to end? If I'd been Cinderella, I'd have stuck around on the top of those stairs.

He steers me away from his bench, his hand low and firm just beneath the spot that burns and aches from his needles. And okay, just above another, slightly more southern spot that also aches and burns because clearly I'm all kinds of messed up.

"Harper?" His mouth brushes the hair by my ear.

"Yeah?" My stupid feet stop moving toward the front desk, where an astronomical bill waits for tonight's piece of folly. Ink and this man do not come cheap.

"I'm sorry I don't remember you and I mean it. I'd be happy to be your booty call," he whispers roughly. "All you have to do is ask, sweetheart."

I just…can't.

Vik disappears while I settle up with his receptionist for my new ink. I shouldn't be disappointed. Obviously, the flirty come-on lines are just part of the service—kind of like a hairdresser chatting you up while you're in her chair and pretending she's super-interested in your life. I force myself not to look around while Gia runs my credit card. After I sign the receipt, however, I discover a logistical problem.

Brooklyn's sound asleep on the couch.

Since leaving her here would be a gross violation of the girlcode (we're besties even if she didn't talk me out of getting a tattoo), I need to get her home. And while I definitely outweigh her, I can't deadlift her. While I consider and abandon constructing a travois out of her borrowed jacket and hauling her ass home, Gia disappears with a little wave. Guess it's quitting time at the zoo.

I could drag Brooklyn outside. The odds of that causing physical damage, however, seem high.

While I'm weighing bruises against camping in a tattoo shop overnight, a bike roars up, the noise of the pipes bouncing off buildings. Vik seems even larger and wilder straddling the enormous bike, which I figure out fast because my eyes just keep checking out his thighs, those long, muscled legs that end in the sexiest pair of boots, the powerful forearms that effortlessly guide the bike to a stop. I can't stop looking, which in retrospect probably should be a red flag that this man isn't easy. That he's capable of riding all over my nice, tidy, way-too-single life as easily as he does the road.

I should have run out of Ink Me screaming.

Instead, I watch him swing off the bike and stride toward me. Possibly, I entertain a few fantasies about pillaging Vikings and village maidens. The fun parts, not the shitty moments involving murder and mayhem. Of course, Mr. Beautiful has no clue about the daydreams playing out inside my head. He's just being a Boy Scout and making sure I'm sorted before he leaves for the night and whatever fun, sexy stuff bad-boy bikers who look like Vikings do in their downtime.

"Called you a taxi," he says when he gets to me, reaching out to touch my arm lightly. The man is definitely snugglier than a cat. A really, really friendly alley cat, I remind myself. Even in high school, his dick had its own frequent flyer club.

"Thanks," I blurt out while he stares patiently at me.

"You want me to follow you home and carry Sleeping Beauty inside?"

"Do you follow all your clients home?"

"Only the cute ones." He winks.

I think about that for a moment too long. Nope. I've got nothing. Flirty banter is not something I excel at—I have a goddamned finance degree from Cornell. Sexy Quips 101 was *not* part of my Ivy League curriculum. Instead, I reexamine Brooklyn, hoping she's magically decided to wake up, sober up and get up.

No such luck.

She snort-sighs, settling deeper into the leather couch. Vik laughs.

"She's out for the night."

Thank you, Captain Obvious.

He puts all those gorgeous muscles to good use, however, sliding his arms underneath her and scooping her up against his chest. They look perfect together, a beautiful blond god and goddess pairing. Her hair trails over his arm as he heads for the door. This is my cue to follow him, and since exhaustion is hitting me hard now, I do. If he's got a solution for my Brooklyn problem, I'll take it.

When we get outside, the taxi is just pulling up. Vik juggles his load of sleeping blonde, and says something to the driver. The guy nods, money changes hands, and then Vik walks around the car, pops open the back door and slides Brooklyn inside. When I open my mouth to protest about his paying, he cuts me off.

"Duane here is gonna see you back to your place. He can carry Sleeping Beauty in if she needs it."

I shouldn't find his ruthless, roughshod side attractive. I blame the broad shoulders stretching the leather of his jacket, or maybe it's the way he leans in to buckle up Brooklyn. He's big but he makes me feel both safe *and* sexy. He's just playing around, but it's been a long time since any guy made me feel like the queen of sexy. Like I don't have to try harder or do more because I'm enough right now, just as I am. I thought I'd have to wait until I met my Mr. Right to feel like that. Looking back, I guess that should've been my first clue that Mark wasn't the guy for me.

"Give me your address." Vik flashes me a wicked smile and I'm grateful I don't have to admit how wet my panties are.

I shoot him a look. He grins. Waiting. I heat up some more. "Because the driver needs it?"

Damn, the man has a sexy laugh. It's low and rough, a dirty, happy-sounding chuckle. I smile back as he saunters back around the car.

"Because I want it, sweetheart."

My girl parts decide this is the best reason ever. In fact, we should totally give Vik whatever he wants. Immediately.

Stupid.

"I'm at the Bellagio," I admit. "I'm between places at the moment thanks to the Douche."

Vik opens the door on my side and hands me in. I'm no dating virgin, but this is the first time any guy has ever physically steered me into a car. I look up at him, intending to protest, and lose my breath. God, he's gorgeous. Gorgeous and so, so close. I can see firsthand that his eyes are still a dark, hard gray...and those beautiful eyes make me forget all about his appropriation of my elbow—and my free will.

My butt hits the seat oh-so-obediently, but he doesn't let go. He cups my elbow with his palm, his fingers stroking briefly over my forearm. It's hardly pornographic but it's been a long time since anyone touched me. Or wanted to. I know Mark didn't, because our California King–size bed had stricter borders than North and South Korea. Mark hadn't crossed those lines to my side of the bed in months.

Vik retreats, shuts the door and then leans down, his big, tattooed hands curling around the open window frame. "Got a proposition for you."

"Okay." I'd like to pretend I don't sound breathless, but this man is like fine wine. He's only gotten better since high school.

"We're having a party out at the clubhouse tomorrow night. Think you'd have fun if you came out."

Is he asking me out on a date? Or maybe this is

the biker version of a coffee? In theory we're old high
school friends who haven't seen each other in years,
so this could be strictly platonic, or him just being
nice because he's aware my life is a mess.

"You're thinking too hard." He looks amused as
he pulls a business card out of his jacket pocket and
scribbles an address on it. He takes my hand, tucking
the card into my palm and closing my fingers around
it. His thumb strokes over my knuckles briefly. "Say
yes. I promise I won't forget you this time."

His eyes dip to my mouth. Is he thinking about
kissing me? Am *I* thinking about kissing *him*?

"Maybe," I blurt out, my good intentions melting
like my panties.

I'm still trying to decide as he saunters back to
his bike, straddles the seat and rides off. Usually,
I'd just admire the view and get on with my life, but
nothing about today has been normal. I've been ren-
dered homeless, dumped and inked. And after an
evening of downing way too many cocktails, I've
also got a monster-size thirst to go with the start of
a headache—and the contacts I've been wearing all
day aren't helping. Hooking up with a biker and tattoo artist is also something I wouldn't usually do.

But I'm painfully aware that the man's ass and
thighs are a delicious work of art that deserve appre-
ciating. Biker. Charmer. Player. Vik is all of these and
more, and the sex appeal just rolls off him. Maybe
we could hook up, but it couldn't end any better than
it did the first time.

Trouble.

That's what Vik is. He's Capital T Trouble.

He's not the Mr. Right I've been searching for, he doesn't fit into my life plan, and that makes him most definitely not the person I need in my life right now. If I were smart, I'd sit out on dating for a few months even if said life plan calls for marriage and kids before I'm thirty-five and my eggs start drying up like water in the desert. It's just that I'd swear Vik looked at me like he liked what he saw. I mean, really, *really* liked what he saw. And he walked me out and gave me his card and God I need to find a life somewhere. I've already taken his dick for a ride, so it's not like I can even blame curiosity for the warm sensation licking my belly and melting all my resolve.

I settle slowly into the seat as the taxi pulls away from Ink Me. Brooklyn makes a face like she's giving serious consideration to puking, so I rub her back and try to not hear the wounded animal sounds she's making.

I should throw Vik's card away. Instead, I turn it over. It's the general card for Ink Me, with all the basic contact information for hitting up the tattoo parlor for an appointment. On the reverse side, however, Vik has scrawled an address and two words.

Come over.

Oh, and he's also sketched a cartoon Viking that's…

Doing something downright obscene.

To a very large penis.

That has…

Ink?

I shove the card into my purse and try not to wonder if Vik has tattoos in some very personal areas. How likely is it that a guy would let a needle and ink anywhere near his favorite body part? Plus, the pain. And how would that even work? Do you ink when you're hard or soft?

He has to be exaggerating.

I make a mental note to Google penis sizes and hand-to-dick ratios. After that, I'll clear my browser cache and get on with my life, curiosity satisfied.

Really.

I will.

Bad boys and bankers don't mix.

CHAPTER FIVE

Harper

MY LIFE DOES not magically sort itself out overnight.

This comes as no surprise, although part of me wishes I'd inherit a fairy godmother or some magic beans. Instead, I wake up alone in my Bellagio hotel room. Since I'm only here for a week or two until I find a new place and I'm paying for my reservation with the Douche's lifetime hoard of frequent flyer miles, I upgraded to a room with a fountain view. This means I don't even have to get out of bed to see the watery fireworks. One push of a convenient bedside button and the blackout drapes part with a dramatic swoosh, sunlight pouring inside as the water below shoots upward to the sounds of "Lucy in the Sky with Diamonds."

I go all in and order room service pancakes. A pot of overpriced coffee, hothouse strawberries and a pound of butter improve my mood substantially. I send emails and make calls, setting up appointments to view various condos because unfortunately I can't live at the Bellagio forever.

I do Saturday things after I've done what I can to organize my life, because it would be a shame to be camped out at the Strip's fanciest hotel and not take advantage of it. I swim in pools surrounded by faux-Grecian statuary spouting water. I lose ten bucks in the slot machines. I pass on visiting the art gallery in favor of the ginormous chocolate fountain in the hotel's candy shop because everything is better with chocolate.

And the whole time I keep thinking about last night. About Vik's casual invitation to join him at an MC party. He might be hot and uninhibited, but he's also a biker, and he's the guy who banged me in the back seat of his car after high school prom…and then promptly forgot my name, my face and every detail of that encounter. I've probably idealized his bedroom skills. He's not worth pursuing, and he likely has zero interest in me that way, even if he did offer to be my booty call. Who says those kinds of things?

Other than company events, I can't remember the last party I went to. There aren't many festive moments on my calendar. Okay, so I could swing by Vik's clubhouse and check out his party. My night's wide-open, and how many opportunities will I get to ogle an entire roomful of bikers? Since I'm most definitely not drinking tonight, I could even drive there, which would give me a handy escape route. I'm assuming a biker event is a little rowdier and grittier than, say, a fund-raiser ball, and it's entirely possible I'll feel too uncomfortable to do more than just look in.

I go through the clothes I've stashed in the closet. Most of them are work things, with a healthy side of yoga pants. Nothing screams *party*. I do a quick Google search for biker get-together dress codes but come up mostly empty. Lots of leather and denim, plus the occasional porn- or Coachella-worthy outfit that makes Princess Leia's slave girl bikini look like a nun's habit.

Huh.

Going naked—or even mostly naked—seems like it would send the wrong message, plus I can't picture myself strutting around in denim shorts and a black bikini top. Maybe it's all in the footwear?

I could go shopping.

Something tells me that Vik would really enjoy a pair of fuck-me Louboutins, for instance. Or I could wear yesterday's heels.

But I feel like something new to go with the new me.

I end up calling Brooklyn for a consult, and then she meets me in the lobby and we hit the Desert Passage Shops at the Aladdin. There's an awesome bar smack in the middle of the mall like the best kind of desert oasis. We make a well-deserved pit stop there for yard-long frozen margaritas that come in fluorescent yellow bongs and manage to achieve both quantity and quality.

After that, we hit the shops. Brooklyn insists that I need to go for a whole new look, and I'm in the mood for a change. She grabs an armload of insanely teeny clothes off the rack in a store I've never stepped foot in before. It's the kind of place that advertises on the pages of *Vogue*, and I'm pretty sure the fabulously gorgeous clothes will be wasted on a bunch of bikers. So it's a good thing I'm dressing for me now.

I come home with a ridiculously expensive black tube top and a pair of wicked stiletto booties with ribbons instead of laces. Outside of work, I avoid anything that adds to my height, but new me, new rules, and apparently New Me has decided tonight's theme is girlish bondage. I shimmy into a pair of skinny jeans that seem to have gotten smaller since their last wash, and then I hit the road.

Vik's clubhouse is not exactly on the Strip. In fact, it's most definitely in East Las Vegas, and the blocks get grittier and more dangerous as I get closer. It's the kind of neighborhood with bars on the windows, bright splashes of graffiti and cars up on blocks. Pots of succulents and geraniums line the walkways adding some hopeful color, and more than one strand of white twinkling lights wrap around palm trees despite the summer weather. Eventually, the houses give way to block after block of slightly run-down, gone-to-seed warehouses. In the movies, this is the point where the bad guys come out shooting or there are gratuitous explosions.

The GPS on my phone announces it's time to turn. I'm not sure what I expected, but Vik's clubhouse looks like all the other warehouses—except for the parking lot full of bikes. Who needs a sign reading Biker Party Here or a clutch of helium balloons with all those Harleys reeking of testosterone?

The bikers themselves don't seem too scary. I mean, they're definitely not firemen, or lawyers, or anything remotely wholesome-looking or suit-wearing, but they're also not engaged in any visible felonies, which I appreciate. They're simply a bunch of guys milling around the bikes, talking and joking. The dress code appears to call for leather and boots. Music pounds out of the warehouse when someone pulls the door open. I don't recognize the singer, but the song has one of those hard-hitting, pulse-raising beats that makes you want to dance in place or screw.

I so don't belong here.

Nevertheless, one of the younger bikers waves me into an empty spot next to a row of trucks. I spot a Camaro, a Dodge Charger and a dented-up minivan that looks about as bikerly as I do, so there's hope for my evening after all. Perhaps the Hard Riders practice a more inclusive form of clubbing?

When I get out, the fresh-faced biker gives me a nod. "You looking for someone?"

I'll bet they don't get too many party-crashers. "Vik."

"Inside," he says. I think he smirks—or possibly rolls his eyes. I'm clearly not the first woman to ask after Vik tonight. "Probably in back by the bar. Might be spinning."

I lock my car (although I'm not sure that's going to stop anyone) and head for the clubhouse. The front door is much more imposing and formidable than the parking lot attendant. In fact, it's clearly been built for mega-giants, and I wrestle with it for a long moment, my glasses sliding down my nose.

A thick, inked arm reaches over me and shoves it open.

"Ladies first," the arm's owner drawls. He looks me up and down slowly, taking in my jeans and dressy boots. I suddenly know how a zebra feels when it accidentally steps into a lion's den. The look on this guy's face is part amusement, part hunger. I'd like to tell him I'm not a steak, but the patch on his vest says PRESIDENT, and I have a feeling that makes him the king of this particular kingdom. If he says I'm steak, I'm steak.

"Is this your club?" I like to know who's in charge, but Mr. I'm-Gonna-Eat-You-Up seems to find my question funny because he just snorts and reaches down to shove my glasses back into place.

"Yeah. I'm Prez. You got an issue with that, sunshine?"

I think about that for a minute and shake my head. Despite my invitation, coming out here seems less smart all the time. Some women like living dangerously, but I've never been one of them. I prefer my life safe and sane, which begs the question of what I'm doing here. Starting over. Taking a chance. About to suffer public humiliation. You can take your pick, but my car and escape looks better and better.

"In," he rumbles, his hand pressing against my shoulder. I decide not to protest, and move forward.

Prez follows me inside, so close that the front of his thighs brush the back of mine. I don't think that's an accident. He cups my elbow, herding me in the direction he wants me to go. This whole life-changing stuff is stupid. Take-charge guys have never been my thing. *Except Vik*, a little voice whispers in my head. *You like* him.

I'm working on that.

You hear things about motorcycle clubs and the Hard Riders have a certain reputation, or so my Google-fu tells me. While they look after their own and spend a commendable amount of time giving back to their community (Vik wasn't kidding about the Christmas toy drive), they also ride hard and party harder. There are darker rumors and whispers, too, about how they have a zero-tolerance policy on drugs and are key players in East Las Vegas's war on illegal substances—although it appears they're big fans of beer.

The place is definitely not the bat cave.

Music blasts from the back of the warehouse. The clubhouse is huge, the entire downstairs floor open and jammed with gyrating, dancing, drinking bodies. Lots of black leather couches have been pushed back against the wall to open up a path to the makeshift bar in the back. Longnecks and red Solo cups are the order of the day. As is skin. I've never seen this much skin on display outside of a beach or a Vegas strip revue. As I scan the crowd, looking for Vik, I realize I'm overdressed.

In fact, clothing seems to be largely optional and I could have saved the money I spent on my shopping trip and just worn my underwear. A brunette in what could be a tube top or a dress brushes past us. The stretchy fabric barely skims her butt, and that's *before* she squeals and throws herself at her dance partner. She scissors her legs around his waist. Everyone here is loud and uninhibited.

A red cup dangles in front of my face.

I take it. I don't know where it came from, so I'm not drinking it but I need something to do with my hands, and I'm *definitely* not doing what the brunette is doing. "Thanks?"

Prez winks at me. "Who're we lookin' for?"

He's got a soft, smoky burr of an accent that makes me think of warm Louisiana nights and the bayou. It's the kind of drawl that almost but not quite distracts you from the fact that this is the guy who runs a biker club and could probably have you killed with one nod of his head.

I really should care about that. Instead, I pony up the answer he's looking for. "Vik."

Prez rubs his free hand over his chin, his pained sigh gusting over my skin. "Figures."

I want to ask what that means, but I'm distracted by the madman bouncing around the dance floor. Shoulder-length blond hair flies everywhere. Vik dances all-out. Muscular, inked arms cut through the air as he thrashes to a beat that bears no resemblance whatsoever to the music vibrating through the warehouse. Faded blue jeans hug his ass and end in a pair of motorcycle boots. Just in case the gift-wrapping on that particular part of the package doesn't scream *open me*, he's wearing his club vest over a fitted white

T-shirt. Muscles bulge as he executes another move and part of me wants to hang all over that arm. See how good it feels. Shove it between my legs.

I'm not the only one with that idea.

A skinny, fabulously gorgeous woman in a barely there black leather dress shimmies up to him and starts using him as her own personal dance pole. They're so close that her breasts press up against his arm and she's riding his thigh as she grinds high and bumps low. I'm so glad I made the effort to come tonight.

And apparently Vik prefers quantity to quality because not one but two more wanna-be dancers latch onto him as he burns up the dance floor. I feel like I should be pulling a wad of one-dollar bills out of my purse and rewarding their efforts.

"Is he always like this?" The words fly out of my mouth before I can stop them.

Prez chuckles. "Pretty much. Man's the fucking Energizer Bunny when it comes to gettin' laid."

Just great.

I take a step backward and bump awkwardly into Prez. Shit. Naturally, my reaction is to lurch forward to put some space between my butt and his groin. Prez laughs again, his hands steadying my hips as I rock on my stupid high heels. He bellows Vik's name, the sound all but getting lost in the general chaos and uproar that is a biker party. Not that I was expecting to be announced by trumpets or a twenty-one-gun salute, but still.

Miracle of miracles, Vik looks toward us. A

wicked grin lights up his face and he dumps the leg-humper off his thigh.

"Harper!" he yells back. His inside voice is loud enough to carry over the deafening beat of the music. So loud that heads turn to stare at me. I consider beating a hasty retreat, but New Me insists on sticking around. She's either brave or horny, and I'm not sure I want to find out which.

Prez chuckles and pats me on the *butt*. "See you later, sunshine."

In a weird way, I don't mind it because the gesture seems less like a creepy grope and more like a friendly overture. Maybe these guys just don't have normal social skills. Or were never housebroken.

Vik bounds over, throwing his arms out. "You found me."

"I did."

People—*bikers*—are still staring.

Possibly, it's because I'm wearing more clothing than all of Vik's previous companions combined. I look down quickly just to make sure that I am fully dressed and not having one of those living nightmares where you waltz into a room buck naked.

I throw caution to the wind and take a sip of my drink, hoping it's magic. A potion like *Alice in Wonderland*'s Drink Me, except maybe it will make me articulate. Give me the gift of gab so that I know what to say to this man. This gorgeous, hot biker who ties me up in knots. Of course, I consumed way more alcohol last night and look how that ended up. I have a tattoo on my back.

Vik grabs my hand. "Dance with me, Harper."

I wait for my drink to kick in, but no luck. Red punch and a truly impressive amount of grain alcohol will not be riding to my rescue tonight.

"Do I look like I dance?" The pole-dancing, thigh-humping antics of his previous partners are not part of my repertoire.

The corners of his mouth quirk up.

I sort of hate him for the way my panties promptly get wet.

Vik sets his hands on my hips—my *hips*—and tugs me closer. He links his hands on top of my butt, fingers skating dangerously close to inked territory, and then he rests his forehead against mine.

"You don't have to dance well," he whispers. I'm pretty sure his mouth brushes my hair. My cup is jammed between us and I have no idea what to do with my spare hand.

"Okay?" New Me, I remind myself. She might turn out to be an awesome closet dancer, so I should make the effort to find out. My feet are still rooted to the floor, though, when somebody jostles us and I slop punch on the front of Vik's shirt. His *white* shirt. Kill. Me.

"God, I, shoot…" I scrub at the front of his shirt. The stain is approximately the size and shape of North America. Possibly South America, too. This is why I don't get asked to parties.

"Hey." He nudges my chin up with his thumb. "No big deal."

He's so beautiful.

I blame my embarrassing muteness on his face. He's the most gorgeous man I've ever seen and he's within touching distance. When he removes his thumb from my face, I almost sigh in disappointment.

And then he flashes a devilish wink at me and shrugs out of his vest. "Hold this for me, babe."

The leather vest he drops into my hands is warm from his skin. You know how there are moments when you can feel your whole life pivot? Because the universe has just served you a red letter day and you need to stop and memorialize that date in your journal? Maybe slap some washi tape and gold stars on that bad boy so that when you look back, fifty years from now, you'll know to tell your grandkids about the day you met dear old granddad and how the trumpets blared and the angelic hosts all pointed at him and declared him to be The One?

I wish I could tell you that's what happens here. I wish I could say I looked at Vik and knew he was a good man and that together we'd have something meaningful.

But I can't.

I am, however, 100 percent in lust with him.

Just look at him.

How could any woman resist?

He hauls his T-shirt over his head in one smooth move and the man could do underwear ads. He's got the most amazing six-pack, all cut muscles dusted with the finest of golden hairs. And the fact that I know this only proves that I'm standing way too close to him. I imagine this must be how Eve looked at

Adam the day she realized he had a dick and he was
naked. My gaze travels down in pure appreciation.
And then goes down some more until all those *pure*
feelings of admiration melt into something far dirtier and hotter. Dear God, the man has been blessed.

"If you wanted me naked, all you had to do was
ask."

And just like that he short-circuits the remaining
brain cells in my stupid, besotted head. Smacking myself upside my head sounds like a plan, except I need
whatever thinking power remains up there. Logic is
my new best friend. Calm. I probably should have
taken one of those yoga classes where they teach you
how to be all Zen and in the moment because right
now I'm practically hyperventilating.

Vik isn't helping. He tugs his vest out of my hands
(I don't particularly want to give it back), shrugs it
on and then tosses the dirty T-shirt onto the floor.
"Come on."

I shove my tongue back into my mouth and let
him lead where he will. Which is apparently from
one group of bikers to the next. And surprisingly, everyone I meet is pretty chill. They tip their heads at
me or wink or flash a killer grin, and…I'm having a
good time. Plus, Vik turns out to be more of a cuddler
than a humper or a groper (contrary to his dance floor
exhibition). He keeps an arm around me, squeezing
me up against his side as he steers us from group to
group. Since he's mostly naked from the waist up, I
find this contact deeply distracting.

The last guy we approach is a biker leaning against

the wall. He's every bit as tattooed, hard and lethal-looking as my Vik. His dark hair is buzzed close to his scalp, and the way he watches us has me convinced he could describe us with perfect accuracy to a police sketch artist. Despite his casual slouch, I get the sense that he's entirely aware of his surroundings and more than prepared to take out or take down anything and anyone that becomes a problem.

Tread carefully.

"Rev." Strong fingers close carefully around mine. His grip is firm but pleasant, and I sense he's being careful not to overwhelm me or squeeze too hard. Or maybe it's just the air of cool containment. This is definitely not a man to fuck with.

Vik's eyes narrow. "I'm going to count to three. If you want to keep all those fingers, you let go before I finish, you feel me?"

Rev laughs. "Feeling possessive?"

Vik nods vigorously. "I'm her booty call. She doesn't have time for you."

"I. We—"

I can feel my face going up in flames, but Rev just laughs.

"She had me undressed within minutes of arriving." Vik gestures down his chest with his hand. As if anyone could have missed all those glorious, naked muscles. And the ridges...the tempting, tempting ridges of his perfect abdomen.

I finally manage to wipe the drool off my chin and respond. "You are *not* my booty call."

Vik winks. "I offered. You didn't say no. Plus, I'm totally fine with you using me for sex."

I think he means it.

This just makes my face redder, which makes Rev laugh harder. It's a vicious cycle, and another example of why I have no business being at a biker party. Vik snags my hand and starts towing me deeper into the clubhouse. Eventually, we hit the bar at the back of the building. It's louder here, the music a deep, throbbing bass that I can feel pulsing through the floor beneath my feet. It's a wonder everyone here isn't permanently deaf.

Vik snags a barstool, deposits me on it before I can protest and then leans back against the bar. His shoulder bumps mine as he grabs my hand and starts playing with my fingers.

"You get a place sorted out yet?"

"I've only been homeless for two days," I point out. I excel at multitasking and getting stuff done, but even I have my limits. "I've got appointments tomorrow to look at a few rentals."

"You could move in with me."

I choke on my drink and he pounds me on the back, careful to avoid my new ink.

"Too fast?" He takes the cup and sets it down on the bar.

"Yes," I wheeze. "When did we discuss this?"

"What?" He blinks at me innocently, but his eyes twinkle.

"Sex. Booty calls. *Moving in.*"

"Yesterday." He settles his hands on my thighs and

pushes gently. My stupid knees part like the Red Sea and he takes full advantage, stepping between them. Dark eyes stare into mine. My nipples don't understand that Vik is like this with every woman he meets. They perk up at his proximity, super-excited that we have a big, sexy biker spreading our thighs.

Stupid nipples.

"Yesterday you gave me a tattoo," I say suspiciously. "At what point did we discuss becoming roommates?"

He rubs my thigh gently. Frankly, this doesn't seem like roommate behavior. Also? I enjoy it way too much. If we actually shared a place, there's no way I wouldn't jump the man.

"You should relax. You're tense."

"Because you're crazy." Someone clearly has to be the voice of reason here. I'm not sure I'm qualified though because his hand drives me crazy and I'm having serious thoughts about wiggling lower to see if he really is as uninhibited as he seems.

His hand moves higher, and all logical thought vacates my brain. Not only is he crazy, but he cheats.

"Tomato. Tomatoh." He looks supremely unconcerned.

Since I'm right, however, I can't let it go. "We never discussed moving in together."

His hand curls around my thigh. Thank God for denim. It's almost thick enough to allow me to block out the fantastic sensation of those fingers easing up my thigh. Or the other places he could put them. Some of my very *favorite* places.

"You were distracted." His breath ruffles my hair. If he gets any closer, he'll either be in my lap or we'll be simulating sex in public. A quick glance around the clubhouse tells me that no one will notice. There are bikers wrapped around girls, and girls wrapped around various combinations of bikers. It's all very un-PG. People dance, they drink and grind, and apparently they fuck.

In *public*.

I yank my gaze away from the pool table in the corner of the clubhouse. There are things you can't unsee, like the penetration occurring on the green felt surface.

"Yesterday," he says helpfully.

"What about yesterday?"

"I volunteered myself as your booty call. You did not say no."

"Silence isn't a *commitment*." For example, I'm totally thinking about a dozen dirty things he could do with his tongue, but none of those are actual requests.

"You're breathing hard. Are you thinking about me?"

Yes, yes I am.

I deflect. "Are you really that conceited?"

"I'm that good." He slides his hand upward.

I think he's fully prepared to finger me in public. I grab his hand, stopping its upward movement.

"We're in *public*."

"So you'd let me touch if we were alone?" He leans in, his mouth brushing my ear. "Good to know."

"No."

He winks. "I'm even better than your imagination. Let me show you. I make the best friend with benefits."

"Vik—"

"My benefits are huge."

"We are not friends with benefits," I say firmly. I need to get out of here before I forget that and launch myself at him. Stupid body wanting its own personal biker toy. I'm ready for my forever man and happily-ever-after, not a fun diversion. I have my life all mapped out and there's no pit stop for Viking pillaging.

"Maybe I inked my number on your ass last night after you expressed your interest in me." He picks up my hand, running strong thumbs over my palm. With each pass, I melt further.

"You told me you were giving me a firebird."

OMG. He didn't, did he?

"Shhh." He keeps a gentle hold on my hand, turning my arm in his grip. From somewhere he magically produces a Sharpie and uncaps it with his teeth. We both lean in, our heads almost touching, as he scrawls a phone number over my skin.

"Something important?"

He draws the Sharpie down my arm. "Mine."

The possessive note in his voice really demands some kind of response. He doesn't let go of my arm, either. Instead, he starts drawing. Roses and vines. Big, bold flowers. I may never wash again.

"Am I your Etch-a-Sketch now?"

"You deserve flowers." He adds another bloom,

smaller and shyer. I'll have to wear a long-sleeved blouse at work this week but I don't want to pull away. Heading straight to Ink Me seems like my best idea. That way I can see Vik's flowers in color.

"Is that your number?"

His hand glides down my arm to wrap around my fingers. "Yeah."

"Most people just put numbers in their contacts."

"Good point." He caps the Sharpie, vanishing it back into a pocket, and then holds out a hand. "Phone."

Not giving it to him doesn't even occur to me. I pull it out of my purse and hand it over. And then when he taps the screen and looks at me, I type in my passcode. His arm comes around me and he snaps a picture of us.

"What should I call myself in your contacts?" He bends his head over my phone, fingers flying. I didn't know adding a contact was such a multistep process, but whatever. I like watching him. Beautiful doesn't cover it.

"Vik," I say, and he makes a face.

"I should have one of those couples' nicknames. Like peaches or love muffin or big daddy. Christen me now."

The giggle flies out of my mouth like some kind of freakish exploding alien baby. I don't giggle. I'm a mature woman with a career, responsible for millions of dollars of other people's money.

I expect him to give the phone back. He doesn't.

He starts snapping pictures of other bikers, adding them to my contacts list.

"I'm curious, Vik. What am I going to need them for? Body disposal?"

He shrugs and slips my phone back into my purse. "Do whatever needs doing. My old man is gonna love you, though. Can't wait for you to meet him."

Say. What?

"That sounds like a pretty big step."

He presses a kiss against the black rose he's drawn on my skin. "When you know, you know, right? And we've got something, babe."

I reluctantly extricate my arm from his hold. I really shouldn't let the crazy man fondle me, no matter how good it feels. "I'm sure your dad's a lovely man."

Vik purses his lips. "He can be difficult."

"So he's related to you," I say drily.

Vik beams. "And he really, really wants me to settle down. It was kinda a surprise to me. We hadn't talked in months, and then boom. He moves in with me because he's lost his place and now he's after me to find The One. I'm not big on planning, though, so we're taking it one day at a time."

I have no answer—just lots of questions. I start with the obvious. "The One?"

Vik hums a few bars of Mendelssohn's "Wedding March." Most guys aren't big on settling down. I know this thanks to years of looking. Vik, however, looks amused rather than spooked.

"I don't look good in white," he confides. "And the jury's out on diamonds."

Ooookay. Next question.

"You didn't speak? And now he's *living* with you?"

We normal people plunge into family life a little more cautiously. Vik, however, apparently believes in doing everything at Mach Seven.

"I'm turning over a new leaf. Gonna need a new biker name." His smile gets more mischievous, and my panties get correspondingly wetter. "The Saint."

"Excuse me?"

"I'll go by The Saint." He practically bounces on his seat. Unless it's opposite day, this man is about as far from sainthood as you can get.

Since there's no point in disabusing him, I nod amicably. "That's sweet of you."

I haven't met too many people who'd just up and move their dad in because he needed a place. Most people would just toss some cash at the problem— or ignore it. It's a little embarrassing how smiley his protectiveness makes me feel. God, I'm so screwed here. There's all this sexual tension between us and while I know it's as temporary as a firefly, it feels good. Vik's fun and he makes me feel fun. He's just drunk and horny, a biker who does God knows what when he's not inking equally drunk girls. I've never had so much as a speeding ticket.

"I have to go," I say, sliding off the barstool. Staying any longer would be stupid. I've come, I've seen and I've conquered the biker party. I can check one more wild thing off my bucket list.

Vik snags my hand, his fingers rubbing the sensitive skin of my inner wrist. "Already?"

"Yes." That sounds firm. That sounds like a woman who's in charge of her life and the new direction it's taken. Hanging out here any longer would be like trying to make a meal out of cotton candy at the fair. By the time you'd eaten enough to feel full, you'd be sick. Vik is pure sweet evil, and I need to be smart enough to walk away.

"Walk you out" is all he says before getting to his feet. His free hand skims my cheek before falling away, while the fingers braceleting my wrist slide down and tangle with mine until we're holding hands. I take a moment to process that.

He prowls toward the door, which seems about as distant and as unattainable as the peak of the Himalayas. Every fourth step or so some new girl seems to detach herself from the dancing, drinking crowd and tries to attach herself to Vik. It's yet more proof of why any attraction between us is doomed. No matter how pretty he is, I'm not into sharing. I'm more ménage à moi than ménage à trois. The girls climb him like a vine, rubbing and grinding and doing a million other sexy, dirty things I've never done even in the privacy of my own place. It's both impressive and off-putting. Eventually, however, we make it to the door, where he shakes off a final admirer wearing an electric blue tube top as a dress.

He doesn't apologize or acknowledge all the girls hanging on him. It's possible he hasn't even noticed them, that accessories with boobs and vaginas are just that common in the Vik-verse. Yuck. I step outside and inhale a clean, fresh, perfume- and skank-free

breath of air. Kissing Vik would be like making out
with hundreds of other people thanks to his probable
man-whore status.

So I'm passing, no matter how pretty his package is. I lean up, press a kiss against his cheek because I'm weak enough to want that much contact,
and step away.

"Thanks. Tonight was fun."

I'm moving toward my car before I've finished
speaking, just in case Vik has other ideas. Because
well-used or not, I won't stand firm if he puts that
mouth of his to good use. His fingers. His pretty,
pretty…package. Yes, I sneak one last look at the
impressive bulge in his jeans as I hightail it away.
It's like taking a final peep at the Grand Canyon or
some other natural wonder. How can you not look?

He raises a hand, looking amused. "Later."

Oh, I hope not.

Don't I?

CHAPTER SIX

Vik

I WAKE UP way too early for a Sunday morning. We had one hell of a party out at the clubhouse. Fun times. When I was twenty-one and wet behind the ears, it was about the booze and the babes, tapping the ass I could and generally showing life my middle finger. I don't like to plan shit out, but now it's about hanging with my brothers, celebrating another day on the road, another milestone, remembering the good times and not forgetting the bad. On Friday, Hun had officially beaten the charges against him and we'd all raised a beer to that.

I've known plenty of bikers, and we all have stories behind our road names. Some stories are funny, others less so, but I've never figured Hun's out. Depending on his mood, he'll give a dozen different reasons for his label, but they boil down to one of two things. Either he fights with the cunning intensity of a Hun, or he possesses legendary aftercare skills with the club's female hangers-on. He claims the ladies nicknamed him Hon', Honey Bunny or Honey Bunches of Oats because he's that goddamned sweet to them. Most of the brothers just take turns punching him when he says shit like that.

Last night, though, was good. Hun walked free, and we celebrated. Party time's not about knocking back the beer and tequila anymore. Life gets all too real, too fast, so it's important to slow down and savor the good moments. Harper is definitely shaping up to be one of those.

Or if I'm a lucky bastard, a really bad, downright filthy moment. No matter what my old man wants, I'm not a long-term man. He'd like me to find an old lady and settle down, but that's not happening. I don't look past the next weekend, although for Harper I might make an exception and give her more than a night or two. She'd be worth at least a week.

I get out of bed before I can do something really stupid like jerk off to a very fucking fond memory of Harper's heels. Black, leather and a bow tie. Those are the ultimate cock tease in shoes and I'm not dead. I love the way she owns her height. Those four-inch heels scream I can measure up or not. She can take me, leave me, do me—*if* I'm man enough.

My dad's parked in the living room in his boxers, watching *Oprah* reruns and eating toaster waffles. I take a better look at the plate he's holding and revise that to syrup with waffles. I need one of those services that ships meals in a box. Or maybe a breakfast place that delivers. Even fruit would be a step in the right direction. That much Mrs. Butterworth's can't be good for his arteries. Fuck if I know anything about taking care of an old man, but I'll learn.

My old man's not perfect, and neither am I. Between him and the club brothers who patched me in, they kicked my ass into a man who I can mostly face in the mirror. My old man's crotchety and he has a sweet tooth—the rest of him is blunt as fuck. Own up to your mistakes and raise a beer to the successes. That's what he taught me, so now that he needs me to be more, I just have to figure it out.

I give him the side-eye as he waves his sticky fork at me in greeting. "Morning."

It would be better if I'd been waking up with Harper by my side. Or underneath me. On top of me. I'm not picky about her position as long as she's naked and screaming my name.

I grunt a greeting in my old man's direction and grab for the coffeepot. After sex, riding and ink, coffee comes next. Some people fantasize about banging on a beach in Fiji, but I've always thought I'd like to give a coffee plantation in Kona a whirl. Wonder if Harper would be up for that?

I resist the thought and stagger back to the kitchen table. "You have a good night?"

He beams. "Played poker with Lora."

Lora's awesome. She sits with my dad when I go out. She's assured me that she's okay with his incessant flirting, and she also does her best to make sure he's fed and safe. She's a good woman, and I don't need my dad cleaning her out.

"You shouldn't take her money." I empty the coffee as fast as I can. It tastes better than the beers I knocked back last night.

"Won two socks, a flip-flop and her bra." My old man cackles like a maniac. "She refused to ante up her panties."

Jesus.

"But she cleaned out that young man you stuck in the hallway." My old man shoots me a sidelong look.

"Goolie?" Goolie's only been prospecting with us for a month. He did two tours in the Middle East and has a strong preference for not shooting shit anymore.

My old man cackles. "She had him down to his boxers in minutes. Think the bra might have been a decoy." He shakes his head. "She's an awesome fucking woman, and that boy didn't know what hit him. She liked the tattoo on his ass, by the way. Told her that was all your work."

If Goolie up and quits the club, Prez will kick my ass. Babysitting my dad isn't club business, but I cleared it with Prez because I'm not taking chances. Not with my dad's safety. I'm new to this whole responsibility thing but I've already learned that old men can get up to more trouble than teenage boys. That, or he's aiming for payback for the shit I pulled in high school. With interest.

Back then life seemed so simple. You drank, you raced, you thanked God for any girl who'd let you get between her legs and worship her on your knees. And yet somehow all those girls have blurred together, and I've forgotten the shot I had at Harper. She's pretty fucking memorable, so clearly this is on me.

Might be a way to see Harper and take care of some family business, too. I have to fix my old man's finances whether he likes it or not. He's been resisting but he needs to know how much he has, and I need to know how I can add to it so he never goes without.

Too bad if that makes him grumpy.

Fuck that noise.

I go into the kitchen and come back with a glass of orange juice. The carton promises it's full of important vitamins and calcium (which might be another vitamin for all I know about nutrition).

I set the glass in front of him. "I'm making us an appointment with a financial planner."

I wait for the heavens to shoot down lightning at the thought of me planning. Nothing. My dad's interest in Oprah, on the other hand, becomes downright fixated. "That so?"

"Yeah."

"Better be discussing your own stuff. I'm good. I don't need anyone poking around my checking account."

We've had this conversation or a variation thereof ever since my dad showed back up out of the blue a month ago. A social worker called and told me to come and pick him up from the Happy Vegas Valley Trailer Park. He couldn't live alone anymore, the chipper voice on the other end announced. I should have noticed this before but our interactions had been limited to my monthly rides out to his neck of the woods, a little barbecue and a little shooting the breeze. Had to confiscate the keys to his bike, too.

Life's problems have three sure fixes: money, kisses or muscle. Options B and C haven't worked out so well in the taking-care-of-Dad department. And while I have enough green stuff to make sure my old man never goes without, money's not all dear old Dad wants. Dad wants to see me settled. Happy. Set for life. The fuck?

Sure enough, my old man launches into his favorite song.

"You meet anyone last night?"

Seriously, does he think an MC party is Tinder central? Harper came out, I danced and a good time was had by all, but no, I'm not dating anyone.

When I tell him as much, he tries again. "You should see someone. Settle a down a little."

"Like you did with Mom?"

This is a low blow, because Mommy Dearest lit out shortly after my birth and never returned.

"You could get it right," he says stubbornly. "What about Amanda What's-Her-Name? Was she there?"

"Nope." Occasionally I throw my dad a bone and name names. Instead of getting him off my back, however, he's turned out to be downright tenacious. He asks after Amanda (and Hope, Janey and Little Bo) every chance he gets. I've learned to nod, smile and change the fucking topic.

Now is the perfect time to zone out and refresh my memory about my favorite parts of Harper. Tits, ass, mouth—there are so many choices.

"You met someone," my dad announces gleefully. "I know that look."

Busted.

"I'm not looking for anything permanent." I'm good for a night, not forever. Just like that, though, last night's memories of Harper pop into my head and refuse to leave. The memories want to stick even if I don't. Those black boots of hers about killed me. The woman practically owes me mouth-to-mouth resuscitation. Or possibly mouth-to-dick. I'm not choosy.

"Thinks he's fine running solo," my old man scoffs. I'm tempted to point out that *he* never settled down much, either. From what he told me, he knocked up my mom, she stuck around just long enough to push me out into the world, and then she took off. Nothing in that story qualifies him to offer romantic advice.

"I'm not the settling-down type," I offer. That sounds so much better than announcing I like variety in my pussy. And that so far, life has been one big all-I-can-eat sex buffet. Why eat à la carte when I can sample every single dish?

My dad's knee starts going up and down like a jackhammer as he picks up his fork. Sets it down. Does the same with his knife. He starts to get up and then sinks back into his chair, his knee jerking wildly. Shit.

Houston, we have a problem.

The doctor I talked with last week said the agitation was a symptom of my old man's dementia. Much of the time, he's still the same person he always was, but other times his brain takes a hard right and it's game over. The doctor said I should make sure that all of his basic needs are met, as if I'd put him on a starvation diet or keep him from sleeping. I'm supposed to be calm and reassuring, a paragon of gentle sincerity.

Yeah. Feel free to laugh your ass off at that one.

As desperate as I am, though, I try. Thank Christ, none of the club is here to see me.

"I'll give it a shot," I say. "I *am* giving it a shot."

My dad's knee slows from its manic pace to something that better resembles a car ricocheting from side to side on the German Autobahn.

"You've met someone?"

"Absolutely." The one upside to dementia is that my old man's bullshit radar no longer functions.

But he nods, his attention slowly returning to the waffles swimming in a sea of syrup. "I'd like to meet her."

"Soon," I promise. "It's early days. I don't want to scare her off."

He flashes me the bird, but we're back on terra firma. There has to be a way to fix this. Without, you know, actually settling down and paying a trip to the drive-through Elvis wedding chapel on the Strip. Sure, one of the club girls would be happy to pretend to be my steady girlfriend, but I don't think that's what my old man has in mind.

I'll just have to improvise.

Harper's face flashes through my head.

As I fix my own plate of waffles—my old man's onto something there and he's definitely getting a waffle-maker for Christmas—I wonder how an investment banker would feel about becoming a biker's pretend girlfriend. I wonder, too, how long she's spent thinking about my booty call offer. Which was 100 percent fucking genuine. I just need to close the deal. Make her see that I'm the perfect guy to scratch all her itches and give her a little under-the-table loving to help her get over the Douche and on with her life. I'm not boyfriend material, but I'm the Santa Claus of fucking orgasms.

You think she's more likely to kick me in the balls?

Good thing I've always loved a challenge.

CHAPTER SEVEN

Harper

WORK IS CRAZY. I stay late each night, retreating back to my Bellagio room with a Subway sandwich or a bag of Mickey D's. It's not even tax season when people get super-concerned about their finances. Yeah, I know they're just looking for a sweet investment to pull in money hand over fist and simultaneously score them some big-ass deduction with the IRS, but their fees keep me employed. And since I only get one chance to make my numbers and impress my bosses, I'm flat-out.

It's not until Thursday night that I return to my old place. Not worrying about Bing is a challenge, but it's not like Mark won't feed him. Plus, even if Mark did forget, Bing would just make Mark's life hell until my ex served up the Fancy Feast. It's no worse than leaving Bing with the cat sitter for company, even if Bing sulks for a week after I've been gone.

Step one in my Break, Enter, Retrieve plan? Getting through the front door. I've banked on Mark's pathological unwillingness to do any household task that he can outsource, and sure enough, he hasn't gotten around to getting a locksmith in. My key still works. There's also no sign of Mark as I open the front door. I breathe a sigh of relief and move on to the second step in the plan. *Retrieve.* Bing likes to hide under our bed, so I scoot up the stairs, cat carrier in hand.

I push the door to the master bedroom open slowly, not wanting to scare Bing. This is a well-executed plan step. The cat doesn't startle.

Hell, no.

I'm the one who freezes in place, peering through the stupid, cracked door.

Turns out, Mark's home after all.

He's eagerly eating out some hussy while she swallows his dick. No. Check that. The woman contorting herself all over my ex is one of Mark's coworkers. The one he used to text and call so often because she had a lousy home situation and lousier husband. They shared a couple of projects. Went out on a few work dinners. Do you hear that sound? It's my rose-colored glasses splintering into a thousand pieces. Fuck me for not recognizing a lie when I heard it. That, or sixty-nine is the new prescription drug for lousy relationships.

The porno moans start up as they round into the home stretch. With each up-and-down, Mark's new friend is practically nose to whiskers with Bing. Bing's eighteen pounds of brown-and-white Siamese love, and he could probably smother that bitch if he sat on her face. Or go to town on Mark's favorite body part. Maybe if I look away, these new-to-me blood-thirsty urges will subside.

Or not.

Mark's replaced me already.

The logical part of my brain (the part not running the odds of a murder conviction if I kill them both now) suggests this might not be the first time Mark's hooked up with his new girl. There's certainly an un-precedented degree of familiarity happening in that bed. Mark's dress pants are unbuckled and shoved down his thighs. Her panties are yanked to the side as if she's so fucking amazing that Mark couldn't wait to undress her. Or maybe he's lazy. God knows, he's never put this much effort into our bedroom time.

The happy twosome shifts and I retreat because I can't handle a close-up of competitor beaver right now. It's not that I want Mark back (especially now I've seen firsthand where he's stuck his dick and his mouth), but I feel like the loser in a race I didn't real-ize I was running. Before I abandon the field to the lucky winner, however, I whip out my phone and snap a couple of pictures. This is immature, but fuck it.

I keep it together as I park my car in the Bellagio's parking garage. I don't break down in the elevator up to my room, and I don't cry the entire, endless length of the hallway. Mark sucks. He's a stupid, cheating, lying bastard and I'm so much better off without him. Screw him.

No, wait. He's already got that well in hand. Or mouth.

Not only is the hussy's beaver now burned into

my brain, but I still don't have my cat. I miss Bing, but what if he decides to cozy up to the new body in the bed? What if my cat falls in love with *her*, too?

I strip down to my panties and shimmy into my Kate Spade sleepshirt. Yes, I'm a big believer in brand loyalty. The shirt is black and has cute little white cuffs that make it the comfortable version of one of the many dress blouses I wear to the office—except for the happy fact that my boobs announce *Eat Cake for Breakfast*. I 100 percent endorse that message. I'm giving serious consideration to room-service-ordering up an entire cake.

The Bellagio's bathroom has more mirrors than a voyeur's bedroom, so it's impossible to turn around without catching a glimpse of myself. The funny thing is I look the same, except with bonus red eyes and blotchy cheeks. Sucks to feel different on the inside where no one can see.

The only thing different on the outside is my new ink. I scooch up to the mirror, hike my shirt up under my armpits in the least sexy move ever and ease my panties halfway down my butt. And then I'm staring at my lower back and ass. You know, just checking shit out.

Even with the tattoo only half-healed, it's clear that Vik is insanely talented with his hands. My firebird explodes up from the base of my spine, wings expanding from my panties and wrapping themselves around my spine. The feathers are this gorgeous red and black, long, sweeping lines of color that soar upward. For all his teasing, Vik didn't ink his number on my butt.

Okay. So he didn't give me his number in permanent color but he's still beneath my skin. There's all that bare skin around the lines he laid down, just begging to be filled. I want more, want that darkness, that sweet pain and the release that comes afterward. The buzz of his needle let me forget so much and then took me to a different place.

I pick up my abandoned clothes. Fold them neatly and stack them on the opulent little vanity bench. The Bellagio has its King Louis the Something-Something going on because my bathroom is practically raining gilt. My black work skirt and Kate Spade blouse look downright sedate, and my beige bra is the cherry on the boring sundae. To be fair, it's not like I can rock red lace underneath a white work blouse, nor do I want to, but still…my underwear covers more than most bikinis. If I got hit by a bus and EMTs stripped me down to check for injuries, my modesty would be safe.

Mark's hussy wore red satin.

I promptly Google selfie tips.

I must be crazy because I'm actually thinking about taking a picture. Of my panties. I recheck the all-knowing Internet, and three minutes later I'm armed, dangerous and pointing my phone at my crotch. Snap, snap, tap. It's not even hard. Sure, I hesitate, my finger hovering over Vik's contact info. For like a nanosecond.

I hit Send. Are these panties boring?

Is sharing mostly naked selfies with an almost total stranger stupid?

Yes.

Yes, it is.

And then, still feeling reckless, I march out and raid the minibar. Never mind that the smallest package of M&M's costs a ridiculous eight dollars or that the price tag on the mini champagne exceeds my last cell phone bill. I'm totally worth it, and today has sucked.

My phone dings with an incoming message.

VIK: You do have my number. Thought you'd never use it.

ME: Answer the question.

VIK: Would look better on the floor. Or wrapped around my dick. Hint hint.

It's silly to be happy because Vik likes my panties. His opinion is hardly statistically significant— I'd have to march my butt out onto the Strip and poll at least ninety-nine other random guys if I wanted meaningful results. But still. *He* likes beige just fine. Of course, that's because he wants to get *in* them but I totally count it as a win for me.

ME: Tried to pick up my cat from my ex. Epic fail.

VIK: Tell me what you need. I'm on it.

ME: Brain bleach.

He's a biker who goes to biker parties, so a random couple 69-ing won't shock him. I text him my new glamor shot of Mark and his colleague. Frankly, the only reason I'm not blasting it to everyone we know is that then I'd have to explain what I was doing in his house after he gave me the boot.

VIK: I'd say fuck him but looks like he's already got that covered. You can do better than him. I can be there in thirty minutes if you decide to upgrade.

See? I'm sexy.

ME: Flying solo tonight but thanks.

VIK: You sure about that?

ME: Not in the mood for company. Swearing off sex forever.

VIK: Give me a shot.

ME: At?

VIK: Changing your mind. You've had the worst. No point in taking a vow of celibacy until you've tried the best.

ME: So you're the best?

Vik texts me back a row of smiley-face emoticons. I have no idea what that means.

Absolutely none.

Is he in a good mood? Laughing at me? Tapped the wrong picture when he meant to send a chorus line of dancing eggplant emojis?

I consider what I know. Item one? I definitely like his body. New Me has fantasized a lot about stripping him down and licking various parts of his anatomy. But those are just fantasies—and Real Me lives firmly in reality. He's hot, and I'm me. Most days, I'm happy to be me. But I'm a conservative investment banker. I wear panty hose. I plan for the long game. No matter how pretty Vik is, he's not my type.

The line of dancing dots appears on my phone.

VIK: Assuming you're not at work?

ME: Nope. Back at the Bellagio.

Ten long heartbeats later, my phone buzzes.

He's sent me a picture.

If I had to pick a word to describe what I'm looking at, I'd be hard-pressed to choose, but *dirty* vies for top position on my list. The shot closes in on his abs and then goes…lower. Much, much, deliciously lower. He's unbuttoned the top buttons of his jeans and he's fisting his dick. The view is both hot as fuck and supremely frustrating because while I know *where* his hand is (squeezing what appears to be a magnificently large penis), I can't see much of anything. Video would be so much better.

VIK: Sweet dreams.

It's definitely time to sign off. Otherwise, I'll be asking him to come over here and show me his Monster Dick in person.

ME: Again? Covered.

I scoop up my snack pile and then text him a picture of my loot. It's not a sexy look, but I'm nervous about taking the next step with him.

VIK: Looks small. The snack, not your tits ;) Perfect mouthful right there.

ME: Girl's gotta do what a girl's gotta do.

VIK: Hear you.

We sign off, and I sigh with relief. I haven't said or done anything too incriminating, like beg him to come over and express his appreciation for my boobs in person. Since the fountain show is scheduled to go off in five minutes, I camp out by the window. The Bellagio has the best furniture—I seriously want to load it all into my car when I check out and take it with me.

The fountains explode, and I hold up my phone, making a video. I'll bet Vik could come up with a dozen different dirty innuendoes for all that water jetting upward. I'll have to challenge him.

The knock on my door comes just as the fountains shoot their final load sky high. After checking through the peephole to make sure it's not a serial killer (bad) or a wayward biker (bad but oh so good), I open the door and let the room service guy in.

"Got a special delivery for you, Ms. George," he says before I can point out that I haven't ordered anything tonight. "Compliments of a Mr. Vik."

And then bless the man, he wheels in a trolley, whips off a half-dozen silver domes and reveals the entire dessert menu. It's like a multiple choice test where you're supposed to choose which plate of decadent goodness is your favorite, A, B, C, D, or E—all of the above. This is clearly a vote for E.

Guess I do get to have cake for breakfast after all.

CHAPTER EIGHT

Harper

THREE DAYS AFTER the dessert incident, I stagger back into the Bellagio clutching a foot-long sub in a bag. Work sucked the big one, and my evening plans consist of mainlining carbs and greasy sandwich meat until I burst. Pepperoni, salami, cheese and banana peppers—what's not to love? Sure, tonight's dinner packs 940 calories and forty-eight grams of fat, but those details are on my to-ignore list for tonight. It would take hours to burn them off on the elliptical machine in the gym downstairs, but I've already decided that they're welcome to take up permanent residence on my hips.

I really need to invest in a place with an actual kitchen, but the last place I looked at was a complete nightmare. The zip code was great, offering a rental in one of those tall, sleek high-rise buildings full of chic condos. New Me liked the white and chrome—it made us feel sexy and sophisticated. Turned out I wasn't the only one feeling the *Fifty Shades of Grey* vibes. From the moaning and thumping echoing through the small space, the neighbors to the left were going at it. The Realtor and I both started giggling so hard that I was afraid I'd interrupt the guy's rhythm.

So now here I am, just me, my sandwich and I. A foot-long dick or margarita sounds like more fun, but I'll have to make do with carbs. When I reach my room, however, the door is ajar on the latch. Since I don't see the housekeeping cart, I ease the door open and peer inside, ready to jump back if there's an assailant hiding in the bathroom.

Nope.

No bad guy—other than the six feet, three inches of biker sprawled on my bed. Vik grins lazily at me as I hover in the doorway.

"You've got four porn channels."

"That cost twenty dollars each."

I step inside and shut the door behind me. I'm not entirely certain what to do or say, but since Vik has made himself at home without an invitation, I figure he has some kind of plan.

"How did you get in? Just out of curiosity?"

He lays his finger beside his nose and winks. "Trade secret, babe. I brought you something. Guess."

I'm sure it's no surprise that I suck at games. "An exercise bike so I can work off some of the calories you had delivered the other night?"

His gaze slides down my body. "We need to be clear on one thing. I don't have to hold back, do I?"

I roll my eyes. "As if you would."

"True." He nods. "So I'm just gonna say that you look amazing. Guess again."

"Flowers." I should be exasperated, but he's so fucking cute. He bounces on the bed, his eyes gleaming with mischief. Whatever his present is, I doubt it's as tame as a florist's bouquet.

He rolls his eyes. "Only roses I do are ink."

He leans over the side of the bed and lifts something up. "Voilà!"

He's brought me a cat carrier. No, *better*. He's brought me *my* cat carrier and that means—

"You stole my cat!" I'm pretty sure I shriek the words, but Bing's already meeping his own hellos and demanding that some human spring him from the carrier *now*. Bing has zero patience and isn't a fan of waiting. If he ever had to live in the wild, he'd starve within a week because he's not the kind of cat that could lay low, stalking its prey for hours on end. Like me, Bing prefers his food hot, tasty and delivered.

"Technicalities. I *sprang* your cat. Set him free. Reunited him with the one love of his life because I'm such a fucking romantic." Vik flops back on the bed dramatically, arms splayed out on either side of him. Whatever point he's trying to make is lost on me because his T-shirt rides up, exposing a chiseled stomach that demands licking.

I err on the side of caution and fly around the side of the bed to spring Bing from prison. Bing's all over me, too, like we've been parted for months and months. He rubs and purrs, and I try to pretend I'm just having an allergic reaction and not tearing up. When a tissue dangles in front of my nose, I take it.

Eventually Bing decides he's had enough of me (or needs to teach me a lesson for abandoning him to Mark's dubious charms) and disappears under the bed to check out his new kingdom. Vik rolls off the bed, saunters over to the table by the window. His butt in those jeans is a work of art. They should showcase it in the fine art gallery downstairs. Better yet, if he were on display, he wouldn't be reaching for my sandwich bag. He pulls my dinner out, unwraps it and takes an enormous bite.

"That's mine."

"I rescued your cat. I don't get a thank-you present?"

"Thank you." I grin happily at him—and stick my hand out for the sandwich. Hello. I haven't had dinner yet.

"Halfsies?" He gives me a charming grin, which is not what I need right now. Hell, now I'm going to have to share with both a biker *and* a cat. I'll be lucky to end up with any sandwich meat at all. It'll be all banana peppers and lettuce for me.

"How did you convince Mark to give up Bing? Wait. Back up." I'm missing a step here. "How did you know where I lived?"

He shrugs like it's no BFD. "You had to give your driver's license to Gia at Ink Me. And Mark the Douche may not be aware that he's a cat light at the moment."

"You stole my cat." I know I've already said this, but it bears repeating.

He hands me half of my sandwich. "That's a technicality. I left the back door wide-open on my way out. Just how much of a dick is your ex?"

Sadly, I don't have to think hard. "Huge. He's a dick of pornographic proportions. Twelve inches of sleazy man schlong."

"Then we're good. He won't want to tell you that he lost your Precious."

I'm not sure what he expects me to say. *Yeah, thanks so much for committing a felony on my behalf. I must be some sort of freak because I find it kind of hot, so maybe we can go knock over a bank or clean out Tiffany's before you ride away?* None of those seem appropriate, so I concentrate on my sandwich.

My *half* a sandwich.

Now that I've got Bing, I'm not giving him back. From the way he's wolfing down salami, I'm not sure Mark was feeding him.

"I can't keep a cat in a hotel room. I don't even have a litter box."

Vik points to the corner. "I brought supplies."

In my reunion glee, I hadn't even noticed the two large carriers from the pet store chain. There's even a giant plastic container of cat litter. I spare a second to wonder how Vik got all this up here. Or if he came on his bike.

"But I've got a better idea." He polishes off his sandwich half and looks hopefully at mine. Not a chance. I shove the rest of it into my mouth, and he snorts. "You don't like to share, do you?"

"Uh..." I work on chewing and swallowing.

"You're in luck, babe. I'm very good at sharing. You and Bing can move in with me."

I choke on the last bite of my sandwich. "You don't think that's a little too friendly? First you offer to be my booty call, and now you're offering to be my roommate?"

"I'll even put out for you." He winks at me. "Total friends with benefits."

"What?" I shake my head, pretending I'm not staring at his chest. He makes it so hard to think straight. "I can't move into some stranger's place. That's like just begging you to be a serial killer and bury me under the porch."

"Don't have a porch, babe. You're safe." He reaches out and tugs me down onto the bed beside him. This is dangerous territory. It's not that Vik doesn't take *no* for answer—it's that I'm all *yes, yes, yes* when I'm around him.

"We barely know each other," I protest.

I sound totally mature, like a grown woman making all the right decisions. Good one, brain. If I'd known he'd be here tonight, I'd have made a list of all the reasons why moving in with him was a really bad idea. In fact, once he leaves tonight, I'll get right on that. And this new plan of mine is totally working, right up until the moment he rolls over and props himself up on one arm. One hard, inked, super-close-to-me arm.

His bare skin is my Waterloo.

Worse, he tugs me closer with his free arm. My stupid, traitorous body rolls right up against him like we fit together. I'm always taller than most of the men I meet. Mark was two inches shorter, although he claimed we were the same height. Vik being built like a mountain, however, almost makes me seem petite. Okay. Not really, but we're a good match.

"I know you're fucking gorgeous." His gaze, full of appreciation, slides over me, and I swear I feel my clothing melting away.

"That's an outside thing, not an inside." I know I'm not making a whole lot of sense but I blame that on *his* outside. He's still way too gorgeous, and whenever I look at him, my brain stops functioning. Plus, now my fingers are sort of petting his arm, tracing the dark swirls of ink that wrap around one hard, perfect male bicep.

Biting him is suddenly way too tempting.

"Inside, huh? Too bad I can't remember our first meeting." He laughs wickedly when I pinch him. Guess he doesn't mind a little pain, either. "I know plenty about you, Harper. I know you like numbers, you count everything, you're way too nice for a guy like me and you're good with animals. Those are all good qualities in a roommate, although your being nice won't stop me from trying to score with you. I'll bet you're also the bomb at paying bills on time and doing all the organizational shit. I should probably be paying you, if we're being honest."

"You're good at this compliment business," I observe.

"You don't believe me?" He rolls and somehow I end up underneath him. This isn't a hardship, particularly when he eases my glasses off my nose and sets them down on the bedside table.

Still, a girl has to have her principles.

"You're a player. I don't think we should be talking about this."

"You don't have anywhere to live. You're looking for a place."

"True." Moving sucks, but getting summarily evicted with zero warning hurts even more. Playing by the rules hasn't won me the prize. I had a master plan and the execution seemed straightforward. Bachelor's degree from an Ivy. Master's from the same. Fill my 401K and my checking account, get a place of my own and conquer the career track before turning thirty. Stay at a prominent investment firm or start my own company—it'll be my choice. I'll find a guy who shares my goals and values and we'll get married. Settle down in our McMansion, discuss whether or not we want our 2.3 kids and when. I thought Mark was that guy, The One, and if he hadn't been my One and Only, he'd have certainly been good enough. Now I have to start all over again.

"So why not live with me?"

"Because it's really freaking hard to find Mr. Right when you're shacking up with...with..."

"Mr. Right Now?" Vik beams at me. "Not a problem."

He has no idea.

I push him up and roll off the bed before I do something really stupid. Such as riding him like a cowgirl. Or reverse cowgirl…yeah. I like that plan. Of course he follows me, putting my strategic retreat at risk.

"You really want to find Mr. Right?"

I stare out the window. The Bellagio has awesome views of the Strip, all blinking, whirring lights and waterworks. If I have to be homeless, this is definitely the place to do it. I shouldn't be whining about being out of a place when I'm here and so many other people are less fortunate.

"I do," I say to my reflection. "I really do. It's what I've been planning."

"And you like your plans." Vik's head nods in the glass. I think he might actually understand, not that it matters. He's not the one in charge of my life or my dreams, although I kind of like hearing that he doesn't think I'm crazy. Not that he's said that, but I'm reading between the lines.

"Being organized is important."

"I'm not looking for any kind of right, Mr. or Ms. I'm not boyfriend material." He plants his hands on either side of me. I could duck. I could go left or right.

I don't.

His mouth finds my ear. "Ask me what I'm good at, Harper."

"Do tell."

"Fuck buddy," he says roughly. "I'm the best toy ever and I don't even need batteries."

The man makes an interesting point. He's not my Mr. Right but since those plans are temporarily on hold…why not seize the moment? We can be friends. Hang out. Explore some sexy side benefits. Maybe he'll even take me for a ride every now and then, and I'll…fuck if I know what I have to offer. I'm solid and stable and way too boring for a man like this.

"You think too much," he says roughly.

"Impossible." I scoot around so I can see his pretty, pretty face because he's even more fun to look at than the Strip.

And then he kisses me, ruining everything.

Vik doesn't kiss me soft, doesn't lead up to the main event. No surprise that he's all in, his mouth taking mine in a hard, thorough kiss as he catches my face in his hands. Heat shoots through me as fast and high as the fountains outside. He knows just how to flip my switch and get me going. Pure animal heat. I've been kissed before but never like this.

I fist his hair, dragging him closer.

I've never wanted anyone more. Or faster. All the hot, painful, pent-up need inside me explodes as I kiss him back. When my knees actually go weak and I sag against him, he chuckles and lifts me like I weigh nothing at all.

"Legs," he whispers against my ear, and I shiver. I do what he says, or try to. His hands bunch beneath my butt, arranging me. Fabric tears because pencil skirts weren't made for man-humping, but do I give a fuck? No, I do not. My legs part around his waist and then I'm grinding against his dick. God, his dick is spectacular. It's as big and thick as every other part of him, and I ride it shamelessly. I don't care that I'm pressed up against the glass, giving the entire Strip a show.

Vik kisses me back like kissing me is the only thing that matters right now. His tongue leaves no inch of me untouched, stroking deep and then light and then who knows what the hell he does but it's so goddamned amazing that I pull at his hair, steering his head in search of more. He hangs on to me like letting go just isn't possible, and I like it. I like him. There's just something about this biker that makes *all* of me weak.

Or to be more specific, his hands *definitely* make me weak. One calloused finger traces the edge of my panties. The big, bad wolf is knock, knock, knocking at my door and I'm ready to beg him to come in and eat me up.

This needs to stop.

But…

He slides a fingertip beneath the lace trim. He's not stopping. He's…

A tease.

Because that finger *does* stop moving, and it takes all the willpower I have not to wiggle until it's right smack on top of my clit. And then I'd have a few directions for him. It wouldn't take long, not the way he has me worked up.

"Test ride," he growls, his mouth so close to mine that I could make him my own personal lollipop and lick him.

"What?" Proximity has short-circuited my brain.

"Take me for a test ride as your fuck buddy. Lemme show you what your new best friend can do."

CHAPTER NINE

Vik

HARPER STARES AT me like I've poured Kool-Aid into the Holy Grail and asked her if she was thirsty. Not sure if that's good or bad, but she's listening.

So I give her the truth even though my finger's inches from sinking into her hot, wet heat. Even though I could make her forget everything—my name, her name, the name of the fucking president. Almost kills me to wait.

"I'm sorry I don't remember you," I admit. "Got plenty of excuses but here's the truth. Forgetting is on me, not you. The fault's all mine, and I'd really like to make it up to you."

We're pressed against the window, my hands wrapped around her ass, and I'm begging. She's not just a woman I want to bang. I can't shove her panties aside and drive deep inside her, not without giving something else up. Don't know what it is or what it'll cost me, but I plan on finding out. I'm not kidding about being her fuck buddy. She doesn't want a relationship with me, but sex?

She's definitely gonna want sex with me.

"Give me ten minutes." That's nine minutes more than I need to make her come, but once won't be enough.

Harper looks at me like she's been stuck in a desert without food or water for the last month, and has just stumbled upon a Vegas buffet in an oasis. I'd love to be on her menu tonight, but I need some words from her first. *Yes, Vik* works. As does *Do me now, Vik* or *For the love of God, give me your dick*. I'm not particular.

"Why?" That's not a *no*—I'm almost in. And then she slides her hands around my neck, fingers tangling in my hair. I don't know what I'll do if she tells me to go. If I can't convince her to give me this shot.

"Because I've got a plan," I whisper roughly against her mouth. Harper fucking loves plans. If I whipped out a PowerPoint presentation, she might come on the spot. It's fucking adorable. "You want to hear it?"

"Is it a good plan?" Her fingers tighten and I hold still. Is she pulling me closer or pushing me away?

"It's a bad plan." I nip her bottom lip. "The very best bad plan ever."

Her grip tightens and she pulls my head back until she can meet my gaze full-on. It's fucking amazing.

"I'm sure a million women have told you how beautiful you are." She stares into my eyes, taking inventory. Don't know what she sees there because inside I'm a whole lot of nothing, but she sighs. A soft tease of sound and air that brushes over my mouth in an almost-kiss, reminding me just how close she is.

"I'm not sure you realize that there's more to you

than just your outside," she continues. "You're a good man, even if you try to hide it underneath all that ink and leather."

"I can't be your boyfriend. I won't be your forever man." Pretty sure I fucking growl the words, but her legs are wrapped around my waist and her pussy's riding my dick. I have zero fucking clues as to what she's talking about, and right now I don't care.

"Got it." She sighs. "You're a loaner dick."

And since I don't know what to say to that, I try kisses instead. I lean in, brushing my mouth over hers, licking at her lower lip.

"Harper." There's no way I forget her, not this time, not ever again.

If you've got amnesia, you revisit all your old haunts, right? To see if anything comes back to you? I skim a finger beneath the edge of Harper's panties, waiting for the memories to rush back. I've got nothing, nothing but a hot, slick path leading straight to temptation. Never has a man been more willing to fall. I stroke higher, taking my time because she feels that fucking good. How could I possibly have forgotten this?

"You need to know something," she whispers.

I stop moving, stop fucking breathing. Take my hand back. If she needs me to listen, that's what I'll do. "Hit me."

"This is just sex, and that's perfect, but I've never been big on one-night stands or quickies so I'm a little out of my league here and I don't want to disappoint.

Also? Seeing as how you're the hottest man I've ever known, I'm a little nervous about doing—"

"Shhhh." I brush my mouth over hers. "Anyone ends up disappointed tonight, it's my fault."

"Are you shushing me?"

"You want to talk afterward, I'm all yours. Give you at least nine minutes then, but this time is mine." I nip her lower lip, leaving the sweetest, pinkest mark.

"I'm timing you," she says breathlessly.

Her phone's halfway across the room, so unless she can count and come at the same time, I'm safe. Just to be sure, I ease my hand up her leg again, curving my fingers around her butt and then sinking lower for gold. I stroke the soft silky fabric of her panties. Christ, she's so wet that I can feel it.

"This is step one in my plan." I drag my fingers up the seam of her slit, circling her clit. She's been so good that she deserves a reward. Or I do. Fuck if I care if it means I get to touch her. "You got any feedback for me, babe?"

And then I kiss her before she can answer me, because it's easier for her to let go and get lost in the pleasure if she's not talking. Plus, I really love kissing her. I slide my mouth hard against hers until she opens up and lets me all the way in.

She tastes so much better than I imagined.

She tastes sweet and ripe as she comes undone for me, and I pull her closer, wanting everything. Her thighs tighten on my waist and she moans. It's not enough. I slide my fingers beneath the edge of her panties, move them over slick, wet pussy. She's fucking juicy. I need to lick her clean, then make her dirty all over again.

"Vik." She whimpers my name, making that one word into a plea. Yeah. I'll give her what she wants. I'm all hers.

"Step two. Gonna owe you some new panties. Take you shopping tomorrow if you want."

I don't wait for her nod—the cream slicking my fingers is all the permission I need. I tear that tiny tease of a panty off her and drop it onto the floor. We don't need anything between us. I circle her clit.

And then she loses it, which has to be the fucking dirtiest, most beautiful thing I've ever seen. She arches against me, bucking and grinding against my dick because now she's taking what she wants, and I can come along for the ride or not. I want to fuck her on the floor, on the back of my bike, down on the Strip in the fountain in full view of the entire world because this woman...

Harper.

She's everything to me.

Just for right now, just for tonight because fuck buddies don't last, but she's the most beautiful woman I've ever seen and she makes me feel like she sees me the same way I do her. I push a finger into her hard, and she takes it. She takes the next one, too, both of us leaning apart so we can see where we're joined together, my fingers stretching her obscenely wide.

Christ, she's tiny. It's gonna be a rough, hard ride.

She's close. Her pussy tightens on my fingers, squeezing hard, and I need to get my dick in her now. I'll give her all the orgasms in the world later tonight, but I have to be inside her this first time. Just to be certain, though, I press the pad of my finger against her G-spot. Her face scrunches up in an almost-frown, her body stilling.

"Vik—"

Gotta love the way she moans my name. I know lots of women believe the G-spot's either a myth or an optional accessory not all of you come with, but I'm a master hunter and I find what I'm looking for. I curl my fingers like I'm trying to stroke her from the inside out, and she loses it. She starts babbling something about seeing stars and she's not even looking at the goddamned sky.

She's looking at *me*.

I unbuckle and unbutton, shoving my jeans down just enough to get free and get a condom out, pressing Harper against the window with one hand and my weight. As if she'd go anywhere now. As if I could let her go. I don't care if the Four Horsemen of the Apocalypse come down from heaven promising orgasms and a million bucks, I'm not stepping aside. Not now.

"Ask me." I know my voice sounds hard and mean but I need her to give me this much. "Tell me to give it to you, Harper. Tell me you want this."

"I want you," she pants out as I roll on the condom.

Thank fuck.

I lift her up, bring her down and give it to her good.

CHAPTER TEN

Harper

THE RETURN TO consciousness is slow. In fact, if it wasn't for the cold glass pressed against my naked butt, I'd stay happily comatose for the next century or so. Unless, you know, Vik has plans for a repeat. I could probably, maybe bestir myself for another epic orgasm.

I bury my face in his neck and zone out for a blissful moment. He mutters something creatively obscene, and then he lifts me off his fantastic dick, cradling me against his chest. My back hits the mattress, but I hang on tighter to my man pillow. As awesome as the Bellagio's four-hundred-count sheets are, Vik's chest is better.

"Should I go? Or can I have ten more minutes?" The mattress dips as Vik follows me down. Not that I'm giving the man much choice—I'm attached tighter than a monkey to a banana.

"Can't," I mumble. "Need some time to recuperate, 'kay?"

He chuckles, a dirty sound that rumbles through my cheek (because I'm still pressed against him) and then down lower. I'm humming and thrumming all over, but particularly in my lady parts. Who knew I could come so hard? Checking the time is low down on my priority list, but I have a sneaking suspicion the man didn't even need the full nine minutes to make fireworks go off in my body.

"Can I recuperate with you?" He rolls us over smoothly, tucking a pillow beneath my cheek. My back's pressed against his front, his arm wrapped around my waist. I spare half a second to wonder where our clothes and the used condom went and then decide I don't care.

"Be my guest," I wriggle backward, getting comfortable. He groans, and things start getting interesting. Too bad for him that he wore me out with his super dick. My last conscious thought is that booty calls rock.

Vik slips away sometime between giving me an epic orgasm and sunrise. Not only does he feed Bing on his way out, but he draws me a note on the pet food receipt—a stick man with an enormous penis waving goodbye. So when he texts me later that morning, I answer. And then he replies, and somehow we fall into a routine of texting.

And it's not just sexy talk, although that part's great. Two mornings after our magnificent bang fest, I ask him what he's working on. I'm up to my eyeballs in client folders, juggling numbers, and I need a break. He takes so long to answer that I decide I've scared him off. Maybe dicks and the activities of said dicks are the only acceptable topics of conversation in the Vik-verse, but it seems weird to me. And then he responds. With a picture. A dozen blackbirds fly free from the tip of a black feather that's all thick, dark lines and shadows. "Take flight, my brother" is sketched beneath the flying birds, and then a pair of dates. I can just see the edges of Vik's rough, beat-up fingers in the shot. It's freaking amazing, but it's also sad and wild and those birds... Vik's birds are going places, and both the journey and the destination seem like they'd be worthwhile.

ME: Who did you lose?

VIK: Ink's for one of my brothers. We like to think Bingo's just riding on ahead scouting. Gonna catch up with him someday.

Sometimes you have to let people go. We both know this. And sometimes...maybe sometimes they're not gone—just riding up ahead and out of sight, and someday you'll turn the corner and catch up. I like the thought of that.

He wants to know what my day looks like, so I send him a selfie of me making crazed eyeballs over an enormous stack of file folders. He offers to swing by my office and help me clear off that desk; I counter by telling him that you have to have an appointment to get anywhere near my...desk.

He likes that.

After that, we just keep texting. Weeks pass like this and in the meantime, I pack up my suite at the Bellagio and move into my newly leased condo—getting Bing back forced me find something quick.

I know Vik and I are just friends with benefits, but apparently one of the unexpected benefits is having someone to talk to. *With*. Because Vik listens and he asks questions and…

Yeah. I don't know what I'm thinking, either.

We had wild, crazy, onetime, up-against-a-window sex, and I liked that. Okay. I freaking loved it, but I'm currently pretending that we absolutely didn't do something so publicly dirty. Or that I kind of want to do it again with my new friend. In fact, thinking about the awesome sex I had two weeks ago with Vik is what makes me late for work this morning. I've never mastered the fine art of jilling in the shower. Balancing and rubbing on all that tile in my new place isn't my strong point, so when the urge to rub one out gets too strong to ignore, I head back to bed.

I slide between the sheets, shove my fingers between my legs and start up a go-to fantasy in my head. I'm backstage at a concert, and the band's just coming offstage. They're all big and sweaty, adrenaline and power rolling off them because they know they've got an entire crowd at their feet and they fucking love it. But then the lead singer spots me waiting by the side of the stage and he beckons me over. We don't make it to the green room. He just yanks up my skirt and tears open his jeans, and then he's

slamming into me and we're perfect together. The rest
of the band is watching or walking on, and I know
other crew members and groupies can see us. But
the singer's mine.

I look up and realize it's no singer. It's Vik pounding into me hard, his eyes watching mine as he gives
me what I want. And I'm right there, teetering on the
brink of a motherfucking huge orgasm, my thighs
and my butt tensing as I ride my fingers straight toward the almighty finish line. Faster and faster, my
fingers rubbing and circling right where I need him
the most, and then what seems like the entire motorcycle club suddenly surrounds us, a band of brothers
dedicated to lending a helping hand, and I come so
hard that I see stars.

So I'm more than a little out of breath after finishing my ménage à moi. My new condo is also farther
from my office than before, and I'm still getting used
to traffic. It's a one-bedroom tucked into a new high-
rise. The walls are white, the carpet's white, even the
appliances are a gleaming stainless steel. I feel like
I've landed inside an igloo or some chic pied-à-terre
in Antarctica—and I like it. It's a fresh start while I
figure out who I am now.

Which is late. Very, very, inexcusably late. So late
that I have to sprint from the parking garage to the
elevator. Eighteen floors are barely enough to suck
in some air and check my buttons and seams in the
elevator mirrors. No woman wants to walk into her
office with her skirt tucked into her panties.

Even if it is a really good skirt. My Dolce & Gabbana

skirt hugs my butt and hips before flaring out over my knees. They make skirts in crazy prints like pineapples, fish and cabbage roses, but this one is a perfectly sensible, entirely professional black. The little black bow at the throat of my Kate Spade blouse is as much fun as I had when I got dressed today. Who's going to trust his bankroll to a woman wearing pineapples on her skirt?

I inhale, exhale. Today's going to be a great day. I've got this. The door dings open softly as I finish my affirmation. I love our office, and not just because it has the kind of steel-and-chrome good looks that star in architectural porn. Money has a smell. On a good day when the market's playing out how we predicted, we practically print that shit here. On a bad day, the senior partners scream at their junior mini-mes and head downtown to drown their woes. Being able to hold your alcohol is a requirement for scoring a corner office and a seat with the big boys, as is an advanced degree in bullshitting and spotting a market trend and riding that big boy straight into the money.

Finance is still very much a boy's world. Like a handful of women, I've muscled my way in and I'm allowed to stay as long as I bring in the green, but despite the ubiquitous presence of both a boys' and a girls' bathroom, finance is a male sandbox. It's just that possessing a vagina instead of a dick is no longer an automatic bar to entry.

Margie intercepts me as soon as I step off the elevator. My usually calm assistant looks flustered. "Your eight o'clock is here."

Rewind.

I had an *eight* o'clock?

Margie makes an apologetic face. "He called and scheduled last minute, so he wasn't on your calendar. He needs to go over his dad's finances and heard you were the best."

He's right but even I need some prep time.

"Give me five minutes and then show him in," I say. "Hit him with coffee and doughnuts or something. A nice bran muffin, courtesy of the house."

No matter how much money they have, people always like free food, and Margie's a goddess at smoothing ruffled feathers. If the newest client on the block is upset by starting at 8:06, she'll fix it. I grab the folder Margie holds out to me. Usually, Margie would enter the client's information into our system, but since he's a last-minute appointment, she hasn't had the chance.

I park at my desk and start flipping through the papers. Jeez. The client's reason for arriving in my office before eight in the morning is painfully clear. The father has some kind of military pension, an annuity, significant gambling winnings and a less lucrative penchant for day-trading. Oh, and a trailer in a park about a hundred miles outside Vegas—not exactly waterfront property.

Margie buzzes, our signal that I should come collect my new clients. Brain working overtime, I head out.

And stop short.

Margie doesn't notice I'm flustered because her own cheeks are pink. Vik has that effect on women.

"Mr. Ash Ilin and Mr. Serge Ilin," Margie says as if she's announcing the King and Queen of England. I practically hear trumpets and a twenty-one-gun salute.

Instead of a crown, Vik carries a cup of coffee. I wonder if the man has ever worn a suit. Bet if he got married, he'd hit the church in jeans and leather. Beside him, an older, more wrinkled and weather-beaten version clutches an enormous stack of doughnuts wrapped in a napkin.

"Thanks, darling." Vik gives Margie a big smile and she beams back like they've been best friends since the second grade. His gaze shifts to me.

Shoot.

That one-night fuck buddy thing we had? I don't think it's over. Completely inappropriate, not-safe-for-work heat stabs through me. And it's a total waste because whatever brought Vik here, it's not me. He's not jonesing for a repeat of our booty call, and whatever he wants from me, it's not a relationship. The man's a man whore, candy of the best kind, and I am officially on a diet.

Starting now.

Maybe I didn't make our onetime status clear. Maybe all the screaming and oh-God-more-now-please confused him. But he's super-cute with his dad.

"What are you doing here?"

"Financial things," he says cheerfully, and tips his head at the old guy by his side. "This is my dad."

Introductions are made, and I can't help but notice that Vik's father checks me out very, very carefully.

Not in a creepy way, but as if he's interested in more than my financial planning skills. He beams at me when he shakes my hand, declaring that he's thrilled to finally meet me.

Finally?

I turn back to Vik. "I'm still confused as to why you're *here*."

Vik winks. "I'm your eight o'clock."

When I said he needed an appointment to get into my...office, I was only playing.

Mostly.

The only thing worse than having a secret crush on a badass biker is having that same biker show up at your office on a Monday morning. Just in time... wait for it...for all the senior partners to walk past on their way to their weekly meeting. The suit parade slows to take inventory. Our clients come in all shapes, sizes and colors, and there's no dress code. Honestly, the only thing that matters is the size of your bank account and your willingness to let us play with it. But even so, Vik sticks out.

Polite surprise is etched across their sober faces. And while I know some of them cut up on their downtime, once they're in the office, it's game time. Our minimum requirement for doing business is usually a cool million—and Vik's dad has a trailer and a military pension. Unless said trailer is parked on top of a massive oil well or perhaps a diamond mine, I'm not sure how I can help—but I want to.

Vik rocks back on his heels—heels in well-worn leather motorcycle boots—and nods agreeably at the parade. He looks every inch the badass biker (except for the little old man accessory that he clearly cares about) and I can feel disapproval from my coworkers and bosses. Or maybe I'm just projecting.

"Let's go into my office and hash this out." I lead the way, pretending I can't feel Vik's gaze checking out my butt.

My office isn't a corner office—not yet—but it's nice. I've got a big black power desk and a pair of expensive black leather sofas. And since I like a little color, I've got a matching set of modern art prints I scored in a half-price sale at West Elm. Most important, however, I have a window. The view mostly consists of pigeons taking craps on the ledge, but it's mine, and unless I get promoted, I'll give it up over my cold, dead body.

Vik settles his dad—Mr. Ilin—in a chair and hands him the cup of coffee. Ilin Senior takes an enormous slurp of coffee and beams at me. "Awesome doughnuts."

"You're welcome." And he truly is.

"So." I sit down behind my desk. Texting is so much easier than this face-to-face stuff.

Vik flashes me a smile. "I really am here to sort out my old man's finances."

"I have it handled." Vik's dad sounds downright grumpy, so I don't think it's the first time they've had this conversation.

"Bullshit," Vik sums up. "You couldn't pay your rent because you'd stashed the cash underneath your couch. What wasn't there was tucked into coffee cans.

None of it was in the fucking bank where it belonged, so you wrote a check that bounced."

He has a point.

"Okay. Since you're a last-minute addition to my schedule, I haven't had a chance to review your portfolio yet, so let's see if I can get a sense of what your assets are."

The old guy pats his crotch. "Keep my assets right here."

Ooo-kay.

Vik clearly inherited his sense of humor from his dad.

CHAPTER ELEVEN

Vik

I MAKE HARPER NERVOUS. She fidgets with the folder she's holding and then twitches the sassy bow tie on the front of her blouse. Fuck me, but that blouse is killing me. The woman has a serious fetish for all things bow-tied and I'm torn between wondering how she'd feel if I showed up at her place wearing just a bow tie and nothing more, and asking her if she'd let me tie her up.

Or untie her.

One swift tug and that bow comes undone. It taunts me as she sashays across the room toward me, all long legs in that prim, black skirt. Am I hard? Fuck yeah, especially when she slides on a pair of glasses. Today's glasses are bright green, beer bottle green, grass green, fucking Emerald City green. A man can only hope she's got the panties to match.

"You got a different pair of glasses for each outfit?"

Harper opens her mouth, maybe to shoot me down, but my dad busts in first.

"So how long have you two known each other?"

Getting my dad here this morning took a combination of bribery and blackmail. Given his never-ending interest in my love life (which is nonexistent, unlike my sex life), I may have let him think that Harper's potential girlfriend material and that he'd be doing me a favor by giving me an excuse to visit her office. Given his unwavering interest in pairing me off, he was happy to help.

Harper looks at him over the edge of her glasses. "Is our being acquaintances a problem?"

"Not at all. You two make a cute couple. You want my blessing, you got it." My dad polishes off doughnut number two as he drops that conversational bomb, and I don't think the look of satisfaction on his face has anything to do with the maple glazed he just consumed. Nope. He's convinced that I've finally found me a girl—and he's not wrong. It's just that we're fuck buddies rather than lovers, and he's gonna find that disappointing.

Harper inhales sharply. Yeah, she's got something to say. "Your son and I are friends, Mr. Ilin."

It's cute how she pokers up. Unfortunately, her righteous indignation is wasted because with each agitated breath she takes, the buttons on her blouse gape. Her eyes sparkle with something. Ire, gas, sheer orneriness—I don't care. She's beautiful. Plus, there's no way I don't admire the show she's putting on for me. I lean sideways just a little. Can't quite tell if that's a beige bra or a white bra she's rocking.

"Eyes up here," she says drily.

See? I still blame her.

My dad nudges me. Any harder and he'd crack a rib. "Always listen to the lady you're dating."

Harper's gaze swings toward him, a look of complete *what the fuck* painted on her pretty face. She's not taking the news of our coupledom without some protests, it seems.

I stretch out my legs, my boots invading her space beneath the desk. She jumps like I've goosed her and glares at me. *Go along with it*, I mouth silently.

She jerks her attention back to the folder in front of her. "I'm not sure how we can help you."

I don't miss a beat. "I can make suggestions."

The look she levels on me is glacial. Christ, that just makes me want to warm her up. "Perhaps you should step outside while I discuss your father's finances with your father."

I shake my head. You know, just in case I'm no longer speaking English. "I stay."

She shoves her glasses farther up her nose and gets this cute, irritated look on her face. "Give me a reason."

Under normal circumstances, she wouldn't be wrong about asking me to leave. But these aren't normal circumstances. Sure, my old man mistakenly thinks that Harper and I are dating. He also routinely thinks it's 1955, that it's Monday and that he has a bank account full of dollars just begging to be spent. Oh, and he also hasn't filed a tax return in five years.

I lean forward, cross my arms over my chest. Harper's eyes fly to my chest and then shoot back to my face. Since we're at her work and we're not alone, I do my best to ignore her interest. I'll remind her about it later. What Harper really likes are numbers, so I'll give her that.

"Item one? He's my dad. That trumps everything as far as I'm concerned. We're family, so I've got him. Item two? He's been supplementing his social security by making personal loans to his neighbors in Happy Vegas Valley Trailer Park. And since he charges 27 percent interest, he hasn't done too badly."

"It's like them small incubator start-up thingies where you crowdfund crap," my old man says defensively. "It was practically public service, if you ask me."

"Item three," I continue, "he stores his profits in a fucking shoe box. For diversity's sake, he also has 'accounts' in his mattress, his bookcase and under his sofa as previously mentioned. That means he's got lots of cash, and no idea how to get it back on the books."

Harper visibly winces. I'm guessing that the shoe box organizational system is her idea of the seventh level of hell. She starts asking my dad a series of questions about how much income he's interested in seeing from his investments and how risk-averse he is.

I snort. My old man and risk are best friends.

For a few seconds, there's nothing but blissful quiet in Harper's office. My dad works on polishing off his muffin, and Harper works out my dad, shifting papers from one stack to another. Where I see a mess, she sees a goddamned puzzle—and she's about to fit the pieces together. And when my dad excuses himself "to find the little boy's room," I seize my chance.

I'm out of my seat and around her desk in two seconds flat. Yes, I'm crowding her. Yes, I have no intention of moving anywhere but closer.

"Space. Give me space." She swats my thigh without looking up.

Nope. That sure as fuck doesn't work for me.

I pull her up out of her seat, slide those glasses off her nose and kiss her. It's a quick kiss because I don't know how long my old man will be gone, but it definitely won't be long enough for the kind of sexual marathon I want when I look at Harper. Christ, she's gorgeous.

Since I have to work with the time I have, I swing her around, shove her folders to one side and plant her cute ass on the freshly cleared real estate. "Have you ever come on your desk?"

"What?" The look on her face is awesome—part cranky, part embarrassed…and part curious. Harper definitely has a dirty side.

"I'll take that as a no. Up." I tug on the hem of her skirt.

She lifts obediently before she thinks about it. "No, wait. What are you doing?"

"Showing you some friendly appreciation." I fold her skirt up to her waist because Harper won't be a fan of wrinkles. She likes her shit well-organized and pressed. She squirms, but I don't think she's trying to get away. More like I've got her off balance and she's deciding if she likes it.

Her panties are a barely-there scrap of yellow, the kind of thong that yields zero panty line. It's probably a purely practical decision on Harper's part, but I can see the outline of her pussy peeking through the lacy front like it's saying *hello*. Or *touch me*. I'm always happy to give a lady what she wants. I yank them off and shove her legs over my shoulder.

"You're gonna have to be quiet, Harper. Can you do that for me?"

She glares at me, but she doesn't close her legs. Of course, given the fact that my shoulders are now holding her thighs apart, shutting me out is gonna be difficult. But her face pinkens up and she's not saying *no*. Since we both know I'm always gonna listen to her, that's a big *hell, yeah* in my book. I get straight to work on making sure that Harper has a very, very good day at work.

She's already wet and slick, so somebody's been thinking naughty, work-inappropriate thoughts. I run my thumbs up her thighs and open her up wide. She squeak-moans, but she keeps the volume low enough that the rest of the office won't come rushing in. Good girls deserve rewards, so I kiss her.

I cover her clit with my mouth, circling it with my tongue.

She moans a little louder and promptly slaps her hand over her mouth. I forgot to specify staying still, so she starts wiggling and bucking around her desk as I tongue her. She tastes even better than I remember. I lick and suck, shoving two fingers deep inside her as I look for and find her G-spot. She moans my name and tenses.

Harper's not a screamer. We established that two weeks ago, when I fucked her senseless against the window in her hotel room. She just sort of melts, coming undone at the edges as she comes. She shudders and tenses and then makes all these cute whimpering noises as I kiss harder and deeper, making her ride my mouth until she's done.

She flops back on her desk, panting. She's all loose and relaxed, and she looks like she just had a midday orgasm. At work. When there are a million suit-wearing people walking past her closed door. She must remember that because about two seconds after I switch her brain off with the mother of all orgasms, she sits bolt upright. Guess the thinking part of her has come back online.

"Your father," she whispers, her face flaming red. She practically throws herself at me, trying to scramble off the desk. Since she's come and I've had my fun, I help her off if only because the way her legs wobble for a second makes me feel like a fucking king. "I'm at *work.*"

"Think of me as a fringe benefit." I pull her skirt down and retie the bow at her throat. I always put away my toys when I'm done playing with them. Her panties, however, go in my pocket. Since I don't get to come, I deserve a souvenir for later.

"He thinks we're *dating.*"

"Yeah." I scrub a hand over my forehead. Harper's scent is all over me and my dick's imitating an iron bar. "Got to admit that's a challenge, but here's what I'm thinking. We're friends, right?"

"Right." She stares at me, suspicion written all over her gorgeous face.

"So that means I have your back," I explain. "And you have mine. Right now, I need to keep my old man happy. What I really want is for him to get off my back about dating someone, so if he thinks we're a couple, problem solved."

"But we're not dating," she protests.

"No," I agree. "I'm not a relationship guy. I don't want to be your boyfriend—just your fuck buddy."

"And friends," she says.

"Friends who bang," I agree. I can hear my old man coming down the hall. He's loud, but he sounds happy and he's taking his sweet time. I suspect this is intentional—after all, we're family and he knows exactly what *he'd* be doing if the situation were reversed and he had a hot investment banker alone in an office.

"He's an old man and he's confused. He'll likely forget the meeting ten minutes after he leaves, so no worries. All you have to do is pretend for now. You do that for me, and I'll owe you one."

From the way Harper's eyes widen, she thinks *owe you one* is code for doing her right in the bedroom. She doesn't say no, though. She stays silent until my dad wanders back in and we resume our meeting.

Exactly thirty minutes after we barged through her office door, she's steering us back out. For two seconds I contemplate refusing to go, but that won't get me anywhere. Plus, my dad really does need her help—and Harper will rock what she does. She'd never settle for coming in second or third when she could be the winner.

"I'll do my best, Mr. Ilin." She pats my dad on the hand and he beams back at her, completely smitten.

I put my old man into the elevator and then I pause, running my fingers down her cheek. Nobody can see us here, not unless they pull the security tapes, so it's safe enough. She's earned the same respect I have when I'm on club business—I won't jeopardize her job.

"Think about my offer," I say. "Booty call. You. Me. Maybe a real fucking bed an entire night this time."

"I—"

She shakes her head like she's got no idea what to say to me. *Yes* works just fine.

"Bring the shoes." I step inside the elevator and let the door slide closed.

CHAPTER TWELVE

Harper

MEN THINK ABOUT sex a lot. Researchers have spent thousands of man-hours studying the issue, and it's a hard one, all puns intended. And so while it might be a stereotype that men think about sex 24/7, they definitely do it often.

And so do women.

Especially *this* woman.

Turns out I'm an overachiever in the thinking-about-sex department, particularly when it comes to Vik. Professionalism flies out the window, and when I work on his dad's portfolio, I daydream about having sex with him. Vik that is—not his dad. Freud would have a field day with that one. My week goes something like this: research investments for Mr. Ilin Senior, contemplate sweeping Vik away to Bora Bora, Paris or the top-floor penthouse at the Bellagio, and telling him he has no choice but to indulge in all my dirty fantasies because I've just earned his dad a million bucks. Drag my head back to the numbers on the computer screen in front of me. Rinse and repeat.

Don't judge. It's no more twisted (or likely) than all those billionaires-buying-virgins schemes that top the bestseller lists.

In reality, I put together a kick-ass portfolio for his dad, and then I do the same thing for ten other new clients. Yes, I've been a busy girl. So busy that on Friday, one of the senior partners stops by to congratulate me and let me know that *they've* got their eyes on me. I can practically smell the promotion.

Better yet, I outperform all my colleagues, which means that I win the Friday prize, a bottle of Veuve Clicquot. Senior management sees the prize-giving as a chance to foster a little friendly competition between us junior firm members, while doling out cheap pats on the back for another successful sixty-hour work week. The champagne's a fun bonus, but it's not the real prize and everyone knows it. There are five of us junior planners, and we're cheerfully cut-throat about the business of getting ahead. No one's going to kneecap me in a parking structure or poach my idea, but everyone wants to be The One, the junior employee who gets the golden invitation to join the big boys and girl at the next level. In this spirit, my coworkers hand me a package of straws to go with my new bottle of fizz, so that I can *better suck up*. I laugh so hard I almost pee myself.

I may not have scored me a badass biker, but my Friday drunky is now a sure thing. I grab my bottle and my things and head home. *Home*. My new condo still feels unfamiliar and sterile, like I'm camped out in a super-chic office or Airbnb. Instead of tackling the sadly small mountain of moving boxes (honestly it's more hill than mountain), I fill up my kitchen sink with ice cubes and submerge my champagne. I'm light on glasses thanks to the Douche's self-serving division of our household goods, so after I change into my pajamas, I end up drinking out of a juice glass decorated with red cherries. I'm not entirely certain that's a regulation-size pour, but down the hatch it goes. In the spirit of adulting, I drop a few raspberries in there, thus covering one if not two of the major food groups.

The three glasses of champagne I down in the next hour undoubtedly explain how my thumbs end up searching for Vik's contact info in my phone. I plan out my approach while I finish glass number four. The beauty of drinking and planning is that every idea seems like genius. Instead of a carefully weighted list of pros and cons, my thoughts gravitate more toward *why the fuck not?*

Remember how I said that women think about doing it, too? I'm all about sexual equality. In fact, the number of times I've fantasized about Vik this week puts me firmly in overachiever territory. Banging, knocking uglies, shaboinking… I've thought about it and then mentally mapped out the steps it would take to bring those activities to fruition.

Okay, fine. Maybe I do spend too much time making lists and outlining steps, but if I ever get my hands on Vik Ilin, I'll be making both of us happy. My phone buzzes in my hand.

Huh.

Some hussy has propositioned my biker while I've been thinking deep thoughts. I have no idea how this happened, but she's quite blunt and straightforward.

ME: U busy? If not, come have sex with me. Plz.

She has lovely manners.

She's also pretty shameless for someone drunk-texting at 11:50 p.m.

Under ordinary, less inebriated circumstances, I'd give that girl a standing ovation. Self-control's not her strong point, but she's identified a want and gone for it.

Fuck me.

What was I thinking? I've just texted Vik and tried to set up a booty call. You know how some corporate email programs have that nifty feature where you can recall an email after you send it because instead of attaching the business proposal your boss requested, you forwarded last night's home porn movie? I totally need that now for my texts. Sure, I pretended to be adding spontaneity to my life. But now that the universe is all *wish granted*?

I need a do-over.

A delete key.

An enormous freaking Magic Eraser to blot the last two minutes out of my life and Vik's memory.

11:53.

11:54.

It's like watching the countdown clock on a deto-
nator that's wired up to a ton of TNT. Any second
now, Vik will glance down at his phone and see I've
propositioned him. Courage seems like a great idea,
the ultimate personal high, an absolute must-do on my
personal bucket list. Now that I've taken the plunge,
however, I realize that the problem with personal
highs is the *plunge*. I'm free-falling off a fucking
emotional mountain and the ground's coming up fast.

11:56.

11:57.

I'm not good at waiting. Timetables are my friend.
Perhaps Vik is asleep. Or his phone is dead. Or he's
busy banging some other chick. No, scratch that. Perhaps he dropped his phone in the toilet and it's permanently ruined and he'll never, ever see my text
message.

Asking him to come over.

For sex.

I pour another glass of champagne (number five
for those of you keeping track at home). Of course,
he could simply be uninterested. We've had sex, but
maybe he's the kind of man who doesn't vacation at
the same property twice, no matter how fabulous the
first experience. Just because I'm up for round two
doesn't mean that he is.

12:07.

Sometimes you need to change your plans.

I fire up my laptop and get ready to go with Plan B:
retail therapy. I swing by Amazon, from whence all

good things come, and fill up my cart with a brand-new, designer wardrobe for a fantasy trip to the Maldives that will stifle the lingering humiliation caused by Vik's silence. Tomorrow, I'll empty the cart and replace its contents with the far more practical cat food and toilet paper deliveries that I actually need, but for tonight…I *totally* need a three-hundred-dollar silk sundress for my hypothetical three-thousand-dollar-a-night bungalow. For that kind of price, Amazon had better be including Chris Hemsworth or Pierce Brosnan in the box.

CHAPTER THIRTEEN

Vik

TONIGHT I WENT to church.

Don't look so shocked. It's a Hard Riders thing, a weekly MC meeting that every brother is expected to attend. Missing one meeting nets you a fine. The second time you ditch earns a personal, hands-on explanation of the attendance policy. Third time? You don't want to go there.

We're not big on rules, although respect is king. This means I've had my phone off for most of the night. We need to up our security, and doing so requires planning. Too many brothers have been shot at or taken hostage this year. Last time it happened, we got our brother back, but several of the Black Dogs MC had gone up on charges for the kidnapping, and it looked like shit might stick. Rev's old lady was making noises about it, too, because her brother, Rocker, was one of those who took a ride downtown in the back of a cop car. Stupid fuck had run drugs and guns. He's looking at some serious time.

The kidnapped brother didn't come out of it the same, either. He's making noises about reaching out to the other club now that they've had their come-to-Jesus moment with the law. Rest of us aren't convinced that the Black Dogs MC have given up on drug-dealing and the cartels. He keeps hinting he has leverage with the other club now that he's been up close and personal with them, but other Hard Riders suggested the *up close and personal* actually occurred with a Black Dogs hanger-on. Specifically, a hanger-on with a super-awesome, miracle pussy. That accusation led to a fight tonight and the argument still isn't settled.

Sucked to be my brother, though, if he's jonesing for a girl who belongs to a rival club. Some shit's just too Romeo and Juliet for words, and I'm not the only brother to notice because Prez has taken to calling him Romeo. I threatened to tattoo his new name on his ass.

Automatically, I turn my phone on as I head out to the parking lot and discover Santa Claus has come early.

HARPER: U busy? If not, come have sex with me. Plz.

Why I'm so tied up in knots about this girl, I don't know. Maybe it's listening to my dad ask if I've met someone. Or maybe it's because inking and fucking go hand in hand more than you'd think. Harper isn't the first to climb into my chair and then drop her panties. She's had a rough time with her ex, and she deserves some sweet in her life. Part of me still thinks hunting the guy down and teaching him some manners is the best idea I've had in a long time. The rest of me thinks we should just focus on getting Harper naked and wet. Get our priorities right.

Romeo shoulders me hard. "Are you buuuuussy, Vik? Or you gonna put out for her?"

"Fuck off." I keep walking toward my bike. Yes, of course I'm headed over to Harper's place. I like her, I like sex, so that's a win-win situation right there.

Romeo's apparently not done giving me shit, however, because he snatches my phone out of my hand. He has to be the biggest brother in the club, and he fills in whenever we need a bouncer or someone requires an ass-kicking. Still not sure how the Black Dogs got the jump on him. We wrestle briefly because I'm determined to get my phone back. I fucking end up on the bottom, too, because the brother's built like a linebacker.

"You gonna hang here?" Romeo laughs down at me. "Or you got other plans?"

He grins at me and reaches between us to shove my phone back into my pocket.

"My dick's got other plans for tonight," I grumble, holding back my own smile. "Don't get too close."

"So you're headed over to see the lovely Harper?" He rolls off me.

"Yeah." I sit up, checking to make sure everything still works. Harper won't enjoy me quite so much if I'm bruised. She likes looking at me.

Romeo slaps me on the back and reaches down a hand. "Who is she?"

I let him pull me up. "None of your business."

Not that she should be my business, either, but we've already established that I don't always do the right thing. Which has to be why I race to Harper's place. Lucky I don't get picked up for breaking every traffic law. She's got a new rental in one of those swank, super-modern high-rise buildings, the kind of place where the windows don't open because the people inside are living in an air-conditioned bubble. Not sure I see the appeal myself, but it's not my call.

I'm standing in front of Harper's door before I realize I probably should have called first. Or texted. Fucking sent a carrier pigeon with roses. Doesn't matter now because I'm here.

I knock. Then fucking knock again. And again. I'm about ready to text Romeo to get his ass over here and help me bust the thing down when she finally yanks the door open.

"Vik?" She sounds part horrified, part dazed.

What the fuck?

"You texted me."

She's wearing a pair of silky pajamas covered with a ridiculous quantity of pink and orange butterflies. The top is one of those camisoles that button up the front and the fabric's sheer enough that I can see the outline of her bra and the soft curve of her belly. Best wrapping paper ever for my Christmas present.

She crosses her arms over her chest. "An hour and a half ago."

"Didn't see an expiration date on your text, so unless you want to fuck in your hallway, let's go inside."

Her mouth falls open and I smell champagne and raspberries. "Excuse me?"

"I'm just keeping my word." Christ, I'm practically a Boy Scout. "I offered to be your booty call. You called, so here I am."

While she splutters, I lean down and kiss her. Our kiss is way too quick but gives me enough time to discover that she tastes like champagne, raspberries and Harper. Not sure what that is other than pure fucking heaven. Letting go requires more self-control than I'd like to admit, but I have plans and it's time to put them into action. Step one? I shrug off my club vest and then whip my T-shirt over my head. I do my best work naked, and something tells me that stripping down in a public place is guaranteed to get a response out of Harper.

Three, two, one…

Sure enough, she goes ballistic.

"You can't do that here!" She grabs whatever she can, yanking at me. Not sure what her objective is, but since it involves her hands touching me in about a hundred different, bare places, I approve. Fuck, she's fun. I start working on my belt.

"Inside," she hisses, hooking her fingers in my belt. Since my dick's huge and my pants hang low, she skims my goodies and jolts backward. I'm commando beneath the denim. While I try not to spontaneously combust, she reaches around me to grab my shirt and vest from the floor outside her door. Guess I'm gonna be her not-so-little dirty secret.

In it is.

"You," she snaps as soon as I'm safely out of the hallway and the door's closed. "You're impossible."

She slaps my chest with her hand, then stares down at her fingers lying right there over my heart. She looks surprised. Not sure if it's my ink or my muscles that's got her going. I'd play show-and-tell with her, but I don't need her distracted right now. Plus, I'm semihard already, so I have better plans for our time together.

I tug her into my arms and spin her around until her back's against the wall. "I'm fucking easy for you."

Probably should have brought wine or flowers or at least asked for a tour of her new place, but we've both waited long enough. Then I'm lifting her up, spreading her legs around my hips and pinning her against the wall. Only thing between my dick and her pussy are my jeans and her shorts, and that's not gonna keep me out of heaven.

She makes the cutest little growling sound in her throat, so I'm half expecting her to go for my balls with her right knee when she surprises me by going to work on my belt buckle. The leather slaps against my abs as she pulls it free so fast I almost get rug burn.

"Don't mark the merchandise." I nip her ear. "You spank my dick with that shit, and I'll get even."

She makes a scoffing sound, even as I wrap the belt around her wrists—loosely because I'm not *that*

much of a jerk—and pull her hands above her head.
I give her a moment to realize her predicament, and
then I lean down and kiss her.

She tastes even better than I remember, and that's
before she shoves her tongue deep into my mouth.
Not sure she knows I'm the one who's in charge here,
and somehow that just sets me on fire more. Fucking need this woman bad because until I'm inside
her, filling up that place she's got for me between her
legs, I'm nowhere.

So I kiss her back, going harder, deeper, until we're
pushing and fighting each other with our mouths because neither of us will back down. Our mouths clash,
all teeth and tongues, and it's wet and slippery, and
absolutely fucking perfect. We don't kiss pretty but
somehow we fit together. We're burning together, and
I don't need words to know that. When I pull back, I'm
panting, and so is she. We're belting out the same chorus of the same song, and it's all halle-fucking-lujah.
I'm not alone in what I'm feeling here.

"Tell me yes," I say. "Also? You got some fucking
specific requests, you make them now."

"Or what?" Her words come out in a pant, and
her tits are heaving up and down like we've just run
a marathon.

"Or you won't get a turn." I nip her unmarked
ear so that now she's got a matched set and drag my
thumb over her cheek. "And you won't like that half
as much as I will."

She glares at me but then she raises her hands over

her head and links them behind my neck. The leather of my belt rubs against me, holding us close.

"You suck," she announces.

"Duly noted." I can't help laughing. "But I do other things, as well."

She shoves at my shoulder, but I don't budge. I'm bigger than her, plus the way she's wriggling against me, I don't think she really wants me to go anywhere. Except down. She smells amazing, like cookies or vanilla, and her body's all sweet curves just begging for a good licking.

She bites my lower lip, and now I'm the one growling. "What was that for?"

"You made me wait. Don't do that again," she orders, looking completely unrepentant.

I shouldn't be this turned on. She bit me, for fuck's sake. Her pretty mouth forms a perfect O that just begs for my dick. My entire body jumps to attention, ready to make that fantasy come true.

"Say it. And don't fucking bite me again, or I'll bite back."

"Yes," she growls.

I twist a hand in her hair, pulling her head back until I have an all-access pass to her mouth. "You like this?"

Her mouth firms, but I'm not giving her a chance to fuck with me. I pull just a little harder and then I kiss her hard and fast, shoving my tongue between her sassy, stubborn lips. And she gives back as good as she gets, shoving against me and driving her own tongue into my mouth. She won't let me dominate her, and I kind of don't want to. I like this. I like the way she more than meets me halfway and won't take my shit.

So I kiss her while she kisses me, her nails scratching my bare back. Bet she's drawing blood. Bet she's inking me in her own way. I fucking love that I'll wear her mark tomorrow on my skin, but she's wearing too many clothes. I pop the buttons open on her top, yank down the cotton bra hiding her tits from me and get my hands on her nipples. I should probably take the time to appreciate her underwear but right now it's just in the way of my worshipping her right.

Because I'm gonna take care of her properly. Make her see the stars, a whole fucking galaxy of sexual pleasure—or just me. Sure, I'm getting inside her, but it won't be without benefits for her. Her breasts pop right out into my hands, the nipples tightening as I rub my thumbs over them. She arches into me, moaning another demand. Fucking love that she knows what she wants.

Me.

And I'm all hers.

Except she's not done talking or thinking, which is something I really need to work on because if I'm doing my job right, rational thought should have been discarded along with her bra. "Lock the door?"

"That a request or a question?" I squeeze her nipples, working them between my fingers.

"Do it," she moans.

Fuck if I'm letting her go, so I walk us over to the door, my hands cupping her ass, and flip the lock.

"We good now?"

When she nods, I set her down, her back against the door. I'm betting she won't be happy if I tear her cute little PJs off her, so it's time to strip. I shove her shirt down her arms, follow it up with the straps of her bra and then go to work on her shorts. I take a brief second to appreciate the hot-pink thong with a big-ass bow parked right over her clit. FYI? That's the best kind of X-marks-the-spot.

I yank my jeans open. Finding a bed seems like a waste of time when I could be balls-deep in Harper. Dick free enough, I grab a condom out of my wallet. It's not my classiest move but Harper likes feeling safe and I'd never do anything to hurt her. Her eyes get wider as I roll the rubber on. Taking her bareback would be something, but that's not for tonight.

She watches me as I suit up, her eyes following my hands as they stroke that shit into place and give my dick a warm-up twist, kind of like a competitive diver throwing in a bonus reverse tuck and a couple dozen somersaults because the judges are watching and that high score beckons. I don't need Harper to tell me that she doesn't do this kind of wild, crazy shit. She's as buttoned-up and cute as the pajamas lying on the floor, but buttons were made to be undone and Harper's fucking perfect. I love that she flies apart for me—now I just need her to do it with me. And like she's reading my mind, she leans up and takes my mouth with hers, kissing me for all she's worth.

So much for foreplay.

I open up, lifting her up. Her hands grab my shoulders, her legs going around my waist. You see that fit? We're absolutely perfect together, and I forget all about being her booty call or her one-time-and-never-again man. She won't forget this when we're over. I won't let her. I'm starting to realize I want something more from her, even if I don't know what that *more* is.

Not yet.

I raise her up and set her on my cock. Just the tip of me teasing that hot, wet doorway to heaven.

Goddamn she's something else.

Hottest thing ever, the way she moans and tries to take me. Right now? She'd let me do whatever I want with her. She's trusting me to make her come hard, and she's not wrong. I push into her, finding her clit with my thumb as she takes me deep. My balls tighten and holding on becomes a fucking torture mission. I work her clit in small, hard circles, and she bucks. Desperate for more. I slam home.

Harper's my kind of girl. She sucks in a breath—releases it on a moan that makes me wish we could go all night because goddamn she likes this. Her hips roll as she rides me, my hands helping her to find the rhythm that's gonna send us both over the edge. I can smell the sweet, salty scent of her and me together and I jerk my fingers away from her clit, licking them. Got to have my taste, and sure enough, she's sweeter than all the fucking cupcakes in this world.

I grab onto her ass, working her on my dick, and she exhales long and soft. And then there's nothing but heat licking through me as I drive into her, the whole world narrowing down to this one amazing woman. I want to make it last forever, but my dick's about to blow. I pound her hard, and she's slamming down to meet me, her nails biting into my shoulders.

She squeezes.

Holds me tight.

It's fucking game over for me and I shoot into her as she comes hard, jerking and twisting. Then she throws her arms around my neck, burying her face against my throat as she loses it. Her pussy clamps down, and I feel each squeeze and pulse as she comes hard. Never felt better.

Can't imagine what I do now.

I've had my share of women, but Harper's someone special, and not just because she's got a magic pussy that makes me come so hard that I'm the one seeing stars. Stars, the sun, the moon and an entire nebulae of shit I never imagined or deserved. Harper might be uptight, buttoned-up and way too *grown* up, but she's also a revelation. No way will I pull out and walk away now.

CHAPTER FOURTEEN

Harper

AFTER VIK BANGS me senseless against my own door, he decides it's time to christen every room in my new place. When I point out the ambitious scope of this plan, he suggests a compromise. He makes me come in each room, and then we end up in my bed. He steals a selfie of the two of us together (from the neck up) to send to his dad, who's still on Vik's case to date "someone nice."

Vik says I'm perfect for the job.

I'm not getting out of bed for at least a day. Too bad there's no Fitbit for sex—I'd have burned a million calories by now. Vik grins down at me. Having me sprawled beneath him appears to be his favorite position, although he doesn't discriminate. We've done it up against the wall, on the floor and doggy style. Right now I've got the best view ever of his gorgeous face. His eyes crinkle up at the corners because the man's that goddamned happy. Or possibly I'm blurry-eyed from all the sex.

"Let's do this again," he says.

Something throbs between my legs, either in anticipation or a warning shot that any more sex and I might be permanently broken.

"Can you die from too much coming?"

He drops a kiss on top of my head. "Not sure we should put that to the test. Sore?"

"A little." I roll over, burying my face in the pillow.

"You want me to kiss it better?"

"I'll take a rain check." There's no way I can hold back my yawn—the man has worn me out.

Vik freezes and there's this moment of awkward silence. Clearly, I've read more into tonight than I should have. Maybe I shouldn't have mentioned the possibility of a next time, but I was mostly joking. I know I shouldn't push for anything more, and frankly I don't know what I want.

Other than his dick.

Vik's dick is my favorite.

And I think I have some body parts that he's rather fond of, too.

"Not sure what's happening here, but I gotta tell you something," he says finally.

"Okay?" I'm really not in the mood for the letdown speech. Last time he snuck out, leaving a cute note. I'd like a little more than that, but I'm honestly not sure how much more.

"You keep calling me, and I'll be the best booty call ever. I promise you this, sweetheart. I'll be your best. Got an orgasm gift-wrapped, with your name on it. Helps to have a face to show my old man, too—

makes him happy to think I'm seeing someone nice. You want to do this again?"

"We can," I say slowly. "And I have to admit that I want to, but I've got to be honest. I'm in the market for a long-term, forever relationship, and that's not us."

He shrugs easily. "Yeah, I'm not into anything permanent, either, babe. Like I said, booty call. You call me when you need some, and I'll call you. It doesn't have to be complicated."

"So just until I meet Mr. Right?" Okay, so I sound less doubtful than I should when he proposes no-strings-attached sex. But his dick's amazing, and I like the guy. We could have fun together.

"That works," he says easily. "I'll even throw in a freebie and help you screen potential dates."

I snort. "You're going to play matchmaker to my Yentl?"

He rubs a palm up and down my back. My tattoo's healed and there's not a lick of pain now. "I'm not gonna get in your way, Harper. We'll do what you want on your terms. You meet a nice guy, good for you. You meet someone not so great, I'll be your own personal bouncer."

It's the craziest idea I've ever heard. But I like Vik, I like his penis, and it's not like I'll stroll out onto the Strip this afternoon and stumble over the perfect man. So why not enjoy Vik in the meantime? We're good together, and I think we could be friends. Plus, there's the whole incredible orgasms thing. The man's a total giver in that department, and it would be a shame to not take advantage.

"Okay." I'm weak. Completely, utterly weak. I blame that on the hot sex. "I'll call you. You'll call me. Somehow this will all work out."

He drops a kiss onto my forehead. "I'll be the best booty call ever. Just wait and see."

Yeah. There's no doubt in my mind that the man can deliver. I drift off to sleep, probably wearing a big, goofy smile because the man has fucked all the common sense straight out of my head. I've never felt this giddy about a hookup. That's never happened before. I mean, he's also my first attempt at casual sex, but I'm giving myself an A for effort. Letting him go would be disappointing.

When I wake up minutes, hours, who-knows-how-much later, there's a heavy, muscled arm draped over my stomach. I consider sucking in my belly because there's more curve there than I like, but on the other hand, Vik doesn't seem to mind. So I give up on miraculously transforming into a Victoria's Secret model and trace my fingers over the ink on his forearm. He has matching bands, dark geometrical scrolls of mandalas that circle upward from the tops of his hands. But because some things can't wait, no matter how beautiful he is, I shift his arm and make for the edge of the bed.

He grunts and rolls over. "You up? You need me to go?"

"Call of nature," I overshare. He nods, settling back into the bed. God, he's gorgeous. Because I've had my fingers in it for the better part of the night, his blond hair is tousled so he looks like some kind of sleeping bear. It cascades over his bare shoulders, almost reaching his chest. He snags my pillow, though, so it's not like he's a saint.

After pulling on his T-shirt to cover up my ass, I grab my phone and snap a picture. Some things are even better with photographic proof. I take care of my business in the bathroom and then step out onto my teeny-tiny balcony. If I twist my head and lean dangerously sideways, I actually have a view of the Strip. While I admire the sliver of pyramid that I can see, I call Brooklyn. That girl's got a sick penchant for running at the crack of dawn, so I'm betting she's already up. Sure enough, she answers.

When she picks up, I just blurt it out. "I had sex."

"Congratulations." She sounds faintly out of breath, so I'm betting she's getting her jog on. "Anybody I know?"

In answer, I send her the picture I took of Vik.

"You screwed the tattoo artist?"

"He's a biker, too, and he's freaking gorgeous," I point out. Strictly in the spirit of being honest, of course, and not because I feel like screaming or doing handstands because I, Harper George, have just banged the ever-living daylights out of a man who is very clearly a ten-plus on the hotness scale.

"Are you seeing each other?" Brooklyn's breathing escalates, so either she's just as affected by Vik's picture as I am, or she's definitely running.

"He's my booty call." God, that sounds weird. I mean, it also sounds downright fantastic, but this isn't something I have any experience with.

I can practically hear Brooklyn rolling her eyes. "You've had your hands on that man and once was enough?"

"We have an arrangement." I hope she doesn't fall over laughing. "We're going to call each other whenever we want sex."

"Wow." For a moment, she says nothing.

"Brooklyn?"

"I'm trying to imagine this," she says. "Which is fun but I'm also a little worried about you."

"Did you look at that picture? We should be cracking champagne to celebrate," I protest.

"Booty calls can be dangerous." She sighs. "It's like buying the ten-dollar box of Star Wars Legos with the super-cool Darth Vader and then suddenly you're upgrading to the four-million-piece Death Star set and every time you step barefoot on the carpet, you find another super-pointy, overlooked piece."

"Is Vik Darth Vader or the Death Star in this example?"

"He's trouble. Hot, gorgeous, bad-boy trouble. He's going to look prettier and easier until you take him out of his box to play, and you need to be careful you don't get hurt."

She's just looking out for me, I remind myself. "Duly noted."

"Okay." She sighs again, sounding a little happier. "But you still have to tell me all the details when we get together, okay? And you're buying since you're the one with the naked hottie in her bed."

We say goodbye and I tiptoe back inside. Or try to.

A big, hard arm swings me around and off my feet. "Morning, babe."

Turns out my biker is even better than that first cup of morning coffee. We end up back in bed so he can kiss all my sore spots better, and then he takes off to do biker things, roaring off on his Harley before I have to invent awkward excuses to get him to leave.

CHAPTER FIFTEEN

Harper

"WHAT ABOUT THIS GUY?" I point to a dark-haired man on my phone while we wait for the light to change. Phone Guy is wearing a well-cut suit, a blue dress shirt open at the throat and no tie. The photo's classy but relaxed, so I think he should go in my keeper pile.

Vik turns his head so he can peer at Bachelor Number Twenty-Two. Since I'm wrapped around his back and straddling his bike, he's got limited viewing options. I wriggle, trying to get comfortable. While he makes a very sexy pillow, the man is *hard* and not just in the dick department. We've been hooking up for the last month, and the sex has been amazing. Vik may not be my forever man, but he's definitely turning out to be perfect for right now.

Taking the phone from my hands, he makes a non-committal noise. "You like the looks of him?"

It's surprisingly difficult to explain why some men look okay when others look all wrong. So far, no one has ticked all the boxes on the Fuck Him and Marry

Him list, but I have time. And while I look, I get hot sex on the side. As long as Vik wants to be friends with benefits, I'm up for it. So far, the orgasms have been as mind-blowing as I expected and the awkwardness has been far less.

"He chose a suit," I point out. "But no tie. He's got a great job and he's open to settling down with the girl of his dreams."

"He likes outdoor sports." Vik lazily hands the phone back to me. "And his idea of the best-ever date is canyoneering in Red Rock Canyon. Are you up for a two-hundred-foot rappel? Maybe you should practice, babe."

I'm sure Vik means that I should practice my outdoor skills, but right now I have other things on my mind. Big, sexy, bad-boy biker kinds of things. I blame Vik. He's the one who came by my place and suggested we go for a ride. He followed up his suggestion by prowling straight into my closet to rifle through my things in search of "riding gear." I got a little of my own back by "helping out" with his plan to dress me like his own personal Barbie doll by stripping down to my panties. That led to a very nice detour on the bed, but now we're riding. Or stopping for every red light in Vegas, which is also okay because I'm not in a hurry to get anywhere. I shove my phone back into my pocket as the light finally changes and we take off.

Vik on his bike gets my panties wet and the bike is just an added bonus. I love riding. It makes me feel like I'm hurtling down the world's shortest, fastest runway and that any second now I'll achieve liftoff and fly. My feet have yet to leave the ground when I'm with Vik, but I have high hopes. He takes me up the Strip today, and even in the sunlight, it's a fun riot of color. It's also extremely congested, which gives me plenty of time to check out the various attractions. The fountains explode as we ride past the Bellagio and I laugh. Seems like the kind of thing Vik would have planned. The man loves over-the-top gestures. Maybe he plans on ending our night by riding off into the sunset.

"Four o'clock," he says when we idle yet again at the next red light. I look and spot a group of men in business attire. "Red tie, navy blue suit, closest to the curb."

I let my gaze roam over Blue Suit as my arms tighten around Vik's waist, my chin resting on his shoulder. Vik's wearing his leather jacket, and beneath that, his club vest and a black T-shirt. His hair's pulled back into a ponytail, exposing the ink that edges his throat. More ink peeks out from beneath his jacket and on his knuckles. This is one of those perfect moments that I'd like to bottle up or freeze so that I can take it out and remember it over and over again in a month, a year, a lifetime. Eventually, Vik and I will part ways, and then these memories will be all I have left of him.

He's so beautiful.

I concentrate on breathing in and out as I tighten my hands over his stomach. He's so solid, so very, very present. Maybe it's because he's built like his medieval namesake, but every inch of me is aware of where I'm pressed up against him.

"Why him?"

"That suit didn't come cheap." Vik shrugs. "And you see the way he pays attention to what his boys are saying? He'll pay attention to you like that."

Blue Suit crosses in front of us, ushering the older man in the group first. He's good-looking but not self-absorbed. Vik's not wrong about his attractiveness, but it's not like I could act on the recommendation. What am I going to do, pass out a business card like those guys who line the Vegas sidewalks handing out cards for lap dances and private parties?

"Two o'clock," Vik says.

"I only need one man," I protest, even as I look.

"You didn't want the first guy," he growls.

No. No, I didn't.

Fortunately, once we leave the Strip behind us, we pick up speed and Vik stops offering to hook me up. He's decided to take me to Red Rock. And since he promises I'll like it, I'm all in. After all, what's not to like about the desert, some cliffs and tons of wildlife?

We abandon the bike in the parking lot, although Vik grabs his saddlebags, slinging them over his shoulder. Then he threads his fingers through mine and heads past the obvious campsites. It's hot, the few tents and RVs almost visibly steaming in the after-noon sunlight. A few steps into our walk, he passes me a bottle of water. I'm not entirely certain if the benefits of hydrating outweigh the dubious charms of the campsite toilets. I much prefer doing my business in the Bellagio's marble stalls to squatting behind a manzanita bush.

Trust and promises of pleasure only go so far with this girl, however. The longer we walk, the more I want specifics. "Tell me exactly where we're going?"

The corners of his mouth quirk up. "You don't like surprises?"

He knows I don't. He teased me mercilessly when he spotted my paper planner. It's the deluxe Happy Planner model, and even though we're months from the end of the year, it weighs about ten pounds thanks to my liberal use of washi tape because I believe you can be both organized and pretty. Thank God he didn't spot my dream board when he rifled through my closet earlier today. I'd never hear the end of that.

"One mile." His fingers squeeze mine. That's the thing about Vik—he teases, but he also makes sure I always get what I need. He seems okay with my quirks. I take a moment to pause and set my Fitbit. This is going to be the mother lode of steps.

Vik's mile turns out to be more of an amble than a hike, if I'm honest. He takes me down a dirt trail, our hands still linked, and I split my time between staring at his butt and the scenery. The famous walls of Red Rock Canyon soar overhead, all stark rock and handfuls of scrubby bushes and grasses. I'm just starting to get into it when Vik stops, looks around and then steps. Off. The. Path.

Hello.

I've seen those movies, read those books.

You don't leave the path. EVER.

I dig in, planting my feet on the well-traveled path. Vik, of course, just grins at me. That smile of his… I'm in so much trouble.

"Problem, babe?"

I point to the trail (such as it is—it's not like he's taking me down a well-paved highway with sanctioned rest stops). "This is where we want to be, *honey buns*."

Every time he calls by one of his ridiculous nicknames, I'm trying on a new one for him. I Googled an entire list and have them stored on my phone.

He tugs lightly on my hand. "Trust me."

And tugs again.

Somehow, just like that, I'm following him off the path and into the brush. After our closet encounter earlier today, I'm ready to jump him again. But we have to establish some boundaries, and I do need to get on with my life. I can't keep letting him do whatever he wants.

But as always, Vik squashes all my logical objections simply by tucking me into his side. He blazes a new path, holding the thornier branches aside for me, and making sure I'm good. If I have to have an up-close-and-personal encounter with Mother Nature, this isn't a bad way to do it. Vik smells fantastic, too, all leather and man instead of the usual Burberry Eau de Toilette I breathe in at work. He hums a heavy metal tune. Since the last time he came over hum-

ming he left me with a Metallica earworm, I'm prepared today. I review my Disney princess knowledge
and get my Pocahontas on. Bet my rendition of "Just
Around the Riverbend" can drown out his rock tunes.

He shoots me a sidelong glance and hums louder.
I counter, and before long we're both shout-singing at
the top of our lungs. God, he's the best kind of jack-
ass. If there's any nature around here, it's completely
drowned out by our noise. Ryan Seacrest will not be
begging us to join *American Idol* anytime soon.

"Time to stop." Vik slaps a big hand over my
mouth and I nip lightly at his fingers. Gag me, will
he? I'm about to up the ante and bite something else
when I hear the water.

I push his hand away. "Are we swimming?"

He swats my butt. "You bet."

The swimming hole comes into view, the blue-
green water so clear that I can see the rocks on the
bottom. Vik drops the bags by the side of the creek
and shucks his jacket and vest, hanging them on a
branch. Then he hauls his T-shirt over his head. Pleasure explodes through me. I love watching him, the
way he moves so confidently, attacking life head-
on. And even though I should question the stripping-
down-in-public thing, I don't. I just stand and stare.

He laughs, the sound low and rough. "Get naked,
Harper. I've been waiting to see you all day."

He makes it sound simple, as if we're not outside
where anyone could see us. This section of the river
may be private, but there can't possibly be any truly

secret swimming holes near Vegas. It's too hot, the weather too perfect for a dip, for those secrets to be kept for long. And yet I start to undress, sliding off the cute, wine-colored leather jacket I impulse-bought online after our first ride together. I toe off my boots, peeling my socks off even more quickly because stripteases are for satin and silk, not moisture-wicking cotton. Vik's shed his own boots, and his hands work his belt open.

"Let me," I whisper, and his fingers still on the buckle.

"Babe?"

I don't want to be *babe* or *sweetheart* or any of the half a dozen other pet names he probably uses on the women who come and go in his life. I want him to see *me*, to need me the way I'm starting to need him. I drop to my knees in front of him and finish what he's started.

The buckle gives beneath my fingers, and then I'm unbuttoning his jeans, forcing myself to move slowly, to wait for his heated curse, even though I want to take him now, to swallow him whole and hang on to him, adding more perfect moments to my secret collection. I cup his balls through the denim. The hot, heavy weight fills my palm, a hard promise of what this man can do for me.

"Please," I whisper.

Vik's hands tangle in my ponytail, tilting my head back. He's fighting for control, but I want him all the way undone, and instinctively I know this is the way to do it. Just as soon as I undo the buttons, he'll be all mine.

I add another moment to my collection as I hold him, wrapping my palms around the thick, hard length, fingertips tracing a dirty song over him. He makes a rough noise, but it's not enough. I want all of him. I lean closer and exhale, my chin bumping against his dick.

He groans. "Stop teasing, princess, and open up."

I glance up at him through my lashes, letting him see the laughter and lo—no, the *pleasure* I have in doing this for him. With him. Each memory that I'm adding to an ever-growing string of favorite moments. This. Kissing him, touching him, adding a different kind of pearl necklace to my dirty collection... I want it.

I want him.

I press my lips against him and he freezes. There's nothing between us and if it feels good to me, it must feel even better for him. The rough curse he lets loose when I rub my cheek against him seems like a good sign. So I make him mine. I kiss my way down and then up, curling my tongue around the head, then sucking him like he's my lollipop. He really likes that—the cursing picks up volume and he shoves his hands farther into my hair.

Despite being on my knees, his hands fisting my ponytail and guiding my head, this doesn't feel like some kind of power play. I'm tight with desire—to come, to please him, to be his in any way I can. And while I'm tempted to slip into the water just in case anyone does come by, I also want to give him this. To trust him. To make this good for him, too.

"Harper," he groans roughly, and when I struggle to take him all, to relax and let him in, I see how much he wants this. Me. *Us*. He's so goddamned big that I have serious doubts about handling this, but I take him anyhow. I relax until my mouth's stretched wide and he's hitting the back of my throat.

He tugs on my hair and I look up. "Okay?" he asks.

I hum a little note of agreement and he groans.

"Fuck, Harper. You're killing me."

He's discovered my secret master plan. I suck and moan, letting him know that we're in this together, letting his hands on my head guide me. He fucks my mouth deeper, faster, harder, and I move with him, cupping his balls and stroking.

He yanks my hair, the sharp sting waking an answering pulse between my legs. "Gonna come, Harper."

I nod around his dick. Yes. That's my plan.

He moves faster, I suck harder, and then he's grabbing my face, holding me still as he comes with a violent shudder. I swallow and then let him go.

"Jesus," he whispers roughly, scooping me up in his arms. "Harper."

He looks a little dazed and a whole lot possessive. Happy, too, which is funny when I think about it because as much as Vik's always laughing and joking, I'm not sure I'd describe him as *happy*. I'm not sure he ever lets down his guard enough to be that. Whatever he is, however, he's definitely mine.

"Good?" My gaze flips up to his and he nods.

"Your turn." There's a wealth of dirty promise in his voice as he wades into the water. The water is beyond icy, but it turns out that Vik knows exactly how to warm me up.

CHAPTER SIXTEEN

Harper

MY RELATIONSHIP WITH Vik feels as if it's shifted somehow, even though we're playing by the same set of rules as before. He always shows up when I text him for a booty call unless he has club business, but that's just sex. Super-amazing, sometimes dirty, but always wonderful sex. I love the sex. And I trust Vik. But it still seems weird, although that's probably my inner good girl making a token protest. *She's* never had hookup sex before, so she just needs to practice some more and then everything will be fine.

God. The *practicing*.

Vik's the sexiest man I've ever met. Honestly, he's set the bar way too high for Mr. Right. Creativity, stamina and a dirty mouth—Vik's bad-boy accessories are perfect. It's almost enough to make me redo the mental job description I've been carrying around for Mr. Right.

Almost. Not quite.

Because there are moments—not all that often,

but they happen—when it's impossible to forget that Vik's a biker. And while the commission of felonies may not be part of Vik's day-to-day, he has club brothers who've served or are serving time. No matter how many Toys for Tots drives they spearhead, the Hard Riders aren't firefighters, Boy Scouts or good-guy material. They're willing to break rules they dislike, and no matter how many marks fill the *plus* column, the number of negatives outweigh them. I'm still getting crap from my coworkers about my biker client, and not one but two of the firm's senior partners made a point of swinging by my office to "see how it's going." Convincing them I'm not laundering money for a drug cartel is harder than you'd think.

So tonight I'm focused on dating. Dating *other* men. Fine, upstanding, suit-wearing guys who have their eyes on a corner office and a home in the suburbs. I won't find Mr. Right if I don't get out there.

I steal a moment to text Vik and let him know about the night's plans. Reaching out to him, though, is a mistake. I can't think about him without remembering what he looked like naked in my bed, his clothes dropped on my floor. It kind of makes me want to invest in new furniture—maybe a four-poster bed I can tie him to spread-eagled. And since I have no plans to bring tonight's date home with me, I really should take care of business now.

Dating feels like I've just stepped into the biggest, baddest all-you-can-eat Vegas buffet—too many choices, a super-long line at the door and my table's *way* over in the corner. Tonight's guy seems like a good bet, though. Swipe right, tap the heart…and then wait to see if he'd done the same for me. He had, and now here I am, getting dressed for a date that feels kind of like cheating on Vik.

Obviously, I'll have to stop sleeping with him if it looks like there could be anything between me and Mr. Tinder. Vik's assured me that he understands, and that our hookups will remain private, but is it something I should tell tonight's date about?

How would I tell tonight's date? *Excuse me, but I've got this awesome friend with benefits who happens to be a badass biker. Oh. You want to know why I'm not seeing him?* Yeah. It's a good question, but I don't think we could have more, something besides the smoking-hot sex and the comfortable rides. We're friends, but I want a lover, and then eventually, I want a partner. Whoever he is, he'll be the kind of guy who will take Bing to the vet with me—not commit a felony to get him back.

And yet I want to go swimming together and barbecue again.

I want Vik full-time, instead of whichever hours he decides he can spare me, and that would mean changing the terms of our deal.

So I'm not really in a dating mood tonight.

I'm still in my yoga pants and an old Cornell T-shirt with no bra when there's a knock on the door followed by a text on my phone.

VIK: Open the door

I shouldn't, but I do. Vik's lounging against the frame, phone in one hand and a candy box tied up with a ridiculous pink-and-white bow in the other. He hands me the box and then gently nudges me out of his way. Of course I cave, and it has nothing to do with the fact that he's brought me my favorite sea salt caramels.

Vik tugs on the hem of my shirt. "Exactly where is Mr. Tinder taking you tonight?"

I shrug. "Dinner on the Strip."

To be honest, I haven't paid much attention to the details. Vik holds out his hand.

"Phone."

I hand it over and he looks up the texts I've exchanged with James the Lawyer. He grins at me. "You need a wardrobe change."

"You don't think this is dinner material?" I smooth a hand down my pants. I'm definitely not rocking a cocktail dress at the moment, and I do want to send the right message.

Vik smacks me gently on the butt. "Come on."

He heads for my bedroom, and I trail after him. It feels sort of weird, since we're not about to have sex, but if anyone knows what guys like, it's Vik. After all, he's dated pretty much everyone with a vagina in the greater Las Vegas area. When I catch up with him, he's already rummaging through my dresser drawers. Things have gotten far sexier—and skimpier—in those drawers since Vik and I hooked up. Case in point? The pale green thong Vik's currently admiring. That barely-there scrap of lace made a big impact on my credit card statement last month. It's too bad Victoria's Secret doesn't offer a travel points card because I'd have racked up enough to fly to Bora Bora and back by now.

It's weird to think that we could have had our last booty call. That if tonight works out, I won't be sleeping with Vik ever again. I don't believe in cheating and an open relationship isn't for me, and I suspect that Vik has the same set of no-cheating rules. For all that he's a lawless biker who probably commits felonies with casual nonchalance, he's got a streak of honor wider than the Grand Canyon.

He tosses the green thong onto my bed, and then rifles through my closet with the expertise of a Nordstrom personal shopper. Of course, watching his big hands move over my clothes just makes me want to suggest that we ax date night and strip instead. We could get naked, watch Sharknado movies together and take turns getting each other off. Or maybe whoever comes last gets to pick the next movie. That seems fair.

"Hey." He snaps his fingers gently. "We gotta get you dressed before Prince Charming shows up."

"You're really okay with this?" I automatically take the dress he hands me. It's an LBD—little black dress—and there's definitely no room in this Kate Spade number for a bra. The silky material hugs my hips but the top blouses gently, hiding all sorts of sins. There are worse choices.

Vik tugs on the satin ribbon that ties around my

neck, checking out my tag. "You and Kate should get married."

We tease back and forth, him making fun of my obsession with Kate Spade, me pointing out that there are more sartorial choices in this world than black T-shirts and jeans. It's fun. It's familiar—and I keep expecting him to go, to leave before my date arrives, but he shows no signs of departing. I'm trying to figure out how to give him the boot when there's a knock on the door.

"Showtime." Vik rubs his hands together as he bounces toward the door.

"Hey," I hiss, grabbing the hem of his T-shirt. "What do you think you're doing?"

"Getting the door." He flashes me an innocent smile. "You should thank me for being so helpful."

"I think you're leaving," I say firmly. No point in beating around the bush—subtlety is wasted on Vik.

"So I'm headed in the right direction." His grin widens.

I elbow him out of the way and make it to the door first. I don't need tonight's date scared off before we even make it to the lobby. Vik grunts but lets me open the door.

The guy on the other side looks exactly like his Tinder picture. His navy blue suit is expensive but not flashy, as are the Ferragamo loafers. He's skipped the tie but gone for a dress shirt open at the throat. The whole effect is very similar to one of those gorgeous, slick Christmas presents you pay to have gift wrapped at Macy's.

"Hi. Harper, I assume?" He leans in and brushes a quick kiss over my cheek rather than sticking out his hand. Jeez. He'd better hope he has the right girl. I can't help but notice that we're the same height. In fact, with my heels I might have an inch on him.

"Nice to meet you, James." I beam determinedly at him and nod like a bobblehead as I step backward so he can come in. Bar meetings are less awkward and I make a mental note for next time. The odds of my finding Mr. Right on my first date are low, so I should learn from tonight's mistakes so I can get it right next time. *Kill me.*

Vik materializes behind my shoulder. He doesn't even try to be sneaky about it—he just stomps right up. James looks slightly concerned.

"Is this your brother?"

Vik snorts. "I'm her best friend."

Huh. That doesn't sound half as crazy as it should.

James looks a little uncertain but game. "Okay, then."

Vik leans against the wall, crossing his arms over his chest and pretty much blocking the entire hallway. "And where are you taking our Harper tonight, James?"

Unless he was hit by the amnesia stick in the last five minutes, Vik knows exactly where we're headed.

"I have reservations for us at Picasso."

Vik nods. "Harper likes the fountain. You want to show her a good time, you make sure she can see it, you feel me? Pretty fucking romantic watching the show."

"Hey." I'm pretty sure my face is moving from peony pink to flaming tomato red. Best friend does *not* mean Vik gets to act like my dad. "I can manage my own date."

Vik doesn't get the hint. "She likes shellfish. Steak so raw you think it's gonna fucking moo at you. Anything with truffles in it or sugar on it."

James smiles, and it's a nice smile. The corners of his mouth curve right up, the smile reaching his eyes. He's decided this is funny, and I can't really blame him. I'm starting to suspect that Vik would wrap me in a chastity belt if he had one handy.

"We'll get the biggest lobsters in Vegas," he promises easily. "Are we ready?"

Vik shoves off the wall. "How are you getting there?"

Jeez. "Vik—"

He holds up a hand. "Let the man answer the question, Harper."

"My car's out front," James says. "Mercedes-Benz C-Class. The National Highway Traffic Safety Administration promises Harper will be safe with me. It's got one of the best ratings for crashes."

"Are you planning on crashing tonight?"

Wisely, James starts heading for the door.

I follow him, snagging my purse from the side table. "We're done here."

Vik ignores me. "Harper's fucking priceless. You treat her like that, you feel me?"

"Absolutely." James pulls the door open and waits for me to go first. God. He's such a gentleman.

"Thanks for having this conversation with me."
Vik slaps James on the back. We're all bottled up
at the door, and I'm starting to get concerned that I
might never get to head out on my date (at least not
without a bonus biker chaperone) when Vik's phone
rings.

That's his dad's ringtone.

"What's up?" he asks as he steps away.

"Are you ready?" James presses his hand against
the small of my back and my new firebird, urging me
toward the door. He's right. We should totally take advantage of Vik's distraction to escape. I'm sure we've
got reservations and shouldn't be late, but something's
up from the way Vik's free hand taps out an impatient rhythm against his thigh. I can't hear much but I
know that Mr. Serge isn't in the best of health, physically or mentally, and Vik worries.

"Is everything okay?" I wait for Vik to hang up
and follow us out before locking up. James moves
down the hall ahead of us, punching the button for the
elevator and generally giving us some space.

Vik shakes his head. "My dad's had some kind of
thing. Don't know what, but Lora's driving him to the
ER because he's refusing an ambulance. She says it's
probably just heartburn, but we should be sure. I'm
gonna go meet them."

"I can go with you."

"I've got this. You go on your date." He pauses, and
for a moment I think he might kiss me—or pull me
into a hug. We're friends. It would be okay. Instead

after a few awkward seconds, he shoots me a careful smile and lopes toward the stairwell.

"See you," he calls over his shoulder.

So I go. I mean, what else can I do? And it turns out fine. Fine but boring. James doesn't have tattoos, doesn't ride balls-out, but he also doesn't judge me. Or fuck me up against a wall, kiss me senseless, make me laugh.

Turns out, a guy can wear a suit and still be Mr. All Wrong.

CHAPTER SEVENTEEN

Harper

VIK'S NOT MY loaner penis.

Okay.

He's not *just* my loaner penis.

He's not *just* anything. How do I know this? Let me count the ways. Item one: I'm reading his texts while I mainline my sad desk salad at work. Usually, I do a quick run-through of the major financial news sites while I work my way through two cups of arugula and a can of dolphin-safe tuna fish. Item two? I spent the weekend texting him and trying *not* to run over to his place to check up on him.

I'm not sure how his dad is doing, or if Vik's okay. He spent the weekend with his dad, which I totally get. The Friday-night ER visit turned out to be precautionary rather than required, and his dad's back home. Vik is still trying to sort out tests and doctors, but he claims everything is more or less fine. I'm not so convinced, even though today's text has me smiling, and it's not even funny. Or dirty. Or *unusual*.

And that's the problem right there.

My phone always starts buzzing at 12:01 because he knows I'll ignore him before I take my solo thirty minutes. At 12:01, however, he'll text What r u doing? and I'll text back. That's how our Mondays go. There are limits, of course, on the shareable stuff. I don't give him details about my trades or the investments I've set up; I don't tell him dollar amounts, names or personally identifying information. We're just swapping stories. He knows about Coffee Man, who never comes in without two Americanos clutched in his hands, and who gets progressively more jittery as our half-hour appointment winds to a close because it's time for his next hit. He laughs his ass off at It Girl, whose portfolio is entirely invested in the fashion industry—and who picks her stocks based on the contents of her closet. He tells me to give Weeping Widow a hug (which I can't, although she really needs it) when she dissolves into tears yet again because I want her to make changes to the investments her husband set up and she wants everything to stay the same even though it's already changed.

Sure enough, my phone buzzes with Vik's favorite question. What r we eating today?

I'm not adventurous when it comes to food. My standard Monday fare is arugula, tuna and feta. For 358 calories, I get 39 grams of protein and 2 measly grams of fiber. I went wild this morning and added a cup of blueberries because fruit is good for me and you can't have too much vitamin C and folate in your life. I send Vik a picture even though my Tupperware

hardly qualifies as food porn. Vik promptly counters with a picture of the taco truck parked outside
Ink Me.

There's only one response besides demanding he
run a bag of that goodness over here. I can hear your
arteries clogging from over here.

I've offered to make him a salad to take to work.
His whereabouts are unpredictable, I've pointed out.
There's zero guarantee he finds a food truck because
he's not always at Ink Me. He doesn't share details
about Hard Rider business, but he's frequently on
the road on his bike or out at the clubhouse. There
are things he can't tell me, just like there are things I
can't tell him. I suspect the key difference is that his
things could get him five to ten years in state prison.

We eat lunch together over our phones, texting
back and forth. When I ask about his morning, he
bitches about a rainbow and unicorn tattoo requested
by a college freshman.

Don't want to talk about that. U got ur next ink picked
out?

I suddenly know how Eve felt when the serpent
started pitching his suggestions. No, I haven't thought
about getting more ink. In fact, I'm still kind of getting used to the newly healed firebird on my back
because it's my first, it was a drunken impulse and
neither of those things gets much play in my life. But
maybe I *should* think about getting more. If the first

was so amazing, how much better will the second one be? Or the third?

I can haz rainbow kitten?

Google produces a truly astonishing number of rainbow-colored kitten images, and I send him a selection. You know. Just to torture him. His response is short and to the point.

Fuck no.

Alrighty then. This would be more fun if I could see his face, but I'll just have to make do.

What would you ink if it were your skin?

He fires back an answer quickly.

Kinda think it is my skin

Huh. That's not disturbing at all.

Brooklyn bangs on my door while I'm still trying to decide how I feel about Vik's inner caveman coming out to play. After I sad-desk-salad and text with Vik for thirty minutes, she and I speed walk around the block half a dozen times. Otherwise, as she's pointed out, we only get up to pee and we hobble like we're eighty. The mile we squeeze in also burns off approximately a dozen lettuce leaves and several bonus blueberries. It's a win-win.

I snap the lid onto my Tupperware, de-mute my phone and follow her outside, squinting. I usually don't see so much sunlight on a weekday. Good thing Kate's got my back with a pair of snazzy sunglasses.

I'm barely outside, however, when my phone goes off, Marvin Gaye's "Let's Get It On" announcing an incoming text from Vik. I should have stayed muted even if I am temporarily out of the office.

"Haaaarper." Brooklyn draws the syllables of my name out.

I concentrate on focusing straight ahead and resist the urge to yank my phone out and see what Vik's said this time.

Undeterred, Brooklyn pokes me in the side. "Is it your pet Viking? Show me."

Ever since Vik sent me a shirtless selfie (his jeans were partially undone as well for added biker badness), Brooklyn has hounded me to share. She claims it's selfish to keep all that hotness to myself.

Brooklyn makes a give-it-up gesture. "Is he wearing the boots today?"

We both take a moment to mentally appreciate the goodness that is Vik in a pair of motorcycle boots.

My phone announces a second new text.

I should get that. I'm sure I need another half-naked selfie from Vik like I need a hole in the head, but screw it. He's gorgeous, I'm weak and hearing from him sort of makes my day. I pull my phone out and we both stop walking, cupping our hands over the screen to see better.

It's a picture of his…stomach. Okay. It's *way* better than it sounds because the man's six-pack hosts its own eight-pack and that much smooth, hard, muscled man begs a girl to lick and touch. Obviously, I need to get a grip, but still.

Brooklyn lets out a little moan of appreciation, and I fight the urge to do a triumphant fist pump. That's *my* man.

Wait.

Rewind.

When did he become *mine*? Because he's totally, absolutely not and any unrequired liking or possessiveness on my part will end badly.

"You're so lucky." Brooklyn's finger hovers over the screen. "You've totally won the boyfriend sweepstakes. Send this to me? Just, you know, so I have something droolworthy for my screensaver?"

"We're not—"

Shut *up*. I start walking. God, I'm in so much trouble.

"Not what?" The mischievous smile curling the edges of Brooklyn's mouth warns me that I'm about to be given so much shit it would take me a month to shovel it. Hercules could clean up a dozen Augean stables in the time I'd need to deal with what Brooklyn's about to land on me.

"Not boyfriend/girlfriend," I grit out.

There's a brief moment of silence broken only by the usual cacophony of Vegas traffic (so okay, it's still really freaking noisy but *Brooklyn* stays quiet), and then she positively cackles.

"How's the weather in the Land of de Nile?" she

asks. "Is it hot enough for you? Because the two of you are a thing. An item. The world's dirtiest and most ill-kept secret."

"We have sex. Nothing wrong with that."

I sneak another peek at the picture he's sent me. He's sprawled in a chair, the phone angled away to take the shot of his stomach. I've got some bonus blue jeans (those buttons are my favorite) and...there's a rainbow-colored kitten cavorting with his belly button. The man definitely shouldn't be left alone with Sharpies.

"Harper." Brooklyn's voice is soft but insistent. "If you're not dating, what are the two of you doing?"

I shove my phone back into my pocket. "Hooking up."

"Uh-huh."

I'm not sure which of us sounds less certain—me or Brooklyn. And she's got a point. No matter how hard I try to spin it, Vik's not just my loaner penis providing physical release. Our hookup is becoming something more...something way too much like an emotional connection for my comfort.

CHAPTER EIGHTEEN

Harper

BROOKLYN'S WORDS STICK with me for the rest of the
day. And then the next day and the next day after
that. In fact, they hang around the entire week and
take up permanent residence in my head. What's up
between me and Vik? I'd like to pretend that I don't
know, but it doesn't take much thinking to figure out.
I'm falling for him.

I'm falling in love with my fuck buddy.

With my best friend.

With Vik.

Our deal was sex with no strings, a hot hookup
when we were in the mood and lonely. I should have
stopped as soon as *lonely* turned into *loving* for me.
Vik doesn't want my feelings. And honestly? I don't
want them, either. They'll spoil everything. Vik has
been clear from the start that he's all fun and no feelings. When it comes to saying three little words, he'll
always choose *on your knees* over *I love you*.

So when he hits my place on Friday night, I open

the door for him. I pretend nothing has changed and everything's perfectly fine. My feelings are my dirty little secret. I'll pretend I'm looking for Mr. Right when it turns out I've been holding him all along. And if my heart gets broken or trampled beneath a pair of too-sexy motorcycle boots, that's my problem.

I make it through the ten cartons of Chinese take-out that Vik adores. I make it through two hours and twelve minutes of the fourth Pirates of the Caribbean movie. And then in minute two hundred and thirteen, I lose it. Jack's cupping Angelica's face and he's finally giving it up, admitting he loves her, and it's so goddamned romantic and yet it's also about to be over. The shooting-each-other and fighting stuff isn't long-term relationship material and Angelica clearly has commitment issues, but I want them to just kiss and shut up. Kiss and be happy. Kiss and sail off into the sunset together to create baby pirates and major mayhem together.

Instead, they part.

"Hey." Vik nudges me. "You okay, babe?"

No. No, I am not. I want to crawl on top of him, wrap my arms around his neck and hang on like a love-deprived baby monkey. I want to stick to him, hold him, wrap myself around him like there's no tomorrow because it sucks to realize that tomorrow might have to happen without him and that I want so much more than sex from this man.

"I can't—"

The words get stuck in my throat. I should tell him that we're over. That I can't fuck my best friend anymore because it feels wrong. Because I've gotten too close and he hasn't gotten close enough.

"Hey." He brushes a thumb over my wet cheek. "What's wrong?"

"Nothing," I say, meaning it. I feel everything, and he feels nothing.

He grabs the remote and hits the power button. Jack's boat disappears as Vik frowns at me.

"Work too much this week?"

Now is not the moment for emotional revelations. Plus, I hate crying. Tears fix nothing; plans are far more effective. Unfortunately, there's no plan to make Vik fall in love with me.

"Maybe we shouldn't do this anymore."

He tosses the remote onto the coffee table. "Do what?"

"Us. Hooking up."

We're sitting in the dark because Vik insists movie-watching must be done in total blackness, so I can't see his face. But I feel him move. He scoops me up like I'm a delicate flower and then he's carrying me to the bedroom. Even when he sets me down on the mattress, I can't turn the stupid tears off.

He hesitates. I know he doesn't know what to do. I never cry, and we're all about having fun anyhow. We laugh together, but the sadder stuff is off-limits. He wouldn't let me in when his dad had that episode, and he's never deliberately let me see him when he was feeling down or vulnerable or anything other than him being a badass and rocking life. And I've kind of been the same way.

He doesn't say anything, but then he follows me down onto the bed, his arms hold me tight, making promises. I'm safe. He's here. If anything needs to be killed or hurt, he's the man to do it. And his mouth…

His mouth kisses away my tears.

He doesn't give me words, but he gives me everything else. He doesn't tell me not to cry. He doesn't ask why. He just holds me, and I can almost pretend that it feels like something. Like he loves me. Like he really, truly is my best friend and my partner and that he's got me. That the heart beating so steadily beneath my folded hands is mine. *Stupid.*

When the tears start to dry up, he kisses the corner of my mouth. And then my mouth. It's a soft kiss, his lips closed, just brushing mine. Letting me know he's here, too, and that I'm not alone. I could get used to kisses like his. Curled up together as we are, however, it's impossible to miss the way his dick tents the front of his jeans, big and hard. Demanding attention.

"Ignore him," Vik says roughly. "He's got no sense of timing, you feel me?"

Happy to oblige, I slide my hand from his heart to his dick because that's what we have, and I want one last time, one last set of memories. If I can't have forever, I'm stealing right now.

"Make love to me." I try not to cringe as the words leave my mouth. He's so big, so gorgeous and so distant. He nods slowly, but I know he thinks my request is just girl wording. That I'm really asking him to fuck or screw or bang me and not for anything more. He'd panic if he knew I loved him.

"You sure this is what you want to do?"

"I am. I do."

He looks down at me, his hands cupping my face. The kiss he gives me is sweet and quick, his lips barely skating across mine. I lift up, chasing his mouth with mine, and he chuckles. Bastard. Stupid, fucking, wonderful, not-mine bastard.

"You got it." He comes down over me, planting his knees on either side of my hips. We're face-to-face, but his mouth is too far away from mine. The handful of inches separating us is wider than the Grand Canyon.

I tug on his T-shirt. "Get naked."

"As you wish." His grin flashes in the darkness.

He looks happier now that the waterworks have dried up and we're back on familiar ground. And me? I want whatever he'll give me, which likely makes me pathetic. I need his skin on mine, nothing between us. He sits back, hauling the shirt over his head, and I watch his big hands work.

The shirt hits the floor, leaving him bare-chested. God, I love his chest. It's all sexy muscles and tempting ridges that ripple with power as he twists to consider his boots. Yeah. Those boots are a problem.

"Be right back." He brushes another kiss over my mouth and then rolls off me. He makes short work of stripping off the rest of his clothes and then he removes mine. He drops carefully back down on top of me.

I spread my legs, making room for him, and wrap my arms around him. And for a moment I hang on. I let myself forget that eventually we'll get up and go about our lives and I won't get to keep him.

"In." I reach between us, going straight for his dick.

His forehead creases. "Condom would be a good idea, babe."

"I'm on the pill." Since condoms are only 75 percent effective, I'm on the pill. Still, we've always used a condom. I've never given him the go-ahead to take me bare. I want to be his first for something.

He hesitates. "Let me touch you."

"Now," I insist. I don't want foreplay, not tonight. I don't want him to drive me any crazier for him. I just want to feel connected to him.

He pushes slowly inside me and I can feel my body opening for him. I don't think we've ever gone slow, and yet it's so good like this. Quieter, softer, but still good. Instead of chasing my orgasm, I just feel him becoming part of me. I feel his thrusts become deeper and harder, his hips slapping softly against mine as he grunts something that might be my name. I think he needs this, too.

"I love you." The words slip out of my mouth, and I don't hold them back. I need to say them. I need him to hear me.

"Harper." He freezes above me.

"I love you." It's the least I can say, and it doesn't feel like enough. Or too much because he's shaking his head.

"You don't love me. You love this."

And then he leans down and kisses me, cutting off the words. His kiss is rough and wet, raw and carnal. His teeth nip, demanding I open up, and then he thrusts inside my mouth, his tongue fucking me to the rhythm of his dick. He rolls, pulling me on top of him so that I'm riding him, his dick shoved deep inside me. Big hands cup my butt, working me against him in a dirty, sexy rhythm. I brace my hands on his chest, leaning down into him, because he's the only solid thing in my universe now, and then he gives it to me hard.

He slams up into me where I'm tight and hot and aching for him, making me gasp as he pushes inside until he bottoms out and there's no more room. I tighten around him, holding on. He doesn't get to leave me. Not yet.

He pulls back. Thrusts into me again.

Heat and fire explode through me, my body going ballistic. It loves dirty sex. It loves this man. He pinches my clit, his devilish fingers circling and teasing until I can't hold back any longer. He's watching me when I come, and because he may own my heart but he doesn't own my mouth or my head or anything else other than that stupid, stupid organ, I tell him the truth he can't fuck out of me.

"I love you."

CHAPTER NINETEEN

Vik

WHAT THE FUCK does Harper mean?

I love you.

We had a deal and nowhere in our discussion of friends with benefits and sexy hookups was love mentioned. The whole faux boyfriend/girlfriend was just to make my old man happy. But right now my dick's in control, and he wants to come, so come we do. I hammer into the sweet, slick pussy clenching around me, and try not to think. The tightness in my balls is all the feeling I need, fuck her very much.

She was looking for a long-term guy. I helped her scope out dates. I practically *gave* her away. *Goddamn it.*

I'm balls-deep in her and she's stripped away more than just the condom. I have no idea what to do next, so I make her come. I touch and tease until she stops shouting *I love you* and makes those cute but indecipherable whimpering noises that herald her orgasm. And afterward, I may sort of pull her close. I mean, we've reestablished our boundaries, right? When she said those words, it was probably just the sex talking. Or hormones. Pheromones. Something.

She rests her cheek against my chest, breathing hard. I probably qualify for bastard of the year, if we're being honest. She cried, and I fucked her. Cowgirl style. The only feelings allowed here are of the orgasmic, blissful kind. I know I'm an idiot for passing on the possibility of something more but that's me. An idiot. No way anything else could work out between us anyhow. It's not like I'm a white-picket-fence kind of guy—or the kind of man she can dress up in a suit and take to her company cocktail parties. I do dirty sex and I do it well. Really, really fucking well. Feelings, however, are not part of our deal.

The sounds of Bon Jovi's "Ride Cowboy Ride" fill the air.

"That's your dad," Harper says. I both hate and love how she knows that I've given my dad that Bon Jovi ringtone. It makes it harder to pretend that we're just sex and nothing else.

I grab my phone from the pile of clothes on the floor and answer. Apparently, it's my night for crying women.

It's Lora on the other end. At least, I think it's Lora. The number's right, but she's crying so hard I'm not certain. Could be some random stranger sobbing into my ear.

"Calm the fuck down." Harper stiffens by my side. Think she's about to rip me a new one for my lack of manners, but then Lora spits out the words she's choking on.

"Your dad's dead."

I turn my phone off when I reach the hospital, and I don't fire it back up for two days. There's no club business that needs me; Prez knows where I am and that I have personal biz. By the time my old man's been gone two days, however, I decide it's time to stop being such a pussy. I turn my phone back on, and watch the screen blow up with messages.

Stupid.

I delete the voice mails straight off. Nothing I need to hear there. The texts are harder. Got plenty from my brothers, reaching out and asking me if I need anything. As if. The practical stuff is harder. I deal with the doctors, the hospital, the funeral home and Lora. Shitload of other people come out of the woodwork, too, needing decisions about this, that and the other thing. And then there's Harper. She must spend every free moment she has texting me because my phone's at 317 messages and counting. The 317th is a fucking doozy—she's been threatening since 246 to track me down and verify for herself that I'm okay. Not that she thinks I am—that's clear. But that's what losing your old man does to you. I get through the first night by shacking up with Jack Daniels, mostly because I'm dumb as shit. Each swallow dulls the memories a little more, but it all comes crashing back in the morning with a souvenir killer headache.

I know Harper and I have unresolved shit, but I'm

in no mood to talk. Whenever I think about her, something twists inside of me. That call could have been about her. The closer someone gets, the more it fucking burns when they go away. By the time my phone lights up with message 318, I'm feeling really fucking sorry for myself.

HARPER: When's the funeral? I want to be there for you.

ME: Not necessary.

HARPER: I want to.

Life's funny—we don't always get what we want. Santa Claus isn't real, and he doesn't give a boo-fucking-hoo about hitting the highlights on Harper's wish list. I don't know what's happening between us right now—other than me avoiding the shit out of her—but I'm telling myself that the only *wants* I've got are sexual. Got a whole list of preferred positions and dirty fantasies she and I haven't worked out yet. The dirty dangle, doing it accordion style, the electric slide…plenty of shit we haven't tried. Or we could just redo a few favorites. She fucking mewls like a kitten when I do her hard from behind—I love that, too.

So what the fuck does she think I need from her right now? I'm not sure what I'm supposed to say. *Yeah, come hold my hand because I need…*what? We're just a hookup. Can't afford to be more. My fingers fly across my phone with a life of their own.

ME: I don't need a girlfriend.

My stupid, stupid fingers.

Harper doesn't text me anymore after that.

I don't bury my old man alone.

My brothers have my back. My dad might not have patched into our club, but he rode and he was mine, and by extension that means he's theirs. Too many fucking pronouns in that mix, but you feel me. Don't need their interference in my life, but it feels good to know that they care.

"You ready to do this?" Prez straddles his bike, hands on his thighs. Could be out for just any ride, but for the black bandanna around his upper arm.

"Yeah," I say, throwing a leg over my own bike. "Time to let him fly."

He nods slowly. "Okay to hold on, though, if that's what you want."

Doesn't matter what I want so goddamned bad because my old man's dead. I won't turn around and find him riding my ass, a grin lighting up his face because he knows he's got me. Old man loved to get a rise out of me. Might have fought over it, but I loved him.

"Let's ride."

"No one else we're waiting for?"

I make a show of looking around the parking lot. "Entire fucking club's here. You think I shoulda hired a brass band, too?"

Prez shakes his head. "Your girl not coming?"

"We covered this before. I don't have a girl."

Prez grunts. "You ask her to come?"

"None of her business," I say slowly. "She's not a biker, doesn't ride with our club. Got no place for her here."

Prez looks over at Romeo. "Jesus, he's stupid."

Romeo's nodding hard enough to fall off his bike. "You fuck it up with her?"

"You ever know me to have a long-term relationship?"

"The kind where you fuck the same woman more than twice and wake up in her bed?" Romeo asks me.

"Sure."

Prez looks me over. "He did."

"Some shit's off-limits," I say. No big surprise that they fucking keep right on talking. My brothers are worse than a bunch of girls when it comes to this feelings business. Must have some of that attitude written on my face because Prez hooks a finger in my vest and pulls me close, dropping a heavy arm around my shoulder. Fucking feels like the man's made out of iron.

"You think there's no place for a woman in this club?" he asks. "Because you take a good look around you. Some of our brothers, they've found themselves an old lady and they've been smart enough to hang on. Put themselves the fuck out there and get down on their knees if that's what it takes to make her stay. And if you think that's a weakness, you're dumber than I think. Those old ladies are the heart of this club, so that makes them the best fucking part of us. Sometimes it's easier to do your thinking with your dick, but they make us more. Make us better."

"Didn't know it was national poetry day. Don't see you wearing any old lady arm candy."

Prez cuffs my head hard. "Just because shit's sweet doesn't make it candy. You find an old lady, you do whatever you need to do to keep her. If fate drops someone into my lap, I'm gonna throw an arm around her and hold her tight. Not ashamed to admit that there can be more than a quick fuck. Sometimes, you meet someone who belongs by your side and at your back, not just under you."

"She's not my old lady," I say.

Not about to share my sex life with my club president. It's none of the club's business, and I'm not a porn channel he can surf. Sex with Harper was amazing. It's just that...Harper's looking for that shit, too. She wants forever and family and a goddamned dozen qualities I can never be for her, and not just because I don't own a suit. Some brothers settle down, while the rest of us ride on.

"Hear you," Prez says slowly. "Not a question of what she is now—because the answer to that would be *not fucking here*. More interested in what she could be if you were man enough to let her."

"Yeah, well, what if I don't want an old lady?"

"Jesus," Romeo mutters. "You don't want to win the lottery, either?"

Harper would not only know the odds on winning the lottery, but she'd know what came next, too. She never could wrap her head around my old man's love of scratch-off tickets. Said it would be just as effective to burn your dollar or use it as toilet paper. Plus, she'd trotted out all sorts of sad sack stories about winners who went bust or ended up worse off than before because a lottery win's a onetime thing and not an evergreen money tree you plant in your backyard.

"Harper and me are over," I tell them.

Prez mimes shooting himself in the head. "Stupid as fuck."

On that we're agreed.

It's time to ride, though, and so Prez stands up on the seat of his bike, hand balanced on Romeo's head. The rest of the club immediately shuts the fuck up.

"We're gonna say goodbye to a good brother today," he says. He adds a few sentences about who my old man had been, his service to his country and how he and Prez had met. They're good words, but I'm itching to ride.

My brothers listen, heads bowed in respect. Planting my old man in the ground had seemed too much like tying him down, so I'd had the body cremated. We'd let him ride, fly free over the highway he'd raced down so many times. I wait for the familiar stab of pain, and sure enough it comes. We'd had our differences, but we'd had our good moments, too.

We hit the highway at sunset, going balls-out as the desert stretches away from us on either side. It's a good night for a ride, and when we crest a little rise in the highway, I know it's time. I pop the lid on my old man's urn and hold it overhead, letting what's left of him fly free. Might be some people who think this is disrespectful, but he loved the road and the desert. He was happiest here, so this is the right spot to send him on ahead of us on his next ride. Someday sooner or later I'll catch up with him, and he'll give me shit for screwing things up with Harper.

I can't wait to see him again.

CHAPTER TWENTY

Harper

I'M SITTING OUTSIDE Vik's place having a painful moment of personal reflection that *Cosmo* promises will bring 100 percent personal growth, but which makes me think the universe is one sadistic bitch. Yes, I've come looking for Vik. No, he didn't ask me to be here. I'm torn between labeling this a gutsy all-in move on my part and recognizing that it smacks of desperation. I know he laid his father to rest today, or tried to. Not one but four bikers texted me. I want to be here for him in case he needs anything, but I've also been sitting outside long enough to realize a few things. The most important revelation is that I don't have a key to his place. I have free access to his dick but not to his front door.

And if I need any confirmation that today's been rough, he arrives in a truck. In the passenger-side seat. Vik hates letting anyone else drive, so he must be half-wasted. The biker doing the driving helps him out, shoving a broad shoulder underneath Vik's arm so he can steer him toward the front door.

"I'm unavailable tonight," Vik announces, bracing his forearm against the door. His voice is a liquid, drunken slur.

"You're unavailable every night," I point out.

Biker buddy just kind of shakes his head. He's built like a mountain, which appears to be a requirement for joining the Hard Riders, and his long blond hair has been pulled back in a thick tail and braided. He's got ink on his forearms, more on his throat, and I'm pretty sure that if I patted him down for weapons, I'd uncover a small arsenal. And yet despite the aura of danger he projects, he gives me a polite tip of his head.

"I'm taking over." I squint (no glasses tonight) to read the patch on his vest. *Romeo*. I hope the story behind his road name is happier than the original.

Romeo doesn't let go until he's wrestled Vik inside and Vik's not only heavy as a bear, but he's also distinctly uncooperative. He bitches and mutters profanities while Romeo sort of accidentally elbows him in the stomach and then transfers him into my custody when we're by the side of the couch. I score a head tip and then Romeo hightails it out the door. Smart man.

This is the point at which I run out of plan. My dress is a black-and-white-striped A-line number with a scoop neck. It stops an inch above my knee. I look cute—and all wrong. Black's the color for funerals, and he doesn't need *cute*. Not now.

"Why are you here?" he asks.

"Holding you up." To prove my point, I let go, and Vik promptly face-plants onto the sofa. "Or letting you go. Take your pick."

He rolls over onto his back, glaring at me. "Did you come here for this?"

This is the monster dick he cups through his jeans.

"I came here for you. You're more than just—*we're* more than just—sex." I drag my eyes back up to his face, needing him to understand. He looks so sad, and I want so badly to fix that.

"No. We're not." He yanks open his jeans and fists himself. He's hard. I'm not sure if I should be flattered or concerned.

And it's totally wrong, but I'm turned on. The adrenaline pumping through me from our almost-fight is heating me up in more ways than one. Or maybe it's because the more I watch him treat his dick like it's the world's greatest plaything, the angrier I get. We may have started as a booty call, but we've moved on. We're definitely something more, even if he doesn't want to hear anything I've got to say. On a scale of one to ten, our emotions are running at twenty, but even if he won't talk to me, maybe I can reach out to him this way. I know it sounds stupid, but that's my plan. I step closer and lean toward him.

"You're in my space," he growls, his hand moving faster. He's going to come without me, and I refuse to be left behind.

"Goddamned straight I am."

I slide my hand up his arm and cup the back of his neck. He doesn't pull away, so that's a green light, right? Plus, his dick is all but stabbing me in the stomach as he continues to work himself with his palm. New plan. I'll kiss that angry look right off his face. I yank his face to mine.

He tastes like the whiskey he's poured down his throat tonight. He tastes like Vik. I kiss him with everything I have until he yanks his head back from mine.

"Leave." The word comes out hoarse and rasping, like he's fighting for air. My own breathing sounds like a freight train, a heavy, panting whine. I need him so badly.

"Bedroom," I snap. "Now."

He gives me a look I can't interpret. Anger, need, rage, possibly homicidal intentions. And then he moves so fast I don't see him coming. He jerks me off my feet, and I'm flying through the air, a completely undignified shriek leaving my mouth. I land hard on Vik's shoulder with a loud whoosh.

"You don't get to give me orders," he snarls. "Not today, not ever. We clear on that?"

"Crystal," I snap in my best Colonel Jessup imitation, jamming the heels of my hands into the small of his back. Don't think Vik likes it because he smacks my butt with his palm. We've done dirty things together, but spanking isn't one of them and I don't think he's playing tonight. How can this be the same man I've held and loved? The laughing man is gone, replaced by a surly-tempered giant with a raging hard-on.

At least the hard-on is familiar. He storms down

the hallway to his bedroom, ignoring my attempts to spank *his* ass and see how he likes it. What happens next is equally familiar. He tosses me onto the bed and shoves his jeans down. Naked, pissed-off Vik is definitely worth looking at. This has to be why I'm not scrambling off the bed and sprinting for the door. The wide-open, not-locked, I-could-totally-leave-through-it door.

"Clothes off," he says, voice hard. "Or get the hell out. Your choice."

"Why?" I must have lost my ever-loving mind because now I'm just taunting him.

"Because I want to have sex with you."

Definitely crystal clear.

"Never mind," he says, and reaches for me. Arousal mixes with a sudden dose of adrenaline. He's my Vik, and yet he's not. He spins me around before I can figure it out and flips up my dress. Hooking a finger in my panties, he tugs them down.

I twist, trying to see his face, but his weight pressing against me on the bed like he's done so many times before. My heartbeat pounds in my ears, but the wave of heat that tears through me drowns out everything else. I may moan. I'm entirely certain I moan. This isn't what I planned but if it's the only way he'll let me get close, I'll take it.

He rolls forward, his weight pushing me deeper into the bed. His dick slides between my butt cheeks and I tense. He's huge, and while so far angry sex is checking all my boxes, other things remain firmly in

my no-fly zone. Like butt sex. I make an embarrassing squeaking sound and he laughs.

"I could make you like it."

He makes the dirtiest, most beautiful promises,
but kink isn't what I want right now.

"Not tonight."

If I have my way, we'll have plenty of tomorrows to
explore what each of us likes or dislikes. Vik brushes
a finger over my tight pucker. And he's right. It does
feel good, all that heat and need prickling through
me as I grind my hips into his mattress.

I twist my head, pressing my lips against his. If he
doesn't want to talk, we won't. His beautiful, sulky
mouth has a fresh bruise at the corner. He's been
fighting, and he's been hurt enough. I nip, harder than
I should. He grunts, deepening both our kiss and his
caress as his hand rubs my butt again, sliding back up
between my cheeks and pressing against my pucker.
Barely touching me, but I know what it feels like
when the big, bad wolf comes knocking at my door.

Good.

It feels good.

"Do you like that?" He rubs his erection against
my butt. *That* is a little vague, and we're in unfamiliar territory, but I've always liked everything Vik has
done to me. With me. For me. I nod enthusiastically
and he taps the back of my thighs.

"Open up. I'll make you feel better."

My knees know who they trust. Unlike my head,
they don't need to think shit over or come up with a

plan. They part slowly, but they hold nothing back. They let him have everything and anything.

A fingertip traces the seam of my folds, teasing. I whimper, trying to force him deeper. Vik's such a gentleman, because he dips his finger deeper and then strokes slowly up. Down. Everywhere he touches me I'm hot and wet, my body aching, begging for more. The tension builds, my body taking over because I'm about to come and I'm right here, bent over Vik's bed and on the edge of falling off into the world's biggest orgasm ever and—

He stops.

"If you didn't come here for sex, you don't need this," he growls.

Logically, I know I can't die from not coming. Vik, however, is looking at a death sentence because I'm going to kill him.

"This night going according to plan, babe?"

He holds me still with an arm at the small of my back when I try to wriggle upright. He is such a bastard.

"I came here for you," I hiss. "Not a hookup."

"This is all I have to give you, babe."

I hesitate. "I want everything you have to give."

He's wrong. He's so much more than a talented set of fingers or a big dick. I need to tell him that, make him understand, but he grabs my hips and positions himself at my entrance.

God, he's huge.

And impatient.

He shoves himself deep inside me, driving home, and fuck words. I scream, letting everything I'm feeling out. Being facedown on Vik's bed helps with that—the sound's muffled and it's just him and me. It feels good and it feels raw and I don't want him to stop. He pounds into me, creating a raw burn that becomes the brightest, strongest pleasure ever. It's like the night we re-met and he inked me, the pain and discomfort becoming a doorway I step through to somewhere pleasurable. I'm making noises and he's grunting, his hips slapping against my ass with each hard stroke. Right now, he's all mine.

And like the pain when he inked me, my anger changes, becoming something else. It's a connection, a feeling, a heated, pissed-off, burning, fucking fantastic sensation that I refuse to feel guilty about because it's not PC. He pushes me open, slamming into me hard and with none of his usual finesse. It's as if everything inside him has burst open, too, and now he can't or won't hold back. My head hits the mattress with each rough stroke, my thighs bowed wide, and it's so impossibly good.

He comes first, holding me wide-open as he empties himself into me, stretching me so he can fill me up. I cry out because he can't leave me behind, not this time, not when it matters so much that we go somewhere, anywhere together. But fuck him. I can take what I want, I can—

He pulls out, flips me over and covers me with his mouth. I'm dripping wet with his come and my own wetness, and I still want more. I ride his face and it's fast and brutal. He pushes me toward my orgasm ruthlessly, tonguing and kissing and sucking me. I come apart in seconds, crying out and squeezing his head between my thighs.

"Harper."

He says my name, and I'd like to think I hear other things in that one word. Things like *I'm sorry* and *stay* and *be mine*. But this is dirty hookup sex, not a box of candy hearts. I don't get my choice of sweet messages. I don't get his heart.

My dress is still up around my waist, and I've completely lost my panties. And my mind.

"This isn't a booty call," I whisper into the sheets. Then I say it again, louder, with different words. "This matters. We matter."

He looks at me and time slows down. I want to grab his shoulders and shake him. Kick him hard in the balls because maybe then he'll finally feel something for me. It's so stupid, wanting more from a man who's told me over and over that he can't. That he *won't*.

"I love you," I say and wait.

There's a long, painful moment of radio silence. I roll onto my side, and he lets me go.

"Fuck, Harper," he says finally.

That is so not an *I love you, too*.

His hand comes up, like maybe he's about to brush the hair back from my face, but I bare my teeth at him and he backs away before I bite his finger the fuck off. It's obvious that *can't* and *won't* mean *don't* and *never fucking ever.* So it makes no sense for me to stick around. To stick with him. He's not in love with me.

I get up.

I get dressed.

And then I leave.

CHAPTER TWENTY-ONE

Vik

WHAT'S WRONG WITH straight-up sex?

Harper's been my dirty girl, my fun girl, my one-night stand on fucking repeat.

Gotta love that.

I've never gone for seconds or thirds. I get around, but when I'm in your bed, I make sure you have a damned good time. Harper just got a little more of me than normal. Nothing wrong with that. No promises, no strings, no meaning. I don't know where she's got this idea that we should be something else. Why fuck with a good thing? Why risk screwing it up?

I think about this off and on for the next week. It's hard. Or maybe that's because after Harper walks out on me, things take on a fuzzy, dazed quality. Isn't that what all those stupid songwriters claim? That they're walking through rainstorms, fog storms, totally apocalyptic storms?

I just sort of want to see Harper again.

A lot.

I ink giggling college freshmen and have no one to tell. I catch myself drawing pictures to capture moments that will make Harper smile, but there's no place to send them.

She's just…gone.

And having just lost my dad, I've got more experience than I'd like with absences. I'd like to believe that someday, on some road, some place, my dad and I will ride together again. Problem is, that's not today and it's sure as fuck not tomorrow. I don't have a choice about that timeline and I'll have to wait, but with Harper?

I kicked her out.

I told her to go, and she did.

That makes this absence my fault. And when it's your fault, you can't just change your mind and, boom, you get the missing person back. But I wish I could. I wish she were right here, in my arms, and we were fighting or loving, laughing, living, inking—doing anything and everything instead of nothing.

CHAPTER TWENTY-TWO

Vik

TO WIN HARPER BACK, I need a plan. A really awesome, kick-ass plan. After all, Harper's almost as in love with her planner as she used to be with me. She loves forethought, organization and ten-step strategies for handling anything and everything. If I want to show her that I've changed and convince her that I love her, it's not enough to drop at her feet and start belting out the *I love you*s. I wouldn't believe me, either.

I'd insist on proof.

Lots and lots of fucking amazing proof that did *not* involve our bodies getting naked and exchanging dirty favors—although I'm totally making a list for our honeymoon. Yes, *honeymoon*. I'm dreaming big. And anyhow, the longer I have to fantasize, the more creative I'll be. It'll be like my really early, super-awesome Christmas present to her.

Huh. Now, that's an idea. I could make Christmas come early. Never mind that it's September, we live in Vegas and we have more palm trees than pines. My planning ahead should just score me bonus points. I whip out my phone and Google-fu nets me the seeds of a plan. You know that song "Twelve Days of Christmas"? If you don't, you're about to.

I kick off Monday by sending a prospect to Harper's work with an early Christmas present. I'd bring it myself, but she's currently pissed off and not answering my texts. Pretty sure I'll get shit from the rest of the club about my presentation, but I'll deal. Goolie certainly isn't happy about the big, pink box he gets to carry on his bike. Or maybe it's the even larger black velvet ribbon that took me fucking forever to tie. FYI, there are much better ways to spend an hour with ribbon. I'm hoping Harper keeps it and I can show her.

Inside the box is a planner. It's pink to match the box, and I nearly gave myself second-degree burns hot-gluing the black bows to the front. From the number of bow-bedazzled clothes in Harper's closet, I've deduced she *really* likes bows—so I'll give them to her. The inside of the planner, however, reflects my tastes. I've cut-and-pasted pages from the *Kama Sutra*. We can pick a different position for each day of the year.

Harper doesn't say anything.

No texts.

No phone call.

No fucking skywriter drawing my name and hers across the Vegas sky.

Sure, that last one's a stretch, but I won't think about failing. Losing Harper isn't an option. Since I have a bike and know where she is, I ride over at five o'clock to wait in the parking garage next to her car. Five o'clock becomes six and then seven. It's ridiculous how much she works. When she finally appears, it's almost eight and she looks exhausted. She also looks good enough to eat. Her pink shirt's got a bow sitting right over her tits and her heart, just pointing the way for me.

She doesn't see me because she's so intent on reaching for her door handle. Her face is strained, and she has the look of someone getting the hell out of dodge. She juggles an impressive mountain of paperwork as she points her clicker at her car. It's definitely intervention time.

"Babe. How was your day?"

She shrieks, paper mountain collapsing in an avalanche, and she points the clicker at me. Thank fuck it's not a gun or I'd be a dead man.

"You." Her eyes narrow.

"Me." I consider going in for a hello kiss, but her eyes promise that would just seal my death sentence. I settle for crouching at her feet and scooping up her papers. Gives me a real nice view of her legs, too.

"What is this?" She smacks me on the head with her new planner. She makes no move to help me in my collection attempts. That's okay—I've got no problem sitting at her feet for hours. Might eventually have to work my way up—with my mouth—but I'm a patient man. Mostly.

"It's a Christmas present," I tell her.

"It's September." The tone of her voice seriously questions my sanity.

"Christmas is coming early this year. That's your first present."

"There are more?" She sounds distinctly *un*thrilled.

I hum a few bars of the "Twelve Days" song and she groans.

"Are you here to torture me?"

"Nope."

"Then what are you doing here?"

"Giving you a heads-up." I grab the last paper, pat the mess into a vaguely rectangular shape and stand up. "I'm giving you the twelve days of Christmas and tomorrow's our first day."

"I don't want Christmas. I don't want twelve days with you. And there's no *us*." She stabs me in the chest with the clicker after each sentence.

I open her car door, drop the stack of paper inside and then hold the door for her like a fucking gentleman. I should paint my Harley white and pretend it's a horse and I'm a knight.

"What do you want, Vik?"

I keep it short and sweet. "You."

She's equally to the point as she drops into the driver's seat. "Fuck off."

Do you know the words to the Christmas song? Because whoever wrote that thing had the world's worst taste in Christmas gifts. Asshole definitely wasn't a Macy's shopper. The first day of Christmas calls for a partridge in a pear tree. Achieving this requires a minor felony on my part and takes the better part of Tuesday. I bribe one of the Bellagio's waiters for one of those silver room service domes and then I load it up with a nice roast chicken and a poached pear swimming in something alcoholic. More money changes hands when I reach Harper's building and it gets me inside to her front door. This is where the second felony comes in.

I'm naked except for the bow around my neck. Harper really, really likes bows. And dinner. And sugar. I'm just hoping she likes me most. I lean hard on her bell because this whole plan will go much better if she spots me before her neighbors do. It's twenty-four long, naked seconds before she opens the door. I count each one, which just goes to show how much Harper's changed me, right?

"Jesus." She stares at me and I refrain from the obvious jokes about not being a deity. Instead, I wave the tray at her.

"Surprise. Can I come in?"

Look at me using my company manners and asking instead of telling.

"You're naked." She looks a little wild-eyed. Also, her gaze may dip beneath my bow. She's welcome.

"I'm apologizing," I correct. "I fucked up big-time, Harper. I get that. You told me that you loved me, and I told you shit. You want me down on my knees? Because I can do that."

"What makes you think this is what I'd want?"

"Me? On my knees? I think you'd fucking love that, babe."

Generally speaking, groveling isn't something I do. Ever. And getting down on my knees only happens when it involves pussy and my tongue. But for Harper? Anything's possible. I drop down and set the tray down on the floor in front of me. This both frees up my hands and prevents her from slamming the door closed.

"Oh my God." Her gaze darts down the hall.

"Can I come in?"

"No."

"Can I apologize?"

Christ, she's fucking beautiful. My dick picks this grossly inappropriate moment to stand up and applaud her.

"Go." She points toward the elevator. "Just—go."

"I brought you dinner. It's a partridge and a pear. Not sure I worked out the 'in a tree' part, but I'm hoping you cut me some slack." I nudge the room service tray toward her, and for a minute, I think I've got her. Then she shoots the tray back toward me, zips inside and slams the door. I retrieve my clothes from the stairwell, get dressed and move on to the next step in my plan. I've got eleven more days, as I explain to the homeless guy I end up sharing the chicken with. We sit on the curb, picnicking, and I figure day one could have gone worse.

The second fucking day of Christmas calls for turtledoves. Since real birds shit everywhere and would disagree with Bing's digestive tract, on Wednesday I clean the drugstore out of Turtles and Doves. I take the whole lot of chocolate over to Harper's office at dark o'clock and let myself in. This requires smiling charmingly at her assistant, who's more than willing to let me wait for Harper in Harper's office. I keep my clothes on this time because Harper loves her goddamned job and I won't do anything to jeopardize it.

"Day two, babe," I tell her when she shows up clutching a coffee. Since I'm sitting on her desk, she can't exactly miss me. Figure I won't scare the shit out of her this time, either.

She jabs a finger at the sugar mountain stacked beside me. "What is this?"

Since she asked, I sing her the verse. "On the Second day of Christmas my true love sent to me two turtle doves and a partridge in a pear tree." I pause. "I didn't bring you another chicken, though. Didn't seem like breakfast food. Guess I could have gone for chicken and waffles. You want a redo?"

She rubs her temples. "Why are you here? Why do you think I'd want you here?"

"I know what you like." The trick is to sound confident. Remember what I said before? Harper. Forgiveness. Another chance. That's all that matters.

"How do ten thousand calories reflect your greater understanding of me?"

"You like candy. You like laughing. You have an awesome fucking sense of humor."

Harper stares at me like I've lost my mind. Which I may have. My dad would have smacked me upside my head, and he'd have been right. Of course, he'd also have laughed his ass off—and then he'd have suggested that we fill Harper's office to the ceiling with candy. Go big or go home, right?

Thinking about him hurts just a little less today, although it still feels like getting a root canal with no drugs. And possibly using a shovel to do the digging around in my gums. Or my heart.

Harper braces her hip against her desk. She hums a bit of the song. "You're really doing the entire song?"

"You bet." And because I'm all in and dignity has gone out the window already, I start belting it out at the top of my lungs. I hop off the desk, grab her hands and dance her around in circles. I even throw in a few pelvis thrusts.

"Oh God. Stop." She's giggling, though. She doesn't look pissed off anymore. She looks...happy.

I stop.

"You want me to strip? I'll give you breakfast and a show."

Don't think I didn't plan for this. Thanks to the staying power of the Sharpie, I've drawn a hundred big, black, loopy bows on the Calvin Kleins I bought precisely for this occasion.

Harper slaps a hand over my mouth. "Not in my office."

"Where?"

This seems promising. Like hot-makeup-sex promising.

"You need to go." She starts shoving boxes of chocolate underneath her desk. She must have an early meeting.

"I'll go if you promise to read the plan I've put together and go over it with me tomorrow."

She pauses in her candy cleanup. "You want me to go over your plan?"

I go with the truth.

"You like plans. You like to know where things are going. So I made one for us."

Honestly? What I want is for her to go out on a date with me. Make love with me. Ride with me, fight with me, love me. It's that last part of the plan that's most important.

She stares at me.

Pretty sure she's trying to figure out the fastest way to get my ass out of her office because she comes to the obvious conclusions.

She gives in.

"Okay." She scowls. "But you have to wait until Saturday. Some of us have bosses that care if we show up."

I ignore the dig because I'm one step closer to my goal. To *Harper*.

Thursday the song calls for three French hens. In retrospect, I should have gone with "99 Bottles of Beer on the Wall." Courting would have been much simpler. Finding French hens in Vegas is every bit as difficult as you think. The only reason I don't visit a damned pet store is that Bing would either vote me off the island or have lunch. Instead of wildlife, I send a six-pack of beer from a brewery that does a Twelve Days of Christmas series. I scribble a note that's three-quarters picture, one-quarter words. The picture is me trying to tree three very reluctant hens in a palm. I think for a minute and then go with more truth. I tell her how much I want to be with her to celebrate all her milestones. And how I'll be there if she lets me for the shitty days, as well, but with an even bigger beer.

Friday I up my game and actually produce four calling birds. Okay. So she doesn't get to take them home with her, but I think she'll like this better. I adopt four black-and-white penguins at the zoo on her behalf. Since my large check comes with naming rights, I christen them Harpsichord, Harpie, Doodle and Monster Dick.

Today, however, is Saturday.

D-Day.

And either Armageddon or the second coming of Christ when I succeed or fail at convincing Harper to take me back. And yes, I'm feeling the pressure. It may have taken me way too long to realize what I feel for Harper, but now I'm hopelessly, headlong in love with her, and she's the only woman for me.

I pick her up and she settles behind me, her arms wrapped around my waist. See how we fit together? The way we move together as we ride down the Strip?

That's the best fucking sign right there.

I just need to convince Harper. When we get to the Bellagio, I pull over. I've got a buddy who owes me and I'm cashing in all my favors.

"You're going to get a parking ticket." Harper's forehead gets these cute little creases when she's trying to figure out what I'm up to.

"Watch." I switch places with her on the bike because I need to hold her.

Her frown gets deeper. "The fountain show doesn't go off for another eleven minutes, Vik."

I slide my arms around her. How can I not hold on to this woman? Not only is she fucking gorgeous, but she's the smartest person I've ever met. She's organized, funny and has a dirty streak that will make me a very happy man.

"Three," I whisper against her hair.

"You're not singing again, are you?"

She doesn't pull away, and I almost get distracted by the amazing way she smells.

"Two."

I kiss her ear just because it's there and I'm weak. Christ, I love every inch of her. Her hair's pulled back in a ponytail that begs for me to fist it.

"One." I bite down lightly because some things won't change.

She rewards me with a little moan—just as the fountains explode. Timing is everything. The water soars upward, "Twelve Days of Christmas" blaring from the hotel's speakers. While she stares slack-jawed at the show, I scoop her up and stride over to the fountains. By the time I've planted her ass on the railing and caged her in with my arms, she's coming back to her senses.

"You planned this?" She sounds dazed.

Mission fucking accomplished.

"You said I never planned anything. That I never

looked ahead. I just never had anyone I wanted to plan for."

"And now?" She licks her lips. I don't think she likes having nothing between her ass and an entire lake but me and a very thin railing. I'd like to tell you that I immediately set her back on her feet, but that would be untrue. I love having her off balance and hanging on to me. I won't ever let her fall.

"I'm hoping I've got you." I wrap my arms around her back, pulling her closer. "You're my tomorrow and my tomorrow after that. Give me a chance to prove that to you for the next sixty years or so."

"Vik?"

"Yeah, babe?"

"I forgive you. Can you let me down now?"

She *really* doesn't like her current position, does she? I take shameless advantage.

"Wrap your legs around me."

She does, and I can't stop myself from patting her ass as I twirl her around in the biggest goddamned circle. Tourists are looking at us like maybe we're an act and they should drop a quarter in our hat. Let them look. I'm holding all I need.

Well, except for one teeny tiny detail.

"Did you bring the planner I gave you?"

"Yes?" She sounds a little breathless. I slide her down my body, making sure I touch every smoking-hot inch of her.

"Take it out."

She gives me a look. I'm gonna become really familiar with that look over the coming years if I'm lucky. That look says we're in public and I just said something filthy. Still, she fishes the hot-pink planner out of her purse and hands it to me.

"Did you read my plans for us?" I drop down onto a bench. The fountain show is wrapping up, and my friend is probably getting all kinds of shit for his off-script performance. I'll make it up to him later.

Harper flushes. "I read through October. You have a filthy imagination and no one could possibly have that much sex."

I look forward to proving her wrong.

"We wouldn't work," she says, shaking her head. "I like rules and plans and sticking to one path. You may want me right now, but at some point—"

"We can argue over which direction we go or what road we take. We'll be like those old couples fighting in the parking lot, and we'll do it with love. I can be your Mr. Right. I can be whoever you need, Harper. You just gotta let me try."

I flip the planner open to the spot I've bookmarked with a hot-pink ribbon. Guys don't hot-glue-gun shit ever. Not unless they're MacGyver and they're building a nuclear reactor out of spare crap in their garage. The lady at the crafts store showed me how to do it, though. Wouldn't let her touch it because it had to come from me. Especially since there's a big-ass diamond ring hanging off the end of the ribbon.

"I love you," I say.

And then I haul my T-shirt up and show her my new ink. Pink, black and right over my heart, Harper's face is inked into my skin. The words beneath it read

Property of Harper. It's my very own property patch. You have to be strong to partner with a man who belongs to an MC. Harper's got that strength. She's always had it. But if I want her to throw in with me, I'll have to be there for her, too.

And I really fucking want to.

"You mean it?" She blinks and for a moment I think she's about to cry, but then a blinding smile breaks through, lighting up her own face. "I love you, too."

"You be mine, I'll be yours and we'll live happily fucking ever after." I gesture toward my bike. "And if that doesn't work, we can at least ride off into the sunset every night."

"Together." She sighs.

And that's it. That's my perfect answer, my second shot at happiness, my whole world, because she throws her arms around me and there's nothing better than this.

* * * * *

LET'S TALK
Romance

For exclusive extracts, competitions
and special offers, find us online:

f facebook.com/millsandboon

◎ @millsandboonuk

𝕏 @millsandboon

Or get in touch on 0844 844 1351*

For all the latest titles coming soon, visit
millsandboon.co.uk/nextmonth